THE BETRAYERS

To Creighton & Pat —

Enjoy —

Aloha,
David P. Penhallow
10/25/03

THE BETRAYERS

A SEQUEL TO
AFTER THE BALL

BY

DAVID P. PENHALLOW

RICE STREET PRESS
LIHU'E HAWAII

Copyright© 2003 by David P. Penhallow. All rights reserved.

No part of this publication may be reproduced, stored in a retrieval system, or transmitted, in any form or by any means — electronic, mechanical, photocopying, or otherwise, without the prior written permission of the publisher.

Printed in the United States.

Published by Rice Street Press
P.O. Box 148
Lihue, Hawaii 96766

Library of Congress Control No.: 2003092805

ISBN: 0-9674147-1-7

Cover Art by Laka Morton, Volcano, Hawaii.

Design and production by Printmaker, Lihue Hawaii.

This book is dedicated to those angels who turned these pages into a reality; I remain eternally grateful:

Candy Aluli

Jim Anderson

Marian Benham

Pali Montoya-Bowman

Sally-Jo Bowman

Booklines – Claudia Cannon & Norma Charlton

Staff of Borders Store 95 – Lihue, Book, Music & Café

Jeanne Childs

Paul Douglass

Leslie "Rita" Fritz

Donald E. McQuinn

Marsha Monro and Steve Wong – Westin St. Francis Hotel

Debbie Gia & Tom Niblick

Ed Goka

Mary and Jim Griffith

Phillip Hirsch

Dick Lyday

Laka Morton

Helene Perl

Anna Ramos

Robert Schleck

Richard Slusarczyk

Pat & Lisa Sullivan

And Daisy, man's best friend.

ACKNOWLEDGEMENTS

Debbie Gia & Tom Niblick
Printmaker
4365 Kukui Grove Street
Lihue, Hawaii 96766
808-245-7203

Dick Lyday
Heritage Graphics
7405 Makaa Street
Honolulu, Hawaii 96825
808-395-4751

Candy Aluli
Aluli Public Relations
Maui, HI
808-669-1993

Claudia Cannon
Booklines
269 Pali'i Street
Mililani, Hawaii 96789
808-676-0116

Laka Morton — Artist — Cover Art
Post Office Box 1121
Volcano, Hawaii
808-985-7216

EDITORS

Richard Slusarczyk

Phillip Hirsch

Mary and Jim Griffith

PROOFREADER

Leslie "Rita" Fritz

Rita Hayworth, photo by Percy.

PROLOGUE

I have two secrets.
Once I floated on top of a coffin in the middle of the Pacific.
The other secret happened to me on the Aquitania.
On December 7th, 1941, at precisely 7:59 a.m., the Japanese bombed Pearl Harbor. While I was eating scrambled eggs, bacon and spooning Best Foods mayonnaise over everything on my plate, an angry Japanese pilot strafed bullets down my street killing my mother. A year earlier, my mother and father fought a bitter and public divorce in the Honolulu newspapers. At age six, I wet my bed on a regular basis.
I blamed my bad luck on my grandmother.
One summer afternoon, long ago, while visiting her family's cattle ranch on Kauai, riding her horse, my grandmother discovered a warrior's skull on top of a sand dune. The skull had a perfect set of white teeth. She took the skull back to a dentist in Berkeley, California. What she didn't know was that the skull had been cursed after an ancient Hawaiian battle. Three months later, my grandmother died mysteriously. My mother and her sisters blamed her sudden death on the curse. From the time I heard the story of the skull, I was determined to return it to the sand dune. From the age of six, it became my life's mission, not unlike King Arthur searching for the Holy Grail.
In February 1942, the Aquitania, a British luxury liner converted into a troop ship, sailed into Honolulu harbor. The ship was destined for San Francisco. My father booked us on it along with other residents anxious to leave Hawaii. Rumors were being circulated that the Japanese fleet was steaming for Hawaii.
I was thrilled to be leaving. My Aunt Momi had volunteered to escort my sister, Marigold, and me to San Francisco. Aunt Momi was my mother's favorite sister. What I loved about her was that she looked like Rita Hayworth, the movie star.

Once in the City, she was to put us on a train for Baltimore. Two old maid cousins had offered my sister and me their cold, drafty attic for the duration of the war.

Marigold was four years older than I, and a real tomboy. My sister had beautiful brown hair and eyes that I envied. She cried leaving our father as she was passionately devoted to him. My father had remarried and was gaga over his newly born son.

Aunt Momi left her own children behind as she was in a custody battle with her former husband, Uncle Hans. My uncle resembled his mean German Shepherds. My mother had nicknamed him Hans the Hun.

Up to that moment, my Aunt Momi always had a man in tow. She never had to make a major decision in her life because she had been spoiled by men since the day she was born. When she walked up the gangplank, she had a sudden attack of the vapors. For the first time in her life, my aunt realized that she was on her own.

In truth, I was one of the reasons she had the vapors. I was an obnoxious, needy, spoiled brat who craved as much attention as Aunt Momi did. No one knew it, because I kept secrets in a child world of my making, but I longed to belong to somebody. I wanted someone to think of me as a hero, like Tyrone Power in the movies. I wanted somebody to genuinely love me as my mother had.

Before Diamond Head was out of sight, the passengers had nicknamed me Goering after General Wilhelm Goering, the Nazi Luftwaffe General who stood next to Hitler in the RKO newsreels. He was a fat, prissy, heavily rouged swine. It was rumored that he had a penis in the shape of a pink ballerina. Gossips in Hawaii said that his pink ballerina was the reason he was so cruel. Marigold overheard talk of Goering's thing in my father's office and afterwards referred to my thing as a pink ballerina. My sister, as I had suspected, had started the Goering nickname with the passengers.

Besides wanting to be a hero, one of my goals in life was to become a movie star. I wanted to sing, dance and become as famous as movie stars Don Ameche, Alice Faye and Betty Grable, who were currently starring in 20th Century Fox Technicolor musicals.

CHAPTER 1

PERCY

"Percy, put that toilet seat down right this minute. Ladies are sleeping in this stateroom and don't you forget it."

"Yes, Aunt Momi."

"We're having rules around here. Rule one: put the toilet seat down. Rule two: don't wet your bed."

"Yes, Aunt Momi."

"Percy, take that cot. Marigold and I are sleeping in these beds. Are you paying attention?"

"He's in lala land," snorted Marigold, unpacking her suitcase.

"I am not. I heard everything Aunt Momi said." I snipped back at my sister. "How come you get to sleep in a Princess Margaret of England's bed and I have to sleep on a Jack the Ripper grungy cot next to the porthole?"

"Jolljamit it, Percy. Shut up."

"I'm going to pray tonight that my Japanese spy friend, Mr. Hamada, orders a submarine to torpedo us because you are being so mean to me."

"Just follow the rules, Percy. Damn it, I wish your Uncle Lono was with me."

My Aunt Momi swore a lot. Damn it and jolljamit were her favorite swear words. My aunt was a Hawaiian princess by marriage. Her second of four husbands, Prince Lono, would have been king of Hawaii if Americans hadn't overthrown the rule of Queen Liliuokalani. Her prince had joined the Merchant Marines and was sailing somewhere in the South Pacific and, according to Aunt Momi, was delivering toilet paper to the troops.

My aunt was never without a cigarette. Her smoking fascinated me. When the cigarette smoke exhaled out of her nose she quickly sucked it back into her mouth making the smoke disappear into her lungs. Aunt Momi learned that trick from watching Bette Davis movies. She considered it very "katish." "Katish" was a word she made up for something really swell.

"Rule Three," Aunt Momi continued. "Behave like a gentleman. Marigold and I have to put up with you in this cabin for the next ten days. We don't want to hear you talk dirty or break wind."

I laughed nervously.

"I don't find that funny and I won't have you smelling up this cabin. If you can't behave like a gentleman, I'll have the captain send you down to where all the bad boys sleep."

"My mother wouldn't do that to me," I said, my bottom lip protruding.

"Stop being a baby, Percy," my sister sneered.

"I hate you, Marigold."

After Mother died, Daddy wouldn't take us to live with him. His new wife, Kathy, considered us a handful. My sister and I hated her and we were always fighting in her presence.

"Rule Number Four: No wandering around this ship telling wild stories about your sister and me. I don't want people thinking that I'm traveling with a cuckoo child."

"Percy makes things up about me all the time." Marigold informed Aunt Momi.

"All the stories I tell about Marigold are true. Everyone knows that you're a mean person. You already told everybody that I have a pink ballerina."

"Stop it! I can't stand your bickering. You're driving me crazy. I can't wait for this trip to be over. When we land in San Francisco, I'm going to have Cousin Oliver put you on the train because, by then, I'll never want to see you again."

Cousin Oliver was a widower who lived in San Francisco. His dead wife had left him filthy rich and it was rumored that my mother and her sisters had been left a small fortune in his will. It was also rumored that he was leaving all his money to his cook, Ellen.

"We have only been at sea for less than three hours and I'm already at my wits' end with the both of you. And furthermore, Cousin

Oliver's old maid sisters in Maryland won't stand one minute of your fighting. They are meaner than polecats. Meanness runs rampant on that side of our family. If you don't behave, Percy, they'll make you clean their house every day and empty their chamber pots like a slave." By the time she finished her lecture, she had lit two cigarettes.

In truth, the two old maid cousins in Baltimore were real sports. They rolled their own cigarettes, drank their scotch straight and, after World War I, tangoed in Paris with slick, dark-haired men in smoky cafes. Behind closed doors, they fought over inconsequential things. I already knew that sibling rivalry was the training ground for combat warfare.

Our cabin was very fancy, except for my World War I Army cot next to the porthole. Our suite was overcrowded with all our steamer trunks making it hard for the three of us to maneuver at the same time. I kept tripping over Aunt Momi's small trunk that she had stored next to my cot. While lying on the cot, I could trace with my finger soldiers' names written in ink on the gold wallpaper.

The bathroom had mirrors that ran from floor to ceiling reminding me of a French palace.

I said, stamping my feet, "I'm going to lock myself in the bathroom and pretend that I am Marie Antoinette sitting on her throne. After I finish going number two, I'm going to guillotine myself."

"Just clean up the mess," barked Aunt Momi.

"At least, I have Johnny to talk to. We can talk man to man things," I grumbled.

"I don't want you running around annoying Johnny. People like Johnny have to perform serious duties on this ship and they have more important things to do than have you pester them," warned Aunt Momi.

"Johnny likes me."

Johnny was a British Naval officer and was the reddest man I had ever met in my life. He had a thick head of red hair, arms tangled with red wire, rosy cheeks, bushy black eyebrows, and dark blue eyes that changed color with the weather. What made him handsome was that his blue eyes were rimmed with thick, dark black eyelashes. He was a bonfire of a fellow.

As soon as we boarded the ship, I became lost looking for an ice box to store my jar of Best Foods mayonnaise. It was Johnny who found me and steered me back to my cabin. Even though he observed that I had a wandering nature, he said that I was a very responsible boy because I had delivered, without losing it, a letter to my aunt from her mother-in-law. I liked him immediately. He treated me like one of his mates.

Johnny informed me that the English government had converted the Aquitania into a troopship in 1938. On its last voyage, when the Japanese began to occupy Southeast Asia, the ship evacuated British soldiers from Singapore to Australia. In Sydney, the Aquitania picked up wounded soldiers to bring them back to the United States of America. In Hawaii, the ship added 400 American evacuees, along with Japanese teachers and Buddhist priests. The Japanese teachers and Buddhist priests were considered dangerous by the FBI director, J. Edgar Hoover. He felt their loyalty remained with the Emperor of Japan. It was rumored among the passengers, that the Japanese were being sent to concentration camps on the Mainland.

Johnny told me that many of the Hawaiian evacuees were crammed down on the lower decks because they had run out of space and that I should consider myself very fortunate to be staying in a suite. From the way he talked, I knew at once that he thought that I came from a very rich family. I wasn't rich. I was just fortunate to have a father who had connections with an Army general. Johnny made it sound that the other passengers near the engine room were broiling like steaks in the devil's kitchen. It must be true because I heard passengers walking past our cabin complaining about their confinement, the blazing heat, and lack of air.

Sitting on the cot, sounding chatty, I said, "I ran into Daisy and Neal. They told me that Auntie Sissy has a fancier cabin than ours because they have a bedroom. Johnny told me that the passengers are jealous of us."

"Yes, we are very fortunate, Percy. So mind your manners and keep your mouth shut. We don't want to bring any undue attention upon ourselves when most of the other people on this ship are less fortunate than we are."

I blurted out, "And we're really fortunate to have Johnny as my friend."

"He's a gentleman and that's the way you should behave. It's nice

The Betrayers

to know that I can count on him especially where you're concerned. And, remember what he told you, Percy. Put your lifejacket on before leaving the stateroom and go to the right, down the corridor, to reach our lifeboat." Aunt Momi slipped out of her dress and put on her nightgown. She was talking nicer now.

Marigold threw a crayon at me, and yelled from her bed. "That's my Superman comic book, Percy. Give it back! You've scribbled on it, Hermann Goering. Aunt Momi, Percy ruined my comic book. Daddy gave that to me as a going away present," Marigold threw her crayons at me.

I threw the comic book at her, apologizing, "I forgot. You can have my Lana Turner paper dolls."

She huffed turning the pages of the comic book. "I wouldn't touch your paper dolls with a ten-foot pole. Your big problem is your pink ballerina. It makes you stupid."

"It does not. Anyway, my thing is part of the curse."

"Stop it. No more talk about pink ballerinas or curses for the rest of this trip." Aunt Momi shimmied under the covers propping pillows behind her. She lit a cigarette. Her hands were shaking.

Moments later, coming out of the bathroom, I informed my sister, "Johnny told me that there are ghosts on this ship. Wouldn't it be spooky to see one? Tomorrow night, let's go find one."

"Okay." She mumbled.

"Not on your chinny chin chins, kids. You are both to always stay in this cabin after dark," Aunt Momi spoke to us looking into a hand mirror, scraping a fleck of lipstick off her teeth with her little finger.

Marigold began moaning, "My stomach hurts. I hate boiled beef and cabbage. That damn dinner was pukey."

The ship began to hit large swells. Johnny warned us that we were heading into a winter storm. My sister became seasick.

"Aunt Momi, I have two bottles of Best Foods mayonnaise in my suitcase. Wasn't that brilliant of me to bring them?"

"You're a pig, Percy. Don't talk about food when I'm sick," moaned Marigold. Her eyes were rolling to the ceiling as she held her tummy.

Aunt Momi said in a calm voice, "Don't think about being sick, Marigold. Percy, don't talk about food in front of Marigold and don't go around telling everybody that you have two bottles of mayonnaise. Some people hate mayonnaise and gag when they hear that word. Remember, dear, we want to make friends on this trip."

"Oh, Aunt Momi, don't you feel sorry for people who hate Best Foods mayonnaise?"

The ship hit a large swell. The boat lurched backwards as if we had smacked into a stone wall. The lights flickered off. In that sudden moment of darkness, the cabin door opened. Bang! A gun exploded. I could hear a bullet ricocheting off the wall into one of the steamer trunks.

In the dark, Aunt Momi yelled, "YA SON-OF-A-BEESWAX!"

Before the ship smacked into another swell, the door slammed shut and the lights flickered back on.

I screamed, "SOMEONE JUST TRIED TO KILL YOU, AUNT MOMI!"

In a sudden frenzy, my aunt threw her purse at the door. She jumped out of bed and slammed her body against the door making sure it was shut. After locking the door, my aunt swore like a sailor.

Wide-eyed, I sat stupefied on my cot smelling gunpowder smoke that hung heavily in the air. I was suffocating. With blood pounding into my brain, I felt as frightened as the day the Japanese bombed Pearl Harbor.

Aunt Momi grabbed her purse off the floor, opened it, pulled out a Lucky Strike cigarette, and lit it. She leaned against the door and with her hands shaking, she shouted out loud, "Damn, damn, damn it to hell. I'm going to kill that sneaky son-of-a-bitch."

CHAPTER 2

OUT OF THE MOUTHS OF BABES

The curse had struck again.

Aunt Momi yelled, "Percy, did you see the gun?"

Standing up on the cot, wagging my finger at my aunt, I screamed again, "SOMEONE TRIED TO KILL YOU."

Shaking all over, she said, "You didn't shut the door properly."

"I did, too. You blame me for everything. I wasn't the last person to shut that son-of-a-beeswax door."

Motioning for me to sit down, Aunt Momi whispered, "Quit swearing. Lower your damn voice."

Looking at her hands, Aunt Momi muttered, "Shitooski." She had broken a fingernail.

"Look, Marigold," I cried. I pointed to a hole above Aunt Momi's bed.

Marigold jumped out of her bed and inspected the hole. After putting her finger into the hole, she yelled, "It's a bullet hole all right and it's still warm. Aunt Momi, you were lucky the bullet didn't splatter your brains all over the place."

"Stop that, Marigold," my aunt commanded. Her ear was pressed against the door. She was listening to the voices in the corridor.

I was too excited to keep my voice down and yelled, "It's the curse, Aunt Momi. Everybody wants us dead. Everybody wants our stateroom. Call for Johnny."

"I can't, Percy, and stop yelling," my aunt yelled. Walking back to her bed, she cautioned us, "Don't let your imaginations run away with you. Keep calm."

The ship suddenly rocked violently, creaking as if it was about to break apart. Marigold jumped back into her bed and smashed her face into the pillow and began wailing, "I'm going to throw-up, Aunt Momi."

I grabbed a Tootsie Roll from under my pillow, gnawing on it, and said cheerfully, "Isn't this exciting, Marigold? I love rough seas. Bring on the big waves, the bigger the better. Big waves make me want to eat a ton of sauerkraut and pickles. And, rough seas will keep the killer away."

From under her pillow, Marigold screamed, "Percy, quit talking about food. You're an evil little brother."

Swaying with the ship, I raised my hand and asked, "Aunt Momi, why don't you want anybody to save us from the killer?"

Chewing on her broken fingernail, my aunt said, "Marigold, you have my permission to throw up on Percy. Percy, get under the covers and be quiet." Pulling a pearl-handle revolver out of her purse, she muttered, "Next time, I'll be ready for that son-of-a-beeswax."

Pointing the gun at the door, she stuttered, "Uncle... Uncle Lono's mo-mo-mother gave this to me for our protection."

"Aunt Momi, you don't know how to shoot a gun," Marigold and I said in unison.

"Hush! I do, too."

With the gun in one hand, a cigarette in the other, my aunt tip-toed back to the cabin door, unlocked it and slowly opened it. Passengers were filing past our cabin lunging into the walls. They looked seasick.

I screamed, "Up there in the porthole."

Aunt Momi slammed the door, locked it, turned around, pointed the gun at the porthole, and hissed, "What is it?"

I said excitedly, "A crazy person was looking at us."

Seeing no one in the porthole, my aunt hissed, "Quit playing games."

"I'm not playing games." I said vehemently.

"One day, Mister Percy, you'll be crying for help. You've cried wolf once too often. Next time, I won't bite and then you'll be sorry. Because that time you'll be in real trouble." She stomped back to her bed, sat down, and laid the pistol beside her.

I said in a smart-alecky voice. "I just wanted to see if you were on your toes. You never believe anything I ever say, anyway. I wish I had never been born and I'm not making that up."

"You don't know how to tell the truth," said Aunt Momi shaking her head.

"I *was* telling the truth. There was an ugly, old man with warts all over his face looking at us." I got up and peered out the porthole looking for someone to show Aunt Momi that I hadn't been lying. On the deck, the sun had set. I couldn't see anything, much less a man with warts all over his face.

Exasperated, my aunt ordered, "Close the curtains. We're not supposed to show any light. Remember what your friend Johnny said about the blackout?"

Marigold jerked the pillow away from her face and said in a know-it-all voice that I hated, "When Percy lies, his mouth twitches. Look at his mouth, Aunt Momi." She imitated the twitches my mouth was making.

I slammed the curtain across the porthole and stretched my lips with my fingers. "My mouth does not twitch. Yours does."

Aunt Momi ordered. "I have had it. Get out of bed, right now. Come here and sit next to me."

I threw the covers back and raced Marigold to sit on Aunt Momi's bed first. Plopping myself next to my aunt, I saluted, "Abbott and Costello reporting for duty, mien herr."

Scratching her legs, Aunt Momi pointed down to where the bad boys slept and said, "Behave."

Marigold took Aunt Momi's hand as the ship rocked back and forth. "Percy pretends he's a big-time movie star all the time acting in some old dumb movie." Leaning to me, she said, "You're not in **Buck Privates** now, stupid mein herr."

"And you're not the Andrews Sisters in **Buck Privates** either, Miss Pukehead."

"Quit it, you two. I mean it!" Aunt Momi looked as if she was about to cry. "Just stop it. I have something very important to tell you. I am in big trouble. I have a big secret to tell you. Percy, you have to keep this secret because this is a serious secret. If this secret gets out, we'll get killed for sure. I am going to tell you why someone just shot at me." As she talked, I wiggled like a worm.

Slapping my leg, my aunt scolded, "Quit fidgeting."

"I'm sitting on the gun, Aunt Momi. It's going to shoot me up my you-know-where."

"Stand up." She grabbed the gun from under me and threw it into her purse. "Now sit and, for heaven's sake, settle down."

Marigold said sincerely, "Aunt Momi, Percy can't keep secrets. That's the truth. Please, don't tell him the secret. Lock him in the bathroom and tell me."

"I can too keep secrets, Marigold. I have a thousand secrets in my belly that I never told anyone about and that's the truth. It's all those secrets in my belly that make me fat."

"The reason you're so fat is because you eat Best Foods mayonnaise breakfast, lunch and dinner. Aunt Momi, don't push your finger into his belly button because a ton of mayonnaise will ooze out."

I answered angrily, "Aunt Momi, I'll bet you a bottle of Best Foods mayonnaise that if you poke your finger up Marigold's you-know-where..."

Aunt Momi yanked my ear. "Stop that right now. Go sit on your bed."

I crawled like a monkey over Marigold's bed, onto my cot, sat down, and placed my hands over my ears. Aunt Momi stared into space.

I mumbled to myself. Thoughts kept popping into my head. "Hummmmmmm. EEEEEEEEboom! Boom! Boom! I'm Tyrone Power flying in an RAF plane dropping bombs. Target tonight: Marigold and Aunt Momi. Bombs away. Bulls eye. Got'em both.

"Boy, this ship is rocking.

"Aunt Momi's got a big nose. When she dies, she's gonna look ugly.

"Goody. Goody. Marigold is seasick.

"Mother looked beautiful in her coffin, that's because she loved me.

"I hate my double chins. I'll be glad when I'm dead. I won't have to look at myself in the mirror ever again."

In my Jimmy Cagney voice, I snarled, "Give up the secret if you don't want to get a plug from my gat, baby."

"Percy, if you don't be quiet, I am going feed you to the sharks. This is not monkey business."

My sister kicked my leg. "Aunt Momi is in danger. Don't you understand that?"

"Quit kicking, Marigold." Continuing with my Cagney voice, I said, "Okay, okay, I get the drift. Let's get down to business because there's a dirty rat outside who wants to rub you out, Aunt Momi."

Aunt Momi rose from the bed, steadied herself against the bureau (the ship was bucking like a bronco), and staggered towards the small steamer trunk next to my cot. "Kids, what I am about to show you is the reason someone wants to kill me."

The Aquitania.

CHAPTER 3

THE SECRET

Aunt Momi with the help of my sister lifted the steamer trunk onto Marigold's bed. Marigold and I held the trunk in place as my aunt reached for her purse. Out of the purse, she retrieved a key, unlocked the trunk, and opened it.

She spoke softly, "I don't know why I consented to do this. I should have my head examined. In truth, no one ever says no to my jolljamit mother-in-law. I never have."

Inside the trunk were little mummies wrapped with strips of muslin. My aunt picked up one of the objects and unwound its protective covering and said, "This... this... is one of the most sacred religious objects in ancient Hawaii. One of the most precious."

She held a wood carving of a Hawaiian goddess with bosoms shaped like two oblong pancakes. The light from the lamp lit the flowing goddess' hair making it look like rivers of lava. "This is human hair taken from a dead warrior after a battle."

"Wow," gasped Marigold. Then she said what I was thinking, "This is spooky, Aunt Momi."

I screamed, "There's a *moʻo* inside her mouth."

"Shush!" Aunt Momi said, slapping my head. "There is no lizard in her mouth."

She rewrapped the wooden god and carefully laid her back in the steamer trunk. Turning to Marigold, whose mouth was open as wide as the whale that swallowed Pinocchio, my aunt explained, "There are a total of eight sacred Hawaiian objects in here along with other valuable treasures." She again reached into the trunk and this time brought out a small purple velvet bag. Untying a satin ribbon, she opened the bag. In her hand, a diamond butterfly sparkled. Two tiny, dark blue sapphires gave the creature eyes to see and its diamond wings fluttered as Aunt Momi moved it around with her hand.

"There are three more bags of jewelry in that steamer trunk," she whispered.

"Oh, gad," gasped Marigold.

"This is more like it," I said, reaching for the brooch.

Aunt Momi smacked my hand away. "This is not a plaything, Percy. This brooch belonged to Queen Kapiolani, dowager queen of King Kalakaua. It is worth thousands and thousands of dollars. To the people of Hawaii, this diamond brooch is priceless."

Marigold whistled, asking, "Why do you have these things, Aunt Momi?"

"Lono's mother, my mother-in-law, doesn't want these objects captured by the Japanese. Percy, what you saw a few minutes ago, the *moʻo*, could have been real. Hawaiians believe all their gods have invisible power. They call it *mana*. I'm not sure Hawaiians would say she has a lizard inside her mouth, but she holds a mysterious power for the Hawaiians. Sacred objects can be used for good or for evil. If these objects fell into the enemy's hands, and used in a sacrilegious manner, terrible things could happen to the people in Hawaii. These treasures are as sacred as a piece of wood from Jesus' cross. Percy, don't ever let me catch you playing with them."

"Oogie. Oogie, Oogie. I wouldn't touch them or a piece of Jesus' cross ever. I'd die." Goose bumps rose all over my body.

Holding my face in her hand, making sure I was listening, my aunt continued. "Bernadette, my mother-in-law's cousin, took them out of the Bishop Museum without permission, as my mother-in-law's requested. Many people back in Hawaii would kill to keep these sacred treasures from leaving the Islands. They would rather see us dead. They would have chosen to hide the treasures in a secret cave or at the Royal mausoleum or locked up in the vault at the Bishop Museum. Hawaiians feel that the artifacts in this steamer trunk don't belong on the Mainland.

"In fact, most of Hawaii's greatest treasures are now in private collections or stored in museums all over the world. That's why what's in this trunk is so precious. Hawaii has few treasures left in Hawaii and these can never be replaced."

Marigold whispered, "You mean your mother-in-law stole the treasures?"

"No. They belong to her family, but they were held in sacred trust at the museum."

"What's the big deal, Aunt Momi?

"Unfortunately, other Hawaiian families claim to be the real owners of these objects. There has been a fight over their ownership since the day King Kamehameha died. Most Hawaiians believe that my mother-in-law is the genuine Princess of Hawaii. Percy, remember, I am just a princess by marriage. My mother-in-law *is* the highest-ranking *alii* in all of Hawaii and feels that it is her responsibility to care for these objects."

"But, why do you have them?" my sister asked.

"She believes that with an imminent invasion by the Japanese, looting would occur and the possibility of the museum and its priceless Hawaiian heritage destroyed is more than she could bear. Bernadette removed the treasures including a very valuable jade necklace that belonged to Queen Liliuokalani's husband, John Dominis. A sea captain, a friend of the Queen's husband, had stolen the necklace from the Imperial Palace in Peking right from under the nose of the Dowager Empress. There is a large reward in China for the return of this necklace. The necklace is as valuable to the people of China as the Great Wall."

Putting the brooch down, she removed a note from her purse. She passed the note to Marigold and said, "I received this note from my mother-in-law. Read it aloud, Marigold."

Marigold read: "Dear Momi, I have bitten off more than I can chew. I am afraid that you and the children are in grave danger. Bernadette died this morning. I feel I have been betrayed. Many on the ship may know what you are carrying in my steamer trunk.

"I believe what I did is the right thing for Hawaii and its people, but your lives are far more important to me than the diamonds or the other sacred objects. If the situation becomes too dangerous for you and the children, throw the treasures overboard. I give you my permission. Lovingly, Mother."

Marigold passed the note back to Aunt Momi. "Whew, we are in some terrible pickle." My sister looked into the steamer trunk and counted the treasures making sure of the number. After counting, she advised, "Maybe we'd better toss the treasures overboard now because next time, he won't miss you, Aunt Momi."

Picking up the brooch that lay on the bed and pinning it on my pj's, rubbing the little sapphire eyes with my baby finger, I offered my opinion that nobody asked for. "I don't think your mother-in-law meant what she wrote in that note. She wants us to save the objects. I vote we don't throw the treasures overboard, no matter what."

Swaying to the rhythm of the rocking ship, I said, "I wish this brooch had magical powers to keep us safe."

"Come here, naughty boy," Aunt Momi ordered. "Take off that brooch. Don't you ever listen?" Aunt Momi unpinned the brooch from my pajamas.

"Aunt Momi, Hitler is going to send his assassins to kill you for everything that's in that steamer trunk. If his assassins don't kill you, a Hawaiian warrior will spear your heart for that lady with the human hair. If that doesn't happen, one of the Japanese prisoners of war is going to shove a bamboo stick under your fingernail for that butterfly brooch. If that fails, a band of Chinese bandits from the Imperial Palace will ram a sword into your belly for that jade necklace. Everyone on this ship, in fact in the whole wide world, has a reason to kill you. Grandma's curse is working overtime. We gotta find the skull on the Mainland or else we are going to be in doodoo for eternity. How come Auntie Sissy doesn't have the treasures in her cabin? She's the real daughter."

Marigold knew that answer. "Because Auntie Sissy drinks too much, that's why. Percy is right, Aunt Momi. It seems we are triple times cursed, if you ask me."

Aunt Momi warned, "Not one word to Sissy or her kids about these treasures. If Sissy finds out that I have them, she'll want the jewels." Aunt Momi's dander always went up when she talked about Auntie Sissy.

As the ship pitched to starboard, Marigold slid off the bed, smacking her fanny on the floor. "Ouch," she screamed. Aunt Momi and I held the steamer trunk so it didn't fall on her head.

"OOOOOOOOOh, damn it," moaned my sister. Her face was pea green.

"Don't get sick, Marigold. Please, I need you," Aunt Momi pleaded. It was too late. My sister ran for the bathroom.

"Marigold is barfing, Aunt Momi."

"I don't need a news reporter telling me what's happening to Marigold."

As Aunt Momi closed the steamer trunk, she prayed, "God, find it in your heart to shut Percy up permanently and keep Marigold from getting seasick. If you do that I promise I will give up smoking."

Sounding hurt, I said, "Aunt Momi, are you talking bad to God about me?"

"Jolljamit, God, please shut him up. Give me a sign." Aunt Momi looked at the ceiling for her answer.

God answered. The handle of the cabin door slowly moved back and forth. Someone was trying to get into the cabin. Aunt Momi and I ran to the door making sure it was still locked. The ship made a sudden lurch to port and the person stopped fiddling with the doorknob.

Standing behind Aunt Momi, I sighed, "I hope that stupid jerk cracked his head and died. If this keeps up, Aunt Momi, you, Marigold, and I are going to be dead before breakfast."

Marigold screamed from the bathroom, "I'm already dead, Percy."

I squeezed Aunt Momi's hand and urged, "Do something brilliant, Aunt Momi."

"What?" she snapped.

I answered annoyed, "I don't know. You're the grownup."

Thump! Thump! Thump! Somebody began to pound on our cabin door.

Aunt Momi cried, "Who's there?"

No answer.

"Who's there?" she called louder.

Still no answer.

The pounding began again.

I whispered, "It's Death knocking. Tell Death to go away. Tell him we're out. Tell Death I'm in Hollywood dancing with Ginger Rogers. I got it. Tell Death we're taking a bubble bath."

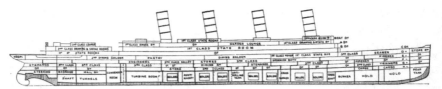

Deck plan of the Aquitania.

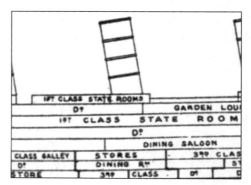

First Class accomodations

CHAPTER 4

DAISY'S TREASURE CHEST

"Let us in!"

We ran to Marigold's bed, pulled the steamer trunk off, pushed it behind my cot, and hid it under a blanket.

Marigold yelled from the bathroom, "Oh, for gaaad's sake, let them in."

I pushed my aunt's fanny toward the door and urged, "Open the door, Aunt Momi."

Pushing me away, she screamed, "Quit it, Percy."

My aunt unhitched the bolt and slowly pulled the door open. In the corridor, two little pink rabbits were jumping up and down screaming, "Let us in!"

Marigold exclaimed, walking out of the bathroom, "Daisy and Neal!" Aunt Momi yanked them into the cabin and bolted the door.

Daisy and Neal were my best friends. Their mother, Auntie Sissy, terrified me. She was blonde, rich and beautiful. Aunt Momi detested her and Auntie Sissy returned the sentiments. Auntie Sissy's passion was playing polo with her husband, Happy. Happy was the saddest looking man I had ever encountered. Auntie Sissy had a temper that sent her husband running for the hills. When my mother was alive, she and Auntie Sissy were best friends.

Daisy was petite, blonde and my age. Sweet as they come. Neal, a skinny gangly kid, was a year younger than Daisy and thought of himself, even at seven, a brain. He bragged that he wore eye glasses because he was a genius.

Daisy clasped her hands to her heart and pleaded, "Princess Momi, loan us Percy. Please. Sissy needs him badly."

Aunt Momi sat on her bed and pulled Daisy to her and brushed a strand of yellow hair from her pretty face. "I'm not a princess. I'm just your old Aunt Momi. Now, tell me in a calm voice, what this is all about?" Aunt Momi never liked to be called a princess, unless, of course, it got her the best table in a restaurant, linen sheets on her bed or a strand of pearls at a discount.

Settling on Marigold's lap, Neal whispered, "We need Percy. That's all we can tell you. Sissy told us to get Percy right away and mum's the word."

"Do you always call your mother Sissy?" Marigold asked Neal.

"She wants us to. Sissy doesn't like to be called mother. She says it makes her feel old and like a mother," said Neal. Marigold wiped his glasses.

"Now dear, tell your old Aunt Momi what this is all about. Forget about mum's the word."

Daisy looked to me for help. I mouthed silently the word, "lie."

Reading my lips and crossing her fingers, she babbled, "It's my treasure chest. Please let Percy come with us because he's the only one who can open it. Please."

Aunt Momi asked, perplexed, "Percy is the only one who can open your treasure chest? That's preposterous. What's in it that is so important?"

Daisy babbled on, "It's true. I shouldn't be telling you this, but if you insist. I put Sissy's emerald bracelet in the chest by mistake — and she wants it NOW. You *know* how *upset* Sissy gets when Sissy doesn't get her way. You don't want her to hit me with her polo mallet, do you?"

Aunt Momi laughed, "I know your mother, all right." She turned to me, "Tell Daisy the damn combination."

I threw myself dramatically against the bureau, slapped my hand against my forehead and wailed, "I can't remember the combination unless I see the lock. You know how stupid I am."

Neal agreed with me saying that he had wanted to say that I was dumb for a long time, adding, "Percy is a dumbbell. Percy is a real dumbbell."

Aunt Momi glared at me, "Percy, you are not going to leave this cabin. I mean it." She looked at the bullet hole.

I blabbed, "No one wants to kill me, Aunt Momi."

Marigold flung Neal off her lap and charged me like a bull, pinning me against the bureau, and threatened, "Someone very close to you is going to kill you right now if you don't keep your trap shut."

In spite of Marigold's stranglehold on my neck, I whispered, "I have to go with them. It's really important. I'll explain later. Be a pal, Marigold. I'm not lying this time."

Marigold looked at my mouth and seeing that it wasn't twitching, (I was chewing on my tongue.), she turned me around and said, "I can't think of anyone who'd want to kill him but me. Let him go, Aunt Momi. He'll be all right."

After Marigold released my neck, I said, "I can't remember the combination unless I see the numbers on the lock."

Looking for her cigarettes, Aunt Momi said, "You're mixing me up. I can't think."

"Pleeeeese," I cried.

"Quit whining." Finding her cigarettes, she relented. "It's against my better judgment… but…"

Before she could say another word, I kissed her hand and used my Charles Boyer accent, "Thank you, Princess Aunt. Youze a scrumptious French tart."

"Don't you tart me, buster! Be back in here as soon as you've opened the chest. Neal and Daisy will escort you back to this cabin after you're finished with that funny business. And don't think, Miss Daisy, that you have fooled me with that lock business." Satisfied that their mission had been accomplished, Daisy and Neal scurried out of the cabin to wait for me in the corridor.

Leaving, I rubbed Marigold's sore tummy as a thank you. At the door, I gave a farewell address, "Friends, Romans and natives that includes Aunt Momi and Marigold. Here's the secret signal to let me back in. I'll knock twice and you say, 'Who's there?' I'll say 'Best Foods mayonnaise.' You open the door and let me in. It's that simple.

"If I say 'Kraft mayonnaise,' the coast isn't clear but you can open the door a crack and let me in, but if I say 'Miracle Whip,' get out the gun and shoot whoever comes through the door. Can you remember that?"

Lighting a cigarette, Aunt Momi laid her head on the pillow and waved me away. "Get out of here, buster. It's way past your bedtime. If you're not back here within the hour, you know what will happen to you. You'll be down in the engine room sleeping with all the other bad boys." She formed her fingers into a make-believe gun and pretended to shoot me.

"I'll be good." With her head resting on the pillow and a cigarette in her mouth, she shut her eyes.

I tiptoed out of the cabin. "Don't forget the secret code. And you know what? I bet Aunt Sissy has a gun. I'm going to find out if she's used it recently." I slammed the door as Aunt Momi yelled for me to come back.

I screamed, "Let's get out of here!"

Running down the corridor, Daisy cried, "You did it, Percy."

"Shhhh," Neal whispered, "Aunt Momi will hear us."

At the far end of the corridor, we formed a huddle.

Gulping out his words, Neal said, "We're in big trouble, Percy."

"I know," I said.

"You know?" gasped Daisy "How do you know?"

"I saw you when you came aboard this afternoon." I startled them even more as I continued on matters that I thought were more important. "There is a dangerous killer roaming this ship and a ghost to boot. I've taken a solemn oath not to tell you about them so erase what I just said. But keep it in the back of your mind just in case you meet the ghost or the killer gets into your mother's cabin. Let's get out of here and open up the treasure chest before the killer finds us and shoots us dead."

Running beside Daisy, I puffed, "I know who's in your treasure chest. That person is in real danger, if you ask me."

CHAPTER 5

OUT OF THE CLOSET

Approaching Auntie Sissy's cabin, we heard what sounded like a gaggle of bearded, tattooed lady wrestlers. Barricading the corridor ahead of us were all types of women from Hawaii sitting cross-legged on the floor. From the looks of their red eyes, they were drunk.

I recognized a bank president's wife, the Liberty House manager's daughter, the Honolulu Garden Club's secretary, and my mother's manicurist amongst them. Propped against the corridor wall, slinging their bare feet out in front of them, drinking from a silver flask, dangling cigarettes in their fingers, shoveling food into their mouths, they were toasting President Roosevelt.

Without anyone taking notice, children always become invisible when adults are tipsy, we entered Auntie Sissy's cabin. Inside, more refugees were sitting on the floor singing and swaying to the sounds of a ukulele.

Uncle Peanut was playing the ukulele. Uncle Peanut was once a professional wrestler and looked like a pirate. He was Auntie Sissy's bodyguard. He wore a patch over one eye because of a childhood accident. His best friend in the sixth grade shot an arrow into his eye.

A tall six-foot Hawaiian woman sat in a chair next to Uncle Peanut. She wore white orchids on top of her hair. The orchids made her look like a queen. Everyone, strangers and friends alike, called her Aunt Rose. Tonight, she wore a black holoku with a long train. I was fascinated by a multi-faceted amethyst brooch pinned at the neck of her dress. Tiny seed pearls encircled an amethyst, making the purple stone look darker than a mountain pool. The old-fashioned brooch matched her ancient face. Once when we met on the streets of Honolulu, I asked, "Who died?" She always appeared as if she was going to a funeral. She was a very famous person in Hawaii.

Aunt Rose's eyes were closed. I examined the deep rivers and tiny tributaries that were etched from her forehead to her neck. Feeling my breath on her face, she opened her eyes, and pointed to the bathroom door.

Out stepped Auntie Sissy, wearing white linen slacks and a white blouse. Surprisingly, a nun in a black habit stood behind her. The nun looked like the Queen of Spades. Even though Auntie Sissy's beautiful face was bloated like a balloon and had red splotches splashed on her cheeks and forehead, she still sparkled like a million dollars because she wore diamonds and pearls around her neck and wrists. She looked richer than Wall Street.

Seeing us, Auntie Sissy clapped her hands loudly and, in a clipped English accent that well-to-do people in Hawaii used when they commanded their servants, grabbed her polo mallet, pounded it on the floor and yelled, "Everybody out. Now! This party is ovah."

Hearing Auntie Sissy's polo mallet strike the floor, the ladies gathered up all the food and drink and left the cabin. The nun, fingering her rosary beads, was the last to leave. Aunt Rose and Uncle Peanut remained in the cabin.

Auntie Sissy barked, "Herman, take Aunt Rose up to the lounge. Bring her back in an hour."

Herman was Uncle Peanut's given name. When he wrestled at the Civic Auditorium, he was billed as Herman the Hunk. Only Auntie Sissy was allowed to call him Herman.

With a great swoop, Uncle Peanut lifted Aunt Rose out of the chair and carried her like a feather out of the cabin. Setting her down in the corridor, he took Aunt Rose's arm gently and carefully led her towards the ship's lounge. As soon as they were out of hearing, Auntie Sissy told us to sit on the floor.

She stalked around the cabin like a caged tigress and snapped, "First off, I want to make it very clear that it wasn't my idea to bring you here. I can't fathom how a little fat boy can help me solve my problem."

After she said that, she looked down to see if I was as fat as she remembered. I stuck my belly out to jolt her memory. She banged the polo mallet on the floor signaling me to quit fooling around.

Before she could conk my head with the polo mallet, I asked, "Do you have a gun?"

"None of your business," she snorted.

I continued, "Where is she?"

"Where is who?" Auntie Sissy said, waving the mallet in my face.

I ducked behind Daisy. "You know who. I saw her when you came aboard this afternoon. You tried to hide her under a horse blanket. You didn't fool me because her spiky hair stuck out."

With the polo mallet touching the tip of my nose, she roared like a dragon, "You didn't tell anyone? Did you?"

"Where is she?" I said, feeling the mallet flatten my nose.

Seeing that I wasn't intimidated, she leaned the polo mallet against the wall and, grinding her teeth, said, "In here." Auntie Sissy opened the closet door. On the floor lay Mina scrunched in a little ball. Daisy and Neal ran to her.

"Mina's dead," screamed Daisy.

I loved Mina the day I met her. She was different like me. What made her different was that she had porcupine black hair sticking out of her head at all angles.

Mina came to Hawaii from a mountain village in southern Japan. She began as a kitchen maid for Auntie Sissy and turned into a nursemaid after Daisy was born. When Neal was born, Uncle Happy and Auntie Sissy built a cottage for Mina and the children far away from their main home. It was there Daisy and Neal were raised and called it home. Daisy and Neal loved Mina more than Uncle Happy, and a thousand times more than their mother. They never became scared pink rabbits when Mina was around.

Mina was "king of the mountain" when it came to her charges and not even Auntie Sissy's polo mallet came between Mina and her babies. The only thing Mina feared was the sea. She dreamt as a child that she would drown, even though she had never seen the sea. She hated the ocean that surrounded Hawaii and Japan with a passion.

Finding that Mina had only fainted, Auntie Sissy picked her off the floor and dragged her over to Aunt Rose's chair. Sitting her down, Auntie Sissy said, "Mina, this is not the time to be a weakling. What on earth could you have been thinking of asking for this pile of blubber to help us?"

Taking in deep breaths and a sip of water that Daisy offered her, Mina answered slowly, "He do crazy things. He smart boy. He help me."

Auntie Sissy sighed, "Okay, Mr. Do Crazy Things, here is the situation. I sneaked Mina illegally out of Hawaii. I planned to hide her in this cabin for the entire voyage, but something's come up. She can't stay in here now. Aunt Rose, the elderly lady with Herman, is sleeping down in the hellhole of this ship and that won't do. I can't have Aunt Rose, my oldest living relative, suffocating in that hellhole for ten days, and I won't have her sleeping next to that dreadful Edwina Brown."

"Why can't Aunt Rose and Mina stay in here with you together? There's plenty of room."

"Aunt Rose isn't about to sleep in this cabin with Mina. Three of her relatives died on December 7th. She can't stand the Japanese people."

"I love Japanese people, even though a Japanese pilot killed my mother. But that doesn't mean all Japanese people are bad. My best friend is a Japanese spy. I love Mr. Hamada and… I love Mina, too. Japanese people are just like us, Auntie Sissy. Maybe not like you because you're really different."

I had a big stupid mouth. I never knew when to shut up.

Fixing a scotch and water in the bathroom, ignoring my offending remark, Auntie Sissy continued, "Mina can't stay in here. That's all there is to it. If someone discovers her on this ship, I'm a cooked goose. Mina will be shot and I will be sent to prison."

"When you're in Alcatraz, before they send you to the electric chair, maybe you can share a cell with Ma Barker, the man killer. **Photoplay** magazine says Bette Davis is going to play Ma in the movies next year."

Auntie Sissy grabbed her polo mallet, screaming, "I hate Bette Davis and I'm not going to share a cell with Ma Barker. Stop fooling around before I kill you. NOW DO SOMETHING! I need Mina to raise my children. But Mina has to leave this cabin before Aunt Rose and Herman return. Think of a hiding place where she won't be discovered."

"I can't think if you keep that polo mallet in your hand." As soon as she laid the mallet against the wall, I walked in circles. Walking in circles always made me think clearer.

I stopped and said, "I've got it. Remember the movie with Bobby Breen, my favorite kid singing movie star? The movie was called

Hawaii Calls. Bobby was a stowaway and sang all my favorite songs hiding in a lifeboat. We're going to do what Bobby did."

"Oh, for Christ sake, Mina isn't going to sing songs!" cried out Auntie Sissy in frustration.

"No. We're going to hide Mina in a lifeboat. During the day, she'll look like a normal passenger. She'll sit in a deck chair, hold a book and wear dark glasses. No one will guess that Mina is Japanese because of my perfect makeup job. Disguised, she can wander on deck all she wants, night and day, because I'll tell everyone that Mina is a mysterious countess from Poland."

Auntie Sissy talked to herself trying to make sense of my idea. "Sleeping inside a lifeboat makes sense but forget the Polish countess..."

"It's the best I can come up with on such short notice. Take it or leave it." I stood facing her with my hands on my hips.

Auntie Sissy picked up the polo mallet, smacked it on the floor, signaling that she had made up her mind. "We'll make it work. Mina, strip the blanket off my bed. Take that pillow. I'll fetch some warm clothes for you. You can have my red scarf. Don't sit there looking like dummies. It beats suffocating in that closet. We'll put everything into my black valise."

I had to work fast. I grabbed Auntie Sissy's makeup off the bathroom counter and snatched a black turban on her bureau. I stuffed the disguise into the black valise.

Daisy and Neal insisted on coming with me. Auntie Sissy didn't argue because she was on pins and needles expecting to hear Uncle Peanut and Aunt Rose's voices in the corridor.

Everything came at me in one fell swoop. I had problems. If I didn't return to my cabin before the hour was up, Aunt Momi was going to banish me to sleep with the bad boys in the engine room. Secondly, I wanted to discover the person who wanted to kill my aunt. Thirdly, I wanted to make the treasures disappear so my aunt wouldn't be killed if I couldn't discover the shooter. My most immediate problem was to find a lifeboat for Mina without having her fall into the rough seas making her nightmares come true.

Inspecting the Aquitania's lifeboats.

CHAPTER 6

MEN OVERBOARD

As we were leaving the cabin, the Aquitania climbed a monster wave and sped faster than a bullet into an ocean valley. We all thought the Aquitania was about to sink like the Titanic.

As the ship steadied herself, I hollered, "That was a reeeally big wave. I'm worried about hiding Mina in a lifeboat. The sea is too rough, Auntie Sissy,"

She snapped, "Get the hell out of here before Rose finds Mina. I mean it. I don't care how rough the sea is."

Holding the black valise in my hand, I walked unsteadily into the corridor. My chums followed behind.

As Auntie Sissy watched us leave, she gasped, "Daisy and Neal, you can't go out on deck like that. Go into the bedroom and put on your bathrobes and slippers. Hurry up before Uncle Peanut and Aunt Rose catch us."

I asked, "What about me and Mina?"

"What about you and Mina? Share the blanket I gave Mina."

Stepping back into the cabin, holding Mina's hand, I pointed to the open closet. "I want that."

"Not my mink coat, young man."

To this day, I can't imagine what prompted me to say this, probably something I remembered in a Betty Grable musical.

"I have to wear something to keep me from catching pneumonia. I'm a very delicate child, Auntie Sissy. I won't leave this cabin until I have that fur coat." I stomped on the floor pretending I was her polo mallet.

"Maybe the captain of the ship would like to know about Mina. I can see it now. Next year, I'll be visiting you and Ma Barker in prison. Of course, I'll be a movie star by then. I'll play the prison warden in the movie they make about you." I put my hands on my hips and stared at her.

Breathing cigarette smoke into my face, she roared, "You're a monster. Your mother would be ashamed of you." She strode to the closet, grabbed the mink coat off the hanger and thrust it at me. "If you ruin this coat, you'll pay for it. Don't think I won't make you pay for it. And, Mr. Percy, at the rate you are heading, you are going straight to hell."

Turning around dragging the mink coat behind me like Betty Grable, I pretended to hear something outside in the corridor and cried, "They're coming!"

Auntie Sissy jumped in a panic.

I turned and pointed to the closet again. "Mina needs that one."

Auntie Sissy screamed, "Not my Persian lamb coat. *That* coat does not leave *that* closet."

"She looks too Japanese in that blanket! In that coat, she could be a Polish countess. Hurry!! They're here!!"

She whipped open the closet door, grabbed the Persian lamb coat off the hanger and threw it at Mina. "Take it. Now, get the hell out of here before they find a fat dead boy on deck tomorrow morning."

Daisy and Neal ran into the stateroom tying on their bathrobes. I wrapped the Persian lamb coat around Mina and pushed everyone into the corridor.

I turned, "May I keep this fur coat, Auntie Sissy?"

Auntie Sissy held a bottle of Scotch in her hand and by the look in her eyes, she was deciding whether to throw the Scotch at me or drink it.

"I could just kill ya," she screamed, banging the polo mallet on the wall.

I yelled, "Run for it."

We raced down the corridor and ran into Aunt Rose and Uncle Peanut turning the corner. Without a backward glance or an exchanged word, we charged past them as the ship roller-coastered into the rough seas. We arrived at a massive wooden staircase buckling under the movement of the waves. The staircase had a carved wooden railing that ran from A Deck to D deck. Grasping onto the railing, we sat on the stairs. The rough seas made it difficult tackling the stairs to the next deck. It looked as difficult as trekking to the top of Mt. Everest. We were fortunate that no one was walking up or down the staircase. The passengers were back in their cabins saying their prayers.

Neal, holding onto the banister, whined, "It's too rough to go outside. We'll wash overboard and die. I'm not going. I'm not stupid and neither is Mina. Mina and I are going to stay right here."

Daisy put her arm around my shoulder. "Percy, if we can't find a lifeboat for Mina tonight, you'll figure something out. I know you will. You have never let me down."

"I'll find a place for Mina to sleep tonight. Don't worry, Daisy."

Mina whimpered, "I scared go outside. I hate ocean. I no can swim. I no like drown. I sleep inside ship."

A light switched on in my head. "I've got it. Remember, I got lost this afternoon looking for the ship's icebox for my mayonnaise. I was next to a room with a plaque on the door that read, 'Writing Salon.' Inside, I saw a huge couch in an alcove. That's where Mina is going to sleep tonight. It's a perfect place. She can sleep behind the couch. Tomorrow, we'll find Mina a lifeboat. Tonight, she sleeps indoors."

The ship leaned hard to port. Neal fell into a potted palm and Mina smacked her head into the wall behind her. Daisy and I grabbed for the banister to keep from rushing into Mina. The ship recovered, groaning louder than an old dog getting out of a chair.

I spoke quickly, "We better find the couch now."

Shaking all over, Daisy asked timidly, "Where is the Writing Salon?"

I pointed up the stairs. "The room is next to a painting of a naked lady. It's where Johnny found me this afternoon. Tomorrow, you're going to meet Johnny and he is going to be your 'bestest' friend, Daisy. I know he is. He knows everything about this ship. He's the one that told me about the ghost. He loves movies and Best Foods mayonnaise as much as I do. Anyone who loves Alice Faye and Best Foods mayonnaise is a person I can trust. He told me that I was named after the Scarlet Pimpernel, a hero in a book that my mother read, as Aunt Momi told me, before I was born. Isn't that thrilling? You see, the Scarlet Pimpernel's real name is… Percy."

"Quit gabbing and get us to the Writing Salon, Percy, Mr. Scarlet Pimpernel. That's a cuckoo name if you ask me," grumbled Neal as he walked up the stairs holding onto the railing. As he climbed, he chanted, "Scarlet Pimpernel is a cuckoo name. Scarlet Pimpernel is a cuckoo name. Pimpernel rhymes with Pimperhell. Percy is a sissy name."

"One more Pimperhell and I'll throw you down the stairs to show you that Percy is not a sissy name."

At the top of the staircase hung a huge painting of a naked lady peeking through bushes showing her two bare breasts. Next to the painting was the sign: Writing Salon. As I remembered, the gilded couch nestled in an alcove. Hustling Mina into the room, we pushed the couch out and helped her crawl behind it, and spread the Persian lamb coat over her like a blanket. I placed the black valise in with her and warned her to be as quiet as a mouse. Moving the couch back in place, I whispered, "If you have to go the bathroom, put on the turban, wrap the scarf around your face and play dumb."

A quivering voice came from behind from the couch. "I dumb stay on ship." She then let out a loud "KAAAACHOO."

"Don't sneeze." I commanded.

"Too muchy dust." She sniffled.

I whispered "sweet dreams" and walked out of the salon. Neal reminded me that we could be shot for smuggling a Japanese person out of Hawaii.

Standing on top of the staircase, Daisy's toes had turned the color of violets. I told my compatriots to go back to their cabin and reminded them to meet me at the salon after breakfast.

"Watch out for the ghost!"

Neal and Daisy ran like gazelles down the rocking staircase.

I had become too excited to return to my cabin. Instead, I decided to look for Mina's lifeboat. I had dismissed all my aunt's warnings from my mind.

Using my ears as a compass, I found a door that led to the outside deck. Wrapping the mink coat around me, I pushed the door open and stepped out into a dark abyss. The waves were wilder than I could have ever imagined with winds blasting me on all sides. I held onto the door with all my might. Suddenly, a gust of wind wrenched the door handle from my hand and slammed it shut. I tried to pull the door back open, but the force of the wind behind me was too great. I turned around and was met by whirling blasts of salt spray smacking me in the face. Another gust of wind knocked me down as a sudden downpour of rain turned the mink coat into a soggy snow sled. As the ship rose onto the next wave, the fur coat slid me at the speed of Superman towards the black ocean that loomed ahead. As I was about to slide overboard, a hand reached out and grabbed the fur coat. Another hand gripped my hair and held me fast. The hands attached to muscular arms with red hair dragged me through a door as a familiar voice muttered, "You're a lucky mate." Johnny!

Righting me against a wall, I asked Johnny with chattering teeth, "W—W—Where'd you come from?"

Spreading his feet apart to keep his balance, Johnny exclaimed, "Looking for you, Sir Percy. Your aunt got worried and asked me to find you. You're freezing, lad."

"I'm lu-lu-lu-lu-lucky to have you around," I chattered, watching a puddle of water around me turn into the shape of Lake Michigan.

He helped me out of the fur coat and gave me his jacket. "You're more than lucky, Sir Percy. A couple of mates of mine almost drowned looking for three escaped war prisoners. I asked if they had seen you; just then you came flying down the deck like a bloody comet."

Looking at the fur coat crumpled on the floor, my teeth chattered, "Wa-Wa-War prisoners?"

"One of them had a gun. Not only could you have drowned but you could have been shot by the bastard," he said.

Hearing the word gun and bastard, I tingled with excitement.

"Yea, my blokes found the prisoners hiding behind a lifeboat. They chased them to the bow of the ship, almost catching them when that 'killer' wave came out of nowhere. We are pretty sure two of them went directly overboard in the wave, but we're certain that one of them survived. What I'm saying ain't for the passengers' consumption, if you know what I mean. Let's keep this between you and me."

"Don't worry, Johnny. I keep secrets," adding Johnny's secret to the other secrets stored in my belly.

Patting me on the back, he said, "I knew I could trust you, Sir Percy, from the first time we met."

"Thanks for saving my life, Johnny. Without you, I'd have been a goner."

Picking the soggy fur coat off the floor, Johnny urged, "Let's get going before you turn into an icicle."

Looking at the dripping fur coat, I moaned, "I'm going to be in big trouble now."

Inspecting the coat, Johnny asked, "Where'd this ugly thing come from?"

"Auntie Sissy. She has oodles of them hanging in her closet. Auntie Sissy is a very rich lady. She's going to kill me with her polo mallet when she finds out that I ruined this coat. She'll make me buy her a new one out of my allowance and that's going to take me a hundred years."

We reached the cabin. "Johnny, keep the fur coat for saving my life. I'll tell Auntie Sissy you have it now. She won't hit you with her polo mallet because you're an officer."

Shaking his head, handing me the dripping fur coat, Johnny said, "No way, mate. I'm not going to get walloped by a polo mallet." Handing him his jacket, he handed me a blanket.

"When I become a movie star, I'm going to buy you a mansion and a hundred bottles of Best Foods mayonnaise for saving my life twice in one day. I deem you my guardian angel, Johnny."

"You and I are buddies, Sir Percy." As he put back on his jacket, a chain popped out of his shirt. A medal hung on the chain.

Touching the medal, I asked, "What's this, Johnny?"

"It's an ankh. It's my good luck piece that I brought back from Egypt."

"It's weird looking."

Stuffing the medal back into his shirt, Johnny grinned, "Someday, I'll tell you about the strange things I learned in the land of the pharaohs."

Standing beside him, looking at him intently, I said, "Someday, I'm going to save people's lives just like you do."

Johnny's blue eyes drifted before he answered, "Keep that thought, Percy. By the way, mate, I have a big surprise for you tomorrow."

"What is it?" I asked.

"If I told you now it wouldn't be a surprise, now would it, mate? It'd be like opening up a Christmas present before Christmas."

"I hate surprises, Johnny. Tell me now." I pleaded.

Johnny pressed his hands on my shoulder and said, "Keep your voice down. The prisoner bloke could be watching us. If I was you, I wouldn't wander about the ship at night. Wrap up in the blanket and get inside your cabin."

I boasted. "Don't worry, Johnny, I'll watch my step. No prisoner is going to shoot me."

Before he left, my new best friend saluted, saying, "Remember what I said. Not a word about this prisoner stuff to anyone."

Johnny disappeared down the corridor, leaving me to think about the prisoner with a gun. Taking a deep breath, I pounded on the cabin door with my fists.

"Who the jollyjamit is knocking?" Aunt Momi called from inside the cabin.

I yelled, "Best Foods mayonnaise."

Aunt Momi opened the door and yanked me inside. Without a word, she wrenched the wet mink coat out of my hands. Keeping her voice low so she wouldn't wake Marigold, she hissed, "Take off those wet clothes and get into bed now! NOW! I'm too angry to speak right now."

In the bathroom, I heard Aunt Momi hanging the fur coat in the shower and growling to herself, "I'm going to send that boy down to the boiler room first thing tomorrow morning. Jolljamit, I wish Lono were here. He'd handle him." I dragged Johnny's blanket onto the cot to keep me warm.

The worst nightmare of the night: I was floating in the ocean wearing a life jacket. Two sharks circled around me. One of the sharks hissed like Aunt Momi, and the other roared like Auntie Sissy.

Aunt Momi's cabin aboard the Aquitania (as seen from Percy's cot).

CHAPTER 7

THE NEXT DAY — THE SURPRISE

I overslept. When I woke, my aunt was dressed for breakfast. From my cot, I called to her, "Our worries are over, Aunt Momi. The man with the gun fell overboard in the big wave last night."

Straightening the seams on her stockings and giving her hair a final brush, she handed me an envelope. "As usual, Mr. Smarty-Pants, you're wrong. Read what's on this envelope."

I grabbed the envelope out of her hand and read the bold print: "NEXT TIME I WON'T MISS!' I opened the envelope and shook a spent bullet into my hand.

"Whew!" I whistled. "When did you find this?"

She grabbed the envelope and cartridge out of my hand. Placing them on the bureau, she said, "I heard a knocking this morning and, when I opened the door, this envelope was lying on the floor. Now, Mr. Smarty-Pants, tell me again about the man with a gun who fell overboard in a big wave."

"Well… well, someone did fall overboard. Johnny told me so and Johnny doesn't lie." I leaned over the cot to make sure the steamer trunk was still under the blanket.

"Well obviously, it wasn't my killer. My killer remains healthy and alive." Placing a straw hat on her head, she dictated a list of instructions. "I'm going to breakfast. Come to the dining room after you've dressed. Put on your life jacket. You forgot your life jacket last night going out on your little adventure. Your sister is still sleeping. Don't wake her. I told Marigold she could stay in bed all day to let her tummy settle down. When you've finished eating breakfast, bring your sister her breakfast on a tray. Can you do that for me?"

"It's perfect, Aunt Momi." I said giggling to myself, "Perfect. Perfect. Perfect!" I clapped my hands like an idiot.

"Mr. Perfect, I don't see anything to clap about. I'd settle down if I were you. We have a long trip ahead of us, and I don't want to have any more of your foolishness. And you know where I'll send you if you don't behave." She pointed toward the engine room.

"I promise to be as good as an angel. Don't forget to use the password to get back in." I mouthed "Best Foods mayonnaise."

My aunt, not having had her first cup of coffee, slammed the door after herself.

As soon as Aunt Momi was out of the cabin, I ran over to Marigold and shook her. She didn't budge. I blew reveille into her ear, "Da da da da da, da, da."

As I finished the last da, the back of her hand smacked my face. "Leave me alone."

"Pleeeease, Marigold, this is important. You have to listen to me."

"Make it snappy and if it ain't important you're going to get another smack on the head." She showed her fangs.

I told her everything that had happened. I emphasized that I was telling her the truth because my mouth wasn't twitching.

"Go get my breakfast and I'll divvy the food when you get back. Where are you going to hide Mina? She can't stay behind a couch all day."

Jumping into my overalls, as my sister fastened the straps to my pants, I told her how I was going to turn Mina into a mysterious lady.

"Better hurry up before somebody finds her. I'm getting hungry." Marigold's tummy wasn't rumbling. Hurrying, I quickly put my arms through the straps of the life jacket and forgot to brush my teeth.

"Marigold, you got funny red things all over your face."

"I do not. Get out of here. When you get back, take that stinking fur coat out of the bathroom. It's beginning to smell like a dead rat."

"It's making me sick, too. Lock the door after me."

I arrived in the Louis XVI dining room in seconds and made a beeline for an empty table. I tossed two hard rolls, a silver knife, a fork, a pot of butter, and three apples into a napkin. Tying them up, I whizzed past Aunt Momi as she was being seated at the Captain's table. I sang all the way back to the cabin, pretending I was Robin Hood. I had stolen from the rich to feed the poor. Before saying the password, Marigold plucked me into the cabin. Picking from the napkin a roll and an apple, she told me to take the rest of the food to Mina.

Hungrily, Marigold took a bite from the apple. The spots on her face looked redder than the apple. I made her get out of bed and look into the mirror. Marigold diagnosed the spots as an allergic reaction to my stinking breath. I agreed by making a bad boy sound.

Before she could kick my behind, I charged out of the cabin praying that Mina hadn't been discovered by the captain. At the Salon, Mina was sitting on the couch talking to the walls.

She zoomed in on me. "Where you been? I scare all time. No sleep. Where you been?"

Spreading the napkin on her lap, I proudly showed her the food. I imitated Spencer Tracy playing the priest in **Boy's Town**. "I've been praying for you all night, dear, and came as fast as I could. Eat your breakfast like a good girl. Let's pray to God to put a smile on your face."

She tweaked my nose. "You talk crazy. I no like eat. I no like you pray to God. You breath stink like one rotten egg. I more bettah jump off ship 'cause you talk crazy and stink. I no like SMILE."

Trying to quell the mutiny, I answered, "Let's put make-up on your face so you'll look like Greta Garbo. That should put a smile on your face. Everybody wants to look like Greta Garbo. She's the most beautiful movie star in the world."

"I hate Greta Garbo. She ugly. You look like Greta Garbo. She stink, too."

I grabbed for Auntie Sissy's makeup out of the valise, and went to work. I first circled her eyes with black mascara and then slashed her lips with Max Factor's "Blushing Bride" lipstick. It looked as if I had gashed her in the mouth with a samurai sword. In seconds, I had changed her face into an exotic raccoon. After I placed the turban on her head and Auntie Sissy's black Persian lamb coat around her shoulders, in my eyes, I had created a Polish countess. I gushed, "You're perfectly perfect. Come, my little Polish countess raccoon, let's beat this joint and join the ladies on deck." I put the makeup back in the valise, and hid the valise behind the couch.

"I no beat this joint. I wait right here for Neal and Daisy!"

"If you stay in here, you could end up in prison with Auntie Sissy. Do you want the captain to find you and send you to Sing Sing with

Auntie Sissy and her polo mallet for the rest of your life? Never see Daisy and Neal again?"

Mina grabbed my hand, put on her dark glasses, wrapped the red scarf around her neck, and pulled me out of the room. "Okay, we beat this joint."

Out on deck, standing at the railing, we took a deep breath. I scanned the horizon. The sea and sky had become the color of a gray tombstone. The Lurline, sailing near us, matched the color of the sea. The few passengers on deck walked around the promenade taking the kinks out of their bodies. Everything and everyone on that February day had turned gray.

I steered Mina to a rickety old deck chair, and seated her in it. I stretched her feet out on the chair's extension and spread the fur coat on her lap. She looked as I had imagined her, a lady of mystery.

As Mina attacked a roll, my name was being hollered in the distance. "Percy. Sir Percy." I turned around. Johnny was loping down the promenade. He had a clipboard under his arm.

"Let me do the talking."

As Johnny approached, I called, "Is Aunt Momi looking for her slave?"

He hollered back, "Not that I know of, Sir Percy."

Standing next to me, taking a deep breath, he said, "We're having a fire drill. I want you to help me take roll."

He handed me the clipboard. "Take this. By the way, lad, can you read?"

I saluted, "Aye, aye, mate. Yo, ho, ho and a bottle of rum. I read the Bible twice before I was four and sailed around the world with Captain Cook three times."

Johnny stared at Mina. "And who is this lady sitting here looking so mysterious? A friend of yours, Sir Percy?" Johnny extended his hand out to Mina.

Mina shook his hand like a stevedore. "This is Madam Theda, one of Auntie Sissy's best friends. Auntie Sissy is the rich woman with the fur coats that I told you about. Auntie Sissy has taken Madam Theda under her wing because Madam is a poor countess from war-torn Poland. She barely escaped the Nazis' tanks. She speaks not a word of

English, poor thing, and has to stay in the sun because she has syphilis."

"I don't think you mean syphilis, young Percy." He laughed.

"Well, it sounded something like that. It is a terrible disease you get from drinking water out of the tap in your backyard. She has to sit in the salt air and sun to get the rust out of her lungs. Doctors ordered her not to speak to anyone, not even in Polish. You also can get this disease from touching dirty doorknobs. That's what Auntie Sissy told me."

"Sir Percy, we have a lot in common. We make up funny stories about our friends. Let's get moving, lad. Madam Theda, do you know where your boat station is located? I hope you're wearing a life jacket under that fur coat?"

Mina nodded.

Johnny helped Mina out of the chair. Playing Madam Theda to perfection, Mina placed the dark glasses over her eyes, re-wrapped the red scarf around her neck, and haughtily headed, I was certain, to hide behind the couch.

The ship's horn blew a series of sharp blasts. The fire drill had begun.

We arrived at our boat station, running, as the horns stopped blowing. The passengers were lined up in three rows. My aunt was pacing the deck looking as if she was about to explode. She grabbed me away from Johnny and pushed me into a corner, hissing, "Where have you been, bad boy?"

"I've been helping Johnny, Aunt Momi." My mouth was twitching.

She burst into tears. "I had to call the ship's doctor."

"Why?"

"Marigold has the measles. Have you had the measles?"

"Hoof and mouth disease, leprosy, pneumonia, chicken pox, whooping cough and… the measles. Aunt Momi, I am a medical marvel to have survived all those diseases."

"Quit fooling around. You're sure you've had the measles?" she asked, looking at my mouth.

"I stayed home from school for a week. That should tell you something." My mouth wasn't twitching.

"Thank God for little mercies. You're turning me into an old woman. I am having the screaming-meemies before my first cup of coffee because of you. And we have other troubles, Mr. Smarty-Pants. The killer tried to get into our cabin again."

Johnny blew a whistle. Before Aunt Momi could explain about the killer, we joined the passengers in line and stood at attention. Johnny clapped his hands and pointed to a thirty-foot lifeboat hanging over the ship.

"Good morning," Johnny began. "This is your lifeboat. This morning, we are conducting our first boat drill. We do this to ensure your safety. Whenever you hear short blasts from the ship's horn, you are to report here immediately. Make sure that your children come straight to this lifeboat, even if they are not with you. Tell them not to return to your cabin. Make that point very clear to them. And keep your life jackets on or with you at all times."

He looked at me. "My assistant will call roll. If your name is not read, see me after the drill. Sir Percy, come here and read off the names. When you hear your name, answer 'present.'"

I marched to the front of the group, pretending that I was Napoleon reviewing his troops at Waterloo. With my right hand tucked behind my back, I blasted out the passengers' names from the list on the clipboard. I skipped over Marigold's name.

I stumbled over one name, Clarence Linden Crabbe. I knew all movie stars real names from reading Photoplay magazine. I looked to see if I could find a movie star in the lineup. Sure enough, there he was. He was the only man in the group. I also knew that sometimes in the movies he was billed as Larry Crabbe.

There were only two male passengers aboard the ship from Hawaii. One was Uncle Peanut and the other was Clarence Linden "Buster" Crabbe. Of course, I was not counting the wounded soldiers lying on bunks on C Deck or the prisoners of war on D deck.

Standing in the back row was an honest to goodness Olympic swimmer, Flash Gordon, Buck Rogers, and Tarzan movie star rolled up into one handsome package. He looked exactly as he did in the movies. Buster Crabbe stood out like a bronzed god in the midst of a tribe of pinched-faced albinos.

After I called roll, Johnny announced that Captain Spaulding had planned a couple of special events for our first day at sea: a bingo game for the grown-ups in the lounge and a double feature for the kids down on D Deck. Everybody applauded enthusiastically.

"There is a mandatory blackout on the ship from sunset to sunrise. No lights are allowed to show outside the ship and that means no smoking on deck after dark. We don't want to make it easy for the Japs to torpedo us."

I tugged on Johnny's sleeve and whispered into his ear. When I finished, he gave me a pat on the back and announced, "I've been corrected by my assistant. I should have said Japanese instead of Japs. I wasn't being respectful to the Japanese people who live in Hawaii. Percy says the Japanese in Hawaii are as American as you and I. Sir Percy swears that his Japanese friends in Hawaii are on our side, loyal, and they love the red, white and blue as much as we do. Thank you, Sir Percy, for correcting me." He paused, "And yet, we have to keep our guard up because the Japanese army right now is killing our men in the Pacific. We wouldn't want one of them Japanese with a gun on this ship attacking us? Now would we, Sir Percy?"

I nodded, remembering the prisoner with the gun who didn't fall overboard.

"At five this evening, the captain will be giving a cocktail party for all the passengers from Hawaii. You don't want to miss the captain's famous martinis." He reminded us, "The bingo game is about to begin and the film starts at ten forty-five sharp. One of the films is especially being shown for my young assistant here." From the look in Johnny's blue eyes, it was my big surprise.

Johnny took the clipboard out of my hand as the passengers screamed for his attention. A gravelly voice sounded from behind me and said, "Good work, boy!" The movie star had praised me and, before I could get his autograph, Tarzan disappeared into the crowd.

The drill over, Aunt Momi grabbed my hand. Riding down the ship's electric elevator to the cabin, I could feel her anger. She didn't speak even when she pushed me into our cabin. The cabin was as dark as night. My aunt stumbled into the bathroom, closed the door, turned on the light, and cried like a baby. I felt like the biggest heel in the world.

A weak voice called in the dark, "Is that you, Percy?"

"It's me. Darned sorry you have the measles, Marigold. Don't die on me." Then I asked what was on the tip of my tongue, "Did the killer really try to get in here while I was gone?"

"Yup!" she said in a John Wayne voice. "The yellow-streaked varmint won't come back here again, I made sure of that. I yelled that I had a pistol and aimed to shoot off his balls. I'm going to ask Aunt Momi for her gun so I can really shoot the varmint's balls off. How's Mina?"

I told her about grumpy Mina and the movies that were about to start, and then I said what was worrying me. "Please, don't ask for Aunt Momi's gun. Please Marigold, come to the movies with me."

"Nah, I don't want to give my measles to nobody, and it's probably one of those sissy movies I hate. I'm happy to stay in here. I still feel a little sick. Don't worry about me. I can take care of myself."

Aunt Momi emerged from the bathroom wiping her face with a washcloth. "I've been thinking. Percy and I should take turns staying with you in the cabin. I don't want you left in here alone with a crazy person running around wanting to steal the artifacts."

"You don't need to do that, please. I want to be alone. You two would bother me all the time and I need sleep. Please, Aunt Momi. You can do me a big favor. Let me have the gun so I can protect myself."

After a little hesitation, my aunt answered, "All right, you can have the gun. Don't shoot it. Well, actually, you can't. My mother-in-law forgot to give me the bullets."

I blurted out, "That's some mother-in-law you got. I wouldn't want her as my best friend. First, she gives you a trunk of stolen treasures that everyone wants to kill us for and then a gun that can't shoot. She's dumber than Goofy, if you ask me."

"I'm not asking you." Taking the gun out of her purse, my aunt handed it to Marigold. Searching through her purse looking for loose change to play bingo, she ordered, "Percy, get a move on if you're going to the movies and, Mr. Smarty-Pants, don't forget to bring your sister her lunch after the movie. You're the man in the family now, so don't forget you have responsibilities to carry out."

"Marigold is at the top of my list of responsibilities," I answered.

My aunt looked at Marigold, "I am having second thoughts about giving you the gun. Guns are dangerous even without bullets and little girls shouldn't have them."

"Aunt Momi, don't think of me as a little girl. Think of me as John Wayne."

I scurried around the room looking for a sheet of paper and a crayon. Finding both, I printed: DO NOT ENTER THIS CABIN. JOHN WAYNE SLEEPS HERE. SHE CAN SHOOT YOUR BALLS OFF WITH ONE SHOT. SINCERELY, THE MAN IN THE FAMILY.

Leaving, I promised Marigold that I would tell her about the movies and, better yet, act them out for her so she wouldn't miss anything. I placed the note in the corridor so the killer could read it easily and went to collect Mina.

Mina was in her deck chair. I grabbed her hand and walked her down the grand staircase to the Grill Room on D Deck. Mina clumped down the stairs. To my happy surprise, Daisy and Neal were waiting for us. We all screamed, cried, jumped up and down, and hugged each other as if we had just been released from Sing Sing. I pushed everyone inside the theater to get seats in the front row.

Daisy and Neal told me that Auntie Sissy had been in a volcanic mood all morning. Out of Scotch, she ordered Uncle Peanut down to the ship's storage room to look for the steamer trunk where she had packed her booze. She needed more of "the hair of the dog that bit her." She told Daisy and Neal that I had given her a hangover. Neal and Daisy couldn't break away from Aunt Rose because Aunt Rose was afraid to be left alone. She had a premonition.

Aunt Rose was a kahuna, a spiritual priestess, who had been indoctrinated into the secret ways of the Hawaiian religion. She not only knew their sacred language but could interpret dreams and saw visions of the good and bad spirits that roamed the earth.

When I confessed that I had ruined Auntie Sissy's fur coat, Daisy and Neal laughed hysterically. I told them that I didn't think it was funny since I was the one who was going to get killed with the polo mallet. Daisy calmed me by pulling two Hershey candy bars from the pocket of her dress. One bar was for Mina and the other for me.

Mina adored four things: Daisy, Neal, Hershey bars and Lucky Strike cigarettes. Taking teensy bites out of the Hershey bar, Mina smiled for the first time that day looking as if she had gone to heaven. From the look on her face, all she needed to make her life perfect was a Lucky Strike cigarette.

The lights dimmed at ten forty-five on the dot. The screaming brats throwing spit balls behind me quieted down. I became spellbound. Nothing mattered to me but what flickered on the screen. One of the films shown was The Scarlet Pimpernel starring Leslie Howard and Merle Oberon. It was Johnny's grand surprise.

After seeing that movie, I wanted to be the Scarlet Pimpernel. He, like Robin Hood, saved people's lives. It was my moment in childhood that I gained a positive direction to the kind of person I wanted to be. I hated the image of fat, sissy Hermann Goering with his pink ballerina.

The sailor turned off the projector. My body ached. I acted out every part in both movies. With the lights back on, Mina was snoring, Daisy was sighing over the Pimpernel, and Neal had tinkled in his pants. I wanted more Scarlet Pimpernel adventures.

It took only seconds for all the kids to empty out the theater and head for hot dogs and ice cream. Running at the end of the stampede, Daisy spied Auntie Sissy and the nun. They were looking for us. The nun's face looked meaner than the witch in Snow White and the Seven Dwarfs and Auntie Sissy's eyes had turned into two pink powder puffs. She had been crying.

"Somebody must have told Auntie Sissy about the fur coat. Let's beat it the other way."

We crept away in the opposite direction, but we didn't move fast enough. They caught us in their periscopes and screeched our names. Reluctantly, we turned around and walked slowly towards the red-eyed goose and the wicked witch.

I lamented, "Auntie Sissy is going to kill me with her polo mallet."

Within arm's reach, the nun grabbed Daisy and Neal away from Mina. Mina, with the strength of an Amazon warrior, pulled her babies back and shielded them behind her. I stood in back of Daisy and Neal and waited to hear my death sentence.

Auntie Sissy leaned her head on the nun's shoulder and cried out, "Aunt Rose has been murdered."

CHAPTER 8

DEAD AS A DOORNAIL

The ship rocked gently as Marigold slurped her tomato soup. I munched on a cookie. When finished, she laid the empty bowl on her lap and said, "Tell me everything!"

I immediately launched into my tales. "Daisy says that the captain is telling the passengers that Aunt Rose's death was an accident. He says that Aunt Rose tripped over Auntie Sissy's polo mallet and broke her neck. That's the official word. For me, it's murder in the first degree because the evidence is as obvious as the nose on Jimmy Durante's face."

"Uncle Peanut thinks it's murder, too, because Aunt Rose's amethyst brooch was stolen. His theory is that Aunt Rose interrupted a robbery. The robber choked her to death to keep her from squealing. The captain calls it an accident because he doesn't want to create panic on his ship. Panic might cause a mutiny."

Marigold asked, "Are you telling me the truth, Percy?"

"Look, my mouth. It isn't twitching, Marigold. Daisy overheard the captain talking to Auntie Sissy and then Auntie Sissy talking to Uncle Peanut but that was before they started fighting like cats and dogs."

Marigold asked, "Why was Aunt Rose alone in the cabin?"

"She got a chill and left the bingo game *alone* to get her sweater in the cabin. Aunt Rose arrived at the right place but at the wrong time."

"Where was Uncle Peanut?" said Marigold, talking like Sherlock Holmes.

Talking back as Dr. Watson to Marigold's Sherlock Holmes, I said, "Elementary my dear Watson, he was down in the storage room looking for one of Auntie Sissy's steamer trunks."

Wiggling a piece of strawberry Jello on a spoon, Marigold asked,

"Who's the nun? She seems a mighty suspicious character to me."

"Sister Mary Louise was one of Auntie Sissy's high school teachers. Auntie Sissy went to a Catholic boarding school in California to learn to become a normal person after she was kicked out of Punahou. At Punahou, in her freshman year, Auntie Sissy was caught drinking gin in the PE locker room with a teacher. The nun, her favorite teacher at the Catholic boarding school, was visiting Auntie Sissy before Pearl Harbor was attacked. Sister Mary Louise is already sleeping in Aunt Rose's bed. Neal and Daisy think that Sister Mary Louise is a German spy because she is baldheaded and has no bazooms. They're sure the nun is a man disguising himself as a nun because she shaves her head every morning. Uncle Peanut is mad because she uses his razor, and he is telling everyone that Sister Mary Louise killed Aunt Rose because she wanted Aunt Rose's bed. Uncle Peanut and Auntie Sissy are fighting over the nun."

Marigold passed me her tray, "Did you feed Mina lunch?"

"Yep, she's eating a cheese sandwich in her deck chair. Marigold, I think even if the nun didn't kill Aunt Rose, she should have a guilty conscience not giving the bed back to Mina."

Marigold ordered, "Take the tray. I'm sleepy. Boy, Aunt Rose's death stinks."

"How does death stink, Marigold?" I asked.

"Bloody." In the next breath, she asked, "How do my spots look?"

"Like death!" I leapt for the door with the tray in hand, and made a dash for the galley, pretending I was flying faster than Superman.

I added Marigold's tray with the dirty dishes in the galley sink. In a corner, seated at a wooden table, the cooks were eating their lunch. One of them grumbled. "That old lady's death is a sign of bad luck. It's as bad as having a bloody albatross hanging around our necks. Mark my words, bad things come in threes." Noticing me eavesdropping, the pasty-face sailor yelled, "Get out of here, little fat boy."

On deck, Mina had hunkered down in the fur coat, trying to protect herself from the cold wind. She wound the red scarf tightly around her neck. Once again, large waves cascaded over the bow of the ship causing mists of salt to stream down the deck. The mists looked like sea ghosts on the prowl. I decided that the sea was as fickle as Marigold's moods.

Standing in front of Mina, I yelled above the wind, "Let's go find your lifeboat." Mina took my hand and we walked up the deserted promenade. I pushed her up a metal ladder to the next deck, where, according to Mr. Know-it-all Neal, we'd find one of the ship's two motor boats. A motor boat was better than a regular lifeboat because it was fastened to the ship's deck and couldn't be swept overboard even by gigantic waves. Mina could get in and out of the boat safely, without falling into the ocean, not like my lifeboat that hung precariously over the side of the ship.

Finding the motor boat, rubbing my hand over the polished mahogany hull, I grinned at Mina. "This is your boat. It's a perfect place to sleep, if I say so myself. " I helped her inside. We found a bench for her to sleep on, portholes to breathe in fresh air and a roof to protect her from the rain and cold.

"I like sleep warm in feather bed."

I cheered, "It's better than sleeping behind a couch sneezing to death. You'll be safe here. After dinner, I'll bring the black satchel and stuff to make you comfy. It's going to be much better than the cabin." My mouth twitched.

Clink. Clank. Somebody joined us on the deck.

I blurted out, "The ghost."

Mina panicked, "We beat this joint." We leaped out of the boat having an ominous feeling that we were being watched.

Back at her deck chair, making light of the situation, knowing the motor boat was the only solution, I said, "I was only kidding about the ghost. I made it up to keep you on your toes. I'm going back to the cabin to see if Marigold is alive and kicking."

"Don't go."

"I'll be back. Promise. Take a nap my little Polish Theda." I tiptoed away when she started talking in her sleep about Japanese *ghosts*.

Aunt Momi hadn't returned. Marigold's mood was as stormy as the weather outside. She was in misery scratching the welts on her arms. "I'll never eat anything from that stinking kitchen again. The tomato soup upset my stomach." Between burps, she told me that Aunt Momi was in the captain's cabin playing bridge, and we were to get her there in case of an emergency.

"Boy, I wish I had Aunt Momi's sex appeal. I'm going to write the killer that Aunt Momi has connections in high places, so he'd better lay off. That'll keep the varmint away."

Marigold belched. "That's not going to do any damn good. He ain't going away. While you were out, I heard him ripping up your note."

"The killer ripped up my note? That's great, Marigold." I had goose bumps on my arms.

"Before the killer left, he made sounds like a wild boar on a rampage into the door."

Scratching my head, I said, "I didn't know you knew any wild boars."

Suddenly, the ship pitched making Marigold drop the gun on the floor. "Tell me about the movies. NOW!"

"Okay. Okay. I think the measles are eating up your brains, Marigold."

To keep my sister from punching me on the nose, I acquainted her with the Scarlet Pimpernel, Sir Percy Blakeney, an aristocratic English nobleman who, with his league of Pimpies, crossed the English Channel. They disguised themselves as hags, beggars, priests and soldiers, rescuing French men, women, and children sentenced to die by the knife of the guillotine. The Scarlet Pimpernel pranced around his wife and friends acting like a sissy to keep his identity from being discovered. That part of the movie appealed to my flamboyant nature. A black bearded, black-hearted villain, M. Chauvelin, was put in charge by Robespierre to capture the pesky Pimpernel and his men. After watching the film, I knew that there was a Scarlet Pimpernel inside of me waiting to surface. I planned to form my own league of Pimpernels on the ship. With my chums, we'd capture the killer with the gun. I envisioned, after the killer was brought to justice, I would no longer be known as the pink ballerina Hermann Goering but as the Scarlet Pimpernel.

"**The Scarlet Pimpernel** wasn't a sissy movie, Marigold. Now, the second movie was hilarious. **Keep Your Seats, Please**, was about twelve dining room chairs. An eccentric millionaire hid a fortune in diamonds in one of them. After the millionaire died, all his relatives ran frantically around trying to find the chair with the diamonds in it. I laughed so hard I hiccupped through the movie. I hate hiccups as much as I hate throwing up."

I stood up and recited a poem from the *Scarlet Pimpernel* movie.
"We seek him here, we seek him there,
Those Frenchies seek him everywhere,
Is he in heaven?—Is he in hell?
That damned, elusive Pimpernel."

Marigold, rubbing her spotted arms, groaned. "If you say that again, I'll shoot your pink ballerina and I won't miss."

I picked up the gun, "Lucky for me, they're no bullets in this gun. Boy, I wish the killer heard you just now. He'd stay away forever because he'd know you're a mean coyote. That's for sure." I paused, "But then again he could break down the door and shoot you."

Marigold growled, "Where's the gun?"

I said smugly, "I have it. You're talking nutty, Marigold, because the measles are eating out your brains making you go crazy. Did you know that *Modern Screen* magazine says that people who come from crazy families become great actors? Between crazy you and nutty Aunt Momi, I'm going to win an Academy Award."

Blowing her stack, blood vessels showing on her forehead, she screamed, "Give me back my gun."

Sounding like the Scarlet Pimpernel, I said, "I'll give you the gun if you promise me you won't shoot my ballerina. You shouldn't have a gun, anyway. Children shouldn't play with guns. But just in case someone gives you a bullet, shoot only if you hear me say 'Miracle Whip.'"

"Percy!" She warned. Seeing that she had an ashtray wavering in her hand, I threw the gun on the bed, and ducked out the door.

Safely outside the cabin, I reminded myself to write another note to the killer: MAD DOG SLEEPS HERE. THE MEASLES ARE EATING OUT HER BRAINS. WARNING: MY SISTER CAN THROW AN ASHTRAY AND SHOOT A GUN BETTER THAN JOHN WAYNE. AUNT MOMI HAS FRIENDS IN HIGH PLACES AND I'M GOING TO BE A GREAT ACTOR SO DON'T FOOL AROUND WTH US!

Feeling the cold wind hitting my face, I skipped down the slippery promenade thinking about my next plan. Dead ahead, Daisy and Neal cuddled Mina like a baby in her deck chair.

I yelled over the wind, "Hey. Hey. Hey. How's everything back in your cabin? In my cabin, Marigold is going nuts."

Daisy shouted, "What did you say?"

I yelled into her ear, "Follow me!"

Collecting my friends, we turned into scraggly nomads hiking the Himalayas in a wind storm. Reaching Mina's lifeboat, I yelled for them to get inside. Once in, we collapsed on the benches.

Rubbing my hands together, I said, "This is Mina's Shangri-La."

Daisy cooed, "That's such a clever name, Percy."

"Everyone, keep your voice down." I was thinking about the intruder.

"I'm sorry," whispered Daisy. Mina buried her face into Neal's skinny chest to keep him warm. Daisy continued in a breathless voice, "Sissy has decided to bury Aunt Rose tonight at sea before the captain's cocktail party. Aunt Rose will be sailing back to Hawaii in a special coffin being built by Uncle Peanut."

"I'm going to the funeral." I said.

Neal, wiping his glasses, asked, "Why would you want to go? Sissy is making me go. Funerals are spooky stuff, if you ask me."

"Spooky or not, this funeral will be a good time for us to look for clues. I bet Aunt Rose's killer will be at the funeral." Looking out the porthole making sure that no one was listening, I continued, "We have to find the killer because Marigold is next on his list. After Marigold, it's Aunt Momi, and then it's me. I'm going to tell you something I have sworn an oath not to tell."

My voice sounded as scary as the wind blowing outside when I said, "The killer is an escaped Japanese prisoner and he has a gun."

"Nooo!" squeaked Daisy.

"Yup!" Then, I blabbed everything I knew. I told about the gunshot and the treasures in the streamer trunk. "If the killer finds out that you know what I know, you could end up dead like Aunt Rose. Or worse. The killer might torture you with an ice pick. That's what the killers do in the movies. Or he could creep into your cabin at night and while you're fast asleep snap your necks off like twigs."

Daisy fell off the bench.

I loved scaring Daisy. "Or else, just when you think you're safe from his clutches, he'll leap out of a dark corner and before you can say eight times eight, he'll stuff you in his laundry bag and toss you to the sharks."

Mina shouted, "Nobody kill my babies. I kill any son-of-a-dog who put my babies in laundry bag."

I brandished an imaginary sword in the air and declared, "To keep the killer from murdering us; we're going to form a secret league like the Scarlet Pimpernel did in the movie today. Our goal is to roam the ship night and day looking for the killer and capture him before he kills Marigold. I've elected myself to be your leader. First, we have to hide the treasures to keep the killer out of our cabin."

Doubting faces stared at me. "I know I mess up sometimes. I have weak points. I tell secrets. I eat too much and I fear being buried alive. I saw a woman being buried alive in a movie with Boris Karloff. Those are my bad points, but I'm working on them. I promise. I have good points but, right now, I can't think of any."

Daisy volunteered, "You tell scary stories. That's your worst fault as far as I'm concerned. My weak points are: I hate centipedes, rats and boogey men. All those things scare me to death."

"I can't swim," said Neal, forgetting to mention that he was the biggest stubborn-head in the whole wide world.

"I'm not afraid of nothing but water, spiders and sleeping behind couches." We were flabbergasted. Mina spoke an entire sentence in English.

I interrupted, "Even with our bad points, we are going to be the best Pimpernels in the whole world."

Neal said, hitting my arm. "I'll keep you from being stupid because every time you do something dumb, I'll kick your fat behind. By the way, I have a perfect plan to hide the treasures."

"Let's think of our motto first," I said, hogging the attention again.

Neal glowered, "Off with his head."

Daisy chirped, "All for one and one for all."

"Sink the Bismarck." "Remember Pearl Harbor." "The pause that refreshes." On and on, suggestions came until Mina stunned us with "The hungry bird eats the worm."

"That's great, Mina!" I exclaimed. "We'll use Mina's motto as our secret code. Let's call our league the Four Shadows."

Daisy came up with our code names. I would be the Scarlet Shadow, Neal the Blue Shadow, Mina the Black Shadow and Daisy proclaimed herself as the Pink Shadow.

I stood and declared:
"We seek the killer here, we seek the killer there,
"We seek the killer everywhere,
"Is he on A Deck or is he below
"Only the elusive Shadows will know."

I heard a noise. "Someone is coming up the ladder. Duck down and be quiet!"

Someone was stomping on the deck in his boots. We heard him pulling back the canvas covers off the lifeboats. He paused in front of our boat and, as he was about to step inside, a door banged open in back of us. A voice yelled, "What are you doing up here?"

"Looking for something, Captain," the man snarled.

"You don't belong up here. Get below where you belong."

The man grunted, "Yes, sir."

"Go on. Get out of here," said the voice with an English accent.

I raised my head to watch the man wearing boots step down the ladder. When he disappeared, the Englishman uttered, "That's a bloody strange one. Where in the hell did he come from?" The man slammed the door.

Wiping perspiration off my forehead, I turned to the Shadows. I had a look of terror on my face.

"You saw him?" whispered Daisy wide-eyed.

"I did. I saw him clearly."

"What did he look like?" asked Neal.

Gripping the bench, I revealed, "He had on a black overcoat and a black knitted sweater underneath the overcoat. A black wool cap covered his hair and a bushy black beard hid his face. He looked exactly like the bad man in *The Scarlet Pimpernel*."

"Who do you think he is, Percy?" Daisy asked, grabbing my hand.

Without a moment's hesitation, I said, "He's the Angel of Death."

CHAPTER 9

OUT TO SEA

By mid-afternoon, wild tales were being told all over the ship about Aunt Rose's mysterious death, causing the ship's captain to send a written memo refuting the rumors. Most of the passengers, out of morbid curiosity, planned to attend her funeral. A few of them were coming out of respect to a beloved friend.

Dressed for the funeral, Aunt Momi dumped the contents of her purse on her bed waiting for me to put on my pants. Rummaging through wads of Kleenex, cigarettes and loose change, she informed us that she told Captain Spaulding about the shooting and the killer's threatening notes. Concerned for our safety, the captain assigned Johnny and his men to patrol our cabin after midnight. The captain made Aunt Momi promise not to mention the shooting incident to the passengers. His motto continued to be, "What the passengers don't know won't hurt them."

Gingerly picking a piece of paper out from the clutter on her bed, my aunt dropped a bombshell, "I found this in my purse not an hour after I left the captain's cabin. Somebody slipped it into my purse while I was in the powder room. I stupidly left my purse on top of the bar."

Marigold grabbed the note and read it aloud, "Don't think I won't get you. Nobody on this ship can protect you, not even the captain. If you leave the treasures outside your door at midnight, you'll never hear from me again. Do not tell anyone about this note or else the next time I won't miss."

Taking the note back from Marigold, Aunt Momi asked, "What should I do?"

I said adamantly, "I've seen enough movies to know once the dodo has the treasures, he'll kill us anyway."

Marigold sputtered, "He's trying to scare you, Aunt Momi."

"Aunt Momi," I said, "we could tell Johnny about the note. After all, he is our bodyguard."

"No," said Marigold, taking the note back, smelling it for clues. "Johnny can't protect us round the clock. Don't forget, I'm the one in here alone all day. The killer has to be someone we know or someone who at least knows that the treasures were taken out of the museum, and that narrows it down to one of the passengers from Hawaii. Only someone from Hawaii could know about the treasures in our cabin. I've been trying all afternoon to figure out who that person could be. And who says it's a he? The killer could be a woman changing her voice to sound like a raging boar."

"It's Auntie Sissy," I yipped. "She's the biggest dodo we know and she certainly acts like a man."

"Don't call your Auntie Sissy a dodo. No matter how we feel about her, she's still Uncle Lono's sister," my aunt scolded.

"Daddy calls her a dodo."

"That's your father." My aunt hated my father since the day he divorced my mother.

"Percy," my sister warned, "Keep your trap shut. Don't tell your bratty friends anything about this. Don't go around being your usual blabbermouth spilling everything to everybody, including Johnny. Understand me?"

She shot her dagger eyes at me, adding, "Blabbermouth, don't forget who is boss around here. The killer is waiting for me to leave the cabin so he can get in here and steal the treasures. I bet he stole a key to our cabin."

Aunt Momi looked miles away, and mumbled, "I've got to be careful myself."

Marigold suggested, "Let's stall for time and write a note to the killer."

"Write that he's a bad shooter," I said, putting in my two cents.

"Percy!" Aunt Momi yelled.

"Well, he missed." I insisted.

"Quiet. Let Aunt Momi think what to write him. Percy, bring that drawing tablet on your bed and a crayon." Marigold helped clean up the mess on Aunt Momi's bed, returning the Kleenex, change, and odds and ends back into her purse.

Marigold and Aunt Momi ignored me as they composed a note to the killer. When they finished, Aunt Momi folded the note, put it into an envelope, licked it, and asked Marigold how it should be addressed.

"To Stupid Who Can't Shoot Straight."

Marigold threw a pillow and at me and snarled, "Quit fooling around." They decided to write something boring: "To Whom It May Concern" and underneath, Marigold underlined the word Treasures.

After tucking my white shirt into my short white pants, I gave a look in the mirror and decided that I looked pretty spiffy for a fat person. I loved the bright blue bowtie that Daddy had given me as a going-away present. I felt as dashing as Bobby Breen, my favorite child movie star, the stowaway in **Hawaii Calls**.

Aunt Momi excused herself into the bathroom. While she smeared "Holiday in Bermuda" on her lips, I cut a black ribbon off her hat and tied the ribbon around my arm to show proper respect for Aunt Rose. I copied what Clark Gable did when his wife, Carole Lombard, died in an airplane crash.

Out of the bathroom, Aunt Momi picked up her hat, cocked it to one side, and tucked a black veil under her chin. She looked as glamorous as any Hollywood movie star. With her shiny black purse under her arm, we left the stateroom.

Waving goodbye to Marigold, I promised faithfully to bring her dinner reminding her not to change the password. I mouthed "Best Foods mayonnaise" in case the killer was listening. Before we walked down the corridor, I wedged the envelope to the killer in the crack of the cabin door.

At the stern of the ship, black ribbons fluttered wildly in the wind. The ship's mahogany deck had been polished to a glistening mirror, reflecting the gray clouds in the sky. A light rain blessed the ship's deck, and the gods turned the sea calm.

Auntie Sissy, Sister Mary Louise, Neal, and Daisy stood straight as ramrods at the stern of the ship. They were silhouetted against the setting sun. Passengers on the upper decks leaned over the railings and ogled us. I couldn't find Mina anywhere in the crowd. To my left, Johnny was shooing a busybody away from the funeral party. The busybody had a Brownie camera pointed at Auntie Sissy.

Standing apart, near the funeral party, stood a tall, skinny lady wearing a long black dress and a large, black hat. A gray veil covered her face. What I liked about her was the way the wind blew her dress in all directions making her whirl like a dervish. She fluttered her hands all around her like a butterfly trying to keep the hat and veil from blowing into the ocean. With the veil covering her face, she looked mysterious and I ached to make her acquaintance.

Auntie Sissy, upon seeing me, scrunched her nose as if she smelled a skunk was approaching her. Aunt Momi nudged my fanny toward the whirling dervish. I obliged without protest. I was scared that Auntie Sissy was going to ask me about the fur coat.

As I sidled next to the tall lady, a cackle came from behind the veil, "What's wrong with you?"

"What's wrong with you?" I answered snottily.

The mysterious lady stepped on my foot.

"That hurt." I looked to see if I could see anything human behind the veil. I couldn't. Her hands held the veil over her face keeping her as mysterious as a sphinx. Using my know-it-all Scarlet Pimpernel deduction, I deducted that a skull had cackled from behind the veil.

I looked at the crowd and spotted Mina hiding in the fur coat watching me from the upper deck. I waved to her. She waved back. I waved again sending her this time a wave of love. Mina looked so helpless.

A sudden gust of wind blew Aunt Momi's hat into the ocean. Her red hair blew wildly all around her making her look like Rita Hayworth dancing with Fred Astaire. Shaking her head, she warned me not to take notice that her hat was floating in the ocean.

Daisy and Neal were having giggling fits to the annoyance of Auntie Sissy. The same gust of wind had blown the nun's veil skyward, exposing her shaved head. As I was about to join in their giggles, Johnny arrived out of the blue. He clutched my hand, stifling the oncoming hysterics. He saved me again. My laughter would have added more blows to my head from Auntie Sissy's polo mallet. Johnny's face looked sadder than an undertaker's face. I copied his sad look.

The winds died down, letting me concentrate on the vibrations from the ship's engines. Beneath my feet, the engines throbbed through my entire body, binding me to the ship. During this lull, I watched a Navy destroyer struggle to keep up with the Aquitania. It made me understand how powerful our ship was compared to any other vessel in the convoy.

Bang! A drumbeat resounded from the upper deck. The ship's officers pushed passengers aside as Uncle Peanut appeared making the passengers gasp. Uncle Peanut had shaved his head and knocked out his front teeth. His change in appearance was a reverent sign of mourning that ancient Hawaiians performed when a person of high birth passed. He was only recognizable because of the familiar black patch that covered one eye. He walked down the ladder like a Roman warrior heading into battle. Behind Uncle Peanut, six men carried the coffin, lifting it high in the air. One of the men lifting the coffin was Tarzan, the rest were sailors.

The captain, wearing a formal blue uniform and holding a Bible under his arm, followed the men and the coffin down the ladder. The coffin was humongous. It was larger than three coffins put together. Uncle Peanut constructed it on the upper deck. Daisy told me Uncle Peanut made the coffin watertight so Aunt Rose would float back to Hawaii. All Aunt Rose's coffin needed to become a true boat was for Uncle Peanut to have added a rudder and a sail.

Uncle Peanut chanted down the ladder to the drumbeats. The ceremony reminded me of a wedding procession. On the deck where Mina watched, two Hawaiian ladies wailed. Wailing was another traditional sign of grief at Hawaiian funerals.

At the stern of the ship, the captain directed his men to place the coffin near the railing. Once the coffin was in place, he raised his hands signaling the passengers to be silent. The drums, the wailing and Uncle Peanut quieted as the passengers on the upper decks bowed their heads in prayer.

The captain opened the Bible and the funeral service began. I couldn't hear a word the captain said because the engine hummed loudly in my ears.

The bony lady murmured, "Make it fast, captain. My feet are killing me."

Under his breath, Johnny replied, "He'll make it quick. The last thing the captain wants is a bloody body decomposing in front of his passengers."

"Hope you got that right, Red," the lady answered, poking her bony finger into his ribs.

Johnny mused, "That one-eyed fellow is wild-looking. He wouldn't let any of my men near him or by the coffin. He threatened to kill us if we came near him."

The bony lady whispered from under her veil, "He feels responsible for Rose's death." She adjusted the veil closer to her face.

Johnny whispered, "He never left the body alone. We offered to weigh the coffin down so it would sink, but he told us to get the hell away from him. I watched him put a small bag inside the coffin, probably her valuables. That coffin is so watertight it'll float like the Queen Mary around the world twice and then some. In the English Navy, we shove our dead overboard in a canvas bag, say a prayer if the bloke is lucky, and then watch him disappear under the sea. That lady was fortunate we had a storage room full of empty coffins. We took four of them apart so he could make that bloody thing. This whole ceremony reminds me of what Egyptians did in ancient Egypt, burying their dead with all their treasures." Johnny stared at Uncle Peanut. Uncle Peanut stared back.

I whispered to Johnny, "Show me the room where you keep the coffins."

"I knew you liked that sort of thing, Sir Percy. If you behave, I'll give you and your pals a tour of the ship tomorrow and show you the coffin room. It's a pretty special room all on its own."

The skinny lady looked up at the passengers and remarked, "Everybody loves a spectacle. No spectacles for me when I die. I want it like you do in the Navy. They can carve fishhooks out of my bones, for all I care. Got to hand it to Peanut, though, he made damned sure that no one will ever hurt Rose again. He should have been with her."

Johnny wondered, "Hawaiians and Egyptians must be bloody relatives, burying their treasures with them. Not me. I'm going to spend all my fortune. Speaking of fortunes, there must be a fortune waiting to be discovered where the Hawaiians buried their kings."

The captain raised his hands and said "Jesus Christ" and "amen." The men tied ropes around the coffin. Uncle Peanut kissed the coffin, straightened up and stared at the setting sun. He was seeing the mountains of Hawaii underneath the clouds. Auntie Sissy watched the sunset with Uncle Peanut. The nun strode back into the ship fingering her rosary beads. Tarzan and the men lifted the coffin over the side and lowered it into the sea. Two Hawaiian ladies on the upper deck sang "Aloha Oe." Others joined in. The coffin floated towards the setting sun, following Aunt Momi's hat. A wounded soldier blew taps. A green flash burst. The sun set as the bugler blew his last note.

Someone yelled, "Let's get drunk." It signaled the end of the service letting the passengers leave for the captain's cocktail party. When I looked beside me, the lady with the veil had vanished. I asked Johnny, "Who was that mysterious lady?"

"She's not liked by your rich friend. No one eats with her or speaks to her and she sits in the lounge all day playing solitaire."

Johnny charged, "Let's go find your aunt. I have work to do. Here." He reached into his pocket and placed something cold in my hand.

"It's an ankh. The ankh is an Egyptian symbol of life and brings good luck and protection to anyone who wears it. So wear it well, mate." He took the ankh out of my hand and hung it around my neck. When the charm touched my skin, I swore I felt it's magic. Blood surged like rivers all over my body.

"This is the best present I have ever had in my whole life. I'll never take it off. Marigold will sure be jealous when she sees this." I hugged Johnny, wishing he was my father.

An eerie blue light turned the Aquitania into a ghost ship. Somewhere out in the dusk, my aunt called my name. She was standing next to the railing where they had lowered the coffin into the sea. I ran and grabbed my aunt's hand making her touch the ankh around my neck. "Look at what Johnny gave me. The ankh is going to protect me from doing bad things, Aunt Momi."

My aunt sighed to Johnny, who was in back of me, and said, "I pray that this thing will keep him out of trouble. May it also protect me and thee from all his foolishness."

"It will, ma'am. Percy promised me that he'll be a good lad from now on, didn't you, Percy?" I loved hearing Johnny build me up in Aunt Momi's eyes.

Touching Johnny's hand, Aunt Momi said, "I'm ever so grateful to you for taking care of this bad boy during the service. I am continually in your debt. Believe me, it will be a miracle to get to San Francisco without having him sink this ship."

"I'll see to it, ma'am. That's a promise." Johnny patted me on the head.

"Now, Percy, escort your old auntie to the cocktail party. I am thirsty for a cold martini. Join me, Johnny?"

"No, ma'am. It's against Navy rules."

"I keep forgetting about your English Navy rules."

Taking my aunt's hand, I asked, "Aunt Momi, stay out here a minute? Can we? Please?"

Brushing hair away from her face, she said, "Only a minute. Your old auntie is very thirsty."

"I'll say goodnight then," Johnny turned and climbed a ladder near us. Aunt Momi cautioned me as he disappeared. "Don't disappoint Johnny. You don't want to lose his friendship."

Facing the ocean, I made a promise, "I'm not going to ever disappoint Johnny. I am going to deserve wearing his ankh."

I caught a whiff of Aunt Momi's perfume floating in the wind. The smell of the perfume made me think of my mother.

A sudden noise came from behind us. Someone bumped into a deck chair. I gasped, "It's the ghost, Aunt Momi!"

"Stop it." She cried.

I looked into the dark and insisted. "Someone is watching us. I can feel it. Didn't you hear that noise?"

"I have warned you about crying wolf."

A bird screeched in the dark. Aunt Momi grabbed my hand and steered me into the ship making me walk in front of her. Before going through the door, I turned around to see if I could discover who had made that noise. A shadow darted behind a post. The bird screeched again.

"Aunt Momi, Aunt Rose is calling us. She wants us to catch the killer."

Hitting my behind with her purse, she steered me down the corridor repeating, "Quit scaring me."

"I'm not crying wolf. This is for real, Aunt Momi."

CHAPTER 10

THE PLAN

When we arrived at the cocktail party, Aunt Momi made a beeline for the bar. Looking around, the Shadows were in a far corner of the room hiding Mina. I waved them over. Seeing my hands signal them, they plunged through the crowd like football players. As soon as we touched hands, they followed me into the foyer for a meeting.

In a huddle, Mina reported that the Angel of Death was sitting at the bar. She knew it was him right away because of his ugly black beard.

Neal butted in saying that Tarzan was drinking with Uncle Peanut and that he was our killer. Neal was prejudiced about actors because Aunt Sissy told him all actors were Democrats which, according to her, was on an equal par with a murderer. Daisy put Sister Mary Louise at the top of her list because she hated her bald head. I said the Angel of Death was our biggest suspect but pondered, "He doesn't look like anybody from Hawaii that I recognize. He dresses like he's going to a Halloween party."

Pointing to a chair in the foyer, I instructed, "Mina, you sit in that and keep your eye on all the suspicious characters who leave the cocktail party, and especially watch when the Angel of Death leaves and look where he goes because we want to follow him."

"I like eat." moaned Mina.

"Neal, get Mina's supper."

Annoyed at my bossiness, he said, "You bet, Pimper*hell*."

"Don't call me Pimper*hell*! We're doing serious business here. I don't want to hear any more sassiness out of you."

Neal replied meekly as if I had hurt his feelings, "Yes, Percy."

Bullies back down if you confront them directly.

"Next, take Marigold her dinner and remember the password.

Don't forget it or she'll shoot you where you don't want to be shot."

I turned to Daisy. "Sit near the nun. She'll do a lot of blabbing tonight because right now she hates Uncle Peanut."

Neal cut back in, "Marigold better not shoot me in the balls or I'll tell Sissy. What'll I do after I get Marigold and Mina their dinners?"

"Come back into the cocktail party. Sit near Uncle Peanut. Tarzan is sitting at Uncle Peanut's table. Remember, Tarzan is your biggest suspect."

"He sure is. Sissy says actors are scumbags."

My eyes lit up and said, "Do you remember where they hid the jewels in **Keep Your Seats, Please**?"

Daisy answered, "They hid the diamonds in a chair."

"That's what we are going to do with our treasures. We're going to hide them in a cushion of a big chair." Neal's jaw dropped after I said that because he said that was his idea. He had come up with it when we were sitting in the lifeboat.

Taking his fingers off my arm, I said, "Okay, it's your idea, Neal. But we have to do it tonight before the killer strikes again. That son-of-a beeswax wrote Aunt Momi another note demanding that we hand over the treasures at midnight or else." After I said "or else," I slid my finger across my neck slowly.

Daisy said excitedly, "We'll do it tonight. Sissy has a sewing basket in the bathroom. Mina can sew the treasures into the chair."

"I sew betta dan one Betsy Ross!" Mina spoke up proudly.

"Great! Now, I have another idea."

Neal's lower lip quivered as I backtracked, "Neal, your ideas are much better than mine, any day. This idea is only second best to any of your ideas. But listen to this. After we hide the treasures, we'll stuff the empty steamer trunk with junk and then in front of the passengers on the ship, we'll throw the trunk overboard. The killer will think the treasures have gone to the bottom of the sea, and then there will be nothing that the killer will want from Aunt Momi. He'll have to shoot somebody else. But if we do this, we have to keep it a secret or else it won't work."

Daisy, gluing her eyes into mine, asked, "When?"

The plan ran through my mind like a movie. "We'll do it tomorrow after lunch. That's when the passengers are walking off their meal."

Wide-eyed, Mina said, "I hope da killer stay watch us."

I grinned. "We'll make such a huge commotion that even if the killer isn't on deck he'll hear about it. We'll yell when we throw the trunk overboard, 'There go the treasures!' Then, there'll be no mistaking what we have done."

In his excitement, Neal's glasses fell on the floor as he insisted, "I'm going to be the one to toss the steamer trunk overboard."

Daisy, acting like a big sister, said to her brother, "Neal, pick up your glasses and behave. You're too small to do that. You'll fall overboard and, remember, you can't swim."

Neal flexed his arms. "I will, too, do it."

I reminded him, "Our goal is to catch the killer. Remember our motto, Neal, 'The hungry bird eats the worm.' We are going to save Aunt Momi's life and, who knows, maybe even Mina's life."

"If Sissy finds out what we're doing, we're all going to get the worst polo mallet licking of our lives. But I don't care anymore. I am gonna save Mina's life." Neal had a new swagger in his voice.

Punching Neal's arm, I cheered, "That's the spirit. Be tough like Superman and just think nobody on this ship is having the adventures we are having. It's just like being in the movies. After midnight, we'll hide the treasures."

Neal made another suggestion. "Let's hide them in the couch where Mina slept last night."

"That's the perfect place," Daisy beamed, as she adjusted the eyeglasses on Neal's face.

I agreed. "That *is* the perfect place. Now we've got that settled, let's go to work. Meet me back here in half hour. Look at them. They're acting crazier than Holy Rollers. One more martini and they'll be blabbing all their secrets to us. Let's hope the Angel of Death is hitting the bottle."

"Are you scared?" asked Daisy.

"Naw," I answered. My mouth twitched.

Pushing Daisy into the cocktail party, I charged, "Let's go find the son-of-a-beeswax."

"Percy, what are you going to do?" she asked.

Hearing Daisy's question, the Shadows stopped and glared at me as if they had discovered a Benedict Arnold in their very midst. I could see from the looks in their eyes they were thinking that I was going into the cocktail party to drink a Coke and have a good time while they did all the dirty work.

"I'm on the scariest mission of all. I'm going to talk to the skinny lady with the veil and learn who she really is. The skinny lady may have the strongest motive of all to kill Aunt Rose, more than anybody on this entire ship. She could be the Angel of Death. Maybe, there is a beard behind that veil. Coming from Hawaii, she could have known that the treasures were taken out of the Bishop Museum and she talks like she can shoot a gun. Anyone who hides behind a gray veil in broad daylight is a very dangerous person."

Wide-eyed, Daisy said, "I'm awfully glad you didn't give her to me. She scares me to death. Sissy hates her. You're very brave to talk to her, Percy."

I bragged, "I'm not scared of her because I'm the Scarlet Shadow and the early bird *is* about to eat that worm."

The Shadows straightened up their spines showing me that they were willing to carry out the orders of the Scarlet Shadow. Turning my back on the Shadows, I walked into the cocktail party and found the lady with the veil sitting at a table nearest the bar, drinking a martini, alone.

The Angel of Death was sitting at the bar next to Aunt Momi.

CHAPTER 11

BEHIND THE GRAY VEIL

I thought she was the strangest looking person in the whole wide world. She sat alone wearing her hat and veil. To see behind the veil, I used my French movie actor, Charles Boyer, accent on her.

"May I ze join youze, dark, dangerous Lady of Mystery?" I was standing at her table.

Making a snorting sound, she said, "The Dangerous Lady of Mystery doesn't seem to have any better offers. Take a load off and sit, my little outcast."

Surprised that she remembered me, I sat down directly across from her. I put my elbows on the table and introduced myself. "Everyone on ze ship says I'm the spitting image of Hermann Goering. I am not. So, don't get confused. I am not the Nazi Hermann Goering. My name is Percy and, after seeing you at the funeral, I have been dying to talk to you, cheri."

She slapped the table. "I like the French talk but quit staring at me like I'm a bug. Take your elbows off the table and keep on saying charming things to me."

Removing my elbows from the table, I kept acting as charming as Boyer did in the movies. I asked, "Cheri, buy me a martini. I've had a very bad day."

The lady with the veil snorted again, this time so loud that the people at the next table turned around and stared at her. "That's not charming, young man. You're not old enough to drink a martini."

"I know. When Aunt Momi is having a bad day, that's what she says. She's drinking a gallon of them right now over at the bar. She's had a terrible day. Between you and me, I was the main cause of her bad day."

The lady swallowed the last of her martini, looked into the empty glass, mused momentarily, and chortled, "I can understand that!"

Pointing to her empty martini glass, the lady with the veil spoke deliberately. "Young man, you are too young to be drinking a martini but, if you'll go up to the bar and order me another martini, I'll treat you to a Shirley Temple."

Putting my elbows back on the table, I looked straight into her veil, lowered my voice, and informed her, "I hate Shirley Temples. Buy me a ginger beer. Princess Margaret Rose drinks them all the time in England. I adore Princess Margaret Rose, don't you?" Without skipping a beat, I asked, "May I have the olives in your glass?"

"Here," she said, shoving the martini glass across the table.

Picking the olives out of the glass, I plopped them in my mouth one by one, trying to think of a way to have her remove her veil.

She slapped my hand and commanded, "Mr. Percy, go to the bar and ask Thomas to make me another martini, and order a ginger beer. Tell Thomas to put the drinks on my tab."

I said, "And who shall I say is treating me?"

Being a fan of Alfred Hitchcock movies, especially my favorite **Sabotage**, I knew that this was the moment when the suspect spills the beans. Seconds went by before she answered, "Mrs. Brown. Edwina Brown. Mrs. Aaron Brown, Mr. Nosy Pants."

Thrilled at my success, I jumped out of my seat and ran to the bar with the order. Thomas, a grizzled old bartender, a Gabby Hayes look-a-like, was pouring martinis as fast as the passengers were drinking them. Waving my hands in his face, getting his attention, I gave him Edwina's order and told him to make it snappy. I couldn't help grinning because I was a great Scarlet Pimpernel. Watching him splash gin into Mrs. Brown's martini glass, I told Thomas to make it a triple. "A hungry bird is about to eat a worm."

On my way back to the table, I stopped dead in my tracks. At the other end of the bar, Aunt Momi was in deep conversation with the Angel of Death. I got a close look at him. The man of mystery resembled Hitler in the newsreels. Both Hitler and the Angel of Death had the same hypnotic eyes. After I finished interviewing the lady with the veil, I planned to sit next to the Angel of Death and discover who was under his beard.

Breathless with excitement, I sat down and passed the martini glass over to Mrs. Brown, thanking her for the ginger beer. Pointing to the bar, I instructed, "Follow my finger, Mrs. Brown. See that oogie man with a beard sitting next to my aunt? My aunt is the lady who looks like Rita Hayworth. Don't you think that man looks exactly like Hitler? Ever seen him before?"

Taking a sip of her martini, she looked closely and revealed something that made the bearded stranger even more mysterious. "That's a fake wig and beard he's wearing. That's not his real hair. I know a thing about wigs. There's something familiar about him that I can't put my finger on." She shook her head trying to think what was so familiar about the mysterious man. Inspecting him again, she shrugged her shoulders and took a sip of her martini.

Drinking my ginger beer, I agreed with Mrs. Brown, "Yes, there is a familiar feeling about him. He gives me the creeps. I call him the Angel of Death."

Raising her martini glass towards me, she said, "A toast to keep the Angel of Death away from our door. While we're at it, let's toast all the outcasts in the world and may God protect all the outcasts from all the angels of death that roam this world." Our glasses clinked sending our toast to heaven.

Downing my ginger beer in three gulps, I asked, "Don't you ever take off your hat and veil?"

"Why?" she asked, fiddling with the olives in her martini glass.

I said nervously, hoping she wouldn't get mad at me, "I keep wondering if I am talking to the ghost of the Aquitania."

She guffawed, "I am. I am. You are talking to the ghost of the Aquitania. Boooooooo!

What would you do for me if I took off my hat and veil?"

I answered quickly, "I'll tell you a secret. I'll tell you a big secret. I've got a million of them stored in my stomach. Some of the secrets in my stomach are doozies."

"Hmmm. We might have a deal here. I like secrets." She asked, "Are they juicy secrets?"

"Humdingers, Edwina." I smiled mysteriously.

With steady hands, Edwina lifted the hat and veil carefully off her head and arranged them neatly on the table before her. "There," she said, looking at me with steely eyes.

"You're not a ghost. I would have fainted if you were. Honest to God, I would have. Boy, you must have been a spiffy dish when you were young."

What struck me and really surprised me was that across from me was the spitting image of Loretta Young. Edwina had the movie star's same big dark eyes, luscious red lips and front teeth that protruded. What made her so striking was that she combed her black hair into a pompadour, making strands of her white hair streak in all the right places.

Taking a long look at her face, I asked, "May I say something else?"

Brushing a loose strand of white hair away from her forehead, she closed her eyes as if she feared that something terrible was about to come out of my mouth. "Make it nice. I have a feeling that I can't stop you from saying anything that comes into your mind. Speak."

"You're a pip. I really mean it. Pardon me for saying this, but you shouldn't hide your face behind that veil. Throw that veil away because you look just like Loretta Young. She's one of the most beautiful pips in Hollywood, California."

Smoothing the veil out on the table, she smiled at me. "I like this veil. It hides things that I don't want people to see."

"Oh," I exclaimed. Not knowing what to say, I said the next thing that came into my mind. "What are those things you don't want people to see?"

Pushing the hat and veil between us, she patted my hand. "I liked being called a pip just now. Mr. Percy, it's your turn. It's time for you to tell me your big juicy secret."

Without a moment's hesitation, I blurted out my life's story from its very beginning and ended with "I'm going to bring back the skull to Hawaii because I don't want to be cursed anymore. Edwina, it's a very tiring thing to have a curse over your head all the time. My Grandmother's curse is giving me fits." Edwina's eyes looked sad.

Snapping my fingers to interrupt her sad thoughts, I inquired, "You look like you have a lot of secrets inside of you, too. Maybe, you should tell me them. Telling secrets will make you feel much better.

Keeping secrets inside of your stomach is very bad for your digestion. It can give you gas. Holding secrets inside of you can make you sicker than a dog. My sister got the measles keeping secrets to herself. Tell me your secrets and you won't catch the measles."

Edwina took the bait.

Her clouded eyes focused on me. "You're dying to know why the people on this ship avoid me like the plague."

I nodded.

Edwina began her story. "My story is about bad things that happen in life. My story is about people you can't trust and people you can. It's about people who betray us. First off, you're sitting with a scandalous woman, a cursed person like yourself. You see, Percy, you don't have a corner on curses. Everyone in this room is afraid to come near me because they are afraid that my curse will rub off on them. You are sitting, my friend, with a living breathing curse. You attract curses."

"You're a living breathing curse?" I exclaimed. "Boy, this is great because I have never known another living curse in my whole life but me."

"Don't think you're so special. Everyone is cursed in some fashion. You were right when you said that there was a ghost hiding behind this veil." She stared at the veil on the table and continued, "I am a dead living person. I feel like a dead living person. If I should die tomorrow, I wouldn't care. That's why I hide behind the veil. I don't want to frighten people. I don't want them to see what I have turned into — the living dead."

"You're a dead person who's living?" I couldn't believe my ears. I found someone who felt exactly like me.

Taking a sip from her martini, she continued, "Cursed as they come. I am cursed through and through — to the very core of my body. When I was a little girl, I thought I had the world on a string. I was so pretty. I turned men's heads. When I became eighteen, I could walk into a room and have every man look at me just like they do your Aunt Momi. Even as a teenager, I understood what their eyes were doing. My mother and I never got along. I was a daddy's girl. One should never go around thinking that you're high and mighty because, one day, somebody or something is going to bring you crashing to earth. I learned that the hard way. One minute I was dancing under a rainbow and the next I was sitting in the rain. Things go wrong when you least expect it. It brought on all these wrinkles. My tragedy turned me into an ugly, old witch. God doesn't play favorites or give a damn whether you're rich or poor, ugly or beautiful when He deals out His cards.

"God dealt me the ace of spades when Mr. Brown arrived from the Mainland some twenty years ago. Everyone in Honolulu hailed him as a real up-and-comer just by his good looks and smooth talk. He had the most wonderful hands. Women notice hands, especially strong, beautiful hands. He had hands of a concert pianist. Someone should have warned me about smooth talkers with long fingers. I was young and I wasn't about to listen to anybody. I loved the heat – the fire – the danger when Mr. Brown was standing next to me. Daddy didn't approve of Mr. Brown and my daddy was always a good judge of character. Daddy told me that Mr. Brown had the soul of a weasel. Strange as it sounds, I called Mr. Brown 'Mr. Brown' till the day he died.

"When Mr. Brown became controller of one of the Big Five Companies, American Factors, we hobnobbed with the best of the sugar aristocracy. Even Sissy and her set sniffed our behinds. We partied with the sugar society on weekends in their Kahala homes. Mr. Brown referred to their Kahala beach houses as villas and was determined to become part of the sugar aristocracy. Weekly, he was written up in the newspapers as Hawaii's financial wizard. He got himself elected as a trustee on all the boards — YMCA, Salvation Army, Central Union Church; you name them, he was on them.

"We were married for over ten years when it happened. One day after lunch at the Halekulani Hotel with my closest and dearest girlfriends, who have since dropped me like a lead balloon, I arrived home to find my front door padlocked. The police were standing outside my home not letting anyone in or out. From the police, I learned that my husband was in jail on charges that he had embezzled millions of dollars from all the institutions he financially handled. He had been robbing them blind for as long as we had been married and I never once guessed it. Believe me, *I never once guessed it.* How dumb can I be? I learned during his trial that his downfall began with whispers at the Pacific Club, then strong rumors circulated on Fort Street, and finally, a formal investigation and his books were secretly audited. Ha! I never saw a dime of that stolen money, and he never told anyone up to the day he died where all that money disappeared to, insisting up to his last breath that he was not guilty of the charges made against him. He was an arrogant bastard to the end."

"Do you have children?"

"Happily, we never had children. Can you imagine children carrying their father's curse for the rest of their lives — a daddy who died in an Oahu prison for stealing from the YMCA? Mr. Brown died a couple of days before the Pearl Harbor attack. I took the trolley out to Oahu prison every day, and not once did he speak about what he did or why or where the money went to. Our visits were long hours of painful silences, but I stayed loyal to the end. The only person he wanted to speak to was the governor, but the governor neither replied nor came near him.

"What happened next?"

"I became a pariah, a curse, and an embarrassment to the matrons of Honolulu society. They treated me as if I had been the one who had stolen the money. The morning I left for that lunch at the Halekulani, I forgot my diamond engagement ring. I left it on the bureau in our bedroom. The police wouldn't let me back in the house to get it. It belonged to my dead mother. Though I never got along with her, there was a sentimental value to that ring. After that lunch, I had only the clothes I wore on my back and had not a penny to my name. Our bank accounts were frozen.

"I begged my father to let me live with him, but he refused. He never spoke to me again. George Moody was good to me. George did for me what he did for so many other women in distress, he hired me in his jewelry store."

"Now, I am off to live with a distant cousin of my mother's in Sacramento, someone whom I have never seen, only communicated with by letter. I'm going to manage one of her dress shops. You talk about being cursed. I was cursed and betrayed real good. Ha!" She finished her second martini.

I whistled. "That's some story, Edwina. Maybe Mr. Brown hid the money in one of your dining room chairs."

Fiddling with her empty glass, she guffawed, "Not a chance, Percy.

All my belongings were sold off at auction to pay back the creditors. He wasn't that creative. He probably lost it all in the stock market or some shady deal with a co-conspirator. There were lots of interesting men at his trial. A dear friend of mine bought my engagement ring and gave it back to me. It was one of the great kindnesses in my life."

"Do you have the ring with you?" I asked.

"It is on me at all times. George Moody says it is quite valuable. The ring is designed in an old Tiffany setting with yellow diamonds surrounding a ten carat blue diamond. It's quite extraordinary."

I warned, "Don't tell anyone on the ship about the ring. You can trust me, but don't tell anyone else about the ring." I was thinking about Aunt Rose's missing amethyst pin.

Handing me her olives, she told me more. "Sissy, sitting over there, thinks that I stole her money. My husband bilked her family estate for over hundreds of thousands of dollars. It drives me crazy thinking about where all that money went to. I keep asking myself, how can so much money disappear without a trace? My father paid a private detective to look into banks all over the United States for the missing money. Even the United States government sent a man to the trial to look into the matter. Of course, when my daddy contacted the Swiss banks, the bank officials were hopeless. Nothing came out of Daddy's investigations. My father died an angry man without speaking to me."

Testing the waters to see if she was Aunt Rose's murderer, I said, "I bet you'd kill to get back that money."

She laughed, "Nothing worse in this world than being a poor, stupid part Hawaiian-German woman who thought she had it all and would be filthy rich till the end of her days. Sure, I want my money back and sure, I want plenty of it, but I wouldn't kill for it."

Looking into her eyes, I asked, "Did you know Aunt Rose?"

"I did!"

"You did?" I gulped.

A wistful expression came over her face as she leaned down to pick a napkin off the floor. "Rose was one of the few friends who stayed loyal to me after the scandal broke. She's the one who loaned me the money to come to the Mainland and she was the friend who bought the engagement ring. She was my bunkmate until Mrs. High and

Mighty took her up to her cabin. Rose was a dear friend and I loved her very much. She was one of the good angels that live on this world and I hope God knows that. If she had stayed with me, she would still be alive. I believe that. I know that."

Putting my Scarlet Pimpernel thinking cap on, I probed, "Why do you know that? Do you have any idea who would want to kill Aunt Rose?"

After folding her napkin into squares, she played with her martini glass before she answered me. "It was a matter of bad timing. I'm with Peanut on that. It happens. Bad things happen to people in this world for no reason at all. You should know that. Rose didn't have an enemy in this world except for that phony baloney nun sitting with Sissy. Rose caught somebody stealing Sissy's things and she got killed for it. It's as simple as that."

I added, "I know all about bad stuff. Look what happened to my mother. She was at the wrong place at the wrong time, and I am at the wrong place all the time. I take after my mother in that department. My mother got killed for trying to keep my sister and me out of danger. Life gets very discouraging at times."

Touching my hand, she asked, "What do you want from your life, young man?"

Without hesitation, I answered, "To be the Scarlet Pimpernel."

"I read that book," she said. "Mr. Pimpernel, let's hope you measure up to your hero and always end up at the right place at the right time. Speaking of time, I've told you more than I have told anyone since forever and I am very tired now thinking thoughts that I hadn't wanted to think about. I ask God every night to give me a bad memory."

"What do you want me to call you?" I asked.

"Edwina. It makes it sound like we are equals. I'll call you Percy and you call me Edwina. Cursed friends — outcasts together." She smiled for the first time. "Will you visit with me again, Mr. Pimpernel?"

My eyes getting misty, I said, "Edwina, you're the cat's meow."

She laughed. "Pajamas, Percy. No, I'm the cat's meow. Look at all those cats talking about us. Now, off with you. It's time for little boys to be asleep in bed."

Looking over at Aunt Momi talking with the Angel of Death, she observed, "Your aunt isn't taking much care of you that I can see." Checking her watch, she gave me a sly look. "One more thing, my little Scarlet Pimpernel, never, ever, believe everything people tell you without checking to see if they are telling you the truth. For you see, if you'd ask anyone in this room about me, each person would tell a different tale about the life of Mr. and Mrs. Brown. Some would say that I married Mr. Brown for his money and got what I deserved."

"Did you?" I asked, looking at the cats meowing in the room.

"Well, if I did, the joke's on me, isn't it? Now off with you, Mr. Percy."

She waved me away from the table.

As I walked over to eavesdrop on the Angel of Death, Aunt Momi screamed, throwing her martini at the Angel of Death. The Angel of Death jumped off the barstool, smashed his martini glass on the floor and ran out of the cocktail party. The Angel of Death must have said something pretty terrible to my aunt, because to my knowledge, my aunt never wasted a martini in her entire life.

CHAPTER 12

THE ADVENTURE BEGINS

Mina slept like a baby. I picked her dark glasses off the floor and woke her gently. Holding her hand, we walked swiftly to the lifeboat. Daisy and Neal followed behind arguing about the Angel of Death.

Next to the Shangri-La, sitting in a circle, Daisy informed us that Sister Mary Louise drank vodka straight and wanted her mother's money. Neal was absolutely certain that one of the sailor pallbearers murdered Aunt Rose for no other reason than he looked mean. I reported that Edwina was not a suspect. Mina spoke revealing that she had only pretended to be asleep in the chair. She placed her dark glasses on the floor because she wanted to see the passengers clearly when they left the cocktail party.

"When Angel of Death ran out, he put face right up here." Pointing to her nose. "He stink more worse dan one rotten mango. He big devil. I think he like kill me." We shivered when she said that.

Clenching her fists, she continued, "He no like Japanese. He like no one." We all agreed with Mina, especially after the incident with Aunt Momi. Settling the argument with Daisy and Neal, the Angel of Death was our prime suspect. But who was he? The Angel of Death remained an unanswered question.

I laid out our plans for hiding the treasures. Neal was to guard the writing salon while we hid the treasures in the couch. "If someone, even the Angel of Death, comes up the stairs, signal us so we can hide. If he catches you, pretend that you are sleepwalking."

"I'm not going to do anything dumb like that. He won't believe me."

Ignoring his bad attitude, I said, "Look, Shadows, our adventure is as patriotic as the American soldiers fighting Hitler. We're going to save the sacred treasures of Hawaii. In King Arthur's time, knights made a sacrifice before they left to fight the bad guys. Even in Hawaii, Hawaiians sacrificed pigs before they went into battle. Sacrificing gets

God's attention to keep us safe."

After a short pause, I continued. "We have to sacrifice. We have to put something into the steamer trunk after we take the treasures out. We don't want the killer to think we are dumping an empty trunk into the ocean. My sacrifice is my last bottle of Best Foods mayonnaise. It is the biggest sacrifice I can think of."

Daisy offered her Loretta Young doll as her sacrifice. Neal pledged his baby pillow. Mina said she'd sacrifice the red scarf as her contribution.

"Mina, keep the scarf. It's cold out here. You're sacrificing enough just sleeping in the Shangri-La. I'll bring you a towel. You can spit on the towel for good luck. People spit in football games for good luck. Spitting is a powerful good luck thing because you are giving up something of yourself that nobody else has… spit. I'll put the spit towel in the steamer trunk as your sacrifice. Your spit will really get God on our side. In fact, let's all spit on the towel for luck. For sure, we'll get God's full attention."

I ordered, "Time for bed. I'll say the prayer tonight:

"Now we lay Mina down to sleep,

We pray the Lord her soul to keep

If the angel of death comes to kill Mina with his stinky breath,

Throw him overboard, God

Amen."

We blessed all the good people in our lives, putting Aunt Rose at the top of the list. We put Auntie Sissy and the nun at the bottom. Neal added, "P.S. God, don't let Sissy hit me with the polo mallet."

I said sincerely, "Neal, if I had to live with Auntie Sissy, I'd jump off this ship. Neal, nothing bad is going to happen to you, because the Scarlet Pimpernel will protect you. Square your shoulders back — stick out your chin. You are now being led by the Scarlet Shadow."

"That's what worries me," he moaned.

We left Mina to sleep in the Shangri-La and disappeared into the shadows of the ship.

I shoved my shoulders back, stuck out my double chins, and ran for the cabin. Whizzing past dark corners, I kept looking for the Angel of Death to leap out and kill me. The Angel of Death had become scarier than any bogeyman that Marigold told me about.

Marigold wasn't asleep. After I called out the password, she opened the door and, before she closed it, I told her everything. Aunt Momi was still drinking martinis at the cocktail party.

Marigold helped me pack the treasures into two pillowcases. My sister, showing her soft side, held out a treasure and cooed, "We are here to protect you so that no harm will come to you." The last things to go into a pillowcase were the velvet bags of jewelry. Unable to resist, I untied one of the bags to peek at the butterfly brooch.

Marigold grabbed the bag away and stuffed it into the pillowcase. "Aunt Momi will be back at any second."

From under my pillow, I took out my last jar of Best Foods mayonnaise and placed it inside the empty steamer trunk. Looking at the mayonnaise jar, I said, "I feel like one of King Arthur's knights off to find the Holy Grail. Knights sacrificed their precious things to give them good luck." Putting the mayonnaise jar in the steamer trunk, I said, "I feel good inside sacrificing like the knights did."

Marigold, saying I was as crazy as a loon, threw a Superman comic book into the trunk. She wasn't taking any chances. Looking at the practical side of life, my sister said, lifting the steam trunk with one hand, "Any dumb bunny would know that this steamer trunk is empty."

A bolt of lightning struck us. We exclaimed, "Auntie Sissy's fur coat!"

I ran into the bathroom, pulled the mink coat off the hanger, Marigold rolled it up and, together, we stuffed it into the trunk. "Yippee!" I said. "Sacrificing Auntie Sissy's fur coat will turn Auntie Sissy into a nice person and at the same time give us good luck to find the killer. Miracles do happen, Marigold."

Suddenly, a key wiggled in the lock. My aunt never used the password. Marigold shoved the steamer trunk against the wall. I dragged the pillowcases behind the cot and covered them over with a blanket.

When Aunt Momi opened the door, we were in our beds pretending to be asleep. I forgot to turn off the lights. Aunt Momi staggered into the cabin as if her world was spinning. She held her high heels and girdle in her hands and tossed them on her bed. Peeping from under the covers, my aunt did a striptease. In the full light, my aunt yanked her dress over her head and threw it over a chair. Next, she shucked her panties doing a wild shimmy. Waving her hands behind her, she unhooked her brassiere dropping it to the floor. After looking at herself naked in the mirror, she hummed "Dancing in the Dark" and waltzed into the bathroom. Reeling out of the bathroom, wearing her nightgown, Rita Hayworth staggered to bed, yanked the covers back and collapsed into it. In minutes, she began to snore like Wallace Beery, my favorite beer drinking character actor, in the MGM movie *Tugboat Annie*.

My aunt had missed her calling. I saw her name in lights — **Madcap Momi starring at the Bijou. She Dances, She Sings And Snores Like A Sailor.**

Marigold snaked out of her bed and handed me her wristwatch. It read ten-thirty. I told her that sleep won't come to the Scarlet Shadow who is keeping an appointment with destiny.

I shined the flashlight at the watch as the hour and minute hands moved slowly towards midnight. When the two hands met, I was older than Methuselah. I slithered out of bed, put on my bathrobe, shook my sister's arm. Together, we dragged the pillowcases to the door watching Aunt Momi snoring. We were safe. She kept snoring in a deep martini coma.

Quietly, we opened the door. Neal, the dependable, was standing in the corridor.

Under his right arm, he held a Loretta Young doll and in his left hand, grasped a baby pillow. Seeing his sacrifices reminded me to fetch the towel for Mina. As Neal handed Marigold his sacrificial offerings, I tiptoed into the cabin to steal a towel from the bathroom. On my way out, I snatched a pack of Lucky Strikes off the bureau.

Back in the corridor, I gave Marigold a big kiss on her puss. She wiped it off and complained that now she had the plague. I didn't mind her saying that because, whether my sister knew it or not, she needed a lot of my kisses on her puss. In a gruff voice, she warned us to be careful, then to my surprise, she handed me Aunt Momi's pistol.

"Take this," she said. Sounding like Sheriff John Wayne sending his deputies off to corral Jesse James, she commanded, "Little brother, you may need this if the killer tries to ambush you. When you catch that varmint, whip out the gun, point it at him, and tell the bastard you'll shoot his you-know-what's."

"Do you mean his you-know-what's are the you-know-what's that you don't have?"

Slapping my head, she groaned, "His balls, stupid."

"I will, Marigold. Promise! And I won't spill the beans that there aren't any bullets in the gun."

Marigold gave me a military salute and crammed Neal's baby pillow into her mouth. The sheriff was about to throw up.

Neal carried the pillowcases. I let him. I really wanted to tell the whiner that the only thing strong about him was his spoiled, muleheaded mind.

I wrapped the spit towel around my neck, stuffed the pistol in my bathrobe pocket and, stealthily, Neal and I rode away on our invisible horses. At every dark corner, I pulled out the gun.

Lifetimes passed before we climbed the grand staircase to the Writing Salon. Like clockwork, Mina and Daisy were at the top of the staircase waiting for us. Daisy, wearing her life jacket, had a sewing kit in her hand. Mina was without her fur coat and looked naked. Again, I had forgotten my lifejacket. Neal wore his backwards. For a band of Shadows going on a dangerous mission, we were a mess.

We huddled and reviewed our plans. I pleaded with Neal to practice sleepwalking, but being a bubble head, he refused.

In the salon, we set the pillowcases on the couch. The three of us pulled the couch away from the wall. Mina scrambled behind it with a pair of scissors. She cut into the fabric and, in minutes, Mina handed us wads of cotton. We piled the stuffing next to the door.

Mina wiggled back out and reported that there was now enough room inside the couch to hide the treasures. Neal whispered, excitedly, that someone was running up the stairs. We scrambled behind the drapes, holding our breaths.

Clump. Clump. Clump. Up the stairs a man ran two steps at a time. I held the pistol close to my chest ready to shoot off his "you know whats." The person raced past the room without looking inside. I peeked from behind the drapes and saw the Angel of Death. He had on a black cape. As his steps faded away, I hissed the all clear signal, "the hungry bird eats the worm." We cautiously stepped from behind the drapes, shaking at the close encounter.

Neal tinkled in his pajamas. I told him he tinkled for all of us. I urged everyone to hurry before the Angel of Death came back. I volunteered to help hide the objects and crawled behind the couch, holding in my fat stomach. Daisy handed me the treasures one by one. First to come were the velvet bags. As I slipped them into the hole, an object fell into my hand. It came from the bag that I didn't tie securely. The diamond butterfly pin lay in my palm. Without thinking, I stuffed the pin into my bathrobe pocket next to the pistol.

The last treasure to be placed inside the couch was the wooden statue of the goddess. I took off part of the goddess' bindings to let her know that I was going to protect her forever and ever and, even if I was tortured, I would never tell anyone where she was until we arrived in San Francisco. I was certain that the wooden lady smiled at me. I wrapped her up again and placed her gently inside the couch with the rest of the treasures.

Mina and I switched places. Quickly, she sewed the treasures into place. While she sewed, we stuffed the cotton into the empty pillowcases. After she finished sewing, Mina asked us to come with her to the lifeboat. She had a big surprise for us.

"On our way to Mina's lifeboat, let's throw the cotton stuffing overboard."

We filed onto the deck, following the same path that the Angel of Death had taken. Before we climbed the ladder to Mina's lifeboat, we emptied the pillow cases over the rail watching lumpy cotton float on the waves. The cotton looked like snow. We threw the pillowcases overboard and they, too, joined the snow floating in the dark water.

Climbing the ladder as panthers, we checked fore and aft, looking for any sign of the Angel of Death. He disappeared as if he had never existed. We sat in our usual circle, hidden in the shadow of the Shangri-La, and made plans for our next excitement.

"First thing in the morning, Johnny will take us on a tour of the ship. If we're going to catch the Angel of Death, we need to know all the secret hiding places on the ship. After lunch, we are going to throw the steamer trunk overboard."

Neal bragged, "I'm going to throw the steamer trunk overboard by myself. I don't care if Sissy finds out. She isn't paying any attention to me, anyway. Since Aunt Rose died, she lets me do anything I want.

Only Mina loves me." He reached over and hugged Mina.

I plotted quickly as I feared the morning sun was about to rise in a couple of hours. "When Neal and I bring the trunk up on deck, we'll make a run for the back of the ship. That's where we'll throw the steamer trunk overboard. It's the exact spot where they put Aunt Rose's coffin in the ocean. Daisy, you scream and point at us when you see us at the railing. Make such a commotion that the killer will know what we are doing."

Adjusting his glasses, Neal pronounced, "Remember, I'm going to toss the steamer trunk overboard all by myself. I don't want your help, Percy." He flexed his tuna can arms to show me that he meant business.

"Okay, but don't forget your glasses so you can see what you are doing. But I don't think you're strong enough to do it by yourself."

He roared, flexing his arms again, "I'm more of a he-man than you are, Percy. I can lift anything."

Mina sneezed, "Kaaaaaachoo," gaining the group's attention.

I asked, "What's your surprise, Mina?"

Mina walked up and down the deck peering into dark corners and, after she was satisfied that the Angel of Death wasn't spying on us, she instructed us, "No move."

She walked up to the boat and whispered, "Toshi." She whispered louder, "Toshi."

Nothing happened.

"Toshi."

Suddenly, a man wearing Mina's fur coat stood up in the lifeboat. He stepped out onto the deck. The man had eyes of a tiger.

Mina, looking pleased as punch, announced, "Daisy, Neal, Percy, this Toshi. He escaped Japanese prisoner. He good boy. He need help."

Toshi didn't look like he needed anyone's help. The way he stood with his feet apart, he looked like a samurai warrior. Without speaking, Toshi indicated that under the fur coat he held a sword and, if he didn't like us, he could slice off our heads with one mighty slash.

I reached for the pistol. Watching my target, I gestured Mina over and whispered, "He could be the Angel of Death, Mina. He could be the one who killed Aunt Rose. He looks dangerous to me, Mina. He could murder us."

Grabbing my hand, she pleaded, "Toshi no killer. Toshi good boy. I trust Toshi. Toshi nineteen. All sailor like kill him. We help Toshi. We *hide* Toshi. Please, Percy."

I had made up my mind the first day I met Mina that I would trust her with my life. I relaxed my hand on the gun and somehow believed that Toshi wasn't our killer.

Keeping my eyes glued on Toshi, I said to Mina, "Okay. But you tell him that if he harms you or any of us, I'll shoot off his you-know-what's. Tell him I have a gun. You tell him that. Tell him I'm tough like John Wayne. Tell him people faint when I walk into a saloon. Tell him that the only reason I don't shoot off his you-know-what's is because you're his friend and in America friends don't shoot things off of other people's friends. In America, we believe in each other and trust each other. You tell him that. Ask him if he has a gun." Mina kissed my cheek and told me that Toshi wanted to be our friend and didn't have a gun.

I whispered, "I hope you're right because if Toshi is the killer, I'm a cooked goose." I whispered softer, "I don't have any bullets in this gun."

Having settled that, I motioned everyone to sit down. Mina took Toshi's hand and made him sit next to her. I sighed, "You know what this means, Shadows. We have another dangerous secret to keep and more food to steal." I reached into my pocket and brought out the pack of Lucky Strikes cigarettes and gave the pack to Mina warning her not to smoke the cigarettes on deck. I added, looking at Toshi, "Mina, we don't want to signal a submarine to torpedo us."

Toshi watched me as a mongoose studied a snake before the kill. I was his snake. His two black eyes showed that he was a survivor and a scar on his face proved it. He was as handsome as Tyrone Power with thick black hair. A tiny wisp of hair growing on his chin gave him a Genghis Khan look.

The moon disappeared behind the clouds. A faint red glow was beginning to show on the horizon. It was time to return to our cabins.

"Shadows, here is one more thing we have to think about. When we get to San Francisco, we have to think of ways to get Toshi and Mina off the ship without the FBI capturing them. Remember, if we are caught smuggling them into America, we are going to end up in the electric chair with Auntie Sissy. Now, let's return to our cabins without getting caught by the Angel of Death. He's probably waiting for us around a dark corner holding a butcher knife. (Daisy had her hands over her ears.) Be brave, Daisy."

Taking the towel off my neck, I told everyone to spit on it. Toshi spit with us. Mina wanted the Japanese warrior to feel that he was part of the Shadows.

I said, looking at Toshi's spit, "That is a big spit if I ever saw one, Toshi. You must eat Wheaties for breakfast. You're tougher than all of us Shadows put together. You got tough spit. I'm going to call you Big Tough Spit Shadow."

"Daisy, I don't know where I came up with the spit idea. I never spit. Marigold spits all the time. Bette Davis never spits in her movies. The Scarlet Pimpernel didn't spit. It must have been something I saw in a Roy Rogers movie. Something Roy did around a camp fire with Trigger."

Mina and Toshi climbed into the lifeboat to spend the night. I carried the spit towel, beckoning Daisy and Neal to follow me down the ladder. I ordered them to run to their cabin before the Angel of Death could catch them. Daisy ran faster than Neal did.

I whispered "Best Foods mayonnaise." Marigold quietly let me into the cabin. Aunt Momi was having a nightmare. She was moaning my name. In the bathroom, I told Marigold about Toshi, and that it was a *go* to toss the streamer trunk overboard after lunch. Marigold offered to come on deck and scream that I was the stupidest brother in the world.

I smiled, "Good, Marigold. Do your brat act or else the killer and Aunt Momi will smell a rat."

Marigold pinched my belly and crept back to bed. I carefully placed the spit towel in the steamer trunk, and put the gun and butterfly pin under my pillow. I wiggled into the cot, pulled the blanket over me, and dreamt that the Shadows were floating on the sea like cotton candy and got sucked into a whirlpool.

Tyrone Power as Percy's hero. 20th Century Fox studio photo.

Chapter 13

IF YOU WANT TO MAKE GOD LAUGH, SPIT ON A TOWEL

There was an eerie calm aboard the ship that morning. The ocean had turned smooth and flat. It was so flat that Sonja Henie, the ice skating movie star, could have whirled around the convoy doing pirouettes. The sun's rays were striking the ship like jagged bolts of lightning making the passengers wear dark glasses. Taking their morning stroll, they talked about drinking gallons of Alka-Seltzer. At breakfast, my waiter observed that most of the passengers had horrific hangovers.

Johnny was in the galley giving the dickens to a sailor who had dropped a coffee pot. I reminded him about the tour of the ship. After a moment's hesitation, he agreed to meet us at the entrance of the dining room, after his men had finished resetting the tables for lunch. Johnny had dark circles under his eyes. He was in a grumpy mood like everyone else. He smiled at me when I showed him the ankh around my neck.

Neal and Daisy were waiting at Mina's lifeboat. Looking around for Mina and Toshi, I asked, "Where are they?"

Mina and Toshi had vanished. Daisy said she put two sweet rolls inside the lifeboat, just in case they had gone to the bathroom. The valise, the pillow and blanket had also disappeared.

As we hurried to meet Johnny, I thought, "Did Toshi kill Mina? Maybe Mina killed Toshi. Maybe they had to hide from the Angel of Death. Maybe the Angel of Death caught them and killed them." We all had the same fearful thoughts.

Trying to cheer up the Shadows, I said, "Once we know the layout of the ship, we'll look for Mina and Toshi."

Johnny, wearing a black turtleneck sweater, leaned wearily against the dining room door, smoking a cigarette. Johnny patted Daisy and

Neal on the tops of their heads and greeted me by mussing up my hair. He took Daisy's hand and told us to follow him. He walked straight to the Shangri-La where he began to lecture us.

"Children, think of the Aquitania as a many-layered cake. Where we are standing is the frosting on the cake. On this deck are the four funnels, the bridge where the captain navigates the ship. Over there, near that funnel, are the officers' sleeping quarters. Look at the smoke coming out of our funnels, and then look at the other ships in the convoy."

Neal interrupted, "Our funnels have heavy black, black smoke belching out of them and the other ships have puny little streams of grey smoke coming out of theirs."

"Correct, mate," said Johnny, patting Neal on the back. "No one knows why, but since the Aquitania was built in 1913, this old lady has belched black smoke. Of all the luxury liners ever built, she's known in the maritime world for her very famous four, black-smoking funnels. Our ship's black smoke can be seen for miles."

"Oh, my goodness," worried Daisy. "I hope the Japanese submarines don't see our black smoke."

"Miss Daisy, don't you worry your pretty head about that. You can be sure that we are ready for them. Now, take hold of my hand, Miss Daisy. Percy and Neal, follow behind us. We are going on the bridge to meet Captain Spaulding. I want you all to behave because the captain has suffered a great tragedy. His wife, who lived in Singapore, is now a prisoner in a Japanese concentration camp. You can understand that he's very sad about that. He's a very strict disciplinarian, runs a tight ship, so speak only when spoken to."

I piped up, "He can't be that sad, Johnny, because he plays bridge in his cabin all day with Aunt Momi."

Johnny looked at me sternly, "Mind your own business, Percy."

Neal and I marched behind Johnny and Daisy until we reached a large wooden door directly in back of the Shangri-La. Johnny knocked hard on the door. A British officer, dressed in starched whites, opened it and saluted Johnny.

We cautiously stepped into the bridge house, staying close together. The bridge was an oblong room. An oak-paneled wall facing the stern of the ship and a series of wooden windows framed the other three sides of the bridge. The windows looked out on the bow of the ship and beyond to a dark blue line where the sky and the sea met. On the right, the ships in the convoy steamed beside and behind us, sailing in a loose formation. At the center of the bridge, a mustached sailor manned the ship's wheel mounted on an oak pedestal. He maneuvered the wheel back and forth steadily with his hands watching the compass in front of him. Three officers stood beside him scanning the horizon. Using binoculars, they were searching the seas for submarines. Four sailors moved frantically like the Marx brothers in an MGM movie. They communicated into mouthpieces, pulled levers and, at the officers' commands, checked the navigational instruments. They were fun to watch.

Captain Spaulding stood in front of a window holding a chart in his hand. We overheard him discussing with his officers the business of the day. After Johnny gave a discreet cough, the captain turned to us.

My first impression of Captain Spaulding was that he resembled the photograph of King George VI hanging on the wall behind us. The king and the captain had the same sad looking eyes and long noses. There were differences, the captain had one eye bigger than the other but most importantly, he didn't wear a crown. All in all, the captain was the spiffiest looking person on the bridge decked out in a blue uniform and gold buttons. I understood why Aunt Momi thought him nifty.

Speaking in precise English, sounding like royalty, the captain remarked, "Ah, Johnny, you've brought your guests right on time. Good show." Looking at Daisy, speaking as a knight to a lady of noble birth, he said "You are the pretty Miss Daisy." Turning to Neal, he added, "You, young man, standing straight as a prince, must be the young Mr. Neal, and you…" He paused and studied me up and down. It was as if he was inspecting one of his sailors. Finished with his inspection, he roared like the lord of a manor, "You are the one who wants to be the Scarlet Pimpernel. Correct me if I'm wrong, Johnny?"

Johnny nodded.

It pleased me to hear that I wasn't the spitting image of Hermann Goering.

Forgetting Johnny's instructions to speak only when spoken to, I blurted out, "I am going to be just like the Scarlet Pimpernel."

Johnny poked his finger into my back.

The Captain seemed a bit flustered at the outburst and said, "How'd you salts like a turn at the wheel?"

Captain Spaulding ushered us over to the navigational wheel and, with the seaman's assistance, we moved the wheel back and forth. The captain explained to us old salts the strange looking apparatuses mounted in front of the windows. All the gizmos had a very specific role that aided the navigation of the ship. One was a compass; the other gismo next to it was to talk to the men in the engine room. In fact, importantly, all the apparatuses enabled the ship to enter and leave a harbor without bumping into a breakwater, a ship or a reef. One of his officers said that the captain couldn't berth the ship in Sydney. The ship's masts were three feet too tall for the bridge that spanned the harbor's entrance. Showing us the chart in his hand, he explained, that before we arrived, he and his officers were completing mathematical calculations making sure that the Aquitania could sail under the Golden Gate Bridge.

The captain stunned me, thinking about my own plans, when he announced, "Scarlet Pimpernel, we are planning to do something exciting after lunch. I have scheduled an hour's drill shooting at a target towed behind one of the destroyers. Our two six-inch guns and our twenty-seven smaller ones will practice at firing at the target. This kind of drill keeps my crew in good fighting form. Someday, we might have to shoot down enemy airplanes. Two of the destroyers are adding to the excitement by dropping depth charges. Submarines, you know. Sounds exciting, doesn't it, children?" The ship's clock chimed four bells.

Captain Spaulding barked at his officers, "I'm off."

Turning to Johnny, he added, "Johnny, take charge of the children. Pressing business, you know. Glad you brought the youngsters up to see me. Children, as you can see, I am mighty proud of my ship. The Aquitania has been a very lucky lady since her maiden voyage." He cracked his knuckles when he spoke the next sentence, "That's why the *accident* of that Hawaiian lady, your Aunt Rose, hit us so hard. Nothing like that has ever happened in the history of this ship. But accidents will happen, I suppose."

Putting his arm around Neal's shoulder, he escorted us to the door as he continued to explain the ship's history. "On our last convoy from Singapore to Australia, we carried five thousand troops without a single incident. I am very proud of our record. No one died or became ill. Can any of you tell me something that my ship does out of the ordinary while traveling in a convoy?"

Mr. Know-It-All raised his hand and answered, "You zigzag to keep the Japanese submarines from torpedoing us."

The captain roared, "Johnny, I'd better mind my p's and q's or I'll find this Mr. Neal the captain of my ship. Take them down to the galley and give them a sweet. I don't think this one needs one." He gave me a jab in the belly.

I blurted out, rubbing my stomach, "Since you're off playing cards with Aunt Momi, would you tell her to be on deck after lunch? I have a big surprise for her. And for you, too!"

Johnny pushed me out the door. Neal and Daisy fled behind me. I had blown the captain's cover. I had blurted out in front of his officers that he was off to play bridge with my aunt. The look on the captain's face told me that he wanted to squash a fat, Hermann Goering toad.

Out on deck, Johnny shook my shoulders. "Percy, that mouth of yours is going to get you into big trouble. Next time, I might not be able to save you like I just did. What is this big surprise after lunch?"

Feeling ashamed that I had disappointed Johnny, I said, "Oh, nothing. I just made that up. It's my big mouth talking again. I can't help being a brat."

Standing next to the Shangri-La, tapping his fingers on the boat, he warned, "Don't do that again."

Johnny shared a secret about the Aquitania. "Now, I'm about to tell you something that the captain didn't tell you. At night, the Aquitania makes an entire circle around the convoy, all alone, by itself. We do that maneuver because, during the day, we have outdistanced the other ships. It's hard for those little pipsqueaks to keep up with us. Every night, like clockwork, we make the rounds. Tonight, watch the stars and you'll be able to see when we are doing the circle. Don't go opening your big mouth about this to anyone, Percy. If there's a spy onboard this ship and the spy hears about it, he could radio a submarine. The ship is a sitting duck for a submarine. We don't zigzag."

Daisy, who hadn't spoken a word since our visit on the bridge, complained, "I don't feel well, Johnny. Pretty please, let's go to the kitchen and have a cookie? I feel dizzy with all this 'making the rounds' stuff."

"Take a deep breath, Daisy. That'll make you feel better. If you want to be considered an old salt, the kitchen on a ship is called a galley. Follow me, mates, but first wouldn't you like to explore the insides of this fine boat next to us? They're only two of them on the Aquitania."

"NOOOOOO!" we screamed.

"Whoa. You've just scared the living daylights out of me. Is there a reason why I shouldn't look inside this boat?"

"Nooooooooooooooooo!" we screamed again.

"Now, my curiosity is up. I'd better take a look inside."

We shut our eyes as Johnny climbed into the boat. We waited breathlessly until, in seconds, he leaped out, reporting, "Nothing much inside but a half-eaten sweet roll. Are you three feeding a rat? Maybe a rat with two legs?"

White as a sheet, I rattled, "No. No. No one stays in there." I quickly crossed my fingers. Crossing my fingers meant that the lie was cancelled on the spot. I never meant to lie to Johnny, ever, but I heard J. Edgar Hoover of the FBI say in a newsreel that there were circumstances in wartime when a person could lie to a friend if it meant saving a life. I was thinking about Mina.

"Hmm, I bet the ghost of the Aquitania lives in that boat. The crew tells me that the ghost on the ship is a man with a black beard who wanders around at night like a madman. He first appeared after we left Singapore. Some described the ghost with fingernails sharp as a knife. So sharp he could cut a throat with a single slash."

"We've seen him," screamed Daisy. "He definitely has a beard. I don't know about his fingernails, but he's scary all right. We saw him at the cocktail party. We call him the *Angel of Death*. Tell us more about him, Johnny."

Making ghostly sounds, Johnny told the story of the ghost. "Angel of Death, now that's a good name for him. The crew swears that he roams the ship after midnight looking for food. The ghost, so the story goes, was a sailor who was locked inside one of the empty food bunkers by mistake. No one found him until three weeks after he died. He had starved to death."

I guffawed, "Johnny, you're like all the other grown-ups. You're trying to scare us to make us behave. Pooh, we don't believe in ghosts."

The Angel of Death is a man just like you."

Daisy screamed, "There's a ghost, Percy, because we've seen him. We better watch out because the Angel of Death is going to eat us up for his supper." Daisy looked wide-eyed at Johnny believing every word of his story.

Changing the subject, Johnny cheered, "Let's go to the galley. I don't want you three to starve to death like the ghost did. We better hurry because I have to be back at work in half an hour."

In the galley, we met the cook and his assistants. They showed us where they stored the vegetables, and what impressed me most was the gargantuan cooler that kept the lettuce fresh and the beef from rotting. I told Daisy and Neal that this was the very cooler where the sailor had starved to death.

Johnny took a sallow-faced cook aside and whispered something into his ear. While they were talking, I slipped a handful of cookies into my pocket. Out of the corner of his eye, Johnny caught me stealing the cookies.

Johnny pulled me away from the cookie jar, saying, "What did I tell you about behaving, Percy. Come on, I'll show you me fancy cabin and the room where they keep the coffins." Mr. Pasty-face returned to his stove and muttered that he cooked thieves in his stews.

I kept trying Johnny's patience with my bad behavior. Deep down, I was testing him to see if he really liked me. I did a lot of testing with adults in those days. Most times, I was disappointed. I had been abandoned by Mother and Hatsuko, the ones I loved most on earth. Since their deaths, I had tested everyone around me trying to find someone to love me with all my faults. Johnny kept passing my tests.

"Follow me," ordered Johnny, pulling me out of the kitchen. As I trotted alongside him, he explained that the captain had assigned him to a suite on B Deck. Because of his position, the captain wanted him close to the passengers, the dining room and all the public areas.

"A Deck," he explained, "is where the first class cabins and public areas were located in the olden days. After the war broke out, A Deck was converted to house officers and troops. A Deck was once a very posh place to stay with cabins fit for kings and queens. Think of A deck as the richest filling in our cake and you lucky mates sleep in some of the cabins we left intact. Most of the fancy furnishings on that deck were thrown overboard during our last voyage. The crew is going to toss the rest of the couches and chairs overboard, when we have time. We want to finish that project before we reach San Francisco because we have to make room for the thousand troops we will be carrying back to Hawaii and Australia."

I gasped, "When are they going to do that?" I feared that our sofa was next on the list.

"Anytime now," he said walking faster.

Oh my God, my God, I panicked thinking that the treasures were sinking to the bottom of the ocean. I planned to check on the sofa as soon as the tour was over. I prayed to God that God was still on our side.

With my mind on the treasures and the afternoon's adventure, I hardly concentrated when Johnny told us that B Deck was the next layer on the cake. That deck was originally set aside for the first class passengers. On C Deck were built the public rooms and cabins for the tourist class.

I said to Johnny, "That's where my friend, Edwina, the lady wearing the veil, sleeps."

Later, Neal found out that D Deck was for the third class passengers. The refugees, prisoners and the wounded were quartered there. E Deck was set aside for the swimming pool, storage rooms, and below that was housed the engine room.

"And below the engine room is Davy Jones's locker," chuckled Johnny.

Arriving on B Deck, Johnny pointed to a brass plate on a door that read: Louis XVI Suite. The door was ajar. Peeping inside, I spied a large photograph of an Egyptian pyramid hanging over a bed. "This is where I bunk," explained Johnny.

Taking a gander in the cabin, I reminded Johnny, "Don't forget, you promised to show me your Egyptian things."

Scratching his head, Johnny mumbled, "I don't remember leaving the door open. One can't afford to be careless on this voyage, mates. I have me here a bad habit. We've all got to keep our doors locked at all times if we don't want our things stolen. If you lose your key or lock yourself out, I have a master key and can always get you into your cabins." Slamming the door shut, locking it, he turned and walked ahead of us. "Hurry," he said. "Let's take a quick look at the swimming pool."

We ran down the grand staircase and arrived on E Deck, out of breath. We passed storage rooms filled with luggage, cases of canned vegetables and sacks of flour. The smell of fuel oil tickled our nostrils. We were directly over the engine room. Stopping at two large steel padlocked doors, Johnny yanked keys out of his pocket; using a brass key, he unlocked the padlocks and pulled a rusted chain to the floor. Pushing his body against the doors, they opened slowly, creaking as if we were about to enter a sacred tomb.

It should have been a king's tomb because the most magnificent, startling, and unusual sight appeared before us. It was the ship's swimming pool. It was Olympic-sized, four feet deep from one end to the other, and tiled in sapphire blue. On the walls were painted mosaics of naked nymphs chasing other nymphs in a dark forest. The pool was empty of water, but inside the pool were wooden coffins stacked in a haphazard fashion. They were all shaped like Aunt Rose's coffin, only smaller versions. Broken pieces of coffins were scattered on the deck of the pool, making it difficult to walk. You had to be careful as you stepped; otherwise, you'd poke a nail in your shoe. Johnny explained the scattered lumber we saw as we walked around the pool. Some had come from the coffins that had been broken apart to make bigger coffins for soldiers whose bodies didn't fit a standard coffin.

I gasped, looking at all the coffins around me. "This is really, really fantastic, Johnny. It's better than being inside a haunted castle."

"I hate this place. Let's get out of here," cried Daisy, standing at the doorway. Neal walked around the pool counting the coffins. He came up with a total of thirty-four.

Johnny, fiddling with his keys, said hastily, "Well, mates, the tour is over. I've got to hustle me bones back on duty. Let's get out of here before I get into trouble showing you this stuff. The swimming pool is kept off limits for the passengers."

"Wait," I said, spotting something familiar near the door. In a pile of books was a bottle of Best Food's mayonnaise. "What's this Johnny?"

As we helped him push the creaking doors shut, Johnny answered, "That, Sir Percy, is the bottle of mayonnaise that you gave me. I store it down here with all my other rare things. With all this funny business going on, and finding my door open all the time, I don't want to lose any of my precious stuff. So, I store my valuables in here hoping they won't get stolen." Locking the chain in place, he urged, "Let's walk quickly."

I gushed, "Thank you, Johnny. Thank you for taking us on the tour. Thank you for treating my Best Foods mayonnaise so extra nice. The swimming pool was the best. It was really scary inside there but exciting at the same time."

Babbling on, I admitted, "My very, very worst nightmare is being buried alive in a coffin. I once saw a movie with Boris Karloff. The movie was called the *Isle of the Dead*. A girl was buried alive in a coffin. Since that time, I have nightmares that I'm buried in a coffin with everyone thinking that I had died. But I am alive. I am inside the coffin with nothing to eat, under tons of earth. I wait for the worms to eat me up. I don't even have Best Foods mayonnaise to eat or *Photoplay* movie magazines to read. I'm all by myself buried under tons of earth, suffocating to death slowly. I pound on the coffin and scream for help. The nightmare ends with me scratching the wood knowing that I will never get out. I always wake up screaming for air. When I die, Johnny, I want you to plunge a wooden stake into my heart to make sure that I am really dead."

"Stop it!" swooned Daisy, wiping her face with a handkerchief.

I continued, "I don't know what makes me say things like that. It's just natural for me to talk about scary things. I was born thinking about ghouls and ghosts, and I love disasters. I dream of wiggly worms, earthquakes, tidal waves, sharks, mummies and vampires."

Johnny cautioned, "Watch out, Percy. Someday, you're going to make all that stuff come true. I'm off, chaps. If I'm not back in five minutes, my mates will think that the ghost buried me alive." He shot off like a cannonball, leaving us behind thinking about the coffins in the swimming pool.

Taking a quick side trip to the Writing Salon, I was relieved seeing the couch safe in the alcove. I told the Shadows that God was still on our side. After we dropped the steamer trunk in the ocean, Daisy and I planned to glue the couch to the floor. I promised myself to return the butterfly pin back to where it belonged, getting rid of a curse that I didn't need. The last words that Daisy said to me before she trotted off to have lunch with Aunt Sissy, were, "Don't forget to wear your life jacket this afternoon. You keep forgetting to wear it and this time you may need it."

The hour arrived. Neal knocked. I opened the cabin door and dragged the steamer trunk over to him. He reminded me to keep my promise and let him throw the steamer trunk overboard or *else*.

We carried the steamer trunk to the elevator, rode it down to D Deck and, miraculously, we were not stopped by one nosy passenger. The steamer trunk was a cinch to carry as the ship was still sailing on a sea of glass. As Neal struggled to lift his end, I bragged that the trunk felt as light as a feather.

Once on deck, we carried the trunk between us hurrying to the stern of the ship. Jumping their cue, Daisy and Marigold began screaming. Aunt Momi was standing on the deck above us with the captain. Recognizing the trunk, my aunt turned into a mad woman and yelled at the captain. The captain yelled at a sailor to catch us.

"Hurry up, Neal," I screamed. "A sailor is coming." We carried the steamer trunk across the deck as fast as I could move Neal.

Neal was having a difficult time because his stubby legs kept him from keeping up with me. His glasses were slipping off his nose. He whined, "My glasses are falling off."

"Go faster," I ordered.

"I can't!" he screamed.

We reached the railing, the very spot from where the pallbearers dropped Aunt Rose's coffin into the ocean. Trying to keep his glasses on, Neal tried to lift his end up onto the railing. He couldn't do it. His little tuna cans weren't strong enough. Neal yelled, "I can't lift it. Help me."

I climbed onto the railing, grabbed the handle of the steamer trunk, and yanked it up.

Neal screamed, "The sailor is coming. Lift it higher."

I groaned, "I'm lifting. I'm lifting. Push, Neal."

Neal put one of his stubby legs on the first rung of the railing, and began to push the trunk up to me. Pulling on the handle, I lifted the steamer trunk and balanced it at the top of the railing.

"Get up here, if you want to push it over." I shouted. The sailor was now upon him.

Neal threw his glasses on the deck, punched the sailor, climbed up another rung and pushed. The force of his push made me sit on top of the railing holding onto the trunk.

"Let me push it over!" shouted Neal. The sailor pounced on him again.

"You can't. He's got you." Neal suddenly grabbed the straps of my life jacket, pulling me backwards towards him bringing the steamer trunk down with me.

In the grip of the sailor, Neal shouted in a rage, "You promised me! You hog everything, big shot Pimperhell!"

Somebody shouted, "Get that other boy before he falls over!" I recognized the captain's voice. He was behind the sailor who was pulling Neal off the railing.

I screamed, "Neal, let GO of my straps." I yelled louder this time, "LET GO, NEAL! PUSH ME!"

Jabbing the sailor with his elbows, Neal yelled, "OKAY, YOU ASKED FOR IT." He let go of my straps and, in a fury, he pushed me so hard that he fell back into the arms of the sailor.

His shove thrust me and the trunk over the railing, plummeting us towards the ocean. Holding on to the steamer trunk, I hollered, "I'M FALLING!"

Together, we plunged into the churning white water. To the passengers on deck watching us, we must have looked like lovers in a suicide pact.

Just before going under the water, I cried out, "JOHNNY, SAVE ME. I DON'T WANT TO DIE!"

CHAPTER 14

FLOTSAM AND JETSAM

My grasp, tightly locked to the steamer trunk, shot us like a bullet toward the bottom of the ocean. Fighting for my life, the propellers of the ship pumped super suds into me as the ship's engines vibrated into every pore of my body. Bubbles filled my nostrils. I held my breath. A voice told me what to do next. I released the steamer trunk and kicked furiously for the surface. With the help of the life jacket, I jerked to the top, gasping for air.

Spitting water out of my mouth, I was blinded by the glittering sea. The sea was a field of diamonds. Bobbing up and down, twirling in the ship's wake, my eyes were focused on the Aquitania zigzagging away from me. I was a piece of flotsam.

The Aquitania's horns blew staccato beats. Suddenly, the horns stopped. The water lapped around my life jacket and made a lonely sound. I scrunched my eyes into little slits. Glittering diamonds were burning them. In the distance, the passengers at the railings were pointing at me. A figure suddenly leapt into the air and dove into the ocean. Johnny was coming to rescue me.

Passengers and crew threw life jackets, a raft and boxes overboard to the diver as he surfaced.

The figure leapt like a porpoise through the waves. Waving my hands, I directed him to where I was floating. Stroking with my arms, I aimed a course for my knight in shining armor.

Ack-ack guns broke the silence. The sky became dotted with puffs of black smoke. The afternoon drill had begun. Two destroyers sounded their horns and circled around the convoy dropping depth charges. Geysers shot into the air.

For a brief second, I was distracted by the explosions. Johnny disappeared. Frantically, I whipped my arms toward the direction where I had last seen him swimming. Johnny surfaced to the right of me. He disappeared again. His head popped up, and I yelled, "Johnny, Johnny, I'm here." Waving my hands frantically, he disappeared again.

Before he vanished, I recognized the swimmer. It wasn't Johnny. It was Tarzan. Tarzan was coming to rescue me and by the look on Tarzan's face, he was in trouble. Within calling distance, Tarzan surfaced again. With great effort, stroking his powerful arms, he swam towards me.

Paddling towards him, I yelled, "What's the matter?"

Tarzan disappeared underwater again. When he surfaced once more, I yelled, "What's the matter?"

"My chest," he cried.

"What?" I said, swallowing water.

"I hurt my chest." He gasped.

"Where's your life jacket?" I screamed.

"Swept under the ship." He slipped under water again.

I hollered, "I'm coming to save you."

He surfaced directly in front of me. His eyes had glazed over. He looked dead. When we could reach out for one another, he cried, "You all right?"

"I'm okay." I quickly untied my life jacket and pushed it to him, gulping in salt water. "Take this. You need it."

Pushing the jacket away, he sputtered, "Save yourself."

I shoved the jacket back into his face, making him grab for it. This time, grabbing the life jacket, it kept his head from going underwater.

Spitting water, I gasped, "Put it on. I can float. Fat people float for hours." Tarzan shoved his arms into the lifejacket and closed his eyes.

Floating with my arms and legs stretched out, I had a ring-side seat watching the Aquitania fire her guns at a target trailing behind a destroyer. In the near distance, a black box caught my eyes as it bobbed up and down on the waves. I paddled for it, hoping that it would keep me afloat.

Grasping it, I pressed my body on it making it sink. Releasing the box from under me, it floated again. Again, I spread out my arms and legs and placed the box carefully on my stomach and began floating again. Whenever Tarzan drifted away, I swam beside him.

The Betrayers

The Aquitania stopped firing its guns. The target practice ceased as quickly as it had begun. The convoy headed into the clouds zigzagging as if a Japanese submarine had sighted the ships in its periscope.

I held the black box and prayed that God would make a miracle and turn the box into a boat to save me and Tarzan. Tarzan, the movie star, floating in my life jacket, looked as dead as a mackerel.

"Tarzan!" I yelled, trying to wake him up. "Tarzan, movie star, wake up. Please wake up." I splashed water in his face. Tarzan kept bobbing up and down in the waves like an empty bottle. I knew he was still alive because he let piggy-snorts out of his nose.

The afternoon wind whipped little waves into my face. I was swallowing the entire ocean. Water goblins were tugging on my legs trying to drown me.

"Tarzan, I can't float anymore." My arms and legs felt heavier than a hundred sandbags.

Tarzan didn't answer.

"Tarzan!" I gasped, feeling the salt water fill up my tummy.

No answer. I was floating alone in the universe.

"Flash Gordon. Calling Flash Gordon." Hearing the name Flash Gordon woke Tarzan up. He opened his eyes, sending snorts out of his nose. It sounded like an S.O.S.

I croaked frantically, "Wake up. Wake up. Calling Flash Gordon! Calling Flash Gordon, spaceship in trouble."

"Percy?"

"It's me, Flash, Percy. I can't float anymore." I was in a panic thinking that I was soon to join the steamer trunk in Davy Jones' locker.

Tarzan fumbled with the life jacket, telling me to hang on. He ignored my pleas for him to keep it on.

Thinking what the Scarlet Pimpernel would do in this situation, I said, swallowing more salt water, "You need it."

Tarzan yelled, "Keep swimming. Keep your head up. I've almost got it off. I'm all right now. I can swim on my own."

"You're not all right," I said, treading water holding the black box in a death grip.

"TAKE IT!" Tarzan commanded. He pushed the life jacket over to me. I shoved the black box towards him.

Hanging onto the life jacket, I wheezed, "Let's share it. You take one end and I'll take the other." He grabbed for the jacket. The pained look in his eyes revealed that he was hurting a lot. The life jacket kept us afloat. Once, when I was getting tired and beginning to sink below the surface, Tarzan let me rest on his arm.

Tarzan inspected the black box and asked, "What's this thing?"

"I don't know. I saw it floating in the water. It came from the Aquitania. Maybe you can float on it. I can't. I'm getting tired, Tarzan." I rested my head on the life jacket, thinking "I'm going to join King Neptune for dinner."

Tarzan jolted me by crying out, "Look over there."

In the glare of the sunlight, I made out a dark object floating near us. It was a log or a part of a raft that was thrown from the Aquitania.

"Let's swim for it, Percy. Can you do it?"

I nodded wearily. "I hope it's the floating island the Hawaiians tell about."

"Swim for it," urged Tarzan. Pushing the life jacket in front of us, we paddled for the floating island. With a new burst of energy, he called to me reassuringly, "Tarzan is going to save Boy."

I gritted my teeth and shouted, "Boy is going to save Tarzan."

As we swam for the mysterious object, I would have sworn that the floating thing was coming directly for us. The closer it came in view the more it looked familiar. Within yards, I recognized it.

Swimming beside it, Buster grimaced as he pushed me on top of the thing, trying not to tip it over. He followed me up, spitting blood out of his mouth. Miraculously, with both of us on it, it floated. I turned to Tarzan and said, "This is oogie spookie."

Rubbing his stomach, he murmured, "Oogie spookie, indeed, Percy."

Balancing precariously on top of Aunt Rose's coffin, I said a silent prayer to Uncle Peanut for making the coffin so huge and watertight that Aunt Rose could float to Waikiki Beach with passengers.

"Where's the black box?" I asked, looking around. Tarzan let it go as we struggled to get on the coffin.

"It's over there," I pointed to the black box floating away. Tarzan slipped off the coffin and swam to retrieve it. Unfazed by his sore chest, Buster swam faster than Superman for the black box. He used the same powerful strokes that won him the gold medals in the Olympics. Grabbing the black box, he tucked it under his arm, and swam back for the coffin. I leaned over, grabbed the black box out of his hands and helped him back onto our floating island.

Tarzan lay down on the coffin, closed his eyes, rubbed his chest, and grunted, "What's in that damned thing?"

"I don't know." I said, hoping to find a tuna sandwich "smooshed" with Best Foods mayonnaise wrapped in wax paper inside the box.

"Open it."

I peeled off the black tape and looked inside. I groaned with disappointment because there wasn't anything inside that looked anything like a tuna sandwich. The box contained four Roman candles, a flashlight and a little round gizmo.

"Tarzan," I said, trying not to hide my disappointment, "it's a pile of junk."

Tarzan reached for the box. Picking out a Roman candle, he mused, "Looks like we have stuff here to signal ships. We have four flares, a flashlight and a thing I've never seen before. This is not junk, Percy. What's in here could save us." He replaced the flare and lifted out the gizmo, and fiddled with a switch. When he turned the switch on, a red light blinked.

"I think this gadget can send a signal to ships to let them know where we are located. Hmmm," he said flipping the switch on and off. "Pretty interesting stuff—if it works."

Becoming excited, I said, "Its right out of a Flash Gordon spaceship movie. Do you really think this thing can bring a ship to rescue us?"

"I don't know." he answered after recovering from a coughing fit. Cradling the gizmo in his arms, he lay back down on the coffin and turned on the switch.

The afternoon sun zapped our bodies like a Flash Gordon ray gun making us turn bright red. Out of nowhere, a blast of cold wind blew over us making us shiver like two strawberry popsicles. One minute we were hotter than the sun, the next minute we were freezing in Alaska.

Looking out to the horizon, the Aquitania's puffs of black smoke had disappeared behind the clouds. The sun was setting and I was floating with Tarzan on top of a coffin in the middle of the Pacific.

"Tarzan, this is the exact same time we buried Aunt Rose." I spotted a star that I had seen while standing with Aunt Momi at the railing. The star predicted that in half an hour, Tarzan and I would be floating in the dark.

"Do you think the Aquitania will come back for us?" I asked, watching Tarzan's face as he again fiddled with the gizmo's switch.

He replied in a low voice, "If this thing can attract ships, it can attract Japanese submarines."

I gulped, "Don't say that. If a Japanese submarine captures us, we'll be sent to a concentration camp with the captain's wife. Or maybe worse, in an RKO movie, a submarine captain gave orders to his crew to machine-gun all the survivors from a torpedoed ship. I know what I'll do, I'll tell the submarine captain to leave us alone and go away. I'll explain that Aunt Rose is in the coffin and she is as famous in Hawaii as Diamond Head and we have to go back with her to Waikiki Beach because she's a single old lady. He's bound to have second thoughts about shooting us because Mr. Hamada says that the Japanese love their old people. Come to think of it, that doesn't make much sense. It doesn't look too good for us, does it, Tarzan?"

Tarzan groaned, "Has anybody ever told you that you talk too much?"

"All the time."

I laid my head down on the coffin and talked to Aunt Rose. "Aunt Rose," I whispered, "do you think the Aquitania will rescue us?"

"Be quiet," Tarzan warned.

"I was speaking to Aunt Rose. I know that movie stars need their privacy. I read that in Photoplay magazine. Tarzan, make believe that I'm not talking to you."

"I'm talking to you, Percy. What I am saying is, SHUT UP!"

"Since you are talking to me, I have a question. Why did you save me, Tarzan?"

He let out a big sigh and said, "If I answer that question, will you be quiet?"

I crossed my fingers and nodded.

"When you fell in the ocean, I was standing next to the captain.

The captain gave me that old 'Tarzan, come to the rescue look.' I had no choice. Make-believe gets mixed up with real life all of the time. No one ever sees me as Buster Crabbe, the barefoot boy from Hawaii. They only see me as Tarzan, King of the Jungle, same as you do. Judging it to be sixty feet to the water from where I was standing, I figured that I had made a similar dive even more daring in one of my movies. The dive from the ship looked easy. Maybe I did it because I wanted to know that I still had it in me. Maybe, I'm not the has-been that Hollywood says I am. When I filmed *Tarzan, the Fearless*, I dove into Lake Sherwood from a tall platform. That dive was more than sixty feet. My stuntman had chickened out so I did it for him, but then again, I was younger.

"I quickly took my bearings, saw where you were floating and dove. Even though I tucked my body in like I did at Lake Sherwood, something went wrong this time. As I hit the water, I hurt myself. It was like Joe Louis had punched me in the stomach. When I surfaced, passengers threw their life jackets and all the other stuff overboard to me because they saw I was hurt. Most of that stuff got swallowed up by the propellers except, it seems, for this black box."

I interrupted, "The captain won't let Tarzan, the movie star, die."

"I hope not, but if someone is coming for us that ship will be taking a big chance. It will be alone and vulnerable for a submarine's torpedo." As Tarzan talked, the light on the gizmo blinked like the evening star that sparkled above us.

Lolling back and forth on the coffin, I said matter-of-factly, "I'm lucky that Tarzan rescued Boy."

"Actually, it was a stupid thing to do," he said, spitting blood in the ocean.

Shifting my body to one side and putting my arm under my head, I said looking at Tarzan's back. "Thank you for doing it anyway. It wasn't a stupid thing to do. I can't die. I know that I'm a big fat, sissy person and to most people on the Aquitania I'm a stupid, fat Hermann Goering person. I know nobody likes me. But before I die, I want to do something great. I want to be a hero just like you."

Buster coughed, "I'm not Tarzan, Percy. I am not a hero. I'm just an ordinary man. Big muscles don't make the man; it's what's inside the man that counts. What is important is what you do with what you are given and do it to the best of your ability. I'm afraid I am about to find out what I have in me and probably how little I'll be remembered if this gizmo doesn't work."

I answered, "If you die, you will be remembered as the movie star hero who sacrificed his life to save a handsome fat boy who looked like the Scarlet Pimpernel. You are going to pass through the doors of heaven without having to knock. You're the kind of hero that everyone reads about in books. How many men do you know who fight alligators, fight lions with one hand, fly spaceships, beat the bad guys to a pulp and saves me?"

He cautioned, "You're like the captain, mixing me up with the Tarzan on the screen. That's all an illusion, what you see on the screen. I say again, it's those things inside of you that are real. I don't even believe floating on this coffin in the middle of the Pacific is real. I think this is an illusion. Life is like the movies; it's only an illusion that we make up in our minds."

I protested. "This is real. I can feel the water. I can feel the cold wind. I know you're here and I know that you are an out and out hero, Tarzan."

Exasperated, he sighed, "Quit calling me Tarzan. Call me Uncle Buster if you have to call me something. Let's make a deal. One, forget that I am Tarzan. Think of me as a guy who got lucky in the movies. Two, stay awake and keep a lookout for a rescue ship and, well, you know what three is." He put his finger to his lips and said, "Shhhhh."

I shut my mouth we rode the coffin over the waves heading for Waikiki Beach. I lay back thinking happy thoughts. If I died, I would get to see Mother and Hatsuko in heaven.

The sky turned crimson. The curtain came down on another day. I remembered Grandma's prediction as a second star appeared in the sky, "Red sky at night, sailor's delight."

My mind is a roving traveler, I started feeling sorry for myself and fancying that everyone on the ship had already forgotten about the Scarlet Shadow. I saw the smiles on their faces when they heard that fat Percy, the stupid half-wit, had stupidly fallen overboard and was lost at sea.

CHAPTER 15

STAR BRIGHT, STAR LIGHT

Looking up at the stars, I cuddled next to Tarzan trying to keep warm. My thoughts spun like a top. An hour passed before I had courage to ask, "Do you like Best Foods mayonnaise?"

"I hate the stuff."

"Dear God," I prayed. "I'd like a toasted tuna sandwich with tomato, lettuce, slices of tangy cheddar cheese, and lots of Best Foods mayonnaise on it. Get it ready. Tarzan and I are coming to your cafeteria pretty soon. Open up them Pearly Gates, God, here we come! Amen."

I rubbed my tummy, "Do you think God heard me, Tarzan?"

Tarzan groaned, "You're making me go crazy."

"I'm thirsty. Can I drink my pee?"

"NO!" he shouted. This time, I thought he was going to strike me.

Thumping my hand on the coffin, I pleaded, "Tarzan, if I don't eat or drink something right now, I'm going to take a Flash Gordon space ship to heaven and live with God and Rudolph Valentino."

"Rudolph Valentino?"

"My mother loved Rudolph Valentino. Whenever my mother was mad at my father she'd tell him that he was no Rudolph Valentino. Daddy would yell, 'He's dead.' My mother would yell back, 'I wish you were.' Rudolph Valentino interests me right now because he's dead and my mother loved him. Dead movie stars are supposed to be very nice. Don't take that as an insult, Tarzan, because pretty soon you're going to be nice, too." I placed my hands on my empty stomach, wanting to telephone Rudolph Valentino to ask a favor.

Tarzan said in a low voice, "Looks as if I can't keep you from talking or can I?"

"The reason I talk so much, Tarzan, is that if I stop talking, I'll die.

That's what I think. You have to talk, too, or else you're gonna die. I was going to telephone Rudolph Valentino and ask him to make my stomach stop aching."

Whoosh. The coffin rode over the top of a big wave and plunged into a valley of water. Seesawing in the trough, I held Tarzan's belt to keep me from falling off the coffin.

As we teetered back and forth, I gasped, "That was some shoot-the-shoot ride."

Tarzan moaned. The bouncing around was hurting his body.

I touched his arm and said, "I know you're hurting, Tarzan, but it's important that you talk. Why aren't you in Hollywood making movies? Tell me."

He muttered in a hoarse voice, "All right, all right, I'll tell you. Everyone in Hollywood thinks I'm shooting *Billy the Kid Trapped*. After December 7th, I couldn't contact my kid brother in Hawaii. One of the admirals in the Navy got me aboard a transport plane. I flew to Honolulu without anyone in the Navy or Hollywood officially knowing what I did. My kid brother and his family are fine, but, of course, they were scared out of their pants. Then, I couldn't get a plane back to Hollywood because my admiral friend went to sea. My only way back home was on the Aquitania. As far as Hollywood knows or cares, I'm at home in bed with the flu. My wife will have a lot of explaining to do if I disappear in the Pacific, and a lot of Navy officers will be court-martialed if that nosy old biddy, Hedda Hopper, finds out how I got to Hawaii. I'm pretty sure I have fooled everyone onboard into thinking that I am my brother, Buddy. I've pretty well covered my tracks there, I think, except for you and your friends."

My throat felt like sandpaper from lack of water. I sounded as gravelly as Tarzan when I said, "I have secrets, too." I told Tarzan about the killer with a gun, the Angel of Death, Toshi, the hidden treasures, the Scarlet Pimpernel, the curse, the steamer trunk, and how I had to catch the killer because he killed Aunt Rose.

He whispered, "You're the reason Aunt Rose saved us."

I knocked on the coffin. "Thank you, Aunt Rose. Thank you for saving us from drowning. Would you put in a good word to God and have Him send someone to rescue us pretty soon? I would float back with you to Hawaii, but right now I'm too hungry and too thirsty to go all the way back with you. I'm sure you can make it back to Waikiki Beach by yourself."

Looking at Tarzan's back, I asked, "Do you think Aunt Rose heard me?"

"She's dead."

Ignoring Tarzan, I knocked on the coffin and said, "Hello again, Aunt Rose. I know you may be dead but you've got a good ear. I know that and I have to talk to someone. Say hello to my friend, Walter. Walter was my best friend, Aunt Rose. He died. I told him about the Boris Karloff movie, and he made me promise to pound a wooden stake into his heart to make sure he was dead. When he died, they took his body away before I could do it for him. I would have. Honestly, I would have. Walter told me in the olden days in England, when people died of the Black Plague and the graveyards ran out of room, they dug up old coffins and took the bodies out to make room for new bodies. In the old coffins, they found scratch marks from the people who had been buried alive. From then on, the rich people tied a string to the wrist of a dead relative. They pulled the string through the ground, and tied the string to a bell in the graveyard. Sons and daughters would sit for days in a graveyard waiting for the bell to ring. Some people were 'saved by the bell,' or as Walter called it, by the 'dead ringer.' Other people were dead as a doornail. Walter had a sense of humor. I don't think Tarzan has one. Aunt Rose, ring God's bell and tell Him I'm still alive."

Pointing my finger to the sky, I took in deep breaths and asked, "Tarzan, what do you think is up there? Playing Flash Gordon in the movies, you've got to know a lot about what's up in the stars."

He muttered, "Stuff." Turning his head to me, he asked in a soft voice, "What do you think is up there?"

"Just stuff, too."

"What kind of stuff?"

"God stuff, like my mother, my cousins and my friends. That kind of stuff. They all live there with other stuff. Everybody is part of that stuff. They talk to us from heaven. Mother talks to me all the time. She talked to me when I fell overboard."

Coughing blood into the ocean, Buster asked, "What is she telling you now?"

"I can't hear her right now. My mind is too busy thinking about eating lamb chops covered with Best Foods mayonnaise."

"Percy, do you pray?"

"Sometimes, mostly before I go to sleep."

"Let's pray right now. Let's pray very hard that tomorrow we'll be back on the ship eating a hot turkey sandwich with gravy and mashed potatoes, because if we're not saved, I'm going to eat you for breakfast."

Boom. Boom. Boom. Whooosh. The coffin rocked back and forth. Something swam underneath us. I grabbed Buster's belt again. Uncle Buster saved us from tipping over by gripping both sides of the coffin, balancing us.

I sighed, "That was God talking, Uncle Buster. He didn't like what you said to me. He sent his favorite angel down to scold you." From the look that Buster gave me, I wondered what part of me Uncle Buster would eat first.

The coffin rocked like a cradle. In a soothing voice, Uncle Buster said, "Sleep, Percy. Please, sleep. Close your eyes and your mouth and go to sleep. Whatever it was that went under the coffin is gone. I promise I won't eat you for breakfast, maybe lunch. Sleep!"

"I can't sleep. My mind won't stand still. And you shouldn't sleep either. Stay awake, Tarzan."

Tarzan spit into the ocean.

I got his message and said, "I'm not going to bother you anymore but I'm afraid to stop talking." My mind was going faster than a merry-go-around. In the whirl, I soon forgot that I was floating on top of Aunt Rose's coffin and fell asleep.

A familiar sound woke me. It was the sound of a ship's engine. Chummmmm, chummmmm, chummmmm. ommmmmmmmmmm. Chummmmmmmmmmm.

"Percy," Tarzan said as he shook me, "where's the box?"

"Here." I was cuddling the box like a teddy bear. I passed it to him.

When he opened it, the red light on the gizmo was blinking like a Christmas star. He reached into the box, took out a flare, broke it, and whoooooosh! Out streamed a rainbow of bright red light that streaked far into the dark sky. It flashed out. The sky turned black again.

The engines hummed closer and closer.

A horn sounded, followed by the sound of ropes running through blocks. A boat was lowered and splashed into the water as a voice called out directions.

I whispered, "Tarzan, mum's the word. If we are being rescued by a Japanese submarine, even if we're tortured, don't tell the Japanese that the Aquitania is carrying precious cargo."

Tarzan coughed. He coughed so loud that all the Japanese in the Pacific must have heard him.

I hushed, "Put your hand over your mouth, Tarzan. I've decided to make you an honorary member of the Shadows. It's my gang. If this is the Aquitania that's rescuing us, whenever we have to meet in secret, I'll say the code, 'The hungry bird eats the worm.' That's our password. Don't forget!"

"Percy, don't forget Buster Crabbe is in Hollywood making a film and never floated on a coffin with you in the Pacific and thank you for…"

I quickly interrupted, "That was nothing. I like to talk. Cross my heart, I do. My talking saved you from dying. I will keep your secret as sacred as the Pledge of Allegiance. Louella Parsons will never hear it from me."

A ship's bell rang.

I sang out, "Tarzan, we've been saved by the bell."

Patting me on the head, he said hoarsely, "I'm glad someone's here to get us. If they hadn't come, I would have eaten your big toe for breakfast."

"You'd be sorry, Tarzan. If you ate my big toe, I'd be talking to you from inside your stomach for the rest of your life."

"You have a point there, Percy."

"Tarzan, you're katish."

"Likewise, Percy. But call me Uncle Buster!"

I whispered to Aunt Rose, "Sorry that I'm not going back to Waikiki Beach with you but I have to return to the ship and find your killer. Promise, I'll find him and send him to the electric chair. If you find yourself at the bottom of the ocean, there's a steamer trunk waiting for you. In the trunk there's a bottle of Best Foods mayonnaise, a

Loretta Young doll, a baby pillow, a spit towel, and a fur coat. They're yours for the ride. Aloha. Have a safe trip home, Aunt Rose."

"One other thing, Aunt Rose, if you find yourself in a bad situation, be yourself and keep talking, even if it means that you might get your big toe eaten for breakfast."

I reached for Johnny's ankh to kiss it. It was gone. It must have been ripped from my neck when I fell into the ocean.

Tarzan took the flashlight out of the black box and blinked it on and off. The ship's bell clanged three times.

Buster Crabbe as Tarzan. – Columbia Studio Photo.

CHAPTER 16

BANISHED INTO EXILE

I was burning in hell. My lips cracked dry as a desert. My arms and legs fried the color of beets. To keep from thinking about hell, I counted shadows tiptoeing past the room. The shadows turned into exotic animals.

My jail was painted sharkskin white and housed four rusty beds. The walls had rivers of gray running down their sides. A naked light bulb guarded me like a policeman. The whiteness of the room couldn't cool the fires of hell.

The door to my cell was wide open.

One of the shadows on the ceiling had a familiar shape. Suddenly, my sister stood looming in the doorway standing with her feet apart. I yelped, "It's about time you've come to spring me from this prison. I could have been dead for all you care. Don't you care that I almost drowned?"

"Cut the crap," Marigold whispered. She furtively looked to her left and right and ran into the room. She slid under my bed whispering, "You're gonna get me into big trouble. Don't talk so loud."

Leaning over the bed, I whispered, "What are you doing under there? Get me out of here."

"I can't. Nobody is allowed to see you. I could be thrown into the brig without bread or water if they found me in here."

"Why?" I asked, leaning further over the bed.

"Keep your voice down."

Annoyed, I ordered, "Get out from under there — *now*."

She spat, "Didn't you hear me? I'm not supposed to be here, numbskull."

I sputtered, "Tell me why not?"

"You're in quarantine."

"Why?"

"Everybody hates you. That's why. I overheard the captain tell Johnny that he'd hang you up on the tallest mast and let you rot if it wasn't against the law."

"That was not a very kind thing to say about me, especially when I almost died."

She yelped, "It's too damn hot down here. I'm coming out." She jumped into my bed, slid under the covers and pulled the blanket over us. Hiding from the world, we looked at each other and giggled.

Marigold tweaked my nose. "Boy, are you red."

Inspecting my face, she quickly gave me the lowdown on what had happened since I fell overboard. "Auntie Sissy and the nun pleaded with the captain to leave you in the drink. Auntie Sissy blames you for putting her babies in danger. She blabbed to everyone that it was you who made us a sitting duck for a Japanese submarine. When the ship went to get you, the captain made us stand at our boat stations for hours. It was freezing cold. Even the prisoners hate you. Two old ladies, who got lost in the engine room, say that you are lower than a rat's behind."

"That doesn't sound very nice for two old ladies to say, Marigold. What about Aunt Momi? Does she hate me, too?"

"She doesn't hate you. She blames herself for you falling overboard because she wasn't around to watch you. She's feeling guilty because she's been playing bridge with the captain all the time. You should see her. Her eyes are really ugly, all red and puffy. Johnny doesn't mention your name without saying 'damn.' The captain blames him for everything and is threatening to demote him. I would say, without exaggeration, your reputation is worse than Hitler's and, personally, I think that's just great. You've got a worse reputation than me and I work at mine. I'm very proud of you, baby brother."

Coming out from under the covers, I sighed, "Boy, I guess I'm in Dutch with everyone. I guess I don't have any friends anymore, not even Johnny."

Marigold added with glee, "Anyone who has ever met you on this ship wishes they hadn't."

"Uncle Buster likes me."

Coming out from under the covers, she continued with more bad news, "Ohhhh, speaking of Uncle Buster, that's even worse." My sister put her hands on her heart and drawled her words out as dramatic as Bette Davis. "Tarzan is recovering in his cabin because he got hurt real, real, real bad rescuing you. He cracked all his ribs, broke his nose in three places, his right arm is bent like a stick, and something else happened that I am sworn to secrecy not to tell."

"What is it?" I asked, fearing to hear the bad news.

Marigold made her face as still as a mummy, and said as seriously as Clark Gable spoke to Scarlett O'Hara. "Frankly my dear, the cooks made me promise not to tell anyone but they heard it straight from the horse's mouth, Johnny, who knows everything that goes on the ship."

"What is it, Marigold?" I squealed, pinching her arm.

"He broke his thing." Marigold giggled.

I groaned, "No! He must have broken it after he swam for the black box. When I pulled him back on the coffin, I must have pulled him too hard."

Whispering into my ear, she added further disaster, "Aunt Momi says if his thing is broken, his career in Hollywood is over. Kaput! No more Tarzan movies, definitely, and maybe no more Flash Gordon movies because he wears those tight gold pants all the time. Think about it, Percy. You've ruined a big movie star's career." Marigold acted very pleased with herself.

Hearing about Buster made me even more determined to escape from my jail. "Marigold, get me out of here. I've got to see Uncle Buster and I've got to find Aunt Rose's killer. If I find the killer, people will like me again. I'll be a hero. I threw the steamer trunk overboard because I didn't want Aunt Momi or you to get killed. You know that. You didn't tell Aunt Momi anything about the empty steamer trunk, did you?"

"No, but if you had died, I would have."

"Thanks for being a pal. Did anything else bad happen while I was drowning in the ocean?"

She scratched her head. Her eyes lit up and said in an off handed way, "Well, kind of. The two old ladies, who hate you, complained that their jewelry was stolen. No one believed them because they complain about everything and they never know where the hell they're going. They can't hear or see. They get lost all the time even going to the bathroom. Johnny found them in the engine room. They thought they were going into the dining room, so no one is taking them very seriously. I hate it when people exaggerate. Nothing much else happened, no more murders, anyway. What was it like drowning?"

I beamed, "Great. Uncle Buster and I would have drowned except we floated on Aunt Rose's coffin. We were going with her to Waikiki Beach but Aunt Rose wanted to do it by herself."

She punched me. "You are such a liar. You didn't float on Aunt Rose's coffin. You're making that up."

Frustrated that my sister didn't believe me, I watched the shadows on the ceiling.

I looked at my sister without my mouth twitching and said, "I think that everyone is going to hate me for the rest of my life. I don't care. No matter what happens to me or what people think of me, I have to be myself. I can't worry anymore that you and everybody think I'm crazy. I have something important to do. Now, get me out of this dump. First off, I have to make sure the treasures haven't been thrown overboard."

Feeling my head for a fever, Marigold said in a sisterly tone, "I can't get you out of here because if I get caught doing it, the captain will tie a rope around my belly and 'keel haul' me under the ship. Everyone hates you so much that if you were to walk out of here right now, all the crazy old ladies on the ship would beat you to death with their umbrellas."

Resting my head next to my sister's, I murmured to her, "Please, Marigold, the Scarlet Shadow promised Aunt Rose to find her killer. Aunt Rose saved my life on the coffin and remember what Mother told us: 'a promise made is a promise kept.' I wish I could turn invisible right now and get out of here."

Marigold choked my neck and warned me for the second time. "Percy, quit talking about Aunt Rose's coffin. I'm telling you the truth. Everyone hates you and will hate you even more if you tell them you were floating on a coffin. Well, everyone except Mrs. Brown."

"Edwina?"

Propping her head up on her arm, she looked at me and said, "Edwina gave the captain hell for not going back for you sooner. If it weren't for Mrs. Brown, you wouldn't be here lying in this bed right now. The passengers hate her as much as they hate you. I'm the only one on the ship that likes her."

Sitting straight up, I vowed, "That's all the more reason I have to get out of here so I can save Edwina's reputation. She's a real pip, Marigold. She's a real friend."

Resting back on the pillow again, my sister sniffed, "Pip or not, she's in doodoo. I was smart. I stuck up for you, but I said it under my breath; that way, people still confide in me."

Facing Marigold, I asked the question that I had been holding back. "Does Aunt Momi still love me?"

"She does, she does. She got crazy, hysterical, when they lifted you unconscious onto the ship. She wouldn't leave your side. She made such a fuss that Captain Spaulding forced her out of this room. The doctor made her take sleeping pills. Because of the pills and a martini, she's knocked out cold. That's why I could sneak out to see you. The way she's snoring, I don't think she'll wake up until we reach San Francisco. Don't worry Percy, she loves you lots. That's true. I promise!"

"I love Aunt Momi. She's a fighter like Edwina." My heart warmed hearing that Aunt Momi and Edwina loved me. Mina flashed into my mind. "What's happened to Mina?"

Marigold began looking at her bare feet. She did that on Sunday mornings while reading the funnies. Picking at her toes, she said, "Mina and Toshi disappeared. Every time Daisy and Neal brought them food, they weren't in the lifeboat. The plate of food remained untouched. Mina and Toshi have disappeared." She shook her head like the prophet of doom.

Touching Marigold's arm, I said, "I never trusted Toshi. Right off the bat, he looked dangerous. I bet you a nickel that Toshi is really Tojo's first cousin. He could have killed Mina because Mina found out that he was the murderer."

People were outside my prison cell walking down the corridor, saying my name. One of the voices belonged to Sister Clarabel. I said excitedly, "Marigold, hide under the blanket! Pretend we're one person. Sister Clarabel is coming. She's crazy."

"Sister Clarabel?"

"A crazy old witch who thinks she's my nurse. She's trouble with a capital T. Just do it." Marigold zipped under the blanket next to me. We became one body.

"The boy's in here."

"Where?" asked a strange voice.

"In here."

I whispered to Marigold that Sister Clarabel wore a starched white nurses' uniform, stood as tall as a beanstalk and had the face of a prune.

The sister walked into the room with a man who looked exactly like Lew Ayres, the handsome actor in the Dr. Kildare movies. "Here's Percy, Doctor," said Sister Clarabel. She sounded as cheerful as if she had just invented Christmas.

I screamed, "Turn off the light. My eyes hurt."

"Goodness, Percy. You didn't say your eyes hurt when I left here." Keeping the light on, the sister stood at the foot of the bed while the doctor inspected me. The doctor peered at me as if I was some exotic bug. He kept staring at my feet.

I squeezed Marigold's hand. "My eyes took their time to hurt. I have delayed eye burn. It's the kind of eye burn you get before you go blind. Please, turn off the light."

In a low voice, the handsome man said carefully, "Percy, I'm Dr. Potter. The captain asked me to look in on you. You certainly are a big fellow for your age. I'd say you're almost as big as two people." He squeezed Marigold's toes making Marigold yelp under the covers.

Trying to drown out Marigold's noise, I said, "Floating in the ocean does that to a fat person. It makes one fat person look like two fat people."

From under the blanket, Marigold sneezed, "kachoo."

"What was that?" asked the sister, looking under the bed.

"I farted. I think my farts sound exactly like sneezes. Ask anyone in my family. Ask my sister, Marigold." Marigold nodded under the covers.

The doctor said, licking his lips, "Sister, I may be imagining it, but I count four legs on Percy. He is an amazing person. I think Percy should be written up in Ripley's Believe It or Not."

"Four legs are better to walk with, doctor," I answered, trying to sound like the wolf in **Red Riding Hood**.

Putting on his black spectacles, he said, "I now believe I detect two heads."

"Two heads are better to think with, doctor," I said, scratching Marigold's head under the covers.

"Hmmm. Sister, let's step out of the room for a minute. I want to get something for Percy that will make him feel well again. Agreed, Sister?" He winked at the nurse.

"You're the doctor." The beanstalk had a devilish look on her face.

They did an about face and left the room. As they walked down the corridor, the doctor was laughing. Marigold threw back the covers, leapt out of the bed, and ran for the door. At the door, she stopped, looked up and down the corridor. Rolling her eyes around like pinwheels, she yelled, "YIKES!" Marigold ran for our cabin.

Within minutes, Dr. Potter and Sister Clarabel walked back into the room. The doctor said, pressing my toes, "Well, young man, you look quite normal again. Sister, I believe we have witnessed a miracle. Percy, I have here in my hand something that will make you feel much better since you're so full of stuff."

"What is it?" I asked, not trusting the funny look in his eyes.

"Castor oil."

"Castor oil?" I screamed. "Listen, doctor, I don't need castor oil. I need oil on my sunburn, an egg salad sandwich with oily mayonnaise, creamed tuna on rice, a chocolate milk shake, not castor oil. I need food. MY KIND OF FOOD. That's what I need. I was floating in the ocean for over twenty-four hours without anything to eat or drink. I almost died. All Sister has fed me is chicken soup. The last thing I need is to take castor oil. What kind of a doctor are you, anyway?"

"I'm a veterinarian. The ship's doctor, Dr. Wallace, is taking care of Mr. Crabbe who has a serious injury. The captain asked me to look in on you."

"I get the leftovers. I get the cow doctor. Moooooooo. Moooooo. Moooooo," I pouted.

"Be a good boy and take your castor oil, and I promise that tomorrow you can return to your cabin." He held the spoon of castor oil near my mouth while Sister Clarabel, standing next to him, made an awful face.

"Promise that I can go back to my cabin tomorrow?" I said, squeezing my fanny.

Bringing the tablespoon closer to my lips, Dr. Potter mumbled two words that didn't sound at all sincere, "I promise."

"Doctor," I said, grimacing like Sister Clarabel.

"What?"

"Just so you don't forget: I'm not a cow." The spoon touched my mouth.

"You could've fooled me. Open up wide." He shoved the spoon into my mouth and the castor oil slimed down my throat, gagging me when it hit my stomach. Dr. Potter turned to the sister who was screwing the cap back on the blue bottle, wiped his hands on a towel and ordered, "The enema, Sister."

I felt hot air on my face. I awoke to find Mina staring at me. Toshi was guarding the door. His beady eyes were on alert. He was afraid of something or someone.

I shot straight up in bed and sputtered, "Mina, where have you been? Are you all right? What time is it?"

Pulling at the red scarf around her neck, Mina's eyes darted around the room like a frightened deer and whispered, "After midnight. We hide in all kind place now. We in big danger. Angel of Death try catch us all time. He like kill us."

"Do you trust Toshi, Mina?" I asked. Toshi stared angrily at me.

She whispered, "He know killer."

"Toshi knows who the killer is? Who is he?"

Toshi ran over and grabbed Mina's arm and dragged her out of the room. I jumped out of bed and ran after them, pleading, "Who is the Angel of Death, Mina? Tell me. Please."

Toshi pushed her down the corridor. Mina called to me, "I find you. Watch babies. Babies and you in big danger."

"Is it Toshi?" Before she could answer me, they vanished.

Five days had passed since I boarded the ship. I had only five days more to find Aunt Rose's killer. In five days, we were to arrive in San Francisco.

CHAPTER 17

COURAGE COMES IN SURPRISING WAYS

Another storm blew down from Alaska bringing the gale force winds and gigantic waves. As on our first day at sea, fifty-foot waves cascaded over the bow of the Aquitania.

I itched from the sunburn. I could strip pieces of skin off my body the size of Band-Aids. I matched the walls in the infirmary. I had stuffed my near-drowning experience into my mind's closet, joining all the other unpleasant events that I kept locked up in there. The Scarlet Shadow wasn't going to be a crybaby.

Back in our cabin, I'd been pressed into maid service. Aunt Momi and Marigold were lying flat on their beds looking like zombies. Marigold upchucked on the hour. Aunt Momi had me press a cold compress on her forehead on the half. My aunt groaned that she was dying. (Marigold whispered that my aunt had mixed sleeping pills with her martinis, and said things to the captain that made her blush.)

Nobody, to my knowledge, had inquired about our health. Our cabin, without official notice, became off limits to the passengers and crew. Treated as lepers, we ate all our meals in our cabin. This situation was entirely all my fault. Marigold's warnings that the passengers hated me on sight and that, outside the cabin, old ladies waited with umbrellas to poke me overboard, made me want to act like the Scarlet Pimpernel and turn the tide of events. I ventured out in the daylight to get our meals, keeping a watchful eye out for any crazy old lady carrying an umbrella. I'd scurry down the corridor five minutes before feeding time putting my head down. Bulldozing my way into the galley, the cooks had our trays ready to place in my hands. Checking the food, I'd scamper back to the cabin like Peter Rabbit. If I met anyone in the corridor, they flattened their backs against the walls trying to avoid me. I was the Hunchback of Notre Dame carrying trays of bubonic plague. With everyone leaving us alone, it gave me time to make plans.

The first day of the second storm, the ship tossed like a cork bobbing in a bucket of water. The now experienced passengers confined themselves to their cabins. With most of the passengers in their cabins except the few hearty folks eating in the dining room, there wasn't much danger, at least to my thinking, of running into the Angel of Death. Even a ghost had to get seasick.

None of my friends had contacted me. I felt that was very strange. I was worried for Johnny, Daisy, Neal and Edwina's safety. Fearing that I had lost Johnny's friendship forever, I kept thinking of a plan to repair it. I pressed my hands against my ears to force my brain to ooze out brilliant ideas. I wanted everything to be back to normal. Thinking all day gave me an earache.

On the first night of the raging storm, believing that everyone was in their cabins sleeping, watching Marigold and Aunt Momi snore in concert, I bundled up my courage and snuck quietly out of the cabin. Stealthily, I roamed the ship as it reared up and down like a bucking bronco. I made the usual rounds. Covering my face with a towel to disguise myself, I fought my way out on deck and headed for the Shangri-La. The stinging sprays of salt water hit my body like pinpricks. Protecting my sunburned face with the towel, leaning into the wind, I staggered step by step up the ladder until I reached the familiar motor boat. Holding onto ropes, I searched for Mina's scarf fluttering in the wind. Not to be seen, I looked inside the boat. Mina and Toshi were not sleeping there. I began to fear the worst. Mina was as dead as a mackerel.

Inside the ship, shaking the salt water off my clothes, I inched forward step by step, carefully looking in back of me, in front of me, to my left and to my right for any sign of the creepy Angel of Death, hoping that he was seasick. As I walked past dark corners, I still imagined him hiding in the shadows waiting for me to show up. In the Writing Salon, to my great relief, the couch stood unmoved from its alcove. I crawled in back of it and touched the fabric. The treasures were safe in their nest. Relieved, I sat on the couch and remembered Mina's warning words, "Babies in trouble."

More secrets: The next night out, as I did the rounds, the seas still heaving mountains of water over the bow of the ship, I came up with a fabulous plan and carried it out as soon as I thought of it. God knew what the plan was — no one else did because I kept that plan in God's hands, hoping He would protect me as I carried it out. To my knowledge, no one saw what I did.

That next morning, lying on the cot, my heart fluttering out of control, my head percolating like a pot of hot coffee, I pleaded with God to tell me how I could right the wrongs I had committed to Johnny, Edwina and everyone else on the ship. It was my mother's voice I heard. It was as if she was standing next to me telling me what to do. That night, I carried out her plan.

Still acting as the maid, picking up the lunch trays in the galley, I overheard the cooks cutting Johnny down to size. They grumbled that Johnny was acting like the king of England. The captain had placed Johnny in charge of catching the thief before the Aquitania docked in San Francisco. Two more robberies had occurred the day the storm hit, and another happened while I had roamed the ship that night. The snot-nose, pasty-faced cook sitting at a table, shoveling spaghetti into his mouth, pointed at me and laughed, "I bet there's the bloody thief."

The pasty-faced cook couldn't talk of anything else but the robberies. He informed his mates that the captain sent a memo to remind all passengers to place their valuables in the purser's office and to keep their cabins locked at all times. "Ha! That won't keep the bloke from stealing anything he wants. He's a clever one, he is."

As the seas calmed and life on the ship returned to normal, the winter storm headed south and the convoy kept its zigzagging course toward San Francisco. Once again, the passengers ate in the dining room without having their dinners slide off the tables. It was now or never to carry out Mother's plan. And, most importantly, I had only a few more days before we sailed under the Golden Gate Bridge.

After lunch, I revealed the plan to my aunt and sister. I was going to make a public apology in the dining room at dinner that night. I'd make my apology at the second sitting. The second sitting was when the captain and Johnny ate their dinner.

Aunt Momi removed the cloth from her forehead, opened her eyes, and asked me to sit by her. She said she was going to take a leaf from my book and ask the captain to forgive her for acting so silly. Thinking there was a glimmer of hope of playing bridge with the captain again, my aunt smiled like a Cheshire cat and kissed my forehead.

Marigold murmured weakly, "Don't you want me to come with you for support?" She ran for the toilet.

I called to her, "This is something I have to do myself, Marigold."

The hour arrived. I dressed up. I wanted to make a movie star entrance in the dining room. I wore the same white pants and white shirt that I had worn to Aunt Rose's funeral. Of course, I wore the blue bowtie that Daddy gave me. I tied the same black ribbon around my arm. I felt I was going to a hanging and the hanging was going to be my own.

"Aunt Momi and Marigold, do I look spiffy?" In reply, my aunt kissed my forehead and Marigold pinched my fanny.

Taking a deep breath, figuring it could be my last, and fearing that at the end of my speech the old ladies would stampede with their umbrellas and toss me overboard. After giving a final farewell, I trotted out of the cabin. I felt like a Christian martyr entering the Coliseum to meet the hungry lions. Passengers going to dinner, seeing me, again flattened themselves against the wall when I passed them. Bubbles churned in my stomach.

At the entrance to the dining room, I stood still as a statue. The captain was already seated at a table with Johnny, Auntie Sissy and the nun. When the captain saw me standing at the entrance, he choked on his soup. When he breathed again, he looked like a red balloon. The other passengers ignored me and pretended to talk about the weather. Behind their napkins, they were pointing their fingers at me.

A loud voice boomed. "Percy."

To my right, Edwina was sitting at her table. She wore her black hat and her oogie veil. She waved me over. Defiantly, sticking out my chins, I marched to the beat of a drum. When I arrived, she had removed her hat and veil. Talking loud enough so that everyone could hear her, she said how much she had missed me. I stood stiff like a soldier as she ordered, "Kiss me." I dutifully kissed both her cheeks.

Rubbing her cheeks, she swore, "Damn it boy, relax and sit down!" I sat next to her. Tears filled my eyes.

I picked up her left hand and kissed it. In a French accent, I murmured, "I mizzed you, Cheri."

"I mizzed you, too!" Growling like a stevedore, her cheeks bright pink, she replied, "That's more like it, kid, but no more of that French mushy stuff between us. I think falling in the drink stiffened your backbone. Damn brave of you coming in here to face all these alley cats. I can see you're the man I thought you'd become. Where's Momi and Marigold?" I told her they were sick and, anyway, I wanted to come by myself.

Calling her waiter over, she barked, "Give my friend here the best meal on the ship. This boy has more guts than anyone on this goddamned ship." The waiter scurried away, saying lots of "Yes, ma'ams."

Touching my sunburned face with a cool spoon, Edwina declared, "You don't look half-bad considering what you've been through. I hear the big fellow got hurt but he's a tough buzzard, so let's not worry about him. I'm sure as hell glad to see you. I've missed you tremendously. No one on this damn ship talks any sense like you do. If they had let you drown, I'd have kicked that horse's ass until he was black and blue in places I'm too ashamed to mention. I really would have."

Watching Edwina take a sip of her martini, I made a request. "I need your help. I'm going to make an apology to everyone for what I did. I want to make right for all the harm I have done. Introduce me, please?"

Daisy and Neal appeared out of nowhere. Neal sat on Edwina's right and Daisy next to me.

"Oh, Percy," squealed Daisy, kissing my cheek, "I missed you so. I cried buckets when you fell into the ocean. I thought you were gone from me forever."

"Me too," mumbled Neal who didn't look me in the face.

Edwina asked, concerned, "Children, won't your mother mind you sitting with this bad boy and me?"

"We don't care," snapped Daisy. "We're the Shadows, and Shadows stick together forever into eternity." Placing her hands on her lap like a lady, she spoke demurely, "You don't mind if we sit here with you and Percy, do you, Mrs. Brown?"

Edwina replied, kindly, "Of course not. It took guts for you and this young sprout to come sit with us because I know what your mother thinks of me and I know what she thinks of this bad boy." She jabbed me in the ribs with her spoon. "I admire young people who have gumption. Remain loyal to their friends. That didn't happen to me. I'm Edwina to you, dear. I gave up being called Mrs. Brown a long time ago." She spoke to Daisy as if they had always been best friends. "It is my honor to have you sitting at my table. Have you eaten, dear?"

"We've had our dinner. But Edwina, may I ask you a question?" asked Daisy.

"What is it, dear?"

Looking at the potato soup the waiter placed in front of me, I cried, "Wait, wait, wait, WAIT! I have something important to do. NOW! I need to do it before the captain leaves the dining room. Daisy, if you keep talking I won't have the courage to do what I came here to do."

Edwina laughed, "Yes Percy, you have the courage. My father once said to me, 'Courage is showing up even if you don't want to. And here you are. It's time, Percy. Go do what you have to do. Daisy will be quiet now."

I screwed up my courage and said, "I have to do it now or I'll never do it."

"What is it, Percy?" said Daisy, touching my hand, gently.

Edwina took Daisy into her arms, and asked me, "What is it you want me to do, Percy?"

My palms moistened as I answered, "Introduce me. (I pointed to the passengers.) I have to make it right for you and everyone else. I'm going to restore your reputation."

Edwina laughed, "It's too late for that, my boy. My reputation was ruined long ago."

Neal whimpered, still not looking at me, "It's my fault. I pushed you over. I made you fall overboard."

"It was my fault, Neal. You and Daisy actually saved my life. You made me wear my life jacket. Let bygones be bygones. Okay?"

Neal looked at me and smiled, "From now on, you can be the big cheese forever and ever. I'll do whatever you ask me to do, promise I will."

I turned to Edwina and said, "Introduce me quick. I'm feeling kind of weak now."

Holding up her spoon, she answered, "It will be my honor. Handsome knights don't ride by my castle anymore and when one does, a lady takes note. Wish it'd been you on that white horse instead of that horse's patootie Mr. Brown."

"You're a pip, Edwina."

Edwina hit her martini glass three times with the spoon and, when the dining room came under her spell, my Guinevere announced, "Ladies and gentlemen, my knight in shining armor has a few words to say to you."

She turned to me and nodded.

I stood on a chair to make sure the captain could see me from where he was sitting.

Johnny was next to the captain. It was the first time since I had fallen overboard that I had seen my friend. For a second we stared at each other, and then he flashed his million-dollar smile. In that instant, we were friends again. The rest of the passengers, by their looks, told me that in front of them stood the hated, fat, sinister Nazi Hermann Wilhelm Goering.

I glanced up at the ceiling. Four eyes were looking down at me from a hole where once hung a chandelier. I could see a red scarf in the hole. Knowing that Mina was alive gave me the strength to begin. I lowered my eyes, turned the passengers into silly goofballs, took a deep breath and spoke from my heart.

The Louis XVI Restaurant aboard the Aquatania.

First class drawing room aboard the Aquatania.

CHAPTER 18

ALL IS LOST

The apology was over. The bubbles popped in my throat. Standing on the chair, feeling as brave as the Scarlet Pimpernel, I waited for the applause. The dining room became silent as a tomb.

In the silence, the captain folded his napkin, rose from his table, pulled the chairs out for Auntie Sissy and the nun and, turning his back to me, left the dining room.

Edwina sprang from her chair and applauded madly. Daisy began clapping her hands like a wild woman. Neal put two fingers in his mouth and whistled like a sailor.

The dining room buzzed like bees in a honeycomb. The passengers rose from their chairs and, en masse, followed the captain and the queen bees out of the dining room.

Feeling I was the biggest failure in the world, I jumped off the chair and sat next to Edwina. The old ladies, who had lunched in the engine room, passed our table tapping me on my head with their umbrellas. I took that as a bad omen. Not knowing what to do next, I twirled a spoon around in my dessert bowl and melted the ice cream into soup. Watching the vanilla ice cream turn into yellow sludge, I wanted to kill myself.

A hand rested on my head. I looked up. Johnny was smiling down at me. He placed his finger in the center of my forehead and said, "You gave a fine speech, Sir Percy. You said all the right things. Don't mind the captain. Thank you, mate, for telling the captain that I wasn't at fault for your shenanigans. You made me and every one of us who love you very proud of you tonight. It takes a big man to own up to his mistakes."

Edwina chortled, "I'll second that, Red. Percy, I think you were a little too lavish in your praise of me, though."

I looked into Johnny's eyes and said, "You do forgive me, don't you, Johnny?"

His steely blue eyes looked back into mine. He paused and made a surprising confession, "I was never mad at you."

"But, Marigold said…" I stammered.

Grabbing my shoulders, he chortled, "What do girls know?"

Edwina slapped Johnny's wrist with the flat of her dinner knife and scolded, "I beg your pardon, Red. Girls know a helluva lot more than you think we do."

Johnny rubbed his hand and apologized, "Excuse me, Mrs. Brown. Exceptions are made at this table."

"I hope so, Red. Remember this, Daisy. Girls are much smarter than men, any day. We just let men think they are smart." Edwina studied Johnny.

Johnny pulled an empty chair to the table, far from the reach of Edwina's knife, and sat next to me. He talked very seriously, "Now, Sir Percy, what was in that suitcase that went overboard? What was so important in that suitcase that you risked your life and ours?"

Before I answered, I took a swallow of ice cream. Looking at Daisy and Neal, then at Edwina, and then back at Johnny, I gulped hoping that what I was going to say wouldn't sound too stupid. "Nothing of importance. Inside the trunk was my last bottle of Best Foods mayonnaise."

Neal broke in, "Don't forget my baby pillow."

"And my doll," chimed in Daisy.

Then I admitted the worst, "And I put Auntie Sissy's fur coat in the steamer trunk."

Edwina yipped as if she had struck gold. "I hope it was her ten thousand-dollar mink coat."

"It was." I said shamefully.

"That's wonderful, Percy. Just wonderful." Edwina's eyes danced a polka.

Neal jumped in again, reminding me, "Don't forget the spit-up towel."

"The spit towel?" asked Johnny.

Neal looked at me proudly that he had remembered it, and boasted, "Yea, we spat on a towel for good luck, for all the luck it did Percy. Maybe we didn't spit enough. Maybe it was Toooshi…"

I reached for Neal to keep him from spilling the beans, and said loudly, "Neal is right. It was my spit that gave me my bad luck."

Johnny looked bemused and asked, "Just that stuff in the suitcase? Nothing else?"

"Just that, Johnny." I said. I didn't want to be asked more questions because if the killer was listening, he'd know the treasures were still onboard the ship.

Johnny asked again, "You're sure? Just that? A spit-up towel and that other stuff?"

Daisy, Neal and I nodded. "Just that."

Johnny exclaimed, "Well, I'll be a monkey's uncle if that isn't the most stupid thing I've ever heard of in all my life. That was a very foolish prank. Think of what it cost us — think of all the people who could have been killed and the money and energy spent in rescuing you. Why?" Johnny asked, shaking his head in disbelief.

"We were playing a game. They dared me. I didn't plan to fall overboard. That wasn't in the plan. That was a mistake. It just happened. Only the steamer trunk was to go overboard." When I said that, I was looking at Neal. "That's why I made the speech, Johnny. Please, Johnny, don't tell anyone what I just told you. I want everyone to think that I threw something very valuable overboard. That was part of the game."

Johnny shook my hand and promised he would keep my secret and again asked, "Mrs. Brown, don't you think that was a very foolish game they were playing?"

"They made a mistake and mistakes happen. We've all made mistakes. Haven't you, Red, ever made a mistake? Kids are kids. With this war going on, I don't think these kids have much of a childhood any more, do you?" She looked quizzically at Johnny.

I chipped in, "I know it was a mistake, and it was a game, but I did it for good reasons. Anyway, I thought they were good reasons." Looking at Johnny, I repeated, "I really thought they were, Johnny. I really did. I did it on a dare."

"It's confusing but I'll take your word for it, Sir Percy. It's all past now." Rising from the chair, he announced, "I have to report to the captain and, I'm with you, Mrs. Brown, I'm very proud of Percy tonight."

Edwina pointed her spoon at Johnny, warning, "You tell that big shot captain to stay out of my way. His behavior was downright rude. This young man gave us his all to make things right for him and the passengers, and all that horse's ass could do was to leave the dining room without saying a word to Percy. That goes for that uppity Miss Sissy and her Friday fish-eating nun."

Edwina turned to Daisy and Neal and apologized, "Sorry, kids, speaking like that about your mother, but it's how I feel." She waved her spoon at Johnny, "Don't forget to tell the captain that Mrs. Brown thinks he's a horse's ass."

"Ma'am, the captain has been at sea most of his life. What he does, he does very well. He's a fair man and treats his ship, his crew and his passengers as if they were his own. Not having kids, he doesn't understand Percy like I do. He has a very sad personal problem that he's dealing with, so give him a little slack." Johnny straightened his tunic, stood tall, nodded, and did an about face.

"That's no excuse."

Johnny turned and said, in his charming voice, "We're on to the robber and we're about to catch the culprit. That's not for anyone else's ears, of course. You're keeping your valuables secured, Mrs. Brown?"

"Safe enough," she bantered. "No pipsqueak is going to steal my diamond ring, believe you me."

"Good enough then, mates. I'll say goodnight to one and all." With that, Johnny left the dining room.

Edwina mused, watching Johnny leave, "He likes you, Percy, and that's a big plus for him in my book, but he's got the most damnable eyes I have ever seen. Did you notice them? They change color as he talks. And that mass of red hair. He's a handsome devil, I'll give him that." Resting her spoon back on the table, she said abruptly, "Turning in. I have a feeling that you three have a few things to discuss without me being around." She picked up her hat and veil, and without a kiss or a goodnight, followed Johnny out of the dining room.

Daisy, Neal and I grabbed each other and screamed. Hearing us scream, the men clearing the tables jumped as if an air raid siren had gone off.

Daisy pleaded, "Let's get out of here, do the rounds and check on the treasures." I assured them that I had made the rounds the night before and that the treasures were still safe inside the couch.

Neal, wild-eyed, said, "Every time we made the rounds after you went overboard, we were being followed. We were watched all the time. So, we had to be careful whatever we did and wherever we went. It scared us because we couldn't see the person, but we knew someone was watching us all the time. We only checked on the treasures once."

"You didn't see who was following you?"

"No. But someone was," said Daisy.

"You're right, Daisy. Someone was following you." I said, remembering Mina's warning.

"Let's go," said Daisy, rising out of her chair. "I'm so frightened. We haven't seen Mina or Toshi since you fell in the ocean. We went to the lifeboat twice but they weren't there. Neal keeps telling me that Mina has been murdered. He made me so scared saying that that I couldn't go back to check on the treasures or the lifeboat."

"That was wise, Daisy. Mina is not dead. Tonight, just before I spoke, I saw Mina's red scarf. Mina was listening to me. When I was in the infirmary, Mina came to see me in the flesh with Toshi." I lowered my voice so none of the helpers in the dining room could hear me. "She knows who the Angel of Death is!"

Neal, rising out of his chair, blurted out so the whole world heard him say, "Who is it?"

"Hush, Neal. Keep your voice down. Mina wouldn't tell me but… but… I think its Toshi." I pronounced Toshi's name so softly that Daisy made me repeat it, twice.

Daisy said firmly, "No. Toshi is a good boy. I trust Toshi because Mina trusts him."

"Well, I don't trust him. If you saw the look in his eyes when he pulled Mina down the corridor, you wouldn't say that." I changed the subject because Daisy was getting upset. Getting out of my chair, I suggested, "Let's check on the treasures."

We took the elevator up to the Writing Salon. The Writing Salon was deserted. Checking the corridor seeing that no one was around, Daisy ran into the room and squeezed behind the couch and screamed, "They're gone!"

"What?" I screamed back.

By this time, Neal had joined Daisy behind the couch. He hollered out to me, "They are really gone. The treasures are gone. Gone. Disappeared."

"Stop saying 'gone.' Let me see." Pulling the couch away from the wall, I crawled behind it and joined them. Sure enough, somebody ripped the fabric from the back of the couch, leaving an empty gaping hole. The treasures had "flown the coop."

I dragged Daisy and Neal away from the couch and pushed the couch back in place. Scared that someone was spying on us, we ran to the top of the staircase. I whispered, "Someone must have followed me last night. I thought I had covered my tracks. They must have been hiding behind the curtain." I quickly looked around to see if anyone was in the corridor.

"Look," I said, remembering Mina's warning, "Go back to your cabin and lock yourselves in. Don't come out until tomorrow morning. Tomorrow, we'll meet at breakfast. You're in real danger."

I led them down the first flight of stairs stopping on the landing, instructing them, "Run the rest of the way. Someone has the treasures now and they will want to shut us up because we are the only ones who know that the treasures didn't go overboard and that someone has to be the Angel of Death. Run like the wind."

"But, Percy..." Daisy protested.

"Do what I say. I know what I'm talking about. Trust me, Shadows. The Scarlet Shadow is going to get to the bottom of this. I promise."

Daisy grabbed Neal's hand. They leapt down the stairs three steps at a time and we're gone in a flash.

Once they were out of sight, I twirled around eight times for luck, climbed back up to the next floor and headed for the Boat Deck. I wanted to find Mina to learn what was behind her warning but, most of all, I wanted her to tell me who the Angel of Death is. Walking out on the Boat Deck, I peered in every lifeboat looking for Mina. Standing next to the Shangri-La, I called quietly, "Mina. Mina." As I waited for her to answer, I looked around to see if she was signaling me with her red scarf. No answer, only the sound of the howling wind flapping the ropes against the mast.

I called louder, "Mina!"

"Who's there?" thundered a voice in the dark.

I hid behind the boat and called out, "It's me."

The voice boomed, "Who's me?"

"Percy."

"Come out from behind that boat and get over here. I'm not going to hurt you,"

I headed for the sound of his voice.

"Come on. Come on. I haven't got all day. Get over here."

Captain Spaulding was leaning against the railing watching the Lurline cut through the water. The ship was outlined by the light of the moon. By the position of the stars, the Aquitania hadn't begun its nightly maneuver around the convoy.

As I approached the captain, he asked, "What are you doing out here?"

"Oh, nothing," I answered.

"Nothing?"

"I came out here to think."

"I have something to say to you. You made a fine apology in there. At first, I didn't know what to make of it. I thought you were just fooling around. Well, I've changed my mind after hearing what you had to say, and also Mr. Crabbe has told me that you saved his life."

I interrupted, "He saved my life." In the next breath, I questioned, "Did he tell you anything else? Did he mention anything about treasures, or talk about a person named Mina or the Angel of Death?" I waited, holding my breath, for his answer.

"What are you talking about?"

"Oh, just kid's stuff." I said, breathing again.

The captain sniffed the air and watched the moon go behind a cloud. "I love to be out on deck on nights like this. I like it when the sea has quieted down and the moon is dim. Before the war, I'd come out on deck on nights like this and smoke my pipe. But the captain has to follow the rules, too. Percy, when you're old enough, smoke a pipe. A pipe is good for a man's soul." He inhaled more salt air and said quietly, "I want to apologize for leaving abruptly."

"Mrs. Brown didn't like it."

"I had to do it. I don't care for scenes and I won't have people at my table making them in public. The ladies at my table were becoming ill-mannered so, before they got out of hand, I made them leave."

"I know all about Auntie Sissy's scenes. When she gets mad, she conks people with her polo mallet. Don't get her mad at you."

"Let's not get into that. Back to our business: I was wrong about you, young man, but you did put my ship in jeopardy. In the British Navy and wartime, that is inexcusable, no matter what the reason. But, on the other hand, any man who admits his mistakes is a man I'll honor."

The captain took a pipe out of his pocket and put it in his mouth and began humming, "A Pretty Girl is Like a Melody." By the look in his eye, I was sure he was thinking of Aunt Momi.

Breaking from his reverie, he spoke, "Two more days and we'll be landing in San Francisco. San Francisco is a great city, a real jewel, but from the weather reports, we're about to hit a fog bank. It's a challenge to sail a ship in fog because anything can happen."

"What kinds of things happen?" I queried him.

"Decks get slippery, ships hit other ships and passengers fall overboard. When ships zigzag in fog, it's even more difficult. I have to take extra precautions. You should do the same. If you fall overboard, you'll be gone forever. I'll never be able to find you. The only good thing I like about the fog is that Japanese submarines have a harder time finding us."

Holding tight to the railing, I said, "I won't fall overboard this time. Promise, I won't. But if I do fall overboard, someone pushed me. Scary things happen in the movies in the fog. Murderers walk the streets in London and knife people. By the way, do you eat Best Foods mayonnaise?" I had asked the captain my favorite question.

"No. Mayonnaise reminds me of scum that floats on top the grease traps in a galley. You have a wandering mind, young lad." He sucked on his pipe, and returned to his reverie. In silence, we listened to the ship plow through the waves.

Acting the captain again, he ordered, "Time for bed, young Percy. By the way, whom were you calling just now?"

"I was calling Johnny," I said, thinking fast.

"He's down on B Deck helping a sick passenger. Go to bed before the fog hits. A word of caution: stay out of dark corners and far away from the railings until we reach San Francisco. Don't trust anyone."

With a salute, he marched off for the bridge. I groped my way back to Mina's lifeboat. Standing beside the Shangri-La, I called out once more, "Mina. Mina." As before, no one answered. I started down the ladder; then out from the corner of my eye, I saw Mina's red scarf fluttering in the wind. I headed for the scarf, calling excitedly, "Mina, come out. It's all right, I'm alone."

Out stepped Toshi with Mina's scarf wrapped around his neck. He was dressed like a sailor with a wool cap covering his black hair. His tiger-eyes glowed in the dark. He moved around like the wolf that had just eaten Little Red Riding Hood.

"Where's Mina, Toshi?"

He grunted something that I couldn't hear.

"Where's Mina?" I insisted.

Toshi challenged me with a ferocious look. A tiger trapped in a cage.

"Where's Mina? I cried.

Toshi held a knife in his hand.

I screamed, "You killed Mina!"

The boat deck.

CHAPTER 19

THE PLOT THICKENS

The tip of the knife glimmered in the moonlight.

I screamed louder, "You're a Jap killer." Toshi ripped the scarf off his neck and threw it at me.

Men's voices cried, "Did you hear that? The bloody bloke is on Boat Deck." I turned to the sound of the voices and, when I looked back, Toshi had run away.

Men wearing boots tramped up the metal ladder, bellowing, "Get that bastard!" They were running towards me sounding as if a posse was out to lynch Jesse James. Afraid that I'd be lynched, I hid in a dark corner, below a fire extinguisher, and curled up into a little ball.

Hooting and hollering, sailors carrying rifles ran past me. They were dressed like Toshi except their black wool caps were pulled over their foreheads, hiding their faces. I didn't recognize any of them. They ran for the stern of the ship. Hearing them in the distance, I cautiously came out of hiding. I grabbed Mina's scarf and ran for the Writing Salon. Inside the Salon, feeling safe, I leaned against a wall and listened to my heart beat. I was scared, excited and exhausted all at the same time. Feeling faint, I lay on the couch to recover my senses. With my eyes closed, I kept seeing Toshi's knife pointed at me. In my dreamy half-awake state, I was glad I had called Toshi a Jap. The Jap word took him off balance; otherwise, he would have knifed me like he knifed Mina.

Thinking about Mina, I put her scarf to my nose. I crinkled my nose, the scarf smelled like Auntie Sissy. In seconds, I drifted into a deep sleep. An odd feeling woke me. The lights in the room had been turned off. The Writing Salon had become as dark as an underground cave and there was a presence in the room. The presence wasn't a bat, it was a breathing human being. Pretending to be asleep, I played possum hoping the strange presence would go away, but it stayed and came close enough so that I could smell it. I sat up and yelled, "Go away, Jap ghost!"

"Go away, Jap ghost?" the voice hummed mysteriously.

"Go away, bad ghost, Angel of Death."

The presence howled, "I don't want to go away. Percy, I am the ghoooost of the Aquitania." When I heard the voice say "Percy," I knew that Johnny was playing tricks on me.

Annoyed that my friend had frightened me, I said angrily, "Johnny, quit it. Quit scaring me. Turn the lights back on."

Johnny flipped on the switch. For a moment, a sheet of lightning blinded me. When I could see Johnny, I demanded, "Why are you scaring me?"

His voice sounding no longer like a ghost, he answered, "I'm the one to ask the questions, Sir Percy. What are you doing in here? Why aren't you in your cabin sleeping like your little friends?"

On a closer look, Johnny was dressed like the men who chased Toshi. Trying to sound as casual as the Scarlet Pimpernel did when he got caught in a pickle, I responded airily, "Resting my eyes, dear boy."

"Don't you 'dear boy' me," Johnny said sternly. He then asked outright, "Was that you out on the Boat Deck just now?"

I paused, thought a minute, and answered, "I was. I was talking with Captain Spaulding."

"What about?" He asked curiously.

"The fog and my speech. The captain liked my speech. He really did. Aren't you surprised? I sure am surprised."

"I'm glad to hear the captain liked your speech, mate. He rightfully should have," said Johnny. There was a sting in his voice.

Taking off his cap, Johnny walked around the room, studying the paintings on the walls. He stopped at a photograph of the Aquitania. With the back of his sleeve, he rubbed a spot of dirt off the glass. Inspecting the photograph again, he turned to me and asked, "Were you talking to anyone else, Sir Percy?"

"Just to myself. I do that all the time." I crossed my fingers but my mouth was twitching.

Johnny sat next to me, looked into my eyes and began to quiz me, "Are you sure you didn't talk to somebody else?"

I looked at my shoes wondering whether I should tell Johnny about Toshi. Not waiting for me to reply, Johnny pressed me. "You wouldn't lie to me, now would you, Percy? We were just about to catch the killer when we heard your voice. Now, this is serious business, mate. We lost him again. We have to find that devil before he does more terrible things on the ship. Once more, did you talk to anyone other than the captain just now?"

I answered adamantly, "I talked to the captain and my imaginary ghost. I'm not lying. I'm telling you the truth, Johnny." My mouth twitched furiously.

"All right," he said, sounding as if he didn't believe me. Noticing the scarf in my hands, he demanded, "Where'd you get that?"

"On the deck. It belongs to a friend of mine. She's the friend I introduced you to, the one with raccoon eyes. She lost it. Actually, it belongs to Auntie Sissy."

His eyes turned watery gray, the exact color of the ships in the convoy, when he asked,

"Mate, are you being straight with me?"

I wrapped the scarf over my head and drawled like Bette Davis, "I am. I am. Please believe me, Johnny. I am, I am, I am. I am your very best friend."

"Where's the ankh?" His question nailed me to the wall. I wasn't expecting it. My shirt was open and he could see that the ankh wasn't hanging around my neck.

Feeling flames of hell licking my behind, I lied, "I left it in the cabin because I didn't want to lose it."

He warned, "Wear it at all times, mate. The ankh can't protect you if you keep it in your cabin. You promised me that you'd wear it at all times."

"I will. I will, Johnny. I will have it on from now on." The devil poked his pitchfork in my behind.

Johnny leaned back on the couch, looked me over and declared, "I think, mate, I have been dead wrong about you."

In a panic, I interrupted him, "No, you're not wrong about me. I am still your Sir Percy. Promise I am, Johnny. Truly, truly, I promise I am. Promise I am still your Sir Percy and you're my very best friend.

Aren't we best friends anymore? We have to be best friends forever, Johnny."

Johnny patted my knee. "Of course, we're friends. It's just that best friends tell each other the whole truth all the time. Best friends tell each other everything even if it hurts for them to say it. It was funny that you called your imaginary ghost a Jap. Remember how you corrected me at the boat station."

"I slipped. It's because, I am not a perfect person. The ghost is an enemy and we call the enemy Japs, don't we Johnny?" I said, stammering out an explanation.

Squeezing my knee, he said, "I just hope you're telling me the truth for your sake and for the sake of this ship and its passengers."

Changing the subject, I said, "Johnny, I'm going to scare you just like you scared me. One dark night, I'm going to pretend that I am the ghost of the Aquitania. When you're sleeping in your bed, I'm going to sneak into your cabin and scare the doodoo out of you."

Slapping me on my back, he laughed, "There's my old Sir Percy. Let me warn you, I'm not the scary type, mate. It'd take more than the likes of you to make me poop in my pants."

"You just wait, because I can be real scary."

Johnny rose from the couch, lifting me up with him. "It's time for this eight-year-old boy to be in bed. I'll walk you back to your cabin." His eyes turned the deepest blue I had ever seen. It was the same shade of blue found at the bottom of the ocean where the ankh and the steamer trunk lay.

Back in the cabin, Aunt Momi and Marigold had waited up for me. I thought I was going the catch the dickens. Instead, they pounced on me, demanding to hear all the news.

Aunt Momi asked, smoking two cigarettes at a time, "How did the captain react to your speech?"

"He liked it."

Aunt Momi looked pleased and then beckoned me to sit beside her on her bed. I rested my head on her bosom and told her about the speech, Mrs. Brown, the captain in the dining room and talking with the captain out on the deck. I left out the missing treasures, Toshi,

Mina, and Johnny's talk to me about the prisoner. Aunt Momi seemed only interested in hearing about the captain.

Nestling closer to her, I sighed, " Aunt Momi, do you ever wonder what's going to happen tomorrow?"

Cuddling me, my aunt said, "All the time. These past few days, I've had time to think. I haven't been a very good aunt to you and Marigold. I'm going to change my ways. I am never going to touch another drop of vodka. Never! This situation with that steamer trunk and all those Hawaiian treasures was just too much for me to cope with. It unnerved me completely. I am ever so relieved that you threw those blasted things overboard. I feel free again."

Marigold kept oddly silent. Her face turned to stone. Something very serious was going on in her mind.

Rita Hayworth blathered on smoking a cigarette. "My job is to see that I get you two onto the train for Baltimore. Into the arms of Nelda and Louisa. My job was not saving those scary, Hawaiian treasures. My job is to keep you both safe. Percy, when we reach San Francisco, we'll find that damned skull. After we find it, I'll take it back to Hawaii and bury it. After that, I promise you that there will be no more curses hanging over our family ever again. Lucky for us, Uncle Lono is on leave and will be meeting the ship in San Francisco."

My aunt lit her fourth cigarette and mused incoherently, "Kids, to tell you the truth, I need a man around. I need to be protected. I'm too dithery. I guess I'm the marrying kind. For better or worse, I need a man to protect me. Even if it's for the worse, it's better than not having a man around at all. That damn steamer trunk threw me for a loop and without a man to tell me what to do, I became a basket case. But, by God, the next time I'll be ready for whatever comes." She looked at the bullet hole and laughed.

My sister asked quizzically, "You really mean that, Aunt Momi? You can take anything now?"

"Of course, I meant it. I'm not a fibber."

Marigold pulled a piece of paper out from under her pillow. "I found this under the door while you were brushing your teeth. It's a note from him again."

Aunt Momi sat up and demanded, "Give it here!"

Marigold passed the note to my aunt. Grabbing the note, she read it silently. Finished reading, she squinted her eyes at me and asked, "Percy, are you sure the treasures went overboard?"

"Why do you ask, Aunt Momi?"

"Read this!" She handed me the note. I read: "This is a threat. Hand over the treasures or you're a dead woman."

Rita Hayworth disappeared and old Aunt Momi asked, "Percy, are the treasures still aboard this ship? I want the truth."

"Yes, Aunt Momi," I answered, "the treasures are still aboard. The trunk that went overboard was filled with junk. I wanted the killer to think that the treasures went into the ocean." Aunt Momi eyed the vodka bottle on the bureau.

"You have nothing to worry about, Aunt Momi. The treasures are gone. They were stolen last night. Someone else has them now, so don't worry about the treasures."

"Give me the note back. Now, let's…let's all go to sleep now. Turn off the lights. We…we won't worry one whit about this stupid note. I know…I know that I'm not going to." When Aunt Momi stuttered, I knew it was a sign that she was going to break her vow to God. That night, she didn't.

My aunt slithered under the covers and amazingly fell right into a deep sleep. Brushing my teeth in the bathroom, Marigold joined me. Shutting the door behind her, she brushed her teeth alongside of me. We talked softly so Aunt Momi couldn't hear us. Between our timed spit-outs of toothpaste, I confided to Marigold everything, especially, that Toshi could be the Angel of Death, and to keep an eye out for a Japanese man with wispy hair on his chin, emphasizing that he looks exactly like Genghis Kahn.

"I'll keep my eye out for the varmint. I'd better watch out for Aunt Momi, too. I think she's about to go bonkers again. Does anyone other than Daisy and Neal know that the treasures are still aboard this ship?"

"Buster, Edwina, and Johnny, and whoever followed me into the Writing Salon. Toshi knows and so does Mina, if Toshi didn't kill her."

I warned, "Marigold, be careful what you do because the captain told me that we are about to enter a fog bank tonight. But, it won't be long before we'll be in San Francisco. There, we'll be safe from the Angel of Death because Uncle Lono and Cousin Oliver will be there to protect us. But right now, the fog is going to make it easy for Toshi to do more awful things. Marigold, the only reason I didn't squeal on Toshi is because he's Mina's friend. Oh, I'm all mixed up."

Marigold's voice, sounding like George Washington at Valley Forge giving his troops a pep talk, said, "Let me figure out the next plan to keep the Angel of Death from killing Aunt Momi. Go to bed and, for the next two days, we'll stick close to the cabin, especially if we're hitting a fog bank." Marigold saluted me and marched out of the bathroom. That night, for the first time that I could remember, Marigold didn't cry over Daddy. That night, she was giggling with excitement.

After I finished gargling with Listerine and washing my face with Irene Dunne's favorite Ivory soap, I tiptoed out of the bathroom just as I spied a note was being slipped under the cabin door. I crouched low so Marigold, who had her eyes shut, and Aunt Momi, who was snoring louder than a sailor, wouldn't see me pick it up. Back in bed, I opened the hand printed note and read it. "I'm not fooling this time. If you don't hand over the stuff, you and your family will all end up like your friend with the red scarf. She's now in a place where no one talks. You don't want to join her there."

Under the covers, I tore up the note and set my course for tomorrow. I made a list of the people I wanted God to protect from the Angel of Death. I put Auntie Sissy at the bottom of the list. With a P.S., I added my name.

The Aquitania's foghorns began to wail mournful sounds. The other ships returned the call. The fog bank was beginning to cover the convoy. In an hour or so, the ships wouldn't be able to see each other. In the fog, as in the movies, murderers roam undetected.

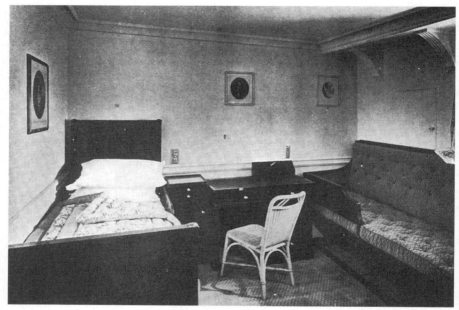
Edwina's new cabin.

CHAPTER 20

MISSING PERSONS

That morning, a sense of dread had swept across the ship. Except for the wails of the fog horns, the silence at sea was deafening.

Even though the sun had risen before six, out on deck, it felt as cold as the inside an igloo. The fog was as thick as pea soup.

I made sure that I could be seen in the fog and wore my yellow sweater and Mina's red scarf. Marigold and Aunt Momi were back in the cabin, asleep.

From Horace, the waiter in the dining room, I learned that Johnny had the morning off. He and his men had been up all night hunting for Toshi. Edwina's waiter, Albert, groused in his peculiar way that Edwina always ate her oatmeal and drank coffee at nine. It was only seven. I couldn't wait, so I ran down to her dormitory where I surprised one of the lady dragons dressing for breakfast. She screamed and quickly wrapped a kimono around her corset. As she pushed me out the door she screeched that Edwina wasn't sleeping there anymore; she had a cabin to herself on A Deck. "Cabin 444," the lady sniffed. "Miss Snooty sure pulled a fast one. One of the officers moved her into grander quarters."

I ran up to A Deck and found her cabin only a few doors away from Auntie Sissy's. On the door hung a "Do Not Disturb" sign. Not wanting to wake her, I planned to look for her after I had found Buster and Johnny.

Back in the dining room, Daisy and Neal were not at breakfast. That was disturbing.

Aunt Momi and Marigold weren't at breakfast either. The missing persons list increased to five.

Grabbing a roll, I ran up to the ship's lounge. Horace was taking a breakfast tray to the captain and "that guy who looks like Tarzan."

Sure enough, the captain and Uncle Buster were huddled in deep conversation with two Naval officers. They were sitting at the same table where I had interviewed Edwina. My stomach did flip flops seeing Uncle Buster. At last, I had someone to interrogate.

Wanting to act tough, I sauntered over to the table using Marigold's John Wayne walk and greeted them with my Jimmy Cagney voice, "Hi ya, ya dirty rats."

After I got their attention, I gave Uncle Buster a Scarlet Shadow once-over look, checking his wounds. Except for a small bandage on his forehead, he looked as fit as when he wrestled the alligators in Tarzan movies. The captain rose from his chair, shook my hand, acting as dignified as the king of England. He saluted me, "A good morning, my friend, Percy." He introduced me to the officers, thanked me for coming, sat down and continued on with his conversation.

I looked at Tarzan and blinked my eyes. I was sending him a Scarlet Pimpernel Morse code message. He wasn't receiving.

Tarzan shook my hand. "It's going to be our last night out. Captain Spaulding just informed me that the convoy is a day ahead of schedule. Tomorrow, we'll be sailing under the Golden Gate Bridge. Actually, you and I helped the convoy arrive in San Francisco a day early by making the other ships steam faster than usual trying to rescue us. Can you believe it? Billy the Kid will be back in front of the cameras shooting the bad guys."

I said out loud, to everyone's annoyance at the table, "THE HUNGRY BIRD EATS THE WORM, UNCLE BUSTER!" I pointed to the men's bathroom.

Buster got the message and winked. He turned to the captain and, under his breath, said, "That's a secret code between Percy and me. Excuse me, captain, I have to meet Percy in the men's room."

I spoke quickly, "Captain, I'm staying out of dark corners and I'm not going to fall overboard. Promise. But, it's important for me to talk to Uncle Buster, alone." Pointing to the sign that read "Men," I walked into the bathroom. It wasn't long before Buster joined me. Luckily, we had the bathroom to ourselves.

Before Buster could ask a question, I attacked him, "Uncle Buster, did you tell anyone that there was only fake stuff in the suitcase and the real treasures are still onboard the ship?"

Taken aback at my outburst, he answered, "No! Why? When I make a promise, I keep it. Since we were rescued, I have spent all my time in my cabin recuperating. I haven't talked to anyone but the captain. I didn't say anything to him about the treasures. Why the question, Percy?"

I gave him the same story I told Aunt Momi. "Someone stole the treasures and the Angel of Death says he will kill us if we don't give them to him. We don't have the treasures. He wrote two scary notes."

My next question preyed on my mind since Marigold had mentioned it. Afraid of hearing his answer, I pointed to his crotch. "Is your thing broken?"

Uncle Buster began to laugh, unable to control himself. When he could speak, Uncle Buster sputtered, "What made you ask me that?"

"Marigold said you broke your arm, your ribs, your face, and your thing."

Brushing his pants, he smiled, "Well, she is wrong. I sprained my arm, broke a few ribs, but my thing as you call it is quite intact, thank you."

Not believing him, I asked again, "You're sure your thing isn't broken? I didn't break it when I pulled you up on Aunt Rose's casket?"

"No, Percy. NO!" he started to laugh again. "But, thanks for your concern."

I squeaked, "You're sure?"

"I am sure! Now, let's drop the subject."

Frustrated at my stupidity, I said, "Marigold is always lying to me. She says my thing looks like a pink ballerina."

What Buster Crabbe did next took away the fears of an eight year old boy who was sensitive to what made him different from his sister and aunt.

"Let me look into your eyes," he said.

Tarzan inspected my eyes as if he was looking at a rare flower and, then, speaking as Dr. Kildare did in the movies, pronounced, "Your thing looks perfect to me. You don't have a pink ballerina. You have a real man's thing if I ever saw one."

"No kidding. Honest injun? Just by looking into my eyes, you can tell that?" I said incredulously.

He smiled at me, I thought, like a proud daddy. Looking into my eyes once more, he said,

"I'm telling the truth, Percy. Men with blue eyes have perfect things. Let's change the subject."

Flabbergasted, I cried, "Wow! That's great. Just great. Now, I can really be the Scarlet Pimpernel, Uncle Buster. Deep down, I always knew the Scarlet Pimpernel didn't have a pink ballerina."

Washing my hands at the basin, looking at my blue eyes in the mirror, I thought out loud. "Uncle Buster, I don't have any men to talk to. I only have women around me. They're nice, and I love them, but they don't understand men things, do they? I need to talk about men things really badly. How can I become a big strong man like you, Uncle Buster?"

Wiping his hands on a towel, he looked into the mirror. He was thinking about my question. Finally, he answered, "Eat spinach. Eat lots of spinach. That's what I did."

"Eating spinach grows hair on chests. You don't have hair on your chest."

Buster corrected me, "Naw, that's made-up stuff. Popeye ate spinach so he can be strong."

Wiping my hands on a towel, I yipped, "That's what I'm going to do from now on. I'm going to eat tons of spinach for breakfast, lunch and dinner."

Shaking his head, chuckling to himself, tucking his shirt into his pants, Buster advised, "I'd keep what I said about blue eyes a secret just between the two of us. Remember, you and I have secrets. Make blue eyes another secret between the Scarlet Pimpernel and Tarzan. Okay?"

"Okay, Tarzan!"

"So now, Mr. Scarlet Pimpernel, what are you up to today?" asked Uncle Buster as I finished washing my hands.

Slicking down my hair with water, copying Uncle Buster, I revealed my plan. "I'm going to find out who spilled the beans about the fake contents in the suitcase. When I find that out, I'll have a good idea who the Angel of Death is."

Buster rested his hand on my shoulder and advised, "Be careful, Percy. I'd stay clear of everyone today because there are dark doings on this ship right now and a bad person is doing them. We were just talking about them at breakfast."

Ready to eat a ton of spinach, I responded to my friend, "I'll see to it, Tarzan, I mean, Uncle Buster. If I'm not at dinner tonight, put me on the missing person list and tell everyone to look for me because, if they don't, the Angel of Death will have got me. He wrote us that he hides people where no one talks."

"Are you playing with me, Percy?" Buster asked, not sure if I was joking with him.

"Kinda, Uncle Buster," I laughed because I didn't want Uncle Buster to worry about me any more.

"Be careful and don't be alone. Stay out of dark corners," he warned.

Sounding now as the Scarlet Shadow, I said, "Funny, that's what the captain said to me last night. Don't worry about me, Uncle Buster, and thanks a million for talking to me man to man. My daddy never ever talked to me like you just did. Tonight at dinner, I want to eat a tuna casserole with Best Foods mayonnaise all over it and a big helping of spinach on the side."

"Best Foods Mayonnaise is where we part company, Percy."

"Uncle Buster, that's all right; nobody is perfect."

We shook hands and left the bathroom. No longer worrying that I had a pink ballerina, I ran back down to Edwina's cabin. The "Do Not Disturb" sign was off the door. I knocked five times. She didn't answer. I dashed for the dining room, hoping I'd find her eating breakfast. Albert said she had come and gone. Daisy and Neal, Aunt Momi and Marigold were not at breakfast, either. They were all on the missing person list. I made a beeline for Johnny's cabin. He was the one person on the ship who could really help me.

Johnny's cabin door was wide open. Peeking inside, the cabin was empty.

Stepping inside, afraid I would trip over a dead body, I was happy to discover Johnny wasn't lying on the floor. I decided to stick around and wait for Johnny. Plus, it gave me the opportunity to look around the cabin for an ankh. I desperately wanted to have one so Johnny wouldn't discover that I had lied to him.

Piles of books on ancient Egypt were strewn haphazardly on the floor. Everything in the cabin was Egyptian. The pictures on the walls were of temples, mummies, King Tutankhamen and Queen Nefertiti. Books next to his bed were on Egyptian curses and charms. A large photograph of the Sphinx hung above his bed.

On top of his bureau, I spied something sparkling. It looked familiar. I hoped it was an ankh. Walking closer to the object, I recognized it immediately.

Aunt Rose's amethyst brooch.

CHAPTER 21

THE ANGEL OF DEATH

In my hand, I held the amethyst brooch the killer had ripped from Aunt Rose's dress. Goose bumps rose like mountains all over my body. I opened the closet door. Hanging in the closet, next to his uniforms, was the Angel of Death's black overcoat. Above his uniforms, a black wool cap, a wig and a beard lay neatly on a shelf.

"What are you doing in my closet, Percy?"

I turned around and shoved Aunt Rose's brooch into my pocket. My mouth twitched as I answered, "I was worried about you. You weren't at breakfast."

Standing in the doorway, Johnny said menacingly, "You were worried about me? I'm flattered, mate. But, as you can see, here I am, fit as a fiddle."

Looking for a way to escape, I moved away from the closet and stood in front of the bureau, hoping he hadn't noticed the brooch was missing.

Approaching Johnny, trying to throw him off guard, I tittered, "I was going to hide in the closet and pretend that I was the ghoooost of the Aquitania. I wanted you to poop in your pants."

Johnny pressed his hairy red hands against the door, blocking my exit. "Did you now, mate? You're sweating like a pig, Percy. Methinks it is you who is pooping in his pants."

Inching towards the door, I laughed, "Ha! Ha! Nah, I'm embarrassed because you caught me red-handed. For your information, the Scarlet Shadow never poops in his pants."

Using a British accent, I chattered nervously, "Jolly good. Well, I've got to 'toodle.' I'm off to meet Aunt Momi and Marigold. I was supposed to have met them ages ago — just ages ago. We're having morning tea on deck. They'll be wondering where I am if I don't show up.

By now, they'll have had a search party looking for me. Well, jolly good to see you, Johnny. Let me by, please."

Johnny reminded me of a cobra. "Don't rush away on my account. Stay awhile. We have a few things to discuss, methinks." He grabbed my arm and closed the door.

My arm in a vise, he said, "No one ever knows who'll pop in to visit, does one, Percy? Or what they'll find while they're snooping around, when they shouldn't be."

Prying his fingers off my arm, I pleaded, "You're hurting me, Johnny. Let me go. I didn't find anything, honest. Honest. All I saw was your Egyptian things. That's all I saw."

"Do you like me Egyptians things, mate?" He pushed me to his bed and forced me to sit on it. Johnny took the ankh from around his neck off and placed it on the bureau. "Fascinating stuff, ain't it, mate?"

He walked to the closet, opened the door, took the black overcoat off a hanger, and put it on. He attached the black beard to his ears, put the wig and cap on, and turned around and grinned. "Look familiar, Percy?" he asked.

I wasn't listening, I was thinking of ways to escape. I didn't hear the question.

"Pay attention when I'm speaking to you," he screamed. Reading my mind, he lashed out, "Don't think of attempting to run for the door. You're too fat and I'm too fast. Now, me lad, I'll ask again, do I look familiar?"

Feeling the amethyst brooch in my pocket, I asked, "Are you the Angel of Death?"

Looking in the mirror on the wall, Johnny moved an eyebrow up and down, and guffawed, "I'm him, Percy. I'm the Angel of Death. I'm the ghost of the Aquitania who kills fat nosy little brats. Ha. Ha. Ha."

Taking the black overcoat off, he hung it back in the closet. With his back to me, he said in a scary singsong voice, "You don't want to leave me. You don't want to leave me all alone. When you don't show up on deck, everyone will think you've fallen overboard again. After all, everybody on the ship hates you. They think you're the dumb little fat boy who looks like Hermann Goering and who is always doing stupid things. In fact, they'll be glad to see you disappear." He turned around and stared at me looking like the devil.

I stood up, holding onto the red scarf, and cried, "I thought you liked me?"

Pushing me back down on the bed, he cooed "Oh, I do, Percy. I do, I do. But you have disappointed me. Real friends never disappoint each other. But you disappointed me because you didn't tell me the truth."

"I didn't lie to you," I protested.

Ripping off the beard, the wig and the hat, throwing them on the closet floor, he whirled around, and snapped, "Yes, you did. You didn't tell me that you hid the treasures in the couch. You lied to me, Percy, from the very beginning. You even lied to me about that scarf." He ripped Mina's scarf out of my hands and threw it on the closet floor.

"Give that scarf back. It belongs to my friend."

Johnny looked at me with contempt on his face.

Breaking the silence, I asked, "How did you know about the treasures?"

"That's a simple answer. Remember, it was I who handed you the letter about the treasures to give to your Aunt Momi. I read the letter."

"You wrote all those notes? It was you who shot into our cabin the first night out."

"You should have figured that out long before this."

I cursed Johnny, "You will go to hell. It was *you* who lied to me. It was *you* who pretended to be my friend just to get at the treasures and to learn about my rich friends."

He took off his dungarees and put on his uniform. "I *was* your friend, Percy. We could have been friends forever. This is my last trip, mate. When we arrive in San Francisco, I plan to disappear. The treasures were a bonus towards my retirement, but you kept getting in the way. I never wanted to harm you. Percy, I have a strong feeling that you know where the treasures are."

"I don't know anything. The Angel of Death took them," I screamed.

Buttoning up his naval jacket, looking movie star handsome, Johnny smirked, "I'm the Angel of Death, remember, and I don't have them. You're lying to me. Percy, you have the treasures, my lad. I know you have them."

"I don't have them, and neither does Neal or Daisy and don't you hurt them!"

"Hurt them? Hmm."

"How did you find out that they were hidden behind the couch?" I demanded.

Looking at himself in the mirror, brushing his hair, he smirked, "From your friend with the red scarf. Percy, there is a point when a person just can't hold anything back. She kept screaming, longer than I thought she would, that she didn't know where they were hidden."

"Mina?"

"Ah, that's her name. I nabbed her right after she spoke to you in the infirmary. Your Jap friend put me off the chase by wearing her scarf. He hid her in a lifeboat. She hurt herself jumping into the lifeboat but the giveaway wasn't her moans but a pack of Lucky Strike cigarettes lying next to the lifeboat. I pulled back the cover on the lifeboat and found her hiding under a piece of canvas. I muzzled her mouth, wrapped her up in a piece of canvas, and took her to a place where no one could hear her scream. It was like I was carrying a sack of straw."

Breathlessly, I interrupted, "Did you kill Mina?"

Johnny fastened his belt and ignored my question. "At first, she wouldn't tell me anything. But before long she told me everything I wanted to know. Small people don't stand pain very well. That little weasel found us and pounded on the door screaming. I ran after him. I forgot to shut the damned door."

"What happened to Mina?" I demanded.

Johnny was shining his shoes. "Wait and see. Be patient, mate. You and me are about to take a little walk."

I threw a pillow at him and yelled, "I won't walk with you. Aunt Momi and Marigold are waiting for me on deck and by this time they'll have the captain send a posse out looking for me."

Johnny grabbed my arm in the same painful grip and threatened, "You *will* walk with me."

Touching the amethyst brooch in my pocket, I asked, "Johnny, before you kill me, tell me about Aunt Rose."

He released my arm. Blood rushed back into my hand, making it tingle. He sauntered over to the bureau, put on the ankh and straightened it on his chest. After he tucked the ankh inside his shirt, he told me what I wanted to know. "You were responsible for that one. It was you who told me about the rich blonde lady who owned the fur coat you ruined. While everyone was playing bingo, I was down in her cabin helping myself to a few of her trinkets when the old lady walked in. I couldn't let her give me away so early in the game, so when she started to scream, I had to do something, didn't I, Percy? Then some damn fool, hearing her scream, banged on the door. I told the banger to scram. I beat it out of there as soon as I heard the banger go away."

"You're a killer," I shouted, hoping someone had heard me.

Johnny slapped my face and told me to be quiet or he'd kill me on the spot like he did Aunt Rose. Grabbing my hand, he pulled me up off the bed. "Keep your voice down. I'm not a killer, Percy, but in my business, some people, unfortunately, just get in the way. Like you are doing right now. Getting in my way."

I rubbed my face, "What are you then, if you're not a lowdown killer? You just said you wanted to kill me and you killed Aunt Rose and I bet you killed Mina."

As Johnny pulled me towards the door, he spoke with a deadly calm. "Percy, I am so disappointed with you. I thought you would understand. I thought you were like me. A bloke, in spite of the odds, wants to make his way up in this crazy world. I vowed when I was just about your age that if anyone gets in me way, well, that's just too bad for them. Life is short and I am going to get what belongs to me and, when I get it, only then will I make peace in this world."

"Let me go. If you let me go, I promise that I won't tell anyone that you're the Angel of Death."

Gripping my arm tighter, he unlocked the door, turned to me and smiled his million- dollar smile, "Of course, you won't tell anyone, Percy. Now, Sir Percy, we're going to take a short walk, and on this walk, you're not going to scream, cry for help or anything. Are you?"

Pulling away from him, I snarled, thinking I had the upper hand, "What makes you think that I won't?"

Looking into my eyes, he said, "Because you won't mate."

"Why?" I asked, disturbed hearing the assurance in his voice.

"Because I think that you want all your friends to live. It would be a shame to have that pretty little Daisy and her brother, the Japanese lady, your Aunt Momi, and your sister die because you didn't follow instructions."

Stunned, understanding now why I hadn't seen any of my friends at breakfast, I sputtered, "You've captured them. You're holding them in a place where no one talks."

He nodded and opened the door, clenching my arm. "Now, will you come with me peacefully?"

I bargained once more with Johnny as he pushed me down the corridor. "Okay, I'll go with you, but you've got to promise me that you'll free them if I come peacefully with you."

In the corridor, he turned back into the old Johnny, the proper officer in the proper British Navy, the person whom everybody loved, and the officer whom the passengers trusted more than any other officer on the ship. "I promise, Sir Percy. Now put a smile on your face and walk in front of me. Act as if we are going to see the captain. I'll be holding your arm just in case you forget yourself. If you do forget yourself, I'll break your arm. If you scream, I'll crack your head against the wall and splatter your brains into scrambled eggs. Did you hear that, mate?"

I mumbled, "I heard that."

He pushed me in front of him and led me down the stairs to the engine room. We passed the storage areas I had seen before and stopped before the two familiar large metal doors. He took a key out of his pocket, unlocked the padlock, dropped the chain to the floor and, with his free hand, opened the doors and shoved me inside. Quick as anything, he closed the doors and locked them from the inside and turned on the lights.

I was standing on the edge of the ship's swimming pool. Thirty-four empty caskets filled it.

CHAPTER 22

DREAMS DO COME TRUE

"Where's Mina?" I said staring at the coffins. Scary thoughts about my friends flooded my mind.

Releasing my arm, Johnny snarled, "Never mind Mina. You and me have a little business to perform before I tell you about *Mina*."

I stomped defiantly over a pile of scattered lumber, growling as nastily as I could. "I'm not going to tell you anything until you tell me what you've done to Daisy, Neal, Mina, Aunt Momi, and Marigold."

He sneered, "Listen to me carefully, Percy. You know where the treasures are, and don't tell me that you don't. I'm in no mood to play games with you. If you tell me *now* where you hid them, I'll let you and your friends go."

I looked back at him with a blank expression on my face.

His face had turned the color of his hair and his eyes had become orange. He screamed, "DO YOU UNDERSTAND ME?"

Lying next to a box of nails and a hammer, was a stick two feet long with a rusty nail pounded through one end of it. Picking my way over pieces of lumber, I edged towards the stick.

I talked as I walked, and made a bargain with Johnny. "Think of me as a frog-prince in a fairy story. If you grant me three things, I'll tell you everything I know. I might even tell you the name of the witch who's guarding the treasures." I was several yards ahead of him when I stood over the stick.

He tripped over a piece of lumber. "God damn it, Percy, come back here. This isn't a fairy tale. I'm not playing Percy games. Come back here."

Rushing to keep up with me, he tripped again and dropped the keys. When he bent down to pick them up, he took his eyes off me. I grabbed the stick and hid it behind my back.

He was having trouble retrieving the keys because they were lodged between two pieces of lumber. I threw a handful of nails to the opposite end of the pool. He instinctively looked to where the nails had landed. Having him off guard, I galloped over the lumber with his back to me, and stabbed him with my weapon. I stabbed him in the back of his shoulder and slashed another hit on his buttocks, ripping his pants. My stabs threw him off balance and he fell headlong onto the lumber. I grabbed the keys and, with the stick in my hand, I ran for the opposite end of the pool.

Johnny screamed as he lay face down on the woodpile. Blood spots stained his white uniform as he screamed that I was a dead person.

Keys in one hand, the stick in the other, I yelled across to him, "Don't come near me if you don't want a rusty nail in your face. The Scarlet Shadow now has the upper hand."

Holding his shoulder, he cursed, "You'll never get out of here alive, you little shit. The doors are on my side, don't forget that, mate. How are you going to get past me? If you try, I'm going to catch you and kill you with my bare hands." Johnny lifted himself slowly off the lumber pile, ripping his tunic as he rose. Rubbing the wound on his shoulder, he yelled, "You only grazed my ass, you weak little nothing."

I yelled, "I wanted to carve an SS on your fanny. Make you remember that you had been beaten by the great Scarlet Shadow."

He stood staring at me with hate in his gray eyes.

As I watched him rub the wound with his tunic, I yelled, "You'll never get the treasures, you big boohooing baby. You and I will be stayin' in here till one of us turns into a mummy." I jingled the keys, and taunted him further, "And, I have these."

"Okay. Okay, what are the three things I have to do?"

Waving the stick around like I was going into battle, I shouted, "Where is Mina?"

He smiled, and said in a sly matter-of-fact way, "She's dead. I brought her in here just like I brought you. After she told me what I wanted to know and as I was going to finish her off, the Jap bastard found us and starting pounding on the door. Of course, that wouldn't do. I opened the door to kill that little bastard but he ran for the engine room. I ran after him..."

I blasted, "He's Japanese."

Johnny laughed, "I heard you on the upper deck calling the little bugger a Jap."

"I'm ashamed of myself. I was wrongheaded. You're the evil one. You're the devil — not Toshi. What happened to Mina?"

He sat on the edge of the pool and rested his feet on the top of a coffin. "You're boring me, Percy. Don't interrupt me again if you want to hear the rest of the story."

Johnny acted calm and cool, too settled.

Chewing on his nails, he continued. "When I ran after that little Jap runt bastard, I, as is my habit, left the door wide open and that little weasel, Mina, escaped. The Jap runt ran too fast for me, so I turned back and ran after the girl. She moved like a cat, up and down ladders, through corridors, sidestepping into rooms, trying to shake me. It was three in the morning with no one around, my mates in bed, so it made for a merry chase. I finally corralled that little bitch at the bow of the ship. She saw me coming for her; she knew the jig was up!"

He paused and beamed, "She jumped overboard." He pressed his fingers on his shoulder and continued, "The little Jap runt bastard was standing on the deck above me with her red scarf around his neck. After he saw her jump, he screamed like a goddamned banshee. Then, right before my eyes, he disappeared. He's been stalking me ever since. I'm going to kill that little bastard, believe me, Percy. I'm going to get him like I've gotten everyone else who has stood in my way, like I'm going to get you. When I find that little Jap bastard, I'm going to peel his yellow skin off in little bloody strips. He has made me very angry, just like you're making me angry right now. When I catch you, Percy, you're going to regret it."

Frightened, I called to him, "You don't scare me, you little baby."

He snorted, "You little prick. What's your number two? My butt hurts like hell. I'm probably dying of blood poisoning because of you. What's your number two? Answer me, you little bloody bastard." He was slurring his words.

Hoping he was dying of blood poisoning, I spoke slowly, "What's the big hurry, you big crybaby?"

"Quit fooling around."

"Why?" I said, hoping a glob of rust was streaking for his heart.

"Why what?" His voice began to sound like he was pooping big rocks in his pants.

"Why did you do it?" I asked.

He hitched himself off the deck of the pool, and stood up and stretched his arms to the ceiling. In a thunderous voice that echoed off the walls, "I did it because I am Tutankhamen."

"You are who?" I watched him strut around the pool acting like a pharaoh. I started to giggle.

"I am Tutankhamen, the boy pharaoh. I was murdered by Ay, my best friend. I want my treasures, Ay. I am Tutankhamen, and I have mystical powers. You are not safe from my great powers."

He was making this all up trying to scare me and make me scream like a girl. What he didn't know was that I had grown up while on top of Aunt Rose's coffin. I wasn't scared of fake pharaohs. I had become the Scarlet Shadow.

As Johnny walked up and down the deck like a frozen mummy, I taunted him, "I never heard of a red-headed pharaoh that came from Australia. You're not scaring me, bubble-head. Do you know who I really think you are?"

He stopped walking and asked, "Who?"

"Hitler. You're just like Hitler and Hitler is a devil. Hitler goes around killing people and stealing treasures from other countries. You're not King Tut, bubble-head. You're just an oogie man who thinks it's okay to do anything, like Hitler. Maybe I'm only eight years old but I know an evil man when I see one and what's more, you're nuts!" I slapped my head realizing that I was the numb-nut believing Johnny's act all this time. Mimicking his pharaoh voice, I called, "King Tut, you're crazy as a loon. You sure fooled me." I moaned, "And I thought you were my best friend."

He looked at me and began pacing the deck like the Angel of Death. The look in his eyes staring over at me told me that he wanted to leap over the pool and devour me.

I yelled, "Johnny, I hope bad things happen to you forever and ever."

Dropping his King Tut act, he called from the other side of the pool, "Crybaby, don't you worry your little head about me. I am protected. I have my ankh. Where's your ankh? No, no. Don't worry about me. I'd worry about little, fat Percy right now. That's who I'd worry about because you are not getting out of here alive."

He stopped abruptly and smiled. His eyes changed to purple. "What is the third thing you want from me?"

I yelled, "Where are my friends? Where is Aunt Momi and Marigold?"

He walked around the pool, oozing evil as he spoke. "I put your aunt in that coffin." He pointed to one of the wooden boxes in the pool.

"I don't believe you. She's not in there." I looked at the coffin to see if it was moving.

Johnny chortled with childish glee, "Don't believe me. But I'm telling you the truth. She's tucked in that coffin neat as a mummy. Her mouth is gagged and I've tied her so tight she can't move. She's alive, but I can't say for how long. It's hard to breathe in there. You can save her if you want to. Now, it's my turn to play fairy tales. By the way, Percy, I sure wouldn't want my aunt's death on my conscience."

"Open up the coffin and show me that she's really in there,"

"Now, why would I want to do that?" he said that doing a little jig. He was so pleased that he had turned the tables on me.

"So that I can believe you," I answered, putting my hands on my hips to show him that I meant business.

Waving his hands in the air as if conjuring a spell, he said, "I have to trust you first before I do that. I did the three things for you and now it's your turn to do three things for me." He walked slowly towards me.

"Freeze! Stay where you are. What are the three things I have to do?"

Back at the entrance doors, he ordered, "Give me the keys." He fiddled with the doorknobs, waiting for my answer.

I thought for a minute and replied, "Come get them." I threw the keys on top of one of the coffins inside the pool.

He growled, "That's not what I meant. I want you to walk over here and hand them to me like a gentleman."

"You didn't say that. I did what you wanted. There are your keys. Go get them. What's the second thing I have to do?" I vowed that no matter what, I wasn't going to let him come near me.

"To set your Aunt Momi free, you have to take her place in the coffin. You have to sacrifice yourself for her life. You know about sacrifices." When he said that, I looked at his face and saw oogie pus coming out his mouth.

I thought to myself, why would I do a dumb thing like that without seeing if Aunt Momi was actually in the coffin? I gave Johnny a look, making him believe that I had bought what he had said. "What's the third thing I have to do?"

Johnny pulled on his chin, and presented the third and the most important condition that he wanted from me. "Tell me where the treasures are hidden."

I yawned. "I have another condition, big baby. I'm willing to do everything you asked if you swear by all that is holy that you are telling me the truth. If you are lying, I swear to you that you will burn in hell for eternity."

Johnny screamed, "I am telling you the truth."

Exhaling slowly, I said, "Okay. I'll get the keys off that coffin. I'll hand them to you like a gentleman. I'll sacrifice myself for Aunt Momi. Only if I get to see her first. Then, you have to set her free before I get in that coffin. Only then will I tell you who I think *might* have the treasures."

Leaning against the doors, rubbing his shoulder, Johnny agreed to my conditions. "Okay, Sir Percy. Get the keys, and throw that goddamned stick away."

Waving the stick at him, I shook my head.

Johnny snapped, "Okay, keep that goddamned stick. Just get over here with those damn keys and help me lift the coffin out of the pool. Your aunt's probably suffocated to death because you've been fooling around, talking too damn much and wasting my time. I need help getting that damned thing out since you've put my arm out of commission with that goddamn stick of yours. It's your fault that you have to come over here to help me. This bloody shoulder hurts like hell. I hope that makes you very happy."

It did. I hoped his shoulder hurt like a million rats were chewing on it. I was tempted to call him a big baby again, but I didn't. I decided not to make him any angrier than he was already. I wanted him to keep weak, thinking he was dealing with a stupid nincompoop. The closer I got to Johnny without him thinking I was up to anything, the easier it was going to be for me to stab him in the heart, slash his face and poke his eyes out with the stick. That was my plan.

I retrieved the keys from the coffin easily. I cautiously walked around the deck of the pool with the stick in one hand and the keys in the other. Nearing Johnny, I stopped. Johnny may be wounded, but he was still bigger and stronger than I was. His eyes had turned to dark blue.

We looked at each other for a few seconds, acting like cowboys at the OK Corral. Johnny broke the standoff, and demanded, "Get over here and give me the keys!" I tossed the keys to him. I wasn't that dumb.

Putting the keys in his pocket, he dictated, "If you want to free your aunt, help me lift the coffin out of the pool." The coffin rested directly below us. Johnny jumped into the pool. His jump proved that he was still tough as nails. He maneuvered the coffin towards me as he talked. "This is a heavy son-of-a-bitch. I'm going to lift it up on my end and push it on the deck towards you. You help me slide it until it rests fully on the deck."

Johnny tipped the coffin on the deck and shoved it to me as if it was as light as a feather. When the coffin reached me, I helped him slide it further away from the edge of the pool. Johnny jumped back on the deck and told me he heard my aunt was calling for help. In my eagerness, I leaned on the coffin, telling Aunt Momi to hold on because I was about to save her.

With a mighty push, Johnny shoved the coffin into my body sprawling me backwards on the deck. With a giant leap, Johnny stood over me and grabbed the stick out of my hand.

"You stupid fat boy, I told you she was gagged. You are an ignorant bastard. Get up and look at your aunt."

He lifted the lid off. The coffin was empty. Johnny pushed me from behind making me tumble into the coffin. I conked my head, making my face bleed. Leering down at me, Johnny poked my stomach with the stick. "What goes around comes around, Percy. You are really one stupid son-of-a-bitch."

Feeling blood trickle down my nose, I whimpered, "Where's Aunt Momi?"

He laughed, "Damn if I know."

Wiping blood out of my eyes, I cried, "You're going to burn in hell forever. You're no pharaoh. You're a nothing. You're just crazy mad for treasures. You're not going to get the jade necklace, the holy lady, or the diamonds from me."

Johnny scratched the nail on my arm and said, "That's what you think. I'm about to turn you into a human pincushion. I'm going to punch rusty nail holes all over your body like you did me. In China it is the worst kind of torture. They call it 'death by a thousand cuts.' Now, Percy," he said sweetly, "I don't want to do this to you, so please tell me where the treasures are hidden or who has them."

I screamed at him, "Do it. Do it. Poke me all over. I'll never tell you anything except a wicked witch protects them and you'll never get them from her because she has powerful magic."

"Brave talk. Very brave talk, mate. Don't play with me, Percy. There's no wicked witch. It won't be long before you'll be screaming wanting to tell me everything I want to know." In a whimpering baby voice, he said, "Please, Johnny, stop… please stop, Johnny." He laughed, "You will scream for mercy. And you will. Trust me. Ask your friend Mina when you see her. Ask her how long it took for me to get the truth out of her. Not long, believe me, just a few cuts in all the right places. By the time I'm done with you, you'll be spilling your guts out. Knowing your big, fat mouth, you'll tell me more than I'll ever want to hear. God, I can hear you pleading now, 'Oh, Johnny, my hero, please, stop.'"

I wasn't listening to him. I was thinking of ways to get out of the coffin.

"Before I start with a few pokes on your legs, is there anything you want to get off your chest, like telling me where the treasures are?"

"I told you the truth. A witch has them and she is more powerful than you are and you'll never get them from her."

Johnny slapped my face. "Tell me who the witch is. Where are the treasures?"

I heard whistles blowing. I listened again. The whistles were real. Signals were coming over a loudspeaker warning that a submarine was lurking in the waters. Because of the hour, the alarm had to be the real McCoy.

Exasperated, Johnny said, "Jesus mate, I can't believe what a lucky son-of-a-bitch you are. I gotta get to me boat station, but I'll be back to finish me work, never you fear. If I'm not back, you'll rot in there until someone finds your putrid dead carcass — maybe in a couple of months, if you're lucky. If a submarine torpedoes us, you're below the waterline and you'll be blasted up to heaven sooner than you think. Pray to God for that death, because that death will be quick. That's not what I have in store for you. My way, death will be slow and painful. Don't have much to look forward to, do you, Percy?"

As he slid the wood cover over the coffin, shutting out the light, he yelled, "I'm tucking you in until I come back." Suddenly, he slid the lid partway open again.

I pleaded, "Don't do this to me. Don't bury me alive. Torture me, anything, but don't leave me in this coffin to die."

"Life is strange, isn't it? Here's a little something to keep you amused until I return. Never say that I wasn't a good friend." He handed me the bottle of Best Foods mayonnaise that I had given him to seal our friendship. He twisted the bottle into my stomach, hurting me and said, "Now Ay is buried like a proper Egyptian with his favorite treasure." I reached for his throat and ripped the ankh off his neck. The ankh fell to the bottom of the coffin, resting under my back.

Johnny screamed, "Damn it, Percy. Give it back."

"I can't. Get me out of here and you can have your ankh back."

He slapped my face. "I'll get the ankh when I return. By the way, when I see your Aunt Momi, I'll suggest that you fell overboard. Later, I'll find out if she's the witch that you've been talking about. I'll bring her down here and do me little business."

He picked up the hammer and, in seconds, pounded nails into the coffin.

I called to Johnny, "You're cursed now because I have your ankh. Better let me out."

As he drove in the last nail, I heard his voice through the darkness, "Johnny doesn't believe in curses."

I shouted back, "I'm not Percy. I'm the Scarlet Shadow. I am the Scarlet Pimpernel!"

There was no reply.

The metal doors slammed shut.

Johnny was gone for only seconds and I already felt that I had been in the coffin for an eternity. The walls of my throat were closing in. I was suffocating.

Mother once warned me, "Be careful what you fear for what you fear will come true."

CHAPTER 23

IN THE BELLY OF A WHALE

I wasn't thinking about the evilness of Johnny lying in the coffin. My sole resolve was to get out and save my life. In retrospect, I don't believe Johnny was a person who had a bad childhood or who turned evil because he didn't have a pet dog when he was a child; Johnny was one of those people who roamed the earth who was inherently evil for no reason that can be discerned. What made Johnny's evilness so insidious was that he was so likeable. Ten percent of the people in the world are truly evil, ten percent are truly good and the rest of us fall in between.

Time had stopped. I was having strange daydreams. In my weirdest dream, a wicked wizard stuffed me into a bottle of pickles. The odor of mold in the coffin was how pickle water smelled in my dream. I pushed my legs against the wood, hoping to break the coffin apart. It wouldn't budge. I twisted my body from side to side, trying to wiggle out. Nothing worked.

Thinking that the sides of the coffin were closing in on me, I'd scream. I finally reasoned that there wasn't any use screaming because I was nailed in a coffin, locked in the swimming pool above a noisy engine room and nobody would hear me scream. But I liked screaming. I felt less helpless, even though it used up the air in the coffin. What bothered me the most: there was only inches between my nose and the lid of the coffin to breathe.

I began dreaming my old dream about being buried alive, and that I would soon wake up in my cot. I heard my mother's voice. "If you don't rein in those wild horses, you'll go crazy like your Cousin Bessie did when she lost all her money in the stock market. Remember, she ran naked all over Honolulu trying to kill her stockbroker."

My mind kept reeling on, "How can I think of anything positive when I'm buried alive in a coffin? Especially, when I'm suffocating in pickle water and I don't have a bell to ring."

Trying to keep negative thoughts out of my head, I'd put a glob of mayonnaise in my mouth. The taste of mayonnaise kept me from thinking about dying. I closed my eyes.

The air in the coffin was heating up. I ate another glop of mayonnaise and thought about Edwina. My toes fell asleep. Wiggling my toes to wake them up kept reminding me that I was in the coffin. I thought of my mother lying in her coffin. I swallowed another glop of mayonnaise. When it slid down my throat, I wanted to throw up. Feeling sick to my stomach, I rolled the mayonnaise bottle down to my feet, spilling goop on my pants and shoes.

I pounded my fists against the top of the coffin. After three tries, I looked up and saw light coming from a little space between the boards.

My stomach gurgled. Mayonnaise was backing up into my throat.

I rolled the bottle of Best Foods mayonnaise back and forth at my feet, trying to keep control of my bodily functions. Pushing the mayonnaise bottle aside, I kicked the lid of the coffin with my right foot and at the same time, pounded the lid with my hands. I had to go. I wasn't going to go in the coffin. With the force that came from my new urgency, I loosened the lid further. Fresh air cooled my face. I kicked harder.

I felt for Johnny's ankh. The ankh was lodged in the crook of my back. I reached for it and put the ankh on my chest next to Aunt Rose's brooch.

I made a bargain with God. "God, if you get me out of this jam, I'll never be stupid again. I'll pray every day and never ask where you came from, but I'd still like to know the name of your mother and father. I want to tell them what a nice person you are. Somebody must have made you, God, just like you made me. I'll even go to Sunday school. That is, on every other Sunday. I'll be nice to Marigold forever, and I'll give up mayonnaise. Anyway, the thought of mayonnaise right now makes me want to puke."

Then, I remembered Hatsuko's egg salad sandwiches.

"God, I've decided to keep mayonnaise as my one weakness. You wouldn't want me to be perfect, now would you? I'd eat one right now, God, even though I feel sick." I saw God eating an egg salad sandwich on a cloud. God's eyes and my mother's eyes looked exactly the same.

It began to sink in what was going to happen to me. I was going to die in the coffin slowly gasping for air. Daydreaming in the coffin became a very negative occupation. I daydreamed of tidal waves covering islands, furry monsters with fangs eating me for supper, sharks feasting on my body, and being buried alive.

I moved my hands over my belly, rubbing the amethyst brooch and the ankh, and listened to the mayonnaise gurgling in my stomach. I fell asleep. In dreamland, Marigold was pushing Johnny overboard. As he fell in the ocean, someone yelled, "Percy." God was calling me home.

"Percy, where in the hell are you?" I opened my eyes and realized that the voice didn't belong to God. God had taken hell out of His dictionary.

"Percy, where in the hell are you?" The voice called again.

The voice was real. In no mood to be poked by crazy Johnny, I played possum.

"Percy, answer me!"

Knowing Johnny would find me sooner, I shouted, "Come get me, stupid. I'll tell you where the treasures are."

First Class swimming pool.

CHAPTER 24

BACK AMONG THE LIVING

"Percy?" the voice called again.

Coming out of my crazy dreams, I answered, "I'm in here, stupid!"

"In where?" the voice asked.

Another voice shouted, "He's over there!" The voice belonged to Aunt Momi. Sure enough, my aunt's high heels were clicking on the deck followed by other footsteps.

The deep voice ordered, "Grab that hammer, James."

In a blink, someone pried the coffin open. A million flashbulbs popped in my face as a blue octopus with wiggling tentacles grabbed for me. With a sudden jerk, arms lifted me up. I creaked as I tried to stand up. A stench followed me. It was the smell of the stinky haze that hovers over a garbage dump. For luck, I held the brooch and ankh in my hand.

I had a hard time standing because the mayonnaise on my shoes made me slide like an ice skater. In the bright light, the people around me appeared to be dazzling ghosts. The officer with the hammer kept me from falling back into the coffin. I laughed like a crazy loon. As I laughed with tears running down my face, holding onto the officer, the ghosts broke into action.

The officer with the hammer helped me out of the coffin, setting my slippery shoes squarely on the deck of the pool. I felt as rubbery as Jell-O.

Standing on my own, I looked at Captain Spaulding and said, stupidly, "Hi!"

He asked, "Where's Johnny?"

I lost my balance. Captain Spaulding grabbed my arm to keep me from falling into the pool. I answered, "That's what I'd like to know."

Shoving the amethyst brooch and ankh into my pocket, I blurted out, "Captain Spaulding, Johnny is the killer."

"We know, son."

Making me walk a few steps on my own, steadying me, the captain revealed, "I've had suspicions about Johnny for a long time now. I couldn't prove anything. At this moment, son, we don't know where he's hiding. He disappeared on us. We'll find him, don't you worry, Mr. Scarlet Pimpernel. Let's get you out of here and cleaned up."

"We'll nail him," said the officer as he led me to the door.

"Percy." Aunt Momi called, looking pale as a ghost. She asked quickly, "Are you all right? How do you feel?"

I whined, "How would you feel being buried alive for years in that stinking coffin by that rotten-egg Johnny." It had been hours but I exaggerated. I couldn't help myself. I wanted sympathy. I couldn't be the Scarlet Shadow all the time.

Aunt Momi stamped her high heels, grabbed my smelly body and sobbed, "Oh, Percy, I'm so sorry. I would have died if we had found you dead in that horrible coffin."

"Me, too, Aunt Momi. I would have died on the spot, too, if you had found me dead." I cried to keep her company.

A friendly hand pinched my fanny, and at the same time, the other hand pinched my arm. From those familiar pinches, I knew Marigold was behind me.

"How did you find me?" I asked.

Holding a handkerchief over his nose, the captain led me to the open steel doors and towards someone crouching next to them. It was Toshi. Toshi was the only one in the room who didn't seem to mind my smell.

Taking Toshi's hand, Aunt Momi explained, "Here is our hero, Percy. Without him, you'd still be laying in that coffin. We would never have found you without the courage of this brave man."

"Toshi saved my life?"

Before anyone could explain, the captain grabbed my hand and steered me out of the room into the corridor. "Yes, it was this brave young man who came out of hiding to rescue you. For his bravery, I am going to see he is rewarded."

At the head of the parade, Marigold bragged, "It was me who convinced Aunt Momi and Captain Spaulding to believe Toshi."

Walking up a flight of stairs, Captain Spaulding instructed his followers, "Let's get this boy a bath." Taking the handkerchief away from his nose, he spoke to Toshi. "Young man, I don't want you hiding on this ship anymore. If you stay with us, I promise you that nothing bad will happen to you when we get to San Francisco. An Englishman never breaks his promises. But I can't promise you anything if you try to escape again. Trust me and I'll see to it that you will be treated well by the United States government. Listen, young man, I believe you're now in as much danger from Johnny as anyone here, perhaps more so because you spoiled the blighter's plans."

Marigold stepped in front of Toshi and translated the captain's words in her own made-up Pidgin English, which included a few Japanese words she knew from Japanese school and lots of sign language. Toshi and Marigold held up my bath as we watched them play charades. After she pretended to slice off Toshi's neck, Toshi nodded to the captain, meaning that he understood everything the captain said and that he was not going to try to escape.

Captain Spaulding spoke to me as if I was now a member of his crew. "Percy, once we've gotten you cleaned up, I want a full report on Johnny. I want to hear in full detail how all of this happened to you."

I saluted and said, "Aye, aye, Captain."

Climbing the stairs at full speed, the captain continued speaking even though he was getting out of breath. "We'll all have to be careful. No more wandering on your own until we catch that blighter. Percy, you, your sister and aunt will be bunking in my cabin tonight. After we land in San Francisco, I'll see to it that the San Francisco police escort you all personally off the ship if Johnny hasn't been caught. My second in command, here, Mr. Anderson, will be in charge of your safety."

We stopped on B Deck to catch our breath. The captain and Aunt Momi weren't used to climbing the stairs two steps at a time like I was. By the way the captain kept looking around, he was on the alert in case Johnny would ambush us before we got to his cabin. I wasn't worried. The captain and Officer Anderson carried pistols in their holsters.

I huffed and puffed to the captain, "I have enough evidence to send Johnny to Sing Sing for life. I'd sure like to be the one to catch the son-of-a-bitch."

The captain took my arm and rebuked me. "Percy, there is an

unwritten law in the world of gentlemen that a gentleman never swears in front of a lady. Only coarse and ignorant people swear in front of ladies. Swearing is a sign that a man lacks vocabulary and is not intelligent. Passengers on D Deck swear and sailors swear but not officers or gentlemen. Using bad words is not the mark of a gentleman. Percy, you do want to be a gentleman?"

I nodded.

"Good!"

I looked back at Aunt Momi following behind us. She had hitched up her dress with one hand and with the other grasped her high heels. She held her head high like a thoroughbred, making her look grander than Lady Astor. Thinking about what the captain said, I wondered if the captain made exceptions for ladies like Aunt Momi, who swore like the passengers and sailors on D deck.

Resting at the top of the stairs on A Deck, before proceeding to the captain's cabin, I made a request, "Captain Spaulding, do you think I could have a mayonnaise sandwich and a thick chocolate milk shake after my bath? I could eat a cow."

Everyone laughed.

There are all kinds of laughter. Hearing their laughter was the most wonderful sound in the world. It was not the crazy laughter that Johnny laughed when he acted like King Tut. It wasn't my hysterical laughter when I was rescued. It was happy laughter from loved ones who were happy that I was alive. They sounded like angels from heaven. Johnny's kind of laughter still gives me "chicken-skin."

At that moment, hearing my rescuers laugh, I prayed to God that Johnny was dying of blood poisoning. I would murder him with the stick, if he ever tried to kill the angels who had rescued me.

After my bath, I smelled like clean sheets.

The captain moved his uniforms into Officer Anderson's cabin to make room for our clothes. Within the hour, Aunt Momi had my underwear drying on the captain's desk, and my washed pants and shirt stretched over the furniture. She made the captain's cabin into a Salvation Army rummage sale. A guard was stationed outside our door and the captain ordered us not to leave the cabin unless he accompanied us.

Marigold and Aunt Momi got the captain's big bed. The Captain, to make me feel at home, ordered a sailor to bring my grungy cot up to his cabin. I had sworn since the day I walked up the gangplank, to the annoyance of Aunt Momi, that a colony of bugs lived with me on my cot. I nicknamed the cot Roanoke Island, after the colony that Sir Walter Raleigh founded in America. On Roanoke Island, the settlers vanished mysteriously. I told Aunt Momi I knew where the settlers had disappeared to. Sir Walter Raleigh's settlers turned into little bugs and set up housekeeping on my cot.

I ate a huge plateful of leftover cold macaroni and cheese. The captain gave an order to cover the cheese with a layer of mayonnaise. It looked like a frosted birthday cake.

After finishing my last bite, wanting to lick the mayonnaise off the plate, I reported everything to the captain, showing him Aunt Rose's amethyst brooch. "Johnny is crazy. All he wants is treasures and will murder anyone to get them. He wanted to know where the treasures were hidden." The captain asked if I had told him.

I shook my head, saying, "I'd never tell Johnny anything. He's worse than ten Hitlers, if you ask me. Look in his cabin, you'll find his disguises and all the things he stole from the passengers."

Turning to Aunt Momi, I said, "Remember the evil looking man with the black beard at the cocktail party? That was Johnny. He was the one who shot at you and wrote all those scary notes and he read the letter from your Princess mother-in-law. That's how he knew everything."

My aunt complained that all this excitement had given her a headache. The captain insisted that Aunt Momi have a cup of tea with him in his cabin. I knew that the "cup of tea" was a round of bridge.

Though it was after midnight, I wasn't sleepy. My stomach was stuffed with macaroni and cheese and mayonnaise, and after all, as I told Marigold, I had been sleeping in a coffin all day.

Marigold sat cross-legged on the bed impatient to tell me of her own tale of danger and daring. Marigold began her story before the sirens sounded the warning that a Japanese submarine was stalking the convoy. The captain told me, before he left for his "cup of tea," that a Japanese submarine had actually followed the convoy and the USS Tucker, one of the destroyers, had blasted the submarine to smithereens with its depth charges.

Turning off the overhead light, Marigold made me pretend that we were in a dark forest sitting around a campfire so she could whisper her story mysteriously. "I got worried. You had been missing since breakfast and it was so foggy outside. After I ate my breakfast, I went to look for you, asking everyone if they had seen you. Daisy and Neal hadn't seen you since last night. They missed breakfast because Auntie Sissy wasn't feeling well and made them stay with her in the stateroom. Tarzan said he talked with you in the ship's lounge during breakfast, but he hadn't seen you since. He said you told him that if you didn't show up for dinner, someone pushed you overboard. He thought you were kidding. I knew you weren't. I got really worried that you fell overboard or were pushed because, after all, you are uncoordinated."

"I am not!"

Walking around the cabin, she continued her story. "Well, being the Sherlock Holmes that I am, I kept sniffing clues, looking for you. I even checked the cook's pantry to see if you were sneaking a mayonnaise sandwich. I had a strange feeling that someone was following me. I finally ended up in the infirmary. Looking for you under one of the beds, someone poked me in the rear. Thinking you were trying to scare me, I crawled back out mad as a hatter, ready to give you the dickens. I screamed because Genghis Khan was standing in the room. Using my Einstein brain, knowing that there weren't too many Genghis Khans running around the ship with hair on his chin, I figured that this person had to be Toshi. I yelled, 'Quit being a brat, Toshi. You just gave me a heart attack?' Well, wouldn't you know it, he bawled like a girl."

"Marigold," I interrupted, "A Japanese samurai doesn't bawl like a girl. Samurai are he-men and never cry. You're exaggerating again."

Sitting back on her haunches, giving me "the stink eye," she resumed her story. "I was scared out of my wits. Toshi kept waving his arms all around like a madman. When he stopped waving his hands, he pointed at the bed you slept in, and then started to choke himself. I knew in an instant that you were in trouble. Understanding that and wanting him to know right off that I was his friend, I walked over and shook his hands, making us friends for life. What really made us friends, I spoke to him in Japanese."

I laughed out loud.

"You're making fun of me."

"I am not."

"You are, too. I'm not going to tell you anything more about Toshi."

I countered, "And I'm not going to show you something I have of Johnny's that he'd kill me for."

She stopped dead in her tracks and asked, "You do?"

"I do! I'll show it to you only after you finish the story about Toshi."

"Promise?"

"Promise," I said, crossing my heart and hoping to die. My mouth wasn't twitching.

Marigold continued, "After I calmed Toshi down *with my vast knowledge of the Japanese language* and my very creative hand signals, I understood immediately you were in danger and that Toshi knew where you were. And, wouldn't you know it, that's when the ship's horns blasted the alarm. I told Toshi to hide under the bed until I came back and, if a torpedo hit us, to jump overboard. Of course, we weren't torpedoed, but had to stand for hours waiting for the all clear signal. All that time, Johnny was acting normal. Luckily, I didn't say anything to anybody until I got the scoop from Toshi."

Getting her second wind, and frustrating me to hear the rest of the story, Marigold described the sinking of the submarine. "Percy, it got real exciting seeing the USS Tucker blasting the submarine. Boom. Boom. Boom." She charged around the cabin like the destroyer dropping depth charges. She spread her arms out wide, crying, "I saw with my own eyes the huge, dark oil slick spread out on the ocean as big as this after the submarine got blasted."

Trying to get her back on track, I asked, "Didn't Aunt Momi wonder where I was? Didn't she worry that I wasn't around?"

"Of course she was worried. She asked Johnny if he had seen you. And do you know what the buzzard said to her? He said you were helping Mrs. Brown to her boat station because she had hurt her leg and needed your assistance."

"And she believed that Hitler?"

"Of course, she believed that Hitler. I did, too. It was only a few hours ago that we all loved Johnny. Remember, you, too. Meanwhile, Mr. Scarlet Pimpernel, when the all-clear signal blew, I ran back to

Toshi and found him hiding under the bed. From the way he talked, he would only tell the captain where you were.

"I told him to stay put, and I'd bring the captain to him. First, I found Aunt Momi and convinced her that you were in terrible danger and we both went to find the captain. After I told the captain about Toshi, and he promised that no harm would come to him if he told the truth, I took him and Aunt Momi to the infirmary where Toshi was hiding under the bed.

"Toshi told him what he knew and the captain kept his promise and treated Toshi like a full American. Feeling that he could trust the captain, Toshi led us to the swimming pool. Captain Spaulding told Aunt Momi that he had his suspicions of Johnny and when Toshi pointed the finger at Johnny, convinced the captain that Toshi was telling the truth. On our way to rescue you, we picked up Officer Anderson. He packed the guns. As we got closer to the swimming pool room, I spotted Johnny walking down the corridor ahead of us. I am sure as shootin' that it was Johnny who ran away from us. We saved you in the nick of time."

I sighed, "Thank you for saving my life." I lay on my back, and held a pillow on my chest thinking that it was only a few hours ago that I lay dying in a coffin.

"It's your turn, Percy. Show me what belongs to Johnny," my sister said, reminding me to keep my promise.

I pulled the ankh out of my pocket and let her hold it. "What's this?" she asked.

"It's an Egyptian good luck charm. It's Johnny's. Johnny will kill to get it back. I ripped it off his neck when he left me in the coffin."

As Marigold examined the ankh, I asked a question that kept bothering me, "Marigold, how did Toshi know that I was in the swimming pool room?"

Marigold sat on the floor, grabbed her hair brush and made me sit up. Pulling my hair back from my forehead with the brush, she looked puzzled. "I never asked him about that."

As she brushed my hair vigorously, which felt like she was pulling the hair out by its roots, I had more questions than answers.

I had to see Toshi.

CHAPTER 25

AUNT MOMI SHOWS HER COLORS

Marigold was asleep on the floor holding the brush as a baton. Running around and telling her wild tales pooped her out.

Tiptoeing into the corridor, I tugged the fuzzy-face sailor's sleeve and pointed to Marigold on the floor, looking dead. "Look at my sister. Take this note to the captain. It's a matter of life and death." I prayed that Marigold wouldn't wake up and give me away.

Fuzzy-Face panicked and ran to find the captain, leaving the cabin unguarded.

In the note, I had scribbled, *"Captin Spaulding, please come. Help. I have to see Toshi tonite. He can help us find Johnny. Percy."*

With the guard gone, I kept a lookout for Johnny. Scanning the corridor from one end to the other, holding onto the doorknob, my feet positioned, I was poised to leap back into the cabin at the first sight of Johnny's red hair. The Scarlet Shadow was on the alert for anyone who looked suspicious. Nobody could be trusted now because anybody on the ship could be part of Johnny's gang.

The captain bolted down the corridor. A raging mama elephant puffed behind him. A fuzzy-face sailor ran in pursuit. The flush on the sailor's face told me that the captain had given him a "helling" for leaving his post. The captain looked at Marigold on the floor, grabbed my shoulders and demanded, "What's happened to Marigold?"

"Shhh. She's sleeping."

"She's what?" he said, looking as if he wanted to throttle me.

"She's sleeping like a baby." Noticing Fuzzy-Face fiddling with his revolver, I added quickly, "Don't blame Sailor Fuzzy-Face. I made him think Marigold was dead so he'd go get you. I was desperate to see you right away. Did you read my note?" I said.

Aunt Momi stepped in front of me and shrieked, "You should be ashamed of yourself, Percy. Haven't you caused enough trouble? Young man, you are to stay put in the captain's cabin and never leave it without my permission. Understand me? Why can't you behave like Marigold? I never have to worry about her. If your Uncle Lono was here, he'd make you mind your p's and q's."

Flashing to Uncle Lono's black belt, I agreed. "You betchum he would, Aunt Momi. Uncle Lono scares me to death. He spanked me once with his black belt and that ONCE was one time too many." Being that Uncle Lono was in San Francisco and being that I was in a smarty-pants mood, I continued, "But he isn't here, is he, Aunt Momi?"

Dragging the captain and Aunt Momi away from Fuzzy-Face just in case he was a spy for Johnny, I whispered, "Toshi knows all the hiding places on this ship. He can give me a good idea where Johnny is hiding. He won't talk to you, Captain Spaulding, because he's scared of you. He won't tell Aunt Momi anything because she's a woman. Mr. Hamada told me that in Japan women walk five steps behind a man. Toshi will tell me everything because he likes me. Look, he saved my life. I can't sleep until I speak to him. I just can't help being a pest, Captain. It's driving me crazy. You wouldn't want me to go crazy, would you?"

The captain sighed, "It's late, Percy. Go to bed."

I insisted. "We have to find Johnny before he kills again. If he does kill again, it's going to be me or Marigold or Aunt Momi. He's now crazier than ten thousand Hitlers and Tojos put together. Toshi can help us. I may be only eight years old, but this eight-year-old Scarlet Pimpernel is dead serious."

The captain roared like a lion. "You are the most damnable, demanding eight-year-old boy I have ever encountered. You're taking me to my wit's end and when I'm at my wit's end, I get VERY angry and you don't want to be around me when I get that angry."

Putting my hands on my hips, I huffed. "If you had been nailed in a coffin and left to die, you'd be damnable and demanding, too. Please?"

Putting his hands on my shoulders, he said, "If I do this for you, I want no more trouble out of you for the rest of the trip. I'm sailing this ship under the Golden Gate Bridge tomorrow, so I don't have time to humor a little eight-year-old boy. Understand me?"

"Deal, Captain. Shake on it." We shook hands as honorable men did in the movies in 1942.

My aunt fluffed her hair and said in a menacing voice that I had heard only once before, "May I remind you, Leslie, that there's a killer still at large on *your* ship who wants to kill me and my family. I resent that you are taking into account the ramblings of an eight-year-old boy. Percy, I am washing my hands of you forever. Men's work, indeed! Leslie, I will hold you personally responsible if anything more happens to this boy on your ship. For God's sake, you don't need to humor him. By the way, men, I could find that son-of-a-bitch, Johnny, in two minutes and string him up by his balls. Percy, for your information, I'd have Toshi eating out of my hand like this." She snapped her fingers.

With her eyes now flaming as red as her hair, she stomped into the cabin and before she slammed the door, she turned to the captain and said, "Our bridge games are over."

I said out loud as the door closed, "I bet Aunt Momi is coming down with the measles."

The captain took my hand and led me away from the sailor. He was still fiddling with his gun. As we walked down the corridor to the brig, the captain looked as if he had a headache. "Women are hard to understand, Percy. When a woman has a bee up her bonnet, she can hold onto that bee for a long, long time and there's no telling when she'll let that bee out to sting you. Percy, my lad, there is much to be said for a career in the Navy. You should think about it."

"Captain Spaulding, Daddy told me that the birds and the bees is an important story. Is this the same story?" I asked.

"In a roundabout way, yes."

I screwed up my courage, looked straight ahead, and lied from my heart. "Captain Spaulding, I taught Aunt Momi her swear words but she doesn't know the meanings of any of them."

Squeezing my hand, the captain said, "Thank you for telling me that, Percy. I wondered where she picked up those bad words."

I smiled and said, "You're welcome. I just didn't want you to think my Aunt Momi isn't a lady."

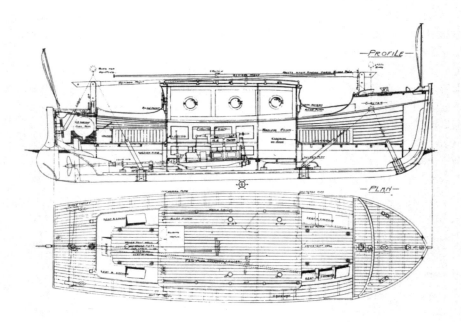

Aquitania's Motor Boat.

CHAPTER 26

TOSHI

The brig was a small room in the middle of the ship, not far from the officer's mess. In the brig was a single bed, a table, a straight-back wooden chair, a single overhead light, and a white porcelain potty next to the bed.

The sailor who guarded Toshi's prison cell looked as ferocious as a black bear. He sent shivers up my spine. Seeing that he didn't have shifty eyes, I relaxed but kept on guard just in case he was a member of Johnny's gang. Before I went in to see Toshi, the captain informed the bear that he was returning to the bridge and would send Officer Anderson, the officer with the hammer, to escort me back into the arms of my angry aunt. He ordered the bear to keep a watch on me through the small window in the door while I was speaking with Toshi.

The bear bolted the door behind me.

Toshi was barefoot, lying on a cot, turning the pages of a Superman comic book. As he tuned the pages, he coughed goop into a handkerchief. He wore prisoner's clothes, a faded blue shirt and dungarees. Toshi laid the comic book on his chest and stared at me. I stared back. Toshi picked up the comic book, laid it over his face, and pretended to go to sleep.

I pleaded, "Toshi, talk to me. Take the comic book away from your face. Look at me, please. I know you can understand what I am saying."

Toshi kept the comic book over his face. In the quietness of the room, he gulped little breaths into his nose and exhaled sharp "ha" sounds.

Samurai breathing.

"Toshi, I am sorry that I called you a Jap. I was mad at you because I thought you killed Mina. I know Johnny killed Mina and you saved my life. I owe you my life. Please, speak to me. We've got to find Johnny before he murders more people like he did Mina. Pleeeese! Pleeese! Pleeese."

Toshi removed the comic book from his face, looked at me and coughed goop into his handkerchief. He had changed since I first saw him at Mina's lifeboat. His hair had grown long and stringy with gray streaks running through it. He was skinny as a stick but hard muscles were still visible on his arms and legs, making him as sleek as a leopard. The skin on his face had tightened tighter over his cheekbones. Toshi and I had only one thing in common. We both needed mothers. The thing we didn't have in common: Toshi was handsome.

"Toshi, did you eat?"

Turning on his side, he threw his handkerchief on the floor and grabbed a clean one from the table next to him. Lying back on the pillow, he muttered, "My name, Toshi Hiranaka. I am samurai warrior."

"You look too skinny for a samurai warrior. Reeeeally, you do," I said, nervously.

He moaned, "I like die. I let Mina die. I no save her."

Walking towards him slowly, I said gently, "You couldn't have saved Mina. Mina knows that. Mina wants you to live. I want you to live. When we arrive in San Francisco, I'll telephone President Roosevelt. He'll give you the Medal of Honor for saving my life. You'll become famous like John Wayne in the movies. The president's wife, Eleanor Roosevelt, will want to meet you personally and take you to lunch. Fala, their dog, will want to meet you, too."

Toshi sat upright and shouted, "No. No. No do that. Relatives in Japan get killed. Relatives get killed if hear I get medal from President Roosevelt. I be traitor. I no like be like John Wayne. I like only be American." Toshi covered his feet with the blanket.

Calming him down, I swore that I wouldn't telephone President Roosevelt or Eleanor or Fala.

"Toshi, how come you are on this ship? Are you really a Japanese soldier?"

Pushing back the covers, rubbing his feet, he answered slowly in broken English, "I born Hawaii. I am American. Fadda work Hawaii plantation. He send me Japan three year ago to go school. Relatives live in Hiroshima, rice farmer. I shame write home because relatives sick all time. They take my money. No can go school. I care for them all time. They cough all time like me. War come, no can go back to United States of America. Japan government say I no can go back. All money from my fadda gone. No can go school. No can go back to Hawaii. I like kill myself."

"How did they keep you in Japan?" I interrupted.

"Japan government say I not American citizen, I Japanese citizen. Tell me only speak Japanese. No English. I keep work on rice farm because only rich boy in Japan go school. Work hard on rice farm. One day, army soldier take me away. Make me join army. Army soldiers all time beat me up, slap face because I American. I hear bad stories about Japan army in China. Only whisper-kind stories like burn Chinese people alive. Do all kind bad things in China. I hear that, it make me want to kill myself. I keep tell everyone I American, but nobody believe me. Every time I say I American, I get beat with stick. Pretty soon, they think I crazy. I escape army. Want to go to America to sister in Washington, D.C. She make things right for me. I go Yokohama, hide on big ship. Ship not go America. Ship go Singapore. In Singapore, I hide on this ship. I good hide on ship. Pretty soon, everybody think I like ghost. Sailors like find ghost and kill ghost.

"When ship leave Hawaii, two Japan boy from Hawaii escape prison on ship. They say they American just like me. They say too muchee hot down in ship. They say more better die in sea than burn up. Two friend go overboard in big wave. red-hair man see me. He like kill me all time.

"I find Mina. She kind girl. I meet you. You give food. I love Mina. Mina smoke Lucky Strike cigarettes all time. Nighttime, we follow red-hair man. See Red-hair man do bad things all time. I watch him. Mina watch him. I cough all time. He too good hear. He listen for cough. One time catch us watch him. He yell he going kill us. I make red-haired man think I Mina. Wear scarf, but no fool him. I cough all time. He chase us. I quick hide Mina in boat. He find Mina, try kill her. She run. Jump off ship. I like kill him. I follow him all time. See him take you swimming pool. You no come out. I know bad thing happen to you like happen to Mina. Find girl walk like cowboy. She get captain. I tell captain red-hair man bad man and you in room."

"Why did you come out of hiding to save me?" I asked.

Toshi answered after he coughed into his handkerchief. "Mina like you like she like other little yellow hairs. I like your name Peeeercy. Percy name made me laugh. Me laugh first time I see you. You in bear coat, slide down ship. Though I sad because friend go in ocean, you make me laugh. You stick up for Japanese people with red-hair man. Then, I like you for all time."

"I make you laugh?" I asked.

Toshi became very animated. "You fat! You fat like sumo wrestler. I love sumo wrestle. Pretty soon when you get more fat, *momona*, bigger like Mount Fuji, then you can be rich sumo wrestler. In Japan, after war, come Japan and be rich sumo wrestler. Sumo wrestler in Japan bigger than John Wayne, movie star."

I said clenching my fists, "I hate being fat. I look like Hermann Goering."

Waving his hands in the air, he spoke fiercely, "Fat good. Look me — all bones stick out here, bone stick out there. Look leg — ugly. I like look big (He flexed the muscles on his arms.) like Gary Cooper, he all time good American movie star. He tall. He brave. He have big muscles, big chest, big teeth, big arms. I hate John Wayne. He have small eyes like red-hair man."

Trying to win his trust, I flashed a big Gary Cooper smile showing lots of teeth. "When we get to America, I'm going to feed you lots of hot dogs and hamburgers and make you look just like a movie star. Promise. I'm going to take good care of you. If you want to look like a sumo wrestler, I'll feed you tons of Best Foods mayonnaise, buckets of rice, and gallons of thick chocolate milk shakes. I'll make you look like a sumo wrestler in no time and then you can become rich."

"B e s t F o o d s m a y o n n a i s e?" he said, looking at me strangely as he stretched out the words.

Thinking that my fifteen minutes were up, I said urgently, "I need your help, Toshi. Where did you and Mina hide on the ship? The bad man with red hair has disappeared. He's hiding somewhere and we don't know where he is hiding. He has to be hiding in a very secret place. You know all the secret hiding places. Tell me where they are so we can find him."

"I tell you if you help me."

"I'll do anything but first tell me," I said.

Toshi described the nooks and crannies he had hidden in since the day he boarded the Aquitania in Singapore. His list included hidden compartments near the engine room, an unused closet in the laundry room, and a small cupboard right under the captain's nose next to the bridge. Toshi said he and Mina had given up hiding in lifeboats, unless they were desperate, because that's where Johnny looked first.

Gluing the list into my memory, I said, "Toshi, you not only saved my life but you're going to save lots of other people's lives. Because of you, we will find Johnny. Toshi, I have a best friend who is a Japanese spy. Honest to God, I do. I'm telling you the truth. He's probably spying in San Francisco right this very minute. His name is Mr. Hamada. He's my guardian angel. If he's around in San Francisco, I'll get him to help you. Now, what do you want?"

"I like go Washington, D.C. My sister work secretary in Peruvian embassy. She help me if I get to her. You help me go to Washington, D.C.?"

"I'll get you to Washington, D.C. Don't you worry. The Scarlet Shadow, who acts like the Scarlet Pimpernel, keeps his word. Someday, Mr. Hamada, you and I will live together on Waikiki Beach and have a big luau for Aunt Rose when her coffin lands on the beach."

I mused, "Wars are strange. Just because we're at war with Japan, you and I are not supposed to be friends. That doesn't make sense to me. When the war is over, everybody in America and Japan will be friends again. I know that. Do you know what I think? I think that Mr. Tojo and Mr. Hitler should fight President Roosevelt and Mr. Churchill in Madison Square Garden. The winner wins the war. Then people like you and me wouldn't have to get killed in the war. Toshi, what do you want most other than seeing your sister in Washington, D.C.?"

"I like go back see my family in Hawaii. They no can help me now. Only big shot sister can. That's why I no get off ship in Hawaii. Only big shot sister can help me."

I had been talking to Toshi way over fifteen minutes and Officer Anderson hadn't come for me. Something was wrong. I knocked on the cabin door to see if Officer Anderson was waiting for me. When the door opened, the pudding-faced sailor from the galley greeted me.

Surprised, I asked, "Where's the bear?"

"He's gone," he said, chewing on his bottom lip.

"Where is Officer Anderson?" I asked, looking into his face.

"He had an emergency. I'm here to get you."

I stared at Pudding-face's eyes, deciding whether I should trust him. I questioned him again. "Where are you taking me?"

"Back to your cabin."

"What's your name?"

"Burt."

That cinched it. Anyone named Burt was not to be trusted. I looked at him again. This time I discovered green specks floating in his eyeballs. All bad men in comic books had green specks in their eyes.

I gulped, "Sailor Burt, excuse me. I have to say goodbye to Toshi in private. One moment, please."

I shut the door in his face and ran to Toshi and whispered breathlessly, "There's a strange sailor out there. I don't trust him. He said that he's going to take me back to *my* cabin. I have a feeling he's going to take me to Johnny because the captain told me that I was supposed to go back to *his* cabin, not mine. He looks like an assassin if I ever saw one."

I whispered, speaking as fast as I could, "I'm going to make a dash for the captain's cabin. I'll be back tomorrow. When I come back, I'll bring you a chocolate bar. Chocolate will make you look like Gary Cooper and stop your coughing. Eat a mountain of mashed potatoes while I'm gone. They'll make you fat. Now, pretend you have a stomachache so I can get Mr. Pudding-face in here while I make a run for it. Scream when I give the signal."

Rubbing his stomach, Toshi moaned, "I no pretend. My stomach hurt like hell. Percy, run like wind. Red-haired man no can run fast. I know. But if he catch you, scream like monkey because Red-hair man will kill you quick."

I whispered frantically, "I know that. I'm so scared but I give you the word of the Scarlet Shadow that I will get you to Washington, D.C. Toshi, I know we're going to be true blue friends for life. I just know that." I shook Toshi's hands like men did in the movies in 1942.

I ran to the door and knocked on it. Pudding-face opened it. I signaled to Toshi. He began screaming. I yelled, "The prisoner is dying! Somebody poisoned him!"

I pushed Pudding-face in his confusion into the cell and ran out. I slammed the door and locked him inside. Speeding down the corridor, running at a hundred miles an hour, I imagined that Johnny was right behind me. I could feel his breath on my neck. As I was about to shoot up the stairs to A Deck, out of nowhere came the sounds of a snake, "Pst. Pst."

I froze in my tracks. I wanted to tinkle but couldn't because the snakes kept telling me to join them in the shadows. The only people who made snake sounds were Johnny and Aunt Momi.

The Garden Lounge.

CHAPTER 27

COME INTO THE SHADOWS, PERCY

A voice kept hissing, "Get in here."

"Hurry up, before he catches you."

"Daisy, is that you?" I tiptoed towards the voice that came from the dark alcove under the stairs. The alcove looked as dark and scary as an underground cave. A hand pulled me into the blackness. When my eyes adjusted to the dark, there was Daisy, Neal and Uncle Buster smashed in the cave like sardines.

I shrieked in surprise.

"Quiet," Uncle Buster ordered. "Crouch down. Is Johnny behind you?"

"No, I don't think so." I tired to wiggle my fat body next to Daisy.

Uncle Buster asked, "Who were you running from?"

"From Pudding-face. He's an agent of Johnny's. I locked him up in Toshi's cell. Pudding-face has green specks in his eyes."

Accepting my convoluted answer, Uncle Buster pushed me out of the hiding place. After peering around to see if the coast was clear, he dragged Daisy and Neal out from the alcove and ordered us to run upstairs.

Taking the stairs two steps at a time, I wheezed, "Uncle Buster, slow down, I can't run as fast as you can. I have a list of all the places where Johnny could be hiding. I've got to tell the captain right now." Following behind Uncle Buster, I asked, "Why were you hiding under the stairs?"

"I'll explain when we get inside my cabin."

He locked the cabin door.

Holding his sides, he gasped, "Jeez, I am getting old." Between breaths, he ordered, "Daisy and Neal, off with your bathrobes and get into that bed."

I watched perplexed as Uncle Buster hustled my friends into one of the single beds. Uncle Buster's cabin was a disheveled mess. Clothes were strewn like fallen leaves over the chairs and tables. Pushing with his feet, Uncle Buster shoved a pair of Neal's pants aside and made an open space on the floor. Pulling a mattress off his bed, he slid it into the empty space, placing a blanket over the mattress.

I yelled in frustration, "What is going on?"

Everyone thought that I had suddenly gone mad.

I repeated, "What is going on?"

Uncle Buster ordered, "Neal, give him a cookie. He needs a cookie." He pointed to a plate of cookies on the dresser.

Neal leapt out of his bed, took two cookies off the plate, and shoved them into my hands. "They're butterscotch." He jumped back into bed.

I snapped, "I hate butterscotch cookies. Will somebody please tell me what is going on?"

Buster sat on his bed, still holding his sides. "Sit here, Percy. Give me a minute. Tarzan is getting over the hill." Taking in a deep breath, he said, "I wanted to wait until tomorrow for explanations. It's late."

I pleaded, "Tell me now, Uncle Buster."

"All right," he wheezed. "Captain Spaulding told me about you and Johnny."

Neal chimed in. "Everybody on the ship now knows about Johnny."

Uncle Buster interrupted, "Neal is right. Everyone on the ship is keeping a watch out for him. I can't foresee how he can escape getting off this ship without getting caught. What we do know is that he will do harm to you because you can send him to the electric chair. That's why you are with me. From now on, you can never be by yourself. No more running down corridors alone like you just did. The captain asked that I bring you here after your meeting with the Japanese boy and that he'd hear your report tomorrow. My cabin is a safer place than your own cabin. Your aunt seems relieved that you are with me."

"Aunt Momi hates me right now. She must be very, VERY RELIEVED that I'm spending the night with you. Go on with your story, Uncle Buster."

Rubbing his forehead, Tarzan continued, "I thought that you were the biggest pest in the world, but you're not. These two babies take the cake. They have been driving me stark raving mad with their constant nagging."

"Percy," said Daisy, "something terrible has happened in our cabin. Sissy and Sister Mary Louise have the measles."

"The measles?" I exclaimed, scratching my head.

Looking like an angel from under the covers, she blinked her big blue eyes at me and said, "Marigold's measles."

"That's impossible," I cried. "They were never near Marigold. Auntie Sissy is making all that up just to get back at me for destroying her mink coat."

"She is not," protested Daisy. "It's true! Sissy got Marigold's measles."

Neal butted in. "It's true. It's true. It's really true, Percy."

Daisy enlightened me. "The night after you ruined Sissy's fur coat, after the funeral, Sissy and Sister Mary Louise went to Aunt Momi's cabin to get back the mink coat. They decided to get it on their way to the cocktail party. What they didn't know was that Marigold had the measles and was sleeping in the cabin. Sissy assumed your family had gone to the cocktail party. What I didn't know is that Sister Mary Louise is a safecracker. She picks the locks on the doors at the convent so she can snoop on her student boarders. Sissy planned to have the sister pick the lock of your cabin, grab the fur coat, and get out.

"While Sister Mary Louise was working on the lock, Marigold heard her, opened the door and spit in their faces. They said your sister screamed that she was sick and tired of being bothered by thieves and murderers and spit again. Sissy said that Marigold laughed like a fiend as they ran down the corridor. That's how they got Marigold's measles. Sister Mary Louise thinks you and Marigold are devils straight from hell and they hate Aunt Momi as much as they hate Mrs. Brown. Their measles didn't break out until last night. Sister doesn't want us around. She says Neal and I frazzle her nerves."

"Marigold didn't tell me about that. Maybe she thought seeing Auntie Sissy and the nun was a nightmare. Marigold had lots of nightmares when she had the measles. Your mother can give anyone nightmares; that's for sure. Daisy, how come you and Neal are staying in

Uncle Buster's cabin?"

Fluttering her eyelashes at Uncle Buster, Daisy continued, "How can I tell you if you keep interrupting me? May I continue?"

I nodded.

"Sister Mary Louise made Sissy order the captain to find us a cabin to sleep in. Of course, there are no empty cabins. Uncle Buster came to our rescue. He didn't want us sleeping in a lifeboat, especially with that awful Johnny running around killing people. So, here we are. Isn't Uncle Buster the biggest sweetie pie in the whole wide world?" Daisy beamed at Uncle Buster. Having used up all her little girl energy telling the story, fairy dust closed her eyes. She nodded off to dreamland without putting a period at the end of her sentence.

Uncle Buster yawned, "Percy, here is your bed on the floor. Tomorrow night, buddy, you'll be sleeping like a prince in a San Francisco hotel, in a real feathered bed."

Feeling the mattress on the floor, I smiled, "Tonight, I am going to sleep in a bed fit for the Scarlet Pimpernel and be near the people I love. What more could a fellow ask for?"

"Here." My real McCoy hero said handing me one of his pajama tops. "Wash your face and rinse your mouth out with Listerine. The Listerine bottle is standing on the counter in the bathroom." With that, Buster flopped on his bed and began to snore without rinsing his mouth out with Listerine.

The pajama top covered me from head to toe. I pretended that I was wearing the same nightgown Marie Antoinette wore on the night before she was guillotined.

The mattress was so much softer than a coffin or even my cot.

Before nodding off, I called out, "Goodnight, Shadows."

Daisy murmured from her dreamland, "Goodnight, Scarlet Shadow."

"Goodnight, Pimpy," Neal yawned, smothering his face into his pillow.

To Buster, who was snoring, I called, "Goodnight, Tarzan. I'm going to grow up to be a hero just like you."

Buster groaned in his sleep, "Eat your spinach, Percy."

CHAPTER 28

GOLDEN GATE IS FALLING DOWN, FALLING DOWN....

"Wake up, Percy!"

Coming out of a Johnny dream, I opened my eyes and asked, "Where am I?"

"Get up. It's almost noon. We're about to sail under the Golden Gate Bridge."

Officer Anderson was standing over me. He was dressed in his whites.

Frightened, I asked, "What are you doing in Uncle Buster's cabin? You are not a friend of Johnny's?"

"I am not. Wash that dirty face and brush your teeth." Slung over his arm were my favorite striped shirt, blue pants and a sweater. In his other hand, he held a lifejacket and a toothbrush.

I kicked back the bedcovers, jumped up, stood in front of Officer Anderson, and saluted him. Taking the clothes and toothbrush from him, I felt dizzy. Questioning him in a rat-tat-tatting voice, I asked "Why didn't Uncle Buster wake me up? Oh boy, the Golden Gate Bridge? Are we almost in San Francisco? Did they find Johnny?"

Pushing me into the bathroom, the officer replied, "I'll answer all your questions as you're getting dressed. Hurry up or you're going to miss seeing the ship go under the bridge."

While washing my face, Officer Anderson sat on Uncle Buster's bed and answered my questions. "Your friends have been up on deck since dawn watching the convoy move into position. It was a pretty impressive sight. We are now the lead ship ready to go under the bridge. The Lurline and destroyers have lined up behind us like ducks in the water."

Rinsing my mouth out with Listerine, I said, "I wish I had seen that."

"Your sister is on the bridge with the captain."

"Marigold gets to do all the fun things," I whined.

"There's plenty of action coming up for you to see. Going under the Golden Gate Bridge and watching the mine sweepers open up the submarine nets is going to be the main show. The captain, right now, is concentrating on hitting low tide at just the right moment or we don't think we can make it under the bridge. Hurry up. On the bureau, Buster left orange juice and sweet rolls for you."

I popped out of the bathroom feeling like a movie star because I slicked down my hair using Uncle Buster's hair pomade and smelled like a barbershop. After drinking the orange juice in one swallow, I inhaled a sweet roll. The other roll, I shoved in my pocket in case of a sudden hunger attack. Putting on the lifejacket, I questioned, "Why are you not on the bridge with the captain?"

Strapping me into the jacket, he explained, "Because you're a very important person, Percy. I'm here to protect you. We haven't found Johnny. We hope with your information from Toshi, we can find out where the blighter is hiding."

I interrupted, "I memorized all the secret hiding places."

"The captain will want to hear about them once we're under the bridge." Making a final inspection that I was dressed properly, the officer grabbed my arm, locked the cabin, and led me up to meet my friends. I was going to watch the Aquitania sail under the fabulous Golden Gate Bridge.

The first sight of the Golden Gate Bridge — well, I was disappointed. It was not what I had anticipated. I had imagined that we were going to sail under a bridge made of pure gold with thousands of diamonds, sapphires, and rubies splattered all over it. Coming into view was an ordinary metal bridge with two twin iron towers sticking out of the water and steel cables that spanned it from one end to the other. The steel cables hung on the bridge like tinsel on a Christmas tree. In between the cables and towers, motor cars zoomed back and forth carrying people over the Bay. What really made the bridge so ordinary and ever so disappointing, was that it wasn't even painted gold. It was painted orange. A color I hated.

My face tingled. Cold air hit it as I stood at the railing. The fog had lifted. A light, gray mist had taken its place. In the distance, the mountains of California looked drab like a Chinese watercolor painting. We had left behind islands that sat in an ocean where the water was colored bright blue and the mountains were painted purple and green. We had fled the colorful Land of Oz and were now arriving in brown Kansas sans "living" Technicolor.

Seagulls swooped in front of me, searching for fish. They squawked like spoiled brats whenever they missed their catch. As we sailed towards the bridge, the ocean lapped in steady rhythmic beats against the hull of the ship. Standing next to Uncle Buster, Daisy, Neal, and I looked at the line-up of ships sailing single file in a row.

The Golden Gate Bridge loomed before us. After the mine sweepers opened up the submarine nets, the captain steered the Aquitania between the two metal towers. We held our breaths as the ship squeezed underneath the bridge. The masts were so close to the bottom of the bridge I would have bet a nickel that we were going to hit it. The captain navigated the ship underneath with inches to spare. I can't tell you how disappointed I was not to see the bridge collapse in the water.

Cars on the Golden Gate honked their horns as the captain sailed the ship under like the queen of the seas into the San Francisco Bay. The people standing along the shoreline cheered us. Sailboats skimmed around us as onlookers onboard waved hats and blew kisses; we gave them the V for victory sign. The winds cleared the mist away, letting the sun shine on us. As the sun warmed our faces, the passengers sang, "God Bless America." In an instant, Aunt Rose, Johnny, and submarine scares were all forgotten. The ten days sailing on the sea had just been a bad dream.

As I was screaming, singing, and waving to the people in the sailboats, someone jostled me. A hand jammed something into my pocket. I pulled out a scrap of paper and unfolded it. Six words were printed on the paper. "I am going to kill you."

I saw Pudding-face running down the ladder to A Deck. I ran over to Officer Anderson and said excitedly, waving the note. "Officer Anderson, Johnny is hiding around here. Pudding-face put a note in my pocket. The note is from Johnny. The note said 'I am going to kill you'."

Officer Anderson put his hand on my shoulder and said, "Slow down, Percy. Calmly, tell me what happened."

After he read the note, I said, "Johnny has to be hiding somewhere near the navigation bridge, in one of the cubbyholes where Toshi and Mina hid. Johnny is in there right now because Pudding-face just handed me the note. Let's go get him. Come on. Come on."

Before the officer could stop me, I raced towards the navigational bridge to search for Johnny. My friends ran after me as Officer Anderson yelled at us, "Don't any of you do anything until I get there."

Next to the entrance to the ship's bridge, I discovered a little door. The door was small, unmarked and blended invisibly into the gray metal wall. I had passed it a hundred times without ever noticing it. I couldn't believe the door had been in front of me all this time. Looking at the door, I couldn't imagine Johnny squeezing his big body into such a small opening. Believing that Johnny was trapped inside, I kicked the door, yelling, "We got you, you big fake Egyptian pharaoh Nazi Hitler. Your days are numbered. You're going to die in the electric chair, you big liar crybaby."

"Stop it, Percy! Get away from that door." Officer Anderson was behind me, holding a pistol.

"Stand away, Percy. He may be armed."

Daisy had cowered behind a lifeboat as I stepped back to join Neal crouched behind a metal chest. My heart pounded as I watched Officer Anderson bring the captain and three sailors out of the bridge holding rifles. I spied Marigold inside waving a sailor's cap at me.

With one mighty thrust, Officer Anderson yanked the metal door open and yelled, "Come out, Johnny. We've got you cornered. You can't escape. Come out or I'll shoot."

Nothing happened.

Officer Anderson looked into the opening. He reached in with his hand and pulled out Mina's red scarf. "That's all that's in there, Captain. Just this scarf. False alarm. Sorry, Sir."

I exclaimed, "Johnny must have gone back to his cabin, taken Mina's scarf and hidden in the cubby hole last night. That proves how sneaky and dangerous Johnny can be."

The captain ordered, "Everyone into the bridge." We pushed in single file and stood around the captain.

"After I've anchored this ship in the bay, we'll continue the search for Johnny. Officer Anderson, stand the children over there and keep them out of my way."

Marigold pinched my behind. I turned and whispered to her, "Where's Aunt Momi?"

"She's in the cabin. Boy, am I glad to be out of her clutches. She's been on a rampage since last night."

"She hates me," I said.

"She doesn't like me either." Marigold crossed her eyes.

Before we could finish our conversation, Officer Anderson caught our attention. "The captain is going to anchor the ship in the middle of the bay. We have to wait out here until the Matsonia leaves from Pier 35 tonight. It's the only pier we can dock this ship into because we're so large. Now, say good-bye to the destroyers. They're sailing up to Alameda to refuel. That tugboat near the Ferry Building is going to berth the Lurline over there. The Lurline usually docks at Pier 35. It's going to be one holy mess in this bay today."

"What's that?" Neal asked.

"That's Alcatraz. That island is where they lock up criminals, like Percy."

Everyone laughed.

"Behind Alcatraz is the Bay Bridge. There in front of you is the grandest city on the Pacific Coast - San Francisco. Look at her today. She is shining in all her glory."

"Wowee," Neal butted in, "That city looks like a big cardboard cutout pasted against a blue sky."

"That's Fisherman's Wharf where all those little fishing boats are tied up. Tomorrow, you eat a big steamed lobster for me. I can't because we'll be preparing to do a quick turnabout to Hawaii."

"We have to catch Johnny today." I said, trying to show the urgency by the sound of my voice.

The ship's anchor hit the water. Captain Spaulding ordered Officer Anderson to take Daisy and Neal back to Auntie Sissy. A tug was waiting to take them off the ship. Auntie Sissy, the nun and Toshi were being sent to St. Mary's Hospital.

"What's wrong with Toshi?" I asked.

The captain replied, "He has tuberculosis. Marigold and Percy, your aunt wants you both back in her cabin. If your aunt agrees, Percy, I want you here on the bridge with me if we can't find Johnny. You're familiar with his ways so I'd like you to observe the passengers as they disembark the ship. In the meantime, you might enjoy being with me on the bridge."

I raised my hand. "I have to say goodbye to Auntie Sissy before she leaves the ship. Officer Anderson, let me have Mina's scarf. I want to return it to Auntie Sissy and apologize to her for ruining her mink coat. Captain, you have to understand that when you're the Scarlet Shadow you have to make things right just like the Scarlet Pimpernel. But the most important thing is we have to find Johnny."

The captain said, "You're correct on that point. I fear that you and I are stuck at the hip until this Johnny affair has ended. Now go with Officer Anderson. But, before you leave, tell me the list of the hiding places, if you please."

From memory, I recited the hidden cubbyholes to a sailor who wrote them down. My business finished, Officer Anderson escorted Daisy, Neal, Marigold, and me with Mina's scarf around my neck, to Auntie Sissy's cabin. Passengers carrying their suitcases stayed out of our way because Officer Anderson held his gun in front of him. Marigold and I guarded the rear and pretended that we, too, carried a gun in our pockets.

CHAPTER 29

FINISHING TOUCHES

When we arrived at Auntie Sissy's cabin, the sounds of wood breaking and glass shattering told us that Auntie Sissy's polo mallet was in use.

Marigold yelled, "Retreat!"

I didn't need her Sherlock Holmes' ears to tell me that Auntie Sissy was inside the cabin going cuckoo.

I warned Officer Anderson, "We'd better get out of here."

There was a loud crash. The silence that followed was ominous. We pressed our ears against the cabin door and heard Auntie Sissy moaning. Then we heard sobs. Auntie Sissy was crying.

Fearing that something dreadful had happened, Officer Anderson pounded on the door. By the force of his fists, the door opened. He flung it wide. Auntie Sissy, with red spots all over her face, was sitting on the floor cradling in her arms her broken mallet. She sobbed like a baby. Looking up, she threw a piece of the polo mallet and screamed for us to get out. Officer Anderson spoke calmly, as if talking to a child, "Calm yourself, Madam, I'm returning your children."

"Where are they?" she sniffed. Her sobbing under control, she then had a fit of hiccups and her nose began to run like a waterfall.

Officer Anderson calmly handed Auntie Sissy his handkerchief to stop Niagara Falls. Indicating with his hands, he pointed behind him, "Your children, madam."

Wiping her nose, Auntie Sissy hiccupped, "Daisy and Neal come away from that man and come sit with your mother."

The door to the bedroom opened unexpectedly and out strode Uncle Peanut, "I'll handle this, Sissy."

Uncle Peanut had changed drastically. His body had withered away and his face was as gray as the Lurline. His face had sorrow written all over it. With his shaved head, he looked like a skeleton.

Daisy and Neal dashed for Uncle Peanut. Putting his arms around them, he kissed the tops of their heads and warned Auntie Sissy to leave her children alone. "Go into the bedroom, Sissy, and finish packing. Just take what you'll need for the hospital."

"I can't pack." She wailed. "I'm sick. I feel weak. I have a fever. You're all against me. I hate these damned spots on my face."

Uncle Peanut commanded, "Get up. You're making yourself sicker sitting on the floor feeling sorry for yourself. I'll take care of the kids' packing. With or without a suitcase, you, the nun, the kids, and I are leaving this ship now."

Auntie Sissy stood reluctantly, dropping the handkerchief on the floor. Standing behind Officer Anderson, I got my first good look at Daisy's mom. In the bright light, she looked like the speckled bride of Frankenstein. I wanted to shriek for joy. Her hair had turned the color of a mouse and her face showed all the meanness that she kept stored inside of her. I giggled. A laugh was forming and was heading for my throat. Sensing what was about to happen, Marigold pinched me so hard a blood blister formed on my fanny.

Seeing the red scarf around my neck, Auntie Sissy screamed, "Give that back to me, you little fat monster."

Protecting me from Auntie Sissy's grabbing hands, Officer Anderson protected me and said calmly, "One moment, madam. Control yourself. You're speaking to a child."

"Child, my ass. He's a monster, and where is my fur coat, you little fat brat?"

Uncle Peanut bellowed at her, "Stop your nonsense right this minute. It's not him you should be angry with but that red-headed haole. He was the one who murdered Rose. He was also the one who murdered Mina who *you* kicked out of your cabin. Forget your fur coat. We haven't time for dramatics."

Picking up the white handkerchief that Auntie Sissy had left on the floor; I waved it at her and walked to her knowing that the polo mallet, her weapon of choice, lay broken on the floor in pieces.

"Auntie Sissy, I want to apologize for ruining your mink coat. It was an accident. I didn't mean to do it. It happened by mistake. If you want it back, the fur coat is in a suitcase at the bottom of the ocean.

Please let me keep this scarf to give to a friend of Mina's. He tried to save her life. Having this scarf would mean a lot to him."

Everybody in the cabin held their breath, waiting for her answer.

A voice shrieked from the bedroom, "Don't give it to that brat. His sister, the she-devil, gave us the measles. They're both devils."

My sister defended us. "We are not devils. I gave you the measles because you were picking the lock to our cabin."

The nun yelled, "That's surely a she-devil talking, Sissy. Don't listen to her. I don't pick locks. Jesus is my witness."

Auntie Sissy yelled, "Shut up, Mary Louise. Jesus is your witness that you do pick locks. This happens to be my affair, not yours."

Auntie Sissy said in a surprisingly calm manner, "I accept your apology, Percy. You may keep the scarf. Now, I want all of you out of this cabin this minute."

She resumed her imperious pose and said with a great deal of ferocity, "And I never ever want to see any of you again and that goes for you, too, Officer Anderson."

"That goes for me, too, Auntie Sissy." I agreed.

"ME, TOO!" said Marigold. **"WE NEVER WANT TO SEE YOU AGAIN, EVER!"** Auntie Sissy ran into the bedroom, passing Uncle Peanut and her children, slamming the door.

I walked over to Daisy and said, "Once a Shadow, always a Shadow. Remember our motto: 'The hungry bird eats the worm.' We'll see each other again, I promise, because we're Shadows for life."

Daisy's eyes filled with tears. "Thanks for trying to save Mina, Percy."

"Goodbye, Pimpy. Goodbye, Marigold," Neal butted in, wiping his eyes. He wouldn't shake my hand.

Daisy broke away from Uncle Peanut and hugged me, crying, "I'll always think of you, Scarlet Shadow. Always." She broke a button off her dress and handed it to me. "A lady always gives a man who acts as brave as the Scarlet Pimpernel something to remember her by."

"And I will always love my Pink Shadow."

Officer Anderson left us at our cabin, promising to return within the hour. I gave him the secret password.

My aunt was still in a bad mood. Shooting daggers from her eyes in the doorway of the bathroom, she pointed to suitcases on the floor.

"Pack! No arguments. Just do it!"

She grabbed dresses out of the closet and threw them into a suitcase. We sat motionless watching her pack her suitcase like a woman possessed.

Aunt Momi slammed her hands on her hips, glared angrily at us, and said, "Didn't you hear what I said?"

"Are we leaving now?" Marigold asked incredulously.

"We are leaving *now*. The captain gave me permission to get us off this ship with Sissy."

I questioned, "We can't. We can't leave with Auntie Sissy. She doesn't like us. Are you sick or something?" I examined her face to see if she had any red spots on her big nose.

Shaking her finger at me, she yelled, "I am sick. I am sick and tired of being on this ship. I am sick and tired of you two disobeying me all the time. I am sick and tired of being worried night and day, wondering if you two are dead or alive. I want to get off this ship now and you both are coming with me. Don't worry your little heads about Miss Sissypants, I can handle her."

"I won't go!" I cried, waiting for a slap in the face.

"Yes, you will," she growled, thumping her forefinger on my chest.

I gritted my teeth. "I'm not going and that's that."

Marigold wrinkled her nose and shouted, "And I'm not leaving this ship without Percy."

A mutiny had started in the cabin.

With a deadly rattle in her throat, Aunt Momi loomed over us and said, "Don't either of you dare threaten me again. I'm warning you. Listen to me carefully; I am not leaving this ship without you two. Do I make myself perfectly clear?"

Putting my hands over my head to deflect the blows that I feared were coming, I peeped, "I can't. I promised the captain that I would help him find Johnny."

She panted, "I don't believe you. The captain told me you can leave with me. Listen, there isn't much time to get packed and I don't want to fight anymore so do me this one little favor, please. For many reasons, I can't stay on this ship any longer. I've made a mess of things. We've lost the treasures and I've made a big fool of myself. I've ruined everything. Just thinking about what I've done is making me sick to my stomach." She ran into the bathroom and threw up.

I called into the bathroom, "If you had the treasures back, would you let me stay and help the captain?"

"What do you mean?" she said, storming out of the bathroom, patting her mouth with a wet towel.

"Yes, what do you mean?" Marigold asked, pinching my arm.

I pulled out a suitcase from under the cot and set it down on Marigold's bed. I opened it. Marigold and Aunt Momi gasped at the sight that lay before them. Lying in neat rows, inside the suitcase, were all the treasures.

Marigold gasped. "How did they get in there?"

I explained quickly, "As you know, the treasures were never in the trunk that went overboard. We hid them inside the couch in the writing room. When I came back after falling overboard, I had the feeling that someone was on to us. Of course, that someone, as we know now, was Johnny. One night, I transferred the treasures all by myself back into this suitcase and hid them under my bed, making everyone think they had been stolen from the couch. I never told anyone what I did, just in case one of us was caught by the killer. That way, no one could spill the beans about the treasures but me. And I promised the treasures that I would never rat on them."

"So, here they are, all safe and sound. I even returned the diamond brooch I took by mistake. I got to tell you the statue of the lady you showed us that first night is a pretty powerful spirit. She's the one with the *mo'o* in her mouth. It was she who protected me from Johnny because I had protected her. That's why I didn't die in the coffin. That's why for Aunt Rose, for the wooden lady inside this suitcase, for Mina, for you and for Marigold's sake, I have to stay behind and help the captain catch Johnny. Aunt Momi, please, let me stay."

In a second, Aunt Momi's bad mood vanished. She began crying and hugging us at the same time and cried, "Oh, kids, I'm not mad at you. I'm just mad at myself for being such a fool."

Marigold and I, both very surprised, said, "You're not mad at us?"

Drying her tears, she sniffed, "I'm not, really."

"Then please, let me stay on board, Aunt Momi," I pleaded, kissing her hand.

After thinking for a second, she said, "All right, you can stay with the captain. But Marigold, you have to come with me. I am not leaving this ship by myself. I'm not brave enough. You can't both abandon me."

"I don't want to go. I want to stay with Percy."

Aunt Momi begged, "I know you want to stay with Percy, but please come with me. Uncle Lono is dying to see you and I need you to protect me and the treasures getting off the ship."

Even though Marigold longed to see the action with me, her John Wayne nature to protect the weak and to see Uncle Lono was stronger. Pinching my arm, she drawled like John Wayne, "You all stay behind and get that critter, pardner. I'm goin' to protect Aunt Momi, and the treasures, and see Uncle Lono."

Aunt Momi got the ball rolling, and in ten minutes all our suitcases were packed. My aunt would take her small suitcase with her jewels and make-up and Marigold would carry my suitcase containing the treasures. Once the Aquitania docked, Uncle Lono would retrieve me and the rest of our luggage from the pier.

As she fluffed up her red Rita Hayworth hair and straightened the seams on her stockings, she looked every inch a movie star again.

Aunt Momi gave me final instructions. "We'll meet you on the dock after the ship docks. Even if it's past your bedtime, I'm going to treat you to a very fancy dinner at Fisherman's Wharf. At Joe DiMaggio's, you can order cracked crab with Best Foods mayonnaise until you burst." She stopped talking suddenly. A bolt of lightning had struck her.

She said, stuttering, "Kids, kids, I need to ask you a favor."

"What is it, Aunt Momi?" Marigold asked.

"This means a great deal to me and we must keep this secret to ourselves."

I answered for Marigold, "We'll promise you anything, Aunt Momi. What is it?" My guess was that she going to make us swear not to tell Uncle Lono that we had almost lost the treasures.

Still stuttering, she said, "Never, never mention Captain Spaulding's name in front of Uncle Lono." Her face blushed after she said that.

Marigold and I looked at each other, thinking the same thoughts, and told Aunt Momi that even if Uncle Lono tortured us, we'd never mention the captain's name in front of him.

"Aunt Momi, remember you promised to do something for me," I said looking into her eyes.

"What is it, Percy?"

"You promised that before we leave for Baltimore, you'll help me find the skull."

Relieved that I hadn't asked for the moon, she kissed my forehead and said, "Of course. Of course, I promised we'd do that. Tomorrow, you and I will go hunting for that old thing."

We all jumped at the sudden rap on the door. A voice called out, "Was it peanut butter? No, no, it was mayonnaise. Darn it, what kind of mayonnaise was it?"

I yelled, "Best Foods." Rubbing Johnny's ankh and Aunt Rose's amethyst brooch in my pants pocket, just in case it was Johnny outside, I opened the door and let Officer Anderson enter. Two sailors accompanied him.

After Aunt Momi pecked my cheek and Marigold pinched my fanny, they walked quickly down the passageway with the tall sailor carrying Aunt Momi's suitcase. Marigold carried mine. My sister wasn't about to let any stranger carry the treasures. A sailor, who was the spitting image of big-mouthed comic, Joe E. Brown, walked bowlegged after them, guarding the rear. Scratching my head, I watched them vanish from sight and felt a sudden pang of loneliness.

Standing in the corridor, I looked into the faces of people walking past me. Fondling the ankh, I was on guard waiting for Johnny to lunge out of the crowd and knife me.

Hawaiian idol from the treasure.

CHAPTER 30

ALWAYS EXPECT THE UNEXPECTED

Touching the scarf around my neck, I asked, "Officer Anderson, please take me to Toshi."

"He's on the tug. We took him off the ship on a stretcher." He gave the cabin a final check and locked it up.

"Is Toshi that bad?"

Leading me down the passageway, he answered, "He's a very sick boy. That's why they're taking him to St. Mary's Hospital. The captain is making sure that he gets the best medical treatment."

Feeling the familiar warm prickles go up and down my back, I groaned, "Please, Toshi can't die. Oh, it's this darn curse. Officer Anderson, don't get close to me or my curse will rub off on you, too, and they'll carry you off on a stretcher."

Out on deck, the ship rested quietly in the bay with its bow pointing like an arrow towards the city. The passengers roamed the deck like cows grazing in a pasture. Beyond the Golden Gate Bridge, out on the horizon, a fog bank threatened the city.

On the bridge, the captain paced back and forth, smoking a pipe. He looked disturbed but upon seeing me, he stopped pacing, smiled, and greeted me. He said dejectedly, "We can't find him. I thought we would have the blighter in the brig by now. Percy, can you think of any other hiding place?"

I shook my head.

Behind the captain, Uncle Buster stood at the windows looking out at the city. He beckoned me to join him.

Holding me back, the captain said, "I'm keeping you with me until the passengers disembark. We'll have supper here as soon as the sun goes down."

I nodded, pleased as punch that he still wanted me to stay with him.

"And, my lad," he said, "you're going to watch me dock this big lady tonight. Not many civilians have that privilege. Keep out of my way, though. That's all I ask."

I saluted him and trying to sound like a seasoned salt, I replied, "Aye, aye, sir."

"Join Mr. Crabbe. Keep Tarzan out of mischief." Winking his eye, he turned back to Officer Anderson, and gave instructions on the order he wanted the passengers to disembark the ship. The wounded men were to come off first.

Tarzan's face looked as troubled as the captain's did. Together, we watched the tugboat carrying Aunt Momi, Marigold, Toshi, Queen Bees, Uncle Peanut, the Shadows and the treasures to the Ferry Building. I had a sinking feeling that I might never see the Shadows ever again.

I studied Tarzan's face, and tried to figure out why he looked so serious. I asked, "What's the matter, Uncle Buster?"

Buster frowned. "I've been thinking, Percy."

"What about?" I asked.

"War. I was just down with the wounded men, saying goodbye. I've been visiting them daily. I'm standing here trying to figure out how to describe war and those wounded men to my children. You see, I am too old to go to war and I don't want my children to go war. I don't like war."

"Did you find a way to tell your children about war?"

He mused, "Can't say that I have and maybe I won't tell them anything. Maybe, I'll tell them about the smell of war."

Squashing my nose into the glass, I muttered, "Johnny wants to kill me."

Putting his face next to mine, making his breath steam on the window, he said. "I know that. There are lots of Johnnys out in the world waiting in the shadows to destroy the good in us, and that will only happen if we let them."

"How can I tell if a person is a bad Johnny?"

"Look into his eyes. If you look into eyes that are empty, you are gazing into a soul that has been over to the dark side. I have met many evil men with empty eyes smoking hundred-dollar cigars sitting behind big, black desks. You can't fool the camera, Percy. A camera can photograph men with empty eyes. I know that. A camera records everything in you, without judgment. The camera sees into the depths of your soul. The lens of a camera has the Wisdom of Solomon. American Indians know that. That's why they won't let you photograph them. They believe when the shutter clicks, the camera is so strong that it can draw a piece of your soul out of your body, taking it away forever."

I said, "Is that why movie stars die young? Like Jean Harlow? I bet they died because there wasn't anything left in their souls." It flashed through my brain about all the times my father took photographs of my mother — maybe that's why she died so young?

Buster blew more warm air on the window causing tears to run down it. "Pay attention to this," he said. "When you leave this ship tonight, you are entering out onto a strange world stage, so be careful. You don't have a mother or father to guide you anymore so you must trust your instincts and not wander into the dark alleys in your mind. It's easy to wander down those dark alleys because fear is a powerful thing. Be brave. Take care of your health. You might not believe this because you're young but your health is your most prized possession, more than treasures. Remember if a man or woman can't look you in the eye, run away from them."

Trying to show Uncle Buster that I understood what he had said, I squeaked, "You have good movie star eyes, Uncle Buster, because your eyes don't look empty."

He growled, "Don't say things because you think that will make me like you. Tell the truth, even if it means that people will get angry with you."

I nodded. "I'll try to remember what you said because I don't want to end up an evil, sneaky, lying, creepy person like Johnny."

"The truth is, Percy, there is a bad Johnny inside all of us and that bad Johnny is far more dangerous than the Johnny hiding on this ship. The bad Johnny inside each of us is hard for us to see or even find. But that is the Johnny we have to seek out before that Johnny kills us."

Smashing my face up against the window, I said, feeling creepy all over, "Do you think Johnny would pretend to be a wounded soldier to try and escape the ship tonight?"

Uncle Buster answered hesitantly, sounding disappointed that I hadn't heard him. "We...we...we have thought of that."

I had heard Uncle Buster but my brain had burst with his thoughts in the back of my head. I asked, "Why are you on the bridge, Uncle Buster?"

"Making this movie star scarce. I think I've blown my cover, but why push it?"

"I have a favor to ask, Uncle Buster. When I come to Hollywood, can I visit you?"

"You bet! When you come to Hollywood, I'll see that you meet all the movie stars you want. I'll take you to lunch at the Brown Derby and we'll eat their famous Cobb salad. Do you like Cobb salads?"

"Does it have mayonnaise and spinach in it?"

"I'll see that Chef Michel makes it special for you."

"Do you really mean that?"

"I do!" Buster said.

Buster looked as shiny as Flash Gordon when he said, "I will always remember our code, Percy, 'the hungry bird eats the worm.' "

As the sun set, the city of San Francisco lit up like a Christmas tree. After enduring blackouts on Oahu and sailing in the dark, seeing all the lights was magical. It was as if the good witch, Glinda of Oz, had waved her magic wand and I, like Dorothy, the Scarecrow, the Lion, Tin Woodsman, and Toto, saw the Emerald City for the first time. I stood in awe, watching diamonds sparkle all over the city.

The captain called "Supper's here."

I looked out the window, the lights were disappearing. A fog bank, traveling as fast as an avalanche, was blanketing the city.

The ship's bells chimed midnight. I leaned on the railing and watched stevedores hitch the gangplank up to the Aquitania. Captain Spaulding was better than a magician because in an hour he had wedged a huge Cadillac into a tiny parking space without the slightest effort.

The captain placed Buster and me above the gangway to have an unobstructed view of the passengers leaving the ship. When the gangplank was secured, stretchers with wounded soldiers were carried off the ship into ambulances parked on the pier. Everyone on the pier stopped talking and stared at the mangled bodies being loaded into the ambulances. For the first time, I smelled the stink of war. Officer Anderson checked off the wounded as he matched dog tags with faces.

Once the wounded were driven away, the Japanese prisoners from Hawaii marched down the gangway. They bowed their heads as they walked. On the dock, Army officers lined them up in three rows and checked their identification papers. Once the officers matched the papers with their faces, they, too, were loaded on trucks and whisked away.

Before the captain allowed the rest of the passengers to disembark, he stationed two officers with Officer Anderson at the foot of the gangway to confirm the women and children's identification. The passengers were gathered at the railings and waved to a small crowd of family and friends who had waited all day to meet their loved ones. At tables on either side of the gangway Red Cross volunteers were poised to pass out woolen mittens and caps to the refugees from Hawaii.

Three blasts of the ship's whistle signaled that it was time for the passengers to leave the ship. Women and children, who had been cooped up for ten days at sea, left their manners in their cabins and pushed their way down the gangplank. Most of them looked like strangers to me.

One person I did recognize was Edwina. She had on her black hat and veil, high heels, and the dress she wore at Aunt Rose's funeral. She seemed ill, hanging onto the rail, trying to keep her balance.

I leaned over the railing and yelled, "Edwina. Edwina, I'm up here. Are you all right? Look at me. I love you. I'm sorry I didn't say goodbye to you. Edweeeeena!"

Edwina kept on moving, not looking back as I called her name. Something was wrong. I turned to Uncle Buster and said urgently, "Uncle Buster, look at that lady with the black hat and veil walking down the gangplank."

"Where?" he said.

I pointed to Edwina just as she reached Officer Anderson. "That's not Edwina! Edwina doesn't have shoulders like that." Goose bumps covered my body when I said, "That's Johnny, Officer Anderson! That's Johnny."

I yelled again, "That's Johnny!"

Officer Anderson couldn't hear me because the noise of the screaming passengers filled the air. In shock, I watched Johnny show his papers to Officer Anderson and disappear into the crowd. In a panic, I ran to the bridge. Uncle Buster ran behind me.

I screamed to the captain, "Johnny got away. He was dressed up as Mrs. Brown." I explained what I saw and the captain immediately contacted Officer Anderson by phone. He ordered him to send out an alert for Johnny dressed as Mrs. Brown. Once the order was given, at my urging, the captain and Uncle Buster, made a beeline for Edwina's cabin. I ran behind them, yelling, "I'm coming, too."

In minutes, we were at Edwina's cabin. The Do Not Disturb sign hung ominously on the doorknob. Using his master key, the captain opened the door. It was obvious that Edwina had struggled for her life. Auntie Sissy's polo mallet couldn't have created the damage that was strewn around the room. Mirrors were broken, the mattress was shredded, and duck feathers ripped out of pillows lay around the room like a heavy snowfall. Everything of Edwina's had been broken or ripped apart. Edwina was not inside the cabin.

"Look in the bathroom, Buster," the captain ordered.

Buster tried the bathroom door. It wouldn't budge. He pushed harder and squeezed his way in. We heard a gasp.

Before the captain could hold me back, I was in the bathroom with Uncle Buster. On the floor, crumpled like a broken doll, lay my dearest friend with a necktie tied tight around her neck. Her beautiful face had been bruised as if she had been in a war. Her eyes were wide open. Her fancy cologne bottle, Mark Cross's Lily of the Valley, had spilled, making the bathroom smell like a funeral parlor. The strong, sweet, smell of death sickened my stomach.

I whimpered, "It's my fault. I told Johnny that a witch had the treasures. Johnny must have assumed that Edwina was the witch. I was making that up."

The captain pulled me out of the bathroom as Uncle Buster covered her face with a towel.

I pushed the captain away and sat down on the bed, and cried, "I killed her!" Captain Spaulding sat next to me and put his hand on my shoulder. Uncle Buster sat with us.

Uncle Buster said gently, "Remember what I told you about evil people? Now you know."

I grumbled, "I already knew about evil people because Johnny killed Aunt Rose and Mina. He didn't have to kill Edwina, too. She had such bad luck in her life. Johnny shouldn't have done that to her. She stuck up for me when nobody else did. She really liked me. Look how I repaid her."

Uncle Buster spoke softly in my ear, "You didn't kill her. Don't think like that. Don't let your mind go down that dark alley. Think about what she gave you and you gave her."

"What did I give her? Nothing," I moaned, wandering down a dark alley in my mind.

"You gave her friendship when she needed a friend and she gave you something good, too. You gave her love. Think of this, she gave you the courage to fight."

I turned to the captain and declared, "I've got to get rid of the curse because if I don't, Johnny is going to choke all the people I love with a necktie. If we don't find him, we're all going to die. I'm not going to let Johnny do that to anyone anymore. I hate Johnny." I reached into my pocket and pressed the ankh against my forehead. Looking into the captain's and Uncle Buster's faces, I said defiantly, "And I'm going to do it."

The captain warned, "Be careful, Percy."

I stood up and said in a determined voice, "He'd better watch out now."

The captain stood and said abruptly. "I'll take care of Mrs. Brown. I'll get word to the San Francisco police about Johnny.

"Percy," said the captain, "in rough times I think of my English teacher, Teddy Turner. He made me memorize Thomas Macaulay's *'Horatius.'* Remembering it has always put me in good stead when I find I am in a difficult situation." He recited:

> 'And how can man die better
> Than facing fearful odds,
> For the ashes of his fathers,
> And the temples of his gods…

> Haul down the bridge, Sir Consul
> With all the speed ye may:
> I, with two more to help me,
> Will hold the foe in play.
> In yon straight path a thousand
> May well be stopped by three.
> Now who will stand on either hand,
> And keep the bridge with me?'

"Horatius saved the city of Rome and you can save the world from Johnnys. Become the man who fights the Johnnys in the world, but do it honorably. Always remember that Mrs. Brown fought a good fight. She was brave to the end. And now, Percy, it's time for you to go."

Standing next to me, Uncle Buster took my hand and said, "I'll take care of him until he's in the hands of his relatives. Come, Scarlet Pimpernel, let the captain take care of business."

As we walked down the corridor, I talked to Edwina. "Goodbye, Edwina, my friend. I'm going to find Johnny and kill him. I wish Mother didn't die; she'd tell me the right thing to do. I know killing is bad, Edwina, but I'm putting you into my closet and closing the door. And when I'm ready, I'll open up the closet and let you out. That's when I will have destroyed Johnny."

Buster escorted me down the gangway. We were the last passengers to leave the ship. It was past midnight and the fog had become as thick as in London and I was freezing cold. When I reached the Red Cross table, all the better woolen caps and mittens had been given away. A lady in a gray uniform fit a maroon woolen cap over my head. It covered half my face. She shoved two huge blue mittens into my tiny hands. With Mina's red scarf around my neck, huge mittens on my hands, and a cap that was too large, the ladies said I looked handsome enough to meet all the pretty girls in San Francisco.

Funny, how the mind works. I should have been thinking about Edwina or the man I hated most in world, but I wasn't. My head was filled with thoughts of a midnight supper on Fisherman's Wharf, eating cracked crab with tons of Best Foods mayonnaise. It was food that ran through my head as I waited for Aunt Momi and Uncle Lono to appear. I felt guilty about that. Meanwhile, I swayed around and around on the pier as if I was still on the ship sailing in rough seas. Even though my feet stood firmly on the wharf, the ocean waves rolled under my feet and the ship's engines vibrated through my body. The Aquitania was keeping me her prisoner.

Someone called Buster's name from inside the pier. A handsome woman with jet-black hair and ruby red lips appeared out of nowhere. She rushed into Uncle Buster's arms. They kissed madly. Jabbering excitedly, she told Uncle Buster that a reporter from the *San Francisco Chronicle* was outside so they had better "beat it" before he was discovered to be the movie star who was rumored to have arrived on the Aquitania. Without a word to me, the lady with ruby red lips pulled Uncle Buster into the fog.

The Red Cross ladies cleaned off their tables and they, too, vanished. I stood under the pier lights, alone. The fog filtered lights made the Aquitania into a ghost ship. In the distance, Officer Anderson was giving orders. A sailor ran down the gangway, passing me, and he, too, vanished into the pier. Except for the sounds of water gurgling out of the ship and a jitney racing inside the pier changing gears, I stood alone. The pier was as quiet as the inside of Dracula's castle. Wrapping Mina's scarf tighter around my neck to keep the cold out, rubbing the ankh and amethyst pin in my pocket, my imagination began to work overtime.

Was Johnny waiting for me inside the pier?

A voice boomed, "Percy?"

As I was about to scramble up the gangplank and yell for help, the voice boomed again, "ARE YOU PERCY?"

Remembering Horatius saving Rome ("And how can a man die better than fighting fearful odds"), I boomed back, "I AM PERCY AND WHO THE JOLLJAMIT WANTS TO KNOW?"

"I DO, YOUNG MAN!"

Out of the shadows appeared a man straight out of David Copperfield's London. His face was as round as a beach ball and he had double chins that covered the knot of his striped tie. He wore an unbuttoned gray overcoat that showed a dark striped blue suit underneath. His suit coat barely covered his watermelon tummy. He reminded me of W.C. Fields because he had a bulbous nose. A shiny gold tooth glittered in his mouth and he was bald. What was troubling: his eyes were so tiny, I couldn't tell if the roly-poly man was an evil sorcerer or a kind nobleman. With a cane, he ambled towards me.

"Who are you?" I called out.

His hooded eyes blinked. Then, sounding as wise as an old owl, he hooted, "I'M YOUR COUSIN OLIVER!"

CHAPTER 31

MR. PICKWICK AND CHARLIE CHAN

Tapping my stomach with his cane, he instructed, "Follow me!"

Puffing like an old steam engine, Cousin Oliver "choochooed" me out of the pier. I followed behind him like a wobbly caboose, trying to copy his waddle, not knowing where he was taking me. On the street, in the fog, I passed a garbage can. I spied Edwina's hat and veil smashed into it. I looked around to see if Johnny was spying on me. I picked the hat gingerly out of the garbage can.

Holding Edwina's hat, Cousin Oliver grabbed it out of my hands and stuffed it back into the can. With a harrumph, he prodded me with his cane into a black limousine. Seated with him in the back seat, he spread a green and red Tartan blanket over our knees and called out like a general, "Home, Charlie!"

An oriental man in the driver's seat, wearing a gray uniform, waved to Cousin Oliver with the back of his hand and answered in broken English, "Yeesee, Mr. Oliver. Charlie startee engine now and takee Mr. Oliver home." The chauffeur put on his cap, turned the ignition key, and started the engine. He shoved the limo into first gear, and we leapt like a panther down the street.

Full of questions and scratching my head, I turned to Cousin Oliver and asked. "Where's Aunt Momi? She promised to take me to Fisherman's Wharf to eat cracked crab. Where's Marigold? Where are my suitcases?"

He answered in short sentences, wiping his nose with a handkerchief. "Slow down, Percy. Slow down. Momi went with her prince. Marigold is with them. They're staying at the St. Francis Hotel. I've invited them for dinner tomorrow night. I've made arrangements to have your bags delivered tomorrow."

Scratching my head vigorously, I asked again, "How come I'm with you and not with them?"

Tapping his cane on my knee, he asked, "Don't you like me?"

Digging into my skull with my fingers, I said, "I don't know yet. We just met. Let me look into your eyes."

He opened his eyes as wide as a dime and asked, "What do you see?"

"I see fat little eyes just like mine and that must mean we are related. I'm glad that you're not an evil sorcerer sent to kill me. I have had enough of those bad doodoos to last me for quite awhile, let me tell you."

He choked on his spit. Catching his breath, he slapped his knees and boomed, "Did you hear that, Charlie? That's a good one. That's a mighty good one. Imagine. I'm an evil sorcerer. I'm glad you made me choose this one over the girl. Percy and I are two peas in a pod."

"You chose me? Why?" I asked.

"The prince had room for only one of you to stay with them in the suite. I took you. You're going to stay with me until you leave for Baltimore. Then, off you go to my old maid sisters in Baltimore. Between you, me and Charlie, my two old miserable sisters are dried-up old prunes. I hope you are going to be a handful for those old tightwads. Imagine, making you sleep in their attic like servants. They could have done much better for you and your sister, but they're always saving a nickel. My sisters are the worst kind of rich people, Percy. They are the stingy kind. They've been stingy girls since the day they were born." He chortled saying under his breath that he hoped he was sending his sisters a truckload of misery.

"How are we related?" I asked, watching him laugh so pleased with himself.

Taken aback at the question, he said, "Don't you know who I am? I'm your Cousin Oliver, your grandfather's first cousin. I'm your rich Cousin Oliver. I am the one in the family who has made a success of himself. Ha! That's who I am. And that means you should be very nice to me because someday I might leave you a big surprise in my will."

"How come you're so rich?" I asked, scratching my head.

"If you will quit scratching, I'll tell you about it. Percy, gentlemen do not scratch their heads while they are talking to other gentlemen." His cane hit my knee making his point.

Pulling the blanket closer to me, I said, "Excuse me. I didn't know I was scratching my head. I've had a very sad day. I'll stop scratching immediately if you will please tell me how you made your fortune. You see, I want to be rich, too." Waiting for his answer, I pretended that I was David Copperfield riding with Mr. Pickwick in foggy Charles Dickens' London, about to make his fortune.

After a pause, my cousin whooped, "Ha! Charlie, did you hear that? This boy wants to become rich like me." He pounded his cane on the floor of the car with glee and began his tale. "This is how I did it, Percy. I left my Quaker family back in Baltimore. Leaving them three thousand miles away in Baltimore was my first big step to success. I started out as a clerk in the Wells Fargo Bank here in San Francisco and worked my way up to become President. It didn't hurt that I married a lovely woman who was heir to the Otis elevator family and who had a large amount of stock in the Wells Fargo Bank. I dearly loved that woman. She died on our thirtieth anniversary. Typhoid fever struck her on our first trip to the Far East. I miss that old dear very much. But you learn in life that a person goes to his Maker when his Maker calls him. Another lesson in life is: it is just as easy to marry a rich woman as it is a poor woman, and if given the choice, always marry a rich woman with a sweet nature. You'll never regret it."

"That's what my father says. You talk just like my daddy. He's a Republican. Are you a Republican?"

Wiping a tear from his eye, thinking about his deceased rich wife, he continued, "We never had children. Children weren't in the cards for us."

Without a moment's hesitation, I said, "Adopt me. Let me be your son. After all, we are related."

The limousine's engine hummed in my ears as I eagerly waited to hear Cousin Oliver's reply. "I quite like being alone and I have become much too old to be a father. I find you a fine, stout young lad, but in my bones, I don't think it's in the cards for either one of us."

"Hmm," I murmured.

Charlie shifted into first gear. He was about to drive the panther up a steep hill. When Cousin Oliver looked away from me, I scratched my head vigorously. In the middle of the hill, the limousine's tires skidded. The hill was as slick as ice. Cousin Oliver roared, "Charlie, put on the brake. The tires are old and rubber tires are hard to find. Don't burn them up. Damn it, Charlie, drive up the hill slowly. This war is getting to be a nuisance."

Shifting the car back into low gear, the chauffeur called back, "Yes, Mr. Oliver. War very troublesome now."

When the limousine reached the top of hill without ruining the panther's tires, Cousin Oliver smiled again. I knew he smiled because his gold tooth gleamed in the dark. In a cheery voice, he continued our conversation, "Let me tell you about Charlie, Percy. Two weeks ago, my old driver, Hop Lee, just up and quit on me, and into my life walked Charlie, with wonderful recommendations. Charlie is a perfect jewel. It's like he's been with me all my life. Charlie knows what I want even before I want it. He is an amazing person, Percy. Watch him and you will learn a few tricks. Even if Hop Lee came crawling back to me on his hands and knees, begging for his job back, I wouldn't give it to him because I have Charlie now." He tapped Charlie on the back of his neck with the cane. "Did you hear that, Charlie?"

"Ah, yes, Mr. Oliver. Ah, yes. Very nice. Very nice," Charlie answered.

"Percy, you won't believe his last name. It's Chan."

I whooped, "He's Charlie Chan, the detective?"

The chauffeur shifted the car into second gear and said, "No detective. Just Charlie Chan. Charlie Chan very ordinary Chinese name."

Keeping with his good mood, Cousin Oliver asked, "What sights do you want to see in San Francisco? You'll be leaving for Baltimore in three days. What would you like to do before you go East?"

"I have to find the skull that Grandma took away from Hawaii. I want a normal life again. I'm tired of having a red-headed man wanting to choke me to death." I had answered him truthfully.

Tapping his cane on my knees again, he warned, "You have a very vivid imagination, young man. You are going to be either President of the United States or…"

Charlie interrupted from the driver's seat and said, "…or another Mr. Oliver." In the rear view mirror, Charlie Chan winked at me.

Cousin Oliver mused, "Quite right. Quite right, Charlie. Another Mr. Oliver. But I'm not sure that I'd want any of my relatives to be

President of the United States after that scoundrel President Franklin Roosevelt keeps leading us down the garden path to ruin. That man is a traitor to his class. It's a wonder that that damned rascal hasn't given our country away to the Communists."

Wondering what my Republican father was doing back in Hawaii, I closed my eyes. The sandman dropped a sandbag on my head and I dreamed that Edwina and I were speeding over the Golden Gate Bridge to rescue President Roosevelt. Cousin Oliver and Daddy were boiling the President in a big pot of vegetable soup. Charlie Chan was peeling the carrots.

In the dream, a thought kept reoccurring, "The chauffeur's eyes aren't Chinese. Charlie Chan is as fake as his name."

Charlie Chan and Number One Son. 20th Century Fox studio photo.

CHAPTER 32

ALL WAS NOT RIGHT WITH MY WORLD

I woke from a sound sleep to the smell of baked bread. The bed I slept in felt soft as sleeping on a fat stomach and the sheets were as slimy as an eel. I longed for my Army cot and coarse blanket. As soon as I awoke, I began to scratch the itches on my scalp. I was worried that Marigold's measles were popping in my scalp.

Yawning, I stretched my arms up to a blue ceiling and looked around the room. Thinking back, I remembered a creaky elevator and Charlie Chan carrying me into this room, washing me and putting me under the covers. I also remembered Cousin Oliver kissing me goodnight.

"Velcome, sleepyhead," a plump woman called, peeking her head into the bedroom.

Frightened by her sudden appearance, I asked, "Who are you?"

"Ellen."

"I'm Percy."

"Ya, I know. Get out of bed. Come to kitchen. Breakfast been ready long time."

"What time is it? Where is Cousin Oliver?"

"Ten o'clock. Out of bed. Put on robe. I vill tell you everything when you come into kitchen," the lady ordered.

After she disappeared from the doorway, I jumped out of bed, put on my bathrobe and followed the smell of bacon frying in the kitchen.

Cousin Oliver's flat felt as long and as wide as the Aquitania. Judging from the musty smell, the flat had been furnished at about the same time the Aquitania sailed on its maiden voyage from England to the United States. It smelled like old people lived here. At one end of the flat, I discovered a solarium stuffed with white wicker furniture and tropical ferns in iron pots. At the other end of the flat, overlooking Gough Street, in a formal parlor, hung large paintings of ships and fierce-looking relatives. Victorian furniture and Oriental knick-knacks filled the empty spaces in the parlor, making the parlor feel claustrophobic. Lace doilies were carefully placed on all the red velvet chairs and sofas. Lace doilies on the furniture marked that a lady of refinement had decorated the room. In the foyer, I found the creaky elevator that I had remembered from the night before. Acting like the Scarlet Pimpernel, I made another reconnaissance of the flat, passing four bedrooms, four baths, a dining room, and a kitchen where Ellen stood patiently waiting for me. I located a stairwell to the street. I was relieved. It made for a perfect escape in case Johnny invaded the flat.

Using my spying techniques, I pried from Ellen that she was from Sweden and had been Cousin Oliver's cook and housekeeper for over thirty years. She was shaped as round as Cousin Oliver and smelled as fresh and sweet as the popovers she was baking in the oven. Ellen reminded me of a Snow Queen because she was dressed in a starched white uniform. The uniform matched the color of her cotton candy hair. We became bosom buddies immediately because we were both fat. Our fatness, I thought, fattened our friendship.

My breakfast was placed on a tray set on a small table next to a window. The window overlooked a park. The park was on a hillside framed by our building, a street above the hill, Gough Street below and a gray-stone apartment building on the opposite side of the park. I was excited about seeing two things, both I had seen recently in a Bette Davis movie. Running over the grass, up and down trees were gray furry animals with tails - squirrels. Ellen pointed out a small patch of white at the top of the park. The white patch was left over from a heavy frost from last night's storm. The patch looked exactly like the *snow* I saw in **The Man Who Came to Dinner**.

Wanting Ellen to like me a lot, I blabbed my entire life story as I ate popovers, scrambled eggs and bacon. As each episode of my life became more dramatic, she'd bustle around the kitchen, tut-tutting, "Oh, my. Oh, my. OH, MY!" Buttering my fourth popover, ladling fresh strawberry jam over the butter, I kept on talking. When it was her turn to talk, she told me about Sweden, and her younger brother, Peter. Peter wrote every Christmas that he wanted Ellen to come home to Sweden to cook for him.

Wiping my mouth, finishing off the last popover, I glanced out the window. Johnny was standing under a leafless tree looking up at me. I gasped, "Ellen, come here. There's the man in the park that I was talking about. Come quick!"

Ellen bustled over to the table and looked out the window, and asked, "Where is he?"

I pointed to Johnny. "There. The man wearing the blue cap. Under that tree."

"I see him. Hmmm. We phone Mr. Oliver to call police right away."

"Too late. He's running away." We watched Johnny sprint down the street looking back at us.

At one-thirty, Ellen began to prepare the dinner for my relatives. We were to dine at eight sharp. The guests had been invited for cocktails at seven. As we peeled carrots, Ellen told me that eight sharp was *the* fashionable time to eat dinner in San Francisco.

"Vat wold you like me to fix special for you for dinner, Percy?" asked Ellen, rolling dough for the lemon pie she was making.

"Spinach. That's what I would like. I have to eat lots and lots of spinach so I can become a big man."

"Spinach. Yah, you good boy. All boys in Sveden eat spinach. Vat you like for lunch?" she asked.

Swiping dough from the cutting board, putting it into my mouth, I pleaded, "If you please, Ellen, an egg salad sandwich. I'd be most grateful if you'd make me one. I've been dying for an egg salad sandwich ever since I left Hawaii." Swallowing the dough, I gave my head a good scratch. I had a strong feeling that Marigold's measles were going inside my head.

"Yah! Yah! I make you my famous egg salad sandwich. I get made already. Secret recipe." Ellen opened the icebox door and pulled out a medium-sized bowl filled with egg salad. The bowl was stored in the lower bin next to two bundles of spinach. Ellen was a mind reader.

Taking a spoonful of the egg salad, I shrieked, "This is exactly the same egg salad that Hatsuko made for me back in Honolulu. No one has ever made it like she did until now. Hatsuko was the maid I told you about. The one who died in a car accident. The curse got her, too. What's your secret, Ellen?"

"You promise you vill tell no one vat I tell you?" What she was about to tell me sounded as an important as an FBI agent revealing his secret code.

I nodded solemnly. Ellen opened up the icebox and showed me her secret. The secret made the molecules in my head go haywire. Learning her secret, I spent the rest of the afternoon in a daze.

Because Ellen had revealed her secret, I embellished Uncle Buster's secret about blue eyes. I told her that spinach made men have blue eyes and big things. She tut tutted that Uncle Buster's secret was a well known fact in Denmark. Eating spinach definitely did not grow hair on Danish boys' chests.

In the afternoon, I assisted the Snow Queen preparing the dinner. Once the leg of lamb was in the oven, Ellen sat at the kitchen table and gossiped about the relatives who were coming to dinner. Hearing their idiosyncrasies, I praised Ellen that she should take the next train to Hollywood and become another Hedda Hopper. As the family scandals were revealed, I kept an eye out for Johnny. He never appeared in the park again.

By four in the afternoon, squirrels no longer ran up and down the trees, and the little patch of frost had long disappeared. The little park was a gray moor in Scotland. To add to the gloom, the sky was overcast and a cold wind blew. San Francisco had turned into the most depressing city in the world.

Ellen and I were alone in the flat all day. Charlie Chan was driving the panther doing errands and Cousin Oliver was sitting in his bank making money. While we peeled potatoes, Ellen soaked her feet in a pan filled with hot water. She never stopped talking all day. Watching her feet turn red, my thoughts were always on Johnny. I rubbed the ankh all afternoon hoping against hope that the police had caught him with his pants down.

All was not right in my world.

CHAPTER 33

DINNER AT EIGHT

The dinner party was a benchmark in my life. It was not only a lesson in family dynamics but it was the first time I had been included at a formal grownup gathering. Previously, I had been relegated to the kitchen to eat dinner with the servants and, if called upon, to pass the hors d'oeuvres. Before the dinner was served, I was always sent to bed after shaking hands with all the guests. I didn't sleep on those nights as I kept my ear to the wall listening to the grownup conversation. That night, I became a participant in the grownup world and was no longer a voyeur.

Being with Ellen, who was alone in a strange country, I realized that, I, too, was alone in a strange country. I was sailing on uncharted seas belonging to no one, and no one belonged to me with the exception of my sister. On the Aquitania, I encountered new adventures that had been life threatening, but I experienced them as Huckleberry Finn floating down the Mississippi river. I had treated those experiences from the perspective of a kid and, after all, I was only eight. Now, alone, in a strange city, in strange surroundings with unfamiliar people, I realized how alone I really was and that I had no one to count on but myself. Talking with Ellen that afternoon made me feel like a grownup.

I learned at that dinner party that all families are different, yet all families are the same. At family dinner parties, it's not what is said that's important but what's not spoken that is real.

There were twelve for dinner that night. Everybody was rich. You could tell they were rich because they talked snooty. After being introduced and shaking hands, I was soon overcome by the energy that each guest shot around the room at each other. Overwhelmed by their powerful personalities, I retreated to a corner and watched them act important.

Aunt Momi, Uncle Lono and Marigold were the last to arrive. Aunt Momi and Uncle Lono were already "three sheets to the wind."

Ginger and Margaret, two maids, having been hired to assist Ellen serve the dinner, passed the hors d'oeuvres in the solarium. The hors d'oeuvres, for my taste, were the best part of the dinner. My favorite was the tiny spoonfuls of Ellen's secret egg salad on crispy rounds of toast. When Ginger offered the egg salad rounds on a silver tray, I grabbed five of them, before anyone else could attack them, and stuffed them into my mouth. With a mouthful of egg salad, I confided to Marigold, sitting next to me, that the hors d'oeuvres were just a mere preview of what Ellen had prepared as her main attraction. I smacked my lips and said, "Leg of lamb, but these egg salad crisps are beyond compare."

Slurping a Coke next to me, Marigold looked as if she had been run through a wringer. The telling tale was the black circles etched under her eyes. At my questioning looks, my sister waved her little finger at Aunt Momi and Uncle Lono drinking martinis. I nodded, knowing I had lucked out staying with Cousin Oliver. I whispered, touching her dress, that I didn't recognize her when she walked in. She had on a blue dress splattered with yellow daisies. But what really changed her appearance was that her beautiful brown, curly hair had been frizzed. I confided to her, as a true blue brother would, that now she looked exactly like the bride of Frankenstein. Marigold moaned that Aunt Momi had dragged her, unwillingly, into the beauty parlor at the St. Francis Hotel. There, under a dryer, my aunt treated her to the "works."

"Boy, did you get the works!"

Scraping her Mary Janes on the parquet floor, Marigold grumbled that she hated being a girl. I told her not to worry. No matter how Aunt Momi had gussied her up at the beauty parlor, she still walked like John Wayne. I told her she should be very relieved that "some things never change." She pinched my arm and told me she'd get even for that remark.

Aunt Momi dressed in a lavish gold lame evening gown that made her appear like a storybook princess, but a princess whose hair had been tangled in trees. I bet Marigold that Uncle Lono had chased my aunt through a magic forest with his martini, and my aunt running away caught her hair on the all the branches in the forest — just like Snow White did when she fled the wicked witch.

While sailing the South Seas delivering toilet paper, Uncle Lono had grown a bushy, black beard. The beard turned him into a Russian prince. He wore a blood-red sash that crossed over his black coat from shoulder to waist. He attached a gold medal to the sash. Queen Victoria of England had bestowed the medal on his family when they attended the queen's Diamond Jubilee. He wore it to remind everyone in the solarium that he was better than they were because he was a prince of Hawaii. My uncle strutted around the solarium showing off the medal, downing one gin martini after the other.

I dressed in long pants (a gift from Cousin Oliver), a white shirt and black bow tie. I looked tidy and grownup but didn't come off looking very impressive because I was surrounded by stout men wearing Brooks Brother's suits and tall ladies gowned from the fitting rooms of the fanciest New York and London department stores.

At dinner, I sat between two lady cousins who fluttered their hands like butterflies. Each one displayed large diamond rings on their fingers. One of the lady cousins had a faint black moustache under her nose. The moustache hypnotized me. I couldn't keep my eyes off her upper lip.

Surveying the people around the table, I thought about the secrets that I had learned about them from Ellen that afternoon. They were so different from what I expected rich people to be. I expected them all to be unusual people. They weren't. They were just ordinary people who chatted on and on about the nuisance of gasoline rationing and the lack of good servants since the start of the war. The rich people in the movies were far more interesting.

At the dinner party, their secrets were not discussed. Secrets such as: Uncle Lono had killed his first wife in a drunken brawl by throwing a plate of kim chee at her and breaking her neck. Aunt Momi never kept kim chee in the ice box. Kim chee brought back too many bad memories of the year my uncle spent in a California prison. That was, of course, all before he married Aunt Momi. The night of his proposal to my aunt, he vowed never to drink again. He broke his vow on their wedding night and Aunt Momi broke hers on the Aquitania. Marigold's secret was that she had a birthmark shaped like an anchor on her right backside. As she grew, the birthmark changed into the Eiffel Tower.

Cousin Oliver lived off his deceased wife's money. Without it, he would have had to live in a simple flat with one bathroom and, of course, without Ellen or Charlie Chan to serve his every need. The moustache cousin, everyone agreed, married out of her class. Pepe, her husband who looked liked Roland Gilbert, the movie star, matched his wife because he had a big, thick black, handlebar moustache under his nose. All evening, he watched me ogling his wife's diamonds and moustache. He was an Argentine horse trainer. Aunt Momi said he was built like a horse. I took that to mean that Pepe's hair was as thick and long as a horse's mane. My cousin on my left was tall as a beanpole and wore diamonds all over her body. Diamonds were on her arms, around her neck, on top of her head. She treated her diamonds as casually as if she had picked them off a beach. The beanpole cousin was the richest in the family. Ellen said that she had diamonds in her dresser drawer, in her laundry bin and in a Swiss bank. "Enough diamonds to sink the German navy."

  The diamond lady's husband was a drunk and obese. At the cocktail party, he matched Aunt Momi drink for drink. Ellen told me that he had the reputation for passing out into his soup bowl at dinner parties. Cousin Oliver ordered vichyssoise whenever he came to dinner. He was called Fat. Tilly, who always sat on Cousin Oliver's right, was Fat's daughter and Bobo, who sat next to Aunt Momi, was Fat's son. They took after their father in the fat department and were an unfortunate looking pair. Tilly had buck teeth and Bobo had moon craters plastered all over his red face. Ducky was the daughter of the cousin on my right. She was beautiful, blonde and, fortunately, didn't take after her mother or father in the moustache department. She rode horses. That was her only topic of conversation. There was a rumor that she slept with her horses. The rest of the guests were an undistinguishable bunch. They looked and talked alike. The men were handsome with determined jaws and the women were blonde, bland and sleek. The women plucked eyebrows into arches, smoked Camels and drank Old Fashions, and the men drank Scotch and smoked Lucky Strike cigarettes. Because of their sameness, I could never remember their names.

  Everyone at the table had inherited their wealth or married into it. Never once was there one word of gratitude at having been born with a silver spoon in their mouths. They all had the most remarkable ability to talk about the most inconsequential things and make them sound earth shattering. Subjects of how they played bridge that afternoon, a new recipe or who didn't buy a table for the hospital fund raiser took up most of their dinner conversation. The other half of their conversation went on about a cancelled safari in Africa, their collection of paperweights, a long ago trip to Venice in the spring, after the floods, of course, and their last crossing on the Normandie before it caught on fire and sank in the New York City harbor. What was left out was that Tilly was" preggie" by a sailor serving on an aircraft carrier. The baby was conceived in a doorway when they were saying farewell. A minister had been hired to greet him on his next leave.

They were a very generous people who sat on boards and gave oodles of money away for good causes. But, if crossed by one of the lower classes, or if one of the lower classes smart mouthed them, the wealthy banished that lowly person into exile with the offhand remark, "Who in the hell does he think he is?" They never said it, and would have been hurt and offended at the mention of it but, because they had money, and from a giveaway flinty look in their eyes, they all felt they were a class above those who didn't have money and especially those who worked for them in subservient positions. The biggest snobs of them all were the ones from poor beginnings who had married into wealth. They acted richer than the rich.

There were many plus sides to their personalities. They loved each other, loved to reminisce about the good old days at school when life was simpler. They had been captains for the football teams, pom pom girls and were elected kings and queens of their senior proms. For them life played out as an extension of high school. Most of all, they remained loyal to each other no matter what they said behind each other's backs.

I would have behaved quite well that evening if it weren't for Cousin Oliver continually harping on me to quit scratching my head. He scolded me in front of everyone. "Gentlemen don't scratch their heads at the dinner table, Percy." He said that to me at least a dozen times before the main course was served. I felt humiliated and picked on. My scalp itched terribly and I couldn't help scratching it.

Cousin Oliver, during a lull in the conversation, after he finished talking about his collection of English Sulphides, said in an off-handed way, "Percy, Ellen tells me that you're the reason we're having fresh spinach tonight."

An observation: most parties are acting performances and, to get along and to have a good time, everyone joins the play, plays their part and they don't disagree, on threat of exile, with the host (the director).

Another observation came naturally to me, being a performer. I learned that if I played my part, the fool, I wouldn't get killed at the dinner party. When I attended the university and read King Lear for the first time, I learned that my role of the fool had been usurped by Shakespeare centuries before. The fool could speak the truth and keep his head.

"Hmm," I muttered to Cousin Oliver. I was determined to be in the cast of his play, to be a good sport, and at the same time cope with the itchy scalp. Inside of me, I wanted to scream at Cousin Oliver at the head of the table to leave me alone.

"Tell me, why does eating spinach interest you so much?" Cousin Oliver pressed me, knowing that Ellen must have told him my secret.

"Hmm," I muttered, praying he would drop the subject.

"Hmm is not a proper response, young man. Speak up." Cousin Oliver kept insisting to keep the topic afloat.

"Do you really want to know about spinach, Cousin Oliver?" I asked, trying to sound like I didn't know what he was up to — in other words — playing the fool.

"Yes, I do," he persisted.

"It's a secret," I giggled, trying to act even more foolish.

"We don't have secrets at this table, young man," he replied with a twinkle in his eye.

I said confidentially in a soft voice, "I'll tell you in private after everyone goes home. It's a personal thing." I looked over at Marigold who was enjoying herself immensely at my discomfort. At Cousin Oliver's cue, each guest had perked up and leaned towards me telling me by words and looks not to hold anything back.

Tapping a dessert spoon on her water glass, Marigold, hoping to create another Pearl Harbor, giggled. "Percy, Percy, come on. Tell us. You're among *friends*."

The cousin with the diamonds nudged me with her elbow, purring, "Don't hold anything back on my account, little boy."

"Okay, if you insist," I said.

"We do insist," said Cousin Oliver. He looked immensely pleased that I was about to drop a bomb.

I said, smiling like the Cheshire cat. "I eat spinach so I can have hair on my chest. Marigold wants hair on her chest just like me." I emphasized Marigold's name to get back at her for being snotty to me. I knew Cousin Oliver and Marigold's balloons had burst that I had not blurted out Uncle Buster's secret, amusing the dinner guests at my expense.

The Argentinean horse trainer whooped, "Zats not why I eat spinach."

"Oh, shut up, Pepe," said his wife, tilting her tiara back, rolling her eyes to the ceiling.

Cousin Oliver, looking grumpy, "Young man, where did you hear that piece of poppycock?"

I said in all seriousness. "A movie actor on the Aquitania told me that spinach grows hair on your chest."

"That explains it. That piece of information is as worthless as the acting profession itself." Annoyed that I didn't mention the unmentionable and didn't create a stir at his dinner party; he countered me with, "It's an old wives' tale. Carrots give you strength."

"When I grow up, Cousin Oliver, I'm going to eat spinach and be another Tarzan in the movies." I flexed my muscles.

Cousin Oliver sputtered, "My boy, acting is not a gentleman's profession. And that's the end of that."

"Why not?"

Acting like the lord of the manor, I was dismissed with, "It's not up for discussion!"

The conversation immediately switched to Horace, a banker who worked for Cousin Oliver at Wells Fargo. He had recently bought acres and acres of farmland from a Japanese family being shipped to a concentration camp in New Mexico. That he had bought it for a song was the theme of the conversation. The Argentinean, in his thick accent, said that the banker wasn't taking advantage of the farmer because, "Yi. Yi. All Japanee are sons of debils." I wanted to punch him in the nose and tell him that the Japanese people in the United States were more American than horse trainers from Argentina who marry rich ladies for their moustaches. I would have done that but I was still playing my part in Cousin Oliver's play.

Instead of speaking my mind, I nodded and sipped from a bowl of clear liquid placed in front of me thinking it was a lemon dessert. (A thin slice of lemon floated in the water.) Everyone howled. Cousin Oliver dipped his fingers into the glass receptacle and showed me the correct way to use a finger bowl. I had redeemed myself by being a fool.

Cousin Oliver brought up Johnny. He regaled everyone how the police came to him that afternoon at the bank and that he had "poopooed" the Johnny business saying that it was all the wild imaginings of a native child from the Hawaiian Islands. "What do you expect from a boy who has walked barefooted all his life?"

I stood up and cried out like Patrick Henry, "It's true about Johnny. When I'm dead, you'll all wish you had listened to me. Ask Marigold. Ask Aunt Momi. Ask Captain Spaulding. Ask Mina. She's dead. Ask Mrs. Brown, but you can't, she's dead. She's dead because Johnny murdered her. Ask Ellen. She saw Johnny in the park this morning. Johnny is real and I have to catch him before he catches me. He wants to kill me because I can send him to the electric chair. That's the truth. It's the solemn word of the Scarlet Shadow."

Without taking a breath, I spouted.

"I seek Johnny here.

I seek Johnny there.

The Scarlet Shadow seeks him everywhere.

Will he go to heaven or will he go to hell.

Only the Scarlet Shadow will tell."

Everyone whooped in unison that I was the most amusing aborigine they had ever met, signaling that no one took me seriously. Marigold gave me the V for victory sign which only added to my gloom.

Cousin Oliver tapped on his glass, and said calmly "Sit down, young man, and behave like a gentleman. And, quit scratching your head."

I sat and watched everyone dab their faces with their napkins. It signaled that the dinner was over.

The ladies were sent to the parlor to drink coffee out of Cousin Oliver's German demitasse cups and Cousin Oliver asked the gentlemen into the solarium. In the solarium, they were to smoke Cuban cigars and sip brandy out of crystal snifters inherited from his beloved

Phoebe. Cousin Oliver was a Quaker to the core. He took every opportunity to remind his relatives that he came from simple beginnings and that the finer things in his life he had inherited from his departed wife.

Watching the guests stroll to their assigned salons, I stood aside not knowing where I was to go, with the men or with the ladies. Observing the squint in Cousin Oliver's tiny eyes, I had the feeling the way I was about to go. He was about to summon Charlie to drive me to an orphanage.

As Aunt Momi was about to leave the dining room, Cousin Oliver called her over. Taking her aside, within my hearing, he said, "Momi, you can have Charlie and my car tomorrow morning. Get that boy a haircut."

Fiddling with her purse, Aunt Momi said, "Cousin Oliver, Percy could be telling you the truth about Johnny." The displeasure that Cousin Oliver immediately showed on his face when he heard that piece of news told me both me and my aunt's surprise had flown out of his will.

Showing his gold tooth, gritting his teeth, my rich cousin said, "That's hard for me to believe, Momi. That child's mind is filled with outlandish nonsense. But I'll take your word for it. I must say this for the boy; he did liven up a dull dinner party. I can't abide that greasy Argentine gigolo. If he said one more 'Yi yi,' I would have booted him out of the house. If what you say about this Johnny character is true, then for the sake of the children, I am glad they are leaving for Baltimore on schedule. Join the women, Momi. What time do you want the car and the boy?"

"Ten would be fine and thank you, Cousin Oliver."

"I hope you haven't made another mistake with your prince, Momi. I'm going into the salon and find out what he's all about."

Aunt Momi interrupted, "A word of caution, Cousin Oliver. Be careful. Lono is called the dark prince in Hawaii." Her fingers shook as she took a Camel out of her gold cigarette case.

"Hmm. I have met many dark princes after the earthquake and in the banking profession. Marauders, all of them. These men appear out of nowhere when the world is at war with itself. The only thing they respect is money and power. I am safe from their reach because I have both. I heard what happened to Lono's first wife." He ended the conversation abruptly and gave a knowing look to Aunt Momi as if to say that she shouldn't be playing with fire.

Planting a kiss on Cousin Oliver's cheek, my aunt sashayed into the parlor wishing that she could make a right turn and drink brandy with the men. Watching Aunt Momi depart, he stared at my aunt with an intensity that foretold of doom. Cousin Oliver pulled a cigar out from his coat pocket and lit it.

Stepping out from the corner, I said, "See, I was telling the truth, Cousin Oliver."

Cousin Oliver, startled at my sudden appearance, poked me with his cane as if wanting to make me disappear. With a loud "harrumph," he stomped into the solarium.

I vanished into the kitchen to join Ellen and the maids. Charlie was at the sink washing dishes. He turned around and, for the first time, I saw him clearly in the kitchen light. Standing at the sink was not Charlie Chan but my friend, Mr. Hamada, the Japanese spy. With a quick glance from his stern eyes, I knew that he wanted me to keep quiet.

CHAPTER 34

THE SILVER TONGUE

We were in Cousin Oliver's panther on our way to pick up Aunt Momi at the St. Francis Hotel. I wore Mina's red scarf and a Buster Brown coat. The coat was a gift from Cousin Oliver. Pulling away from the curb, I asked Mr. Hamada questions that had been plaguing me all night.

"What are you doing in San Francisco? Shouldn't you be in Tokyo doing something really important? Are you still a spy? Don't you think Charlie Chan is a pretty stupid name to use? Even the Scarlet Pimpernel would have come up with something better than Charlie Chan. Choo Choo Chan, Chopped Liver Lips, Sun Fat Moon, or even Hong Kong Billy would have been a hundred times better than stupid Charlie Chan."

"Percy," he said, interrupting my chatter. "Look for Bush Street. I left my glasses on the kitchen sink."

"You need your glasses because you're driving like a maniac, Mr. Hamada. Slow down. You're going too fast. I can't read the signs if you drive like mother did." I shoved two pieces of chewing gum in my mouth as he sped down the street like a lunatic.

"Answer my questions," I demanded.

Mr. Hamada's eyes squinted to make sure of a street sign before he made a sharp left. As we turned, the tires on the panther screeched. "Don't call me Mr. Hamada. Do you want to get me arrested? Look for Powell Street."

Taking the gum out of my mouth, I panicked, "Do you really think the FBI would shoot me for knowing you?" My mind flashed to a firing squad. I was standing blindfolded in front of a brick wall. A soldier hollered, "Ready, aim, and fire."

Thinking about the firing squad, I watched the people walking on the streets of San Francisco, bundled in their heavy coats, pointing their noses into an icy wind as if nothing bothered them. To me who was in real danger from a firing squad and Johnny, they were but silly penguins waddling over an Arctic ice field blowing steam out of their mouths.

Mr. Hamada kept interrupting my thoughts to look at the street signs. Licking his chops, he turned the wheel a hard right and headed downhill on Powell Street. He made another sharp right on Sutter Street and swerved into the curb, parking the panther next to the Metropolitan Club. Pulling the key out of the ignition, he rested his hand on my shoulder and asked, "Mind if I smoke?"

"Smoke all you want, Mr. Hamada." Looking into his face, I said, "You don't have to tell me how you got to San Francisco. That's top secret, I know. And I would definitely be killed by the FBI if they knew that I knew that piece of information. But, please answer my other questions and talk fast because we haven't much time. Aunt Momi expects us to pick her up at ten."

Taking a drag on his cigarette, after rolling down the window, he asked, "What do you want to know?"

"Why are you here?"

Resting the key on his lap, he began a tale. "I have been sent on a peace mission. That's all I can tell you. One thing I can tell you is that the Japanese government wants an agreement with the American government that Kyoto and Nara be kept out of bounds from the American bombers. Kyoto and Nara are sacred places to every Buddhist all over the world and should be protected from American bombs."

"Why should President Roosevelt listen to you? Didn't you bomb Pearl Harbor? Why did you bomb Pearl Harbor and kill people?" I questioned.

"That's a complicated question. But I will try to attempt to answer it for you, Percy. Since the day we first met, I have never treated you as a little boy. You know that. I see something in you that you have yet to experience. But, being a little boy, I will make my explanation simple so that you will understand it." He paused, took another drag from his cigarette, and began. "My country, Japan, felt trapped and humiliated by the other more powerful countries in the world. Our oil supplies were drying up and we needed oil badly to run our poor island's economy. There was an embargo. Oil, if you don't know it, makes the world run. Along with oil, we were running out of everything else to survive on our islands and to compete with the other countries in the world. So, we became a conquering country to survive. We miscalculated the American people's resolve. We thought that the American people were weak and spoiled and wouldn't react as they have done."

"What do you mean?" I asked.

"We thought the American people were soft and fat. We were wrong. We let a ferocious tiger out of its cage. Let me say this in defense of my country. No country thinks they are the aggressor; every nation thinks that they are defending something precious when they go to war — their religion, their race, their pride and for their very survival from being wiped off the face of the earth. For Japan, we needed more land for food to keep our people from starving to death. In the beginning that was Hitler's thinking, too. He also had a poor country recovering from a bad depression and he, like Japan, wanted to create a great empire to protect and keep his country strong. It became Mussolini's mission, too. Actually, these men betrayed their people because they enjoyed the war, the killing, the lust for their enemies' blood that has turned into the ultimate battle for power. The men that run our military have become vampires. Once they tasted blood, they can't get enough of it trying to conquer the world. I am here to represent the Emperor of Japan, not Tojo. I have come in peace. The Emperor is now surrounded by a band of Judas' followers."

He frowned and stared ahead smoking his cigarette.

"Why are you at Cousin Oliver's playing Charlie Chan, the chauffeur, and not in Washington D.C. on your mission?"

Closing his eyes, he said, "You know that answer."

"You're playing Charlie Chan because you made that promise to me a long time ago when we first met at the air show in Honolulu. I remember that. That's when I got lost in the parking lot. That day, you said you'd protect me for the rest of my life because I didn't tell anyone that you were a Japanese spy."

He opened his eyes and looked at me. "How did you know that I was a spy?"

"Oh, you were easy to spot. In your chug-a-lug truck, you had all those maps of Pearl Harbor spread out on the front seat. Any stupid numbskull seeing those maps of Pearl Harbor would have guessed that you were a Japanese spy. I don't think you're much of a spy, if you ask me. You should go to Hollywood and learn how to become one. I've got pull with Tarzan in the movies and he'd get you into a Charlie Chan picture. You'd be perfect playing Charlie Chan's number one son with that dopey chop suey accent you are using. Maybe, playing in a few murder mysteries you could learn some tricks."

"What do you mean my dopey chop suey accent? I think I talk good." he said, putting the car key back into the ignition.

I folded my hands in my lap and said, "You speak fake Chinese like Charlie Chan's number one son does in the movies. No real Chinese man speaks like you do. You'll need lots of work on accents if you're going to be successful in the spying business."

I looked into Mr. Hamada's eyes to see what he was thinking. "I know why you like me. It's because of Hatsuko. Hatsuko thought you never loved her because you were always on a spying mission. Did I ever tell you she was my second mama? She told me everything about you except that you were a spy. She didn't know that part of her father. I think you are really doing this for me to make up to Hatsuko because you treated Hatsuko just like my daddy treats me, and that was not being a good father, Mr. Hamada, if I may say so."

Thinking back to the happy days when Hatsuko was alive, I reminisced. "Hatsuko made the best egg salad sandwiches in the whole wide world. Imagine this, I just found out her secret recipe yesterday from Ellen. I had stopped eating egg salad sandwiches after she married Charlie, the sailor, because nobody made them like she did. You must feel bad that Charlie got killed on December 7th." I paused, thinking about the bombs falling on the Arizona. "That's why Hatsuko killed herself. Japan made a big mistake killing Charlie and Mother. That was their big mistake."

Squashing the cigarette into the car's ashtray, Mr. Hamada murmured, "I loved Hatsuko."

"I know you did. I swear in heaven that she knows how much you love her now. Charlie in heaven knows it, too. My mother loves you, too, even if a Japanese pilot killed her in front of my house."

Feeling mushy inside, I said, "Hatsuko's baby, your granddaughter, is living with my Aunt Ella and Uncle Will in Hilo. Lucky for Mary

Emily, being both Japanese and American, whoever wins the war, she'll be on the right side."

"No more talk, Percy."

Before he could shut me up, I got down to business and told him everything that had happened to me on the Aquitania, especially about Toshi and Johnny. I said proudly, "I am now the Scarlet Shadow." Moving closer to Mr. Hamada, I whispered, "We have to be careful because Johnny is here in San Francisco and he could be spying on us right now. He knows that I'm staying at Cousin Oliver's. Yesterday, he was standing in the park watching me. He wants his ankh back, and the treasures. He'll kill me to get them."

Cracking his knuckles, Mr. Hamada grimaced, "An ankh? My friends will find him."

I pulled the ankh out of my pocket and showed it to Mr. Hamada. "Here's the ankh. I'm scared for Toshi because Johnny wants to kill him, too. He's being kept a prisoner-of-war at St. Mary's Hospital. He is actually an American because he was born in Hawaii. Nobody will believe him. He wants to go to Washington, D.C. to see his sister. She is a very important person and she can help him."

Mr. Hamada became animated and said, "I have friends at St. Mary's. I'll see that he gets to his sister in Washington D.C."

Taking the scarf from around my neck and laying it on Mr. Hamada's lap, I made a request, "Since you have friends at St. Mary's hospital, will you see they give this to Toshi. It belonged to Mina. After the war, let's you, Toshi, and me all live on Waikiki Beach. I'll make Hatsuko's egg salad sandwiches all day. We'll eat them till we burst. Oh boy, that sounds like heaven to me."

"At my age, Percy, too much mayonnaise gives me gas," Mr. Hamada confided.

Watching me fiddle with the ankh in my hands, Mr. Hamada looked concerned, and asked, "Let me have that."

Looking at the ankh, I asked, "Why?"

"So I can protect you. People who wear that belong to a secret society. I know that. They have no allegiance to any country or to anyone but their master. They work for the dark side."

"The dark side?"

"They are a group of evil men sworn to do evil deeds. With me having that ankh, Johnny will leave you alone. That's all he wants from you is the ankh. I agree with you, he will kill you to get it."

"He gave me one as a present. It's at the bottom of the sea."

"You are lucky it is there. He probably wanted to make you one of them. Let me have the ankh."

Taking Tarzan's advice to look people in the eyes when in doubt, I studied Mr. Hamada's eyes. His eyes looked at me as kind as my mother's eyes did. I placed the ankh into his waiting hand and he shoved it into his pocket.

I had a sudden feeling of shyness come over me knowing that Mr. Hamada still wanted to protect me. Nobody had wanted to protect me for a long time. I mumbled softly, knowing that samurai warriors didn't like to hear mushy things but said it anyway, "You're the father I've always wanted."

He turned the key making the engine hum, shifted into first gear, and steered the panther up Sutter Street. As we passed a nosy bus blowing diesel smoke into the open window, the samurai warrior mumbled something under his breath that I couldn't quite hear.

Driving up Sutter Street, I said, "Mr. Hamada, sometimes I hate the Japanese."

"Why?"

"A Japanese pilot killed my mother."

"I know."

"I'm sorry to have to say that to you, Mr. Hamada, you being Japanese and all."

"Have you *ever* thought that there might be a boy in Japan, just like you, who hates Americans because an American soldier killed his father?"

I put my hands over my face and replied, "Life gets so complicated, doesn't it? That's why I like going to the movies. In the movies, I can forget things."

One of Mr. Hamada's connections stole a copy of the Aquitania's manifest. Written next to each passenger's name was the name of a sponsor or relative on the Mainland. Next to my name was Cousin Oliver's with his address on Gough Street. Mr. Hamada bribed Cousin Oliver's chauffeur with gold coins to take a long vacation, which he did. Mr. Hamada with his counterfeit recommendations was hired on the spot as Cousin Oliver's new chauffeur.

Mr. Hamada parked the limousine on Geary Street, next to the St. Francis Hotel. The St. Francis Hotel was known throughout the world for its perfectly chilled martinis. I stepped out of the car, skipped around the corner, and twirled around through the hotel's revolving door letting its momentum "ush" me into the lobby.

The lobby was as dark and somber as Dracula's castle. Massive Italian marble columns held up the ceiling and a large mural hung over the front desk. On the mural an artist had painted pale, half-clothed men and women lounging around a lake dying of tuberculosis.

Brown leather chairs surrounded a table in the center of the lobby. Middle-aged women sat in the chairs, dressed to the nines, looking around for a friend to show up. The ladies wore hats and gloves and crossed their legs as demurely as did Kay Francis, the katish movie star. Adding to their sophistication, they painted black lines up the backs of their legs to simulate silk stockings no longer available because of the war. Crossing their legs, and wearing open-toed six inch high heel shoes, they talked to themselves in lady-like whispers.

What caught my eye was a polished brass spittoon at the entrance to a bar. The Oak Room was the only happy sounding place in the entire lobby. Maybe, it was because women were forbidden in the bar. Laughter erupted from inside the dark cavern in loud staccato jolts. It was common knowledge that in the afternoons, starting at four, the Prince of Hawaii and his warriors drank chilled martinis in the Oak Room.

On this morning, the lobby was jammed with soldiers, sailors, and marines. The grand, gloomy Old World lobby had turned into a Greyhound bus station. Servicemen, off to war, were cooing farewells to pretty young girls wearing wilted orchid corsages. The men in uniform grabbed the girls around their waists, saying feverish good-byes. It gave me the same old, familiar feeling that I first felt on the day I looked into my mother's coffin.

I pushed my way through the crowd. A freestanding sign stood next to an open door. The sign announced that Harry Owens and his

Hawaiian orchestra, starring the comic hula dancer, Hilo Hattie, were entertaining nightly in the Mural Room. A wave of homesickness crashed over my head. I wanted to be back on top of Aunt Rose's coffin sailing for Waikiki Beach. Seeing the sign, I had a stomachache longing for my home.

I maneuvered through the crowd, coughing on the cigarette smoke, elbowing couples in the ribs, seeking Aunt Momi. Not finding her anywhere in the crowd, I asked at the front desk for Princess Momi's suite. Acting more queenly than Bette Davis did playing Queen Elizabeth, the desk clerk said in a grand manner, "My dear sir, the madam you are requesting is residing in the royal suite."

On my way up to the suite, the elevator, frustratingly, stopped at each and every floor. To keep from going mad, I observed the people. The elevator had to be crammed with everyone who ever lived in San Francisco. A fat old man wearing a dark suit, a brown and white striped tie, and a felt hat on his head took up most of the room. He brandished a cigar in my face as if he owned the hotel. Next to me, a young lady painted her lips bright red. She grabbed a serviceman's belt. The serviceman, in turn, smiled down at her like a wolf ready to unbuckle his belt and eat the girl up for breakfast. An older woman kept staring at her reflection in the elevator door preening like the Queen of Sheba. She had to be somebody very important. A slim, young woman with a tiny, moustache above her lip looked exactly like my cousin had who married Yi Yi Pepe, who was hung like a horse. In contrast, my mother was a lady. She took off her moustache with hot wax on Sundays.

I knocked on a door with a sign that read, The King Kamehameha Suite. A voice boomed from inside calling me to enter.

I opened the door carefully. The King Kamehameha suite didn't look at all royal Hawaiian that morning. Uncle Lono and his boy friends had been having luaus in the suite since the day Aunt Momi arrived. It looked as if my uncle and his warriors had played war. Ahead of me, on the carpet, was a minefield of paper takeout cartons from Trader Vic's. A cart was to the side of me overfilled with empty gin bottles and plates stacked haphazardly leaning like the Tower of Pisa.

What completely took the wind out of my sails was seeing the treasures laid out on a table behind the couch. The diamond butterfly pin sparkled next to the wooden lady with her long chichis. All the treasures were accounted for except for the jade necklace.

Uncle Lono, framed against the window, boomed, "Shut the door."

I whirled around, shut the door, and stood at attention waiting for my next order.

"March!" I goosed-stepped over to him, pretending I was a Nazi soldier parading in front of Hitler. I tried to keep my eyes only on my uncle.

As I marched, I wavered and spied the red sash that Uncle Lono had worn hanging over a chair near the bar. The gold medal from Queen Victoria lay on the floor discarded. When I stood in front of my uncle, he ordered me to turn around and face the table with the treasures on it.

I did a perfect about-face. Standing behind the treasures were Aunt Momi, Marigold and another woman who looked just like Aunt Rose, only younger. They smiled at me. I gave them back the same smile that Mata Hari gave before they shot her as a spy.

The Hawaiian lady took my breath away. She was movie-star gorgeous. My knees wobbled looking at her. I memorized her every detail. She had on a brown suit, carried a mink coat over an arm, and a fur hat cocked on her head. She was a Russian countess in a Greta Garbo movie.

"Percy," boomed Blackbeard's cannon from behind.

"Yes, sir!" I squeaked.

"This is my sister, Princess Alice Kapiolani."

I turned around and asked Uncle Lono, "Is Princess Alice a movie star?"

"Alice is not a movie star." He continued, "Young man, my mother, Alice and I want to thank you for saving our Hawaiian heritage." He pointed to the treasures on the table. "It would have been a terrible loss for the Hawaiians and our family if our heritage had fallen into the wrong hands or were lying at the bottom of the sea."

Softening his voice, he asked, "Percy, which of these treasures is the most powerful?"

I remained silent.

"This one!" my uncle said, pointing to the wooden god whose face looked as if it wanted to kill me. The god had angry eyes made out of shells and an open mouth with a protruding tongue.

"Look at him carefully. Does he frighten you?" I nodded, waiting for the wooden statue to leap off the table and bite me.

Standing next to me, Uncle Lono asked, "Do you know what part of the body Hawaiians believe is the most powerful? Look at the god closely and see if you can discover the answer to my question. What part of him stands out prominently?" I shrugged.

"It is this!" my uncle said, pointing to the god's protruding tongue. "The tongue is the most powerful part of our body because the tongue speaks all the things our head thinks. It is the tongue that creates the beauty in the world. It is the tongue that destroys the beauty in the world. The tongue addresses all that is good and all that is evil in each one of us. The tongue can speak the truth or the tongue can lie. The Orientals call it the yin and the yang. Peace and war. What comes out of our mouths, what we say, is our most powerful weapon. Remember, it is the tongue that lies for us and it is the tongue that speaks our truth. So, we need to choose our words carefully or not speak at all. I have learned the hard way and still am learning that some things are best left not said."

"Gaze into that warrior's face. That face was carved centuries ago so fierce that when a Hawaiian made a request from this god for something that he wanted to happen to him, a wish he really wanted to make come true, the person making the request would be very, very careful in the asking. That is why the tongue protrudes so. It is to remind us to be careful what we ask for. For what we ask for will come to pass, as surely as I am standing next to you. But, everything we ask for comes with strings attached to it. Wishes do come true, Percy, but they come in their own time and always at a price. Sometimes, the price is so high that you wish your request had never been made. Make sure that when you ask for something it is really something you want, something you really need. For when the request is granted, you may no longer want it or need it or may have even come to *hate it*. Can you understand that?"

"I think so." I said, looking at the ferocious god and thinking about my wish to be the Scarlet Pimpernel, wondering what price I would have to pay to become a hero.

I remember standing in the middle of the room that morning wondering what Uncle Lono had wished for. Was he talking about himself? Uncle Lono wished to marry Aunt Momi because she was a beautiful princess. Aunt Momi came with strings. She swore. She had children from Uncle Hans, and now he was saddled with Marigold and me. Aunt Momi wished for a handsome prince to ride up on his white steed to sweep her off her feet and take her to his castle to live happily ever after. Uncle Lono had a black Packard and a house in the country. His string was that he had a terrible temper and that he was a two-fisted drinker.

Pressing his hands on my shoulders, Uncle Lono spoke to me like a prince, "My sister and I want to give you something for your bravery." From his pocket, he brought out a small black box and handed it to me. I opened the box and pulled out a silver chain. Hanging on the chain was a tiny silver tongue.

As I rubbed the silver tongue with my fingers, Uncle Lono decreed, "This silver tongue will help you remember to speak wisely and know that all wishes can come true." He took the chain from my hand and handed it to Princess Alice. She placed the chain over my head and kissed my forehead. I was going to explode. Beautiful women make fat, ordinary people weak at the knees.

I knew at that moment the silver tongue was far more powerful than any ankh. Johnny's ankh symbolized evil. The silver tongue symbolized life's possibilities.

Wearing a yellow sweater and pleated blue skirt, Marigold pranced around the room showing off a silver tongue around her neck, too. Princess Alice gathered Marigold and me together and waved her hand over our heads and blessed us. "To you, children, who are about to embark on your new adventure for Baltimore tomorrow night, God bless you and may this silver tongue let you speak the truth and keep you from all harm."

I looked at Aunt Momi. She was dressed very "San Francisco katish." She had on a gray Chanel suit with cuffs trimmed in black fur, and a dead mink biting its tail. She wrapped it around her neck. The velvet turquoise squashy hat on her head matched a blue-green emerald ring on her index finger. Gold bracelets jingled when she moved her hands, making her tinkle like a Japanese wind chime.

The ceremony finished, Uncle Lono patted me on the back, walked to the bar and fixed his favorite breakfast, a gin and tonic. I loved Uncle Lono when he wasn't drinking gin.

Aunt Momi looked around the room for her purse and, sounding as if she was reading off a grocery list, instructed Uncle Lono, "I'm taking Percy to find Mama's skull. You, Alice and Marigold are to meet Sissy at the Cliff House for lunch. Noon sharp. Don't get Sissy mad, Lono. She's in a bad mood. She spent last night with the drunks. She checked herself out this morning and is suing the hospital. She's not over her measles. Sister Mary Louise, thank God, was sent back to the convent. Be sweet to Sissy if you want to use her house in Carmel next weekend. She won't be there; she's visiting Neal and Daisy in Pasadena. You'll need her house if you're playing in the Brown golf tournament at Pebble Beach. After lunch, take Marigold to the Fleishhaker Zoo and after that, treat her to a roller coaster ride at Playland on the Beach. You promised her a roller coaster ride last night just before you and the boys started dumping water on the pedestrians."

Marigold's eyes danced the minuet when she heard the roller coaster word. No way was she now going to join us on what she had teased was a mad, wild goose chase to find the skull.

When Uncle Lono was around, Marigold forgot me. That was fine because my sister hadn't been happy since the day my father left us for Kathy. Having fun with Uncle Lono was as if she was with our father.

As everyone snuggled into warm coats, I reminded Uncle Lono and Princess Alice about Johnny wandering around San Francisco, and warned, "Johnny could be casing the joint right now. I don't think the treasures should be left on that table unguarded."

"I've taken care of that." He snapped his fingers and Uncle Peanut, wearing a coat and tie, not looking as sad as when I last saw him, sauntered out of the bedroom. He winked at me. I winked back, showing him the silver tongue around my neck. I gave him my million dollar smile.

My uncle ordered, "Herman, pack these things up. Take them down to the manager's office while we're gone. Have the manager keep them in the hotel safe until we check out!"

Watching Uncle Peanut pack up the treasures, I knew without a doubt, it was Uncle Peanut who put in a good word for the Scarlet Shadow.

Princess Alice excused herself to get her purse from her suite across the hall. As soon as she left the room, Uncle Lono groaned, "She's going to do it, Momi. I know it. Couldn't you talk her out of it?"

"I tried to reason with her, Lono, but she'll have none of it," my aunt sighed, lighting a cigarette.

Marigold whispered into my ear that Princess Alice hated her brown skin on the mainland. When she walked the streets of San Francisco, she did not like the strange way haoles stared at her.

Sure enough, when the beautiful princess returned, her face was caked with Max Factor makeup five shades lighter than her skin. The most beautiful woman in the world, in three minutes, turned herself into a painted circus clown.

Before we left to ride the elevator down to the lobby, I shook Uncle Peanut's hand and thanked him on behalf of the Scarlet Shadow. In the elevator, I tenderly took Princess Alice's hand into mine and, on my tiptoes, whispered into her ear, "I want you to know, Princess Alice, brown is my very favorite color."

I knew that the silver tongue would say it was alright for me to lie to make a princess feel beautiful. The princess kissed my forehead as we exited the elevator. Blue is really my favorite color.

Mr. Hamada stood next to the brass spittoon searching for us. It was a half past ten. I panicked thinking that most of the morning had flown away. Uncle Lono had complained to Aunt Momi that he really didn't want to have lunch with his sister. Aunt Momi and Princess Alice reminded him that Auntie Sissy was paying the bill. Hearing that, the royal party slid regally into a taxi with my uncle telling the driver to head for the Cliff House.

As the taxi rounded the corner, Marigold waved to me from the back seat. She had gone to seventh heaven. From the smile on her face, Daddy was sitting next to her.

Aunt Momi turned to Mr. Hamada. "Charlie, do we have time to get this ragamuffin a haircut? The barbershop is just down the hallway, off the lobby, and it won't take long. I can't, in good conscience, send him back to Cousin Oliver looking like a shaggy dog. And, my cousins in Baltimore would never forgive me for sending them this scruffy looking thing."

Playing the inscrutable Charlie Chan, Mr. Hamada, talking in his B-movie Chinese accent, agreed with my aunt, saying that it was a great "egg fu yung" idea. I wanted to laugh in his face. I was itching to tell him to get into another line of work. Thank God, the silver tongue was working overtime and kept me from blowing his cover.

Walking on either side of me, Aunt Momi and Mr. Hamada escorted me down a long carpeted hallway. We passed fancy shops that advertised thousand-dollar dresses, five thousand-dollar diamond bracelets, and in one shop a jade necklace was on sale for $200,000. It was the jade necklace we had brought from Hawaii.

The hair on the back of my head stood straight up. I turned around and looked up at the second level of the lobby. On the balcony, a man with red hair disappeared behind a pillar. I faced forward and kept walking knowing that, as long as Mr. Hamada was beside me and he had the ankh in his pocket, and that I had a silver tongue hanging around my neck, I had nothing to fear. Nothing bad could happen to me anymore.

I sat in the barber's chair. The barber lifted a clean, starched white sheet over my belly and prepared to cut the long blonde locks off my head. Max, the barber, said he was one of the last survivors of the 1906 earthquake. I could tell he was old without him telling me. His skin smelled like an old wet dog. He raised his hand, opening and closing his shiny scissors rapidly. In the mirror, he resembled a mad scientist about to operate on a munchkin's brain.

As Max prepared to make his first snip, he adjusted the eyeglasses on his nose, and closely inspected my hair. Stretching the strands of my hair apart, he jumped back banging into the mirror behind him. I thought he had caught on fire because he yelped so loud that everyone sleeping on the benches in Union Park must have woken up. He gasped, turned to Aunt Momi and in a horrified voice, said, "Madam, this boy is loaded with nits!"

CHAPTER 35

THE RUBBER BAND WITCH — A GATEKEEPER

"Nits?" I cried, as the barber probed my scalp with his comb.

"Nits!" thundered the voice of God.

The word, nits, sent everyone in the barber shop running for a bomb shelter. A nit bomb had exploded. "What are nits?" I asked Max.

"Lice," he said, pulling apart the strands of my hair. Aunt Momi and Mr. Hamada retreated to the corner of the barber shop and looked at me as if I was a three-headed monster.

"Are they little?" I asked.

Max sang out like an Italian tenor. "Tiny bugs with little fat legs that lay eggs."

I pouted, "Aunt Momi, I told you there were bugs on that old Army cot. But, oh no, you wouldn't believe me. Nobody ever believes me. Now, do you believe me? And because you wouldn't believe me, bugs with fat legs are eating out my brains."

My aunt walked tentatively to the barber to examine the bugs with Max. Watching my nits having babies, my aunt said calmly, "It's not that bad, Percy. Lots of people have nits. Nits are very common in Hawaii and, I dare say, in San Francisco. Isn't that true, Max?"

"Not in my barber shop, madam."

Sticking out my lower lip, I grumped, "If they are so darn common, you take 'em.

Consider my nits as an early Christmas present. Let them have babies in your hair. They'll build castles in your red hair because you're a princess. I can hear them crying for you in my hair. 'We want to live with royalty.' Wish Johnny was around; I'd give him a fistful of my nits."

Mr. Hamada, scratching his head, put in his inscrutable two cents, "No worree, Percy. Nits very easy to cure. I have many times."

Max said, "Madam, I have the very thing that will do the trick." He stooped down, opened a cabinet door and pulled out a tall, skinny bottle filled with what appeared to me to be lemon soda. Max presented the bottle to Aunt Momi and made her smell it.

"Ooooowee," she said, crinkling her nose, "if that doesn't kill the bastards, nothing will."

"Let me smell it," I demanded.

Max put the bottle under my nose. "That stuff is not going on my head. It's pure turpentine. It's gonna make me smell like a painted house. I'll go bald like Uncle Peanut and the nun."

"Quit fussing, Percy. Get it over with, Max. Pour it all over his head. We're already late looking for that damn skull."

Max cut my hair short after he washed it, and the coup de grace came as Max's yellow nit medicine was poured all over my scalp making the barber shop smell of stale pee and old paint.

Getting out of the barber's chair, breathing in the fumes of the medicine, I put my hand on my chest and spouted patriotic thoughts. "Attention America: Nits rule the world. The rich, the poor, the black, the white, the yellow, Cousin Oliver, Marigold, Mr. Hamada, Johnny, Hitler, and all the brown people like Uncle Lono and Princess Alice are someday going to be conquered by nits. Nits hate nuns, fascists and Uncle Peanut because they are baldheaded. Viva la nits! God Bless Everyone in the Whole Wide World."

"Simmer down, young man," was the only applause I received for my patriotic presentation.

Aunt Momi gave Max a lavish tip to keep his mouth shut and swore me to secrecy threatening to send me to a prison where they served dry tuna fish sandwiches without mayonnaise. "If Cousin Oliver learns that he is housing a nit carrier, you will be booted out and forced to sleep like a hobo on the streets of San Francisco." My aunt emphasized that my nits were to be the best kept secret since the surprise Japanese attack on Pearl Harbor. I promised Aunt Momi that I would kill myself before Cousin Oliver knew that nits were having babies in his flat. Leaving the barbershop, Aunt Momi added Ellen to the list of "don't tells." Cooks, she informed me, were the biggest blabbermouths in San Francisco, especially those born in Sweden. Uncle Lono was also added to the list. She told me I could tell Marigold only after the train passed Chicago.

"Aunt Momi, just think of it, if you had nits, you'd have to shave your head like Uncle Lono."

"Yes, dear, that's just what I was thinking about."

Aunt Momi and Charlie sped me through the lobby of the St. Francis Hotel like a freight train hauling a caboose filled with dangerous chemicals. My stink drove the people to spread apart as I choochooed between them. I pretended that I was Moses parting the Red Sea.

Out in the sunlight, I zigzagged like the Aquitania through the streets of San Francisco, trying to get to the panther without being sunk by the hoards of people. I had never seen so many men and women walking so fast, going nowhere, and heading straight for me. Aunt Momi let go of my hand and, before I knew it, I was swept away with the hoards up the street. I was drowning inside the current of people. Charlie Chan grabbed my hand like a lifeguard, and steered me once again for the panther. It was my first experience walking in a real city.

When we arrived at the panther, Aunt Momi was already sitting in the backseat and ordered me up front with Charlie. Her hat lay beside her. She was vigorously brushing her hair. In the rearview mirror, I saw her examine the brush carefully for signs of my critters.

"Where we go, missy?" Mr. Hamada asked.

"Let me catch my breath, Charlie."

Looking relieved, she returned the brush back to her purse. She smiled to herself as if she had just received a pardon from going to the electric chair. Interrupting her celebration, I said, "I'm glad you don't have nits, Aunt Momi. Now, let's get down to business and go to the house where you lived as a little girl. The dentist that had the skull lived next door to you, right?"

"That's my idea exactly, Percy." She was checking her face with an open compact.

"Where's that, missy princess?" Charlie Chan asked.

"Charlie, it's on the other side of the Bay Bridge. Do you know how to get to Berkeley?" She smeared a layer of lipstick on her lips.

"I do, missy," Charlie answered.

"Once there, I'll direct you to the Uplands. That's the street where I lived as a child. Let's be on our way, Charlie." Aunt Momi waved her little finger at Charlie as she closed her compact.

Mr. Hamada adjusted his chauffeur's cap, sprang the panther into action, rounded the next corner swiftly, crossed Market Street, and headed for the Bay Bridge. I looked back to see if we were being tailed. Once on the bridge, the panther gracefully slid over the metal bumps making soothing humming sounds. We were riding over Hatsuko's metal washboard. We stopped at a toll booth.

While the engine idled and Mr. Hamada handed coins to a man in the booth, I spotted Johnny three cars behind us. He was driving a red roadster convertible. I didn't say anything because I didn't want Aunt Momi to faint. I was sure that Mr. Hamada spotted him because, after he paid the toll, he gunned the panther over the bridge faster than Flash Gordon drove his rocket ship to the moon.

Flying past the University of California, a clock in a tall stone tower chimed twelve bells. It signaled that time was running out. It was already noon on my last day in San Francisco. Aunt Momi directed Charlie to the Uplands. The red roadster kept following us.

Thinking that, in a few minutes, I would be holding the skull in my hands, I could feel blood boiling in my head. In my excitement, I knew deep down inside of me that once I held the skull in my hands, no more bad things would ever happen to me or to the people I loved. I would be protected from the killing hands of Johnny. Even better, once the skull was buried in the Hawaiian sand dune, the curse would be lifted off my entire family. The Johnnys in the world would disappear and I would live happily ever after.

Mr. Hamada took a left at the Uplands and headed up a hill. "Charlie, stop in front of that white three-story house. That one on the right nestled in the hillside."

It was my grandparents' home where my mother and her sister had spent their childhood. Next to the home was a two-story brown, wooden Victorian mansion. The house was old, worn, very dilapidated, and had seen years of neglect, a house that looked as if it had barely survived the 1906 earthquake. This was the home where the dentist had lived.

Mr. Hamada parked the car next to the curb. I thought I was going to faint from all the excitement. I was tingling all over. Taking a deep breath to calm myself, I smelled the scent of the eucalyptus trees.

The scent snaked into my nostrils weaved its way into my head and cleared my head of all the cobwebs. I became focused again.

I insisted on accompanying Aunt Momi to the front door. The Scarlet Pimpernel would never let a lady sally forth into danger alone. Outside of the car, the smell of the eucalyptus trees was far stronger than the smell of the nit medicine radiating from my head. Hand in hand, we walked up a series of red brick steps to the front door. Aunt Momi coughed as she climbed the stairs, complaining that the "goddamn cigarettes" were going to kill her someday. Holding onto me, she took off her gloves and knocked on the large oak door.

Aunt Momi banged again, this time using the large, tarnished brass knocker hanging on the door. She banged many times before the door opened slowly.

Peering around the corner of the door was a middle-aged woman with black hair pulled to the back of her head. The hair was pulled so tight that it stretched her face as if two rubber bands were attached to the back of her neck. Her lips snapped when she talked. She wore a gray suit trimmed in black, with large, round black buttons running down the front of her jacket. A strand of white pearls hung lonely around her neck. Her neck reminded me of a turkey without the wattle.

Pawing at us like a cat, she shooed us away from the door, flicking her fingers. Kicking me with her clunky Brooks Brothers loafers, she growled, "Go away." Without speaking another word, the lady slammed the door in our faces.

I hated her on sight. Determined to find the skull, my aunt rapped on the brass knocker, this time making believe she was punching the lady in the face.

The door jerked opened. I turned the lady into a witch. The witch yelled, "Stop knocking. I'm going to call the police if you don't quit pestering me."

Aunt Momi, using her sweet as pie voice, asked, "May I speak to you for a moment?"

The witch raised her nose in the air, lit a cigarette in a long brown tortoise shell holder, arched her eyebrows up and said flatly, "No."

"Excuse me," Aunt Momi said, continuing to speak sweetly, "I used to live next door."

"What has that got to do with the price of eggs? Get away from my door or else I'm going to call the police. I am very busy. I have something boiling on the stove." She was cooking poisoned apples for Snow White.

Aunt Momi's eyes radiating danger, said, "My dear, two quick questions and we'll be out of your hair."

"Make it snappy."

My aunt asked politely, "Are you related to the dentist who lived here?"

"No!"

"Do you know where he or his family went to?"

"He died." The witch flicked the cigarette off the holder and with her two hands began to close the door.

Feeling desperate enough to jump off the Golden Gate Bridge, I wedged my fat body in the door before she could close it. Remembering how the Scarlet Pimpernel dealt with desperate situations, I yelled, "Stop, villain!"

The witch screamed, "Get out of my house. I'm calling the police right now. I'm warning you, fat boy. Get out of my house."

"You're not going to call the police!" I shouted, jumping into the vestibule of her home.

"Why... why not?" the witch stuttered. Taking a good look at me, she yelped, "You're the spitting image of Hermann Goering."

That made me reeeally angry. I yelled, "Don't you mention that horrible Nazi's name in my presence."

Looking frightened, the witch asked, "Tell me, little fat Nazi, why shouldn't I call the police?"

"Let me think about that."

Quickly, I turned and slammed the front door, leaving Aunt Momi stranded on the front porch.

I cased the joint. The witch's house was decorated in shades of gray, white and beige. Nothing was out of place. The house was as antiseptic as a hospital. I found my plan of attack.

"You won't call the police because I have nits. Nits are lice. Lice are very catching! Call the police. See if I care. While you're telephoning them, I am going to walk around your house placing nits all over your furniture. Nits, if you don't know it, eat your brains out slowly and if you don't die, you'll have them in your hair for life. By the time the cops arrive, your brains will have turned to mush and your perfectly perfect house will be ruined."

"Stop," she shrieked. "Don't go any further into my living room. If you and your nits get out of my house now, I won't call the police. Now, be a good boy and leave my house. Your dirty shoes are ruining my carpet. Stop doing that to my furniture. Are you listening to me?"

I pulled an imaginary sword out of my belt and challenged her, "I'm not leaving here until you tell me everything you know. Rubber band witch, I want the truth NOW!"

"I — I — I will tell you everything if will you get out of my house NOW!"

"I will," I said, putting the imaginary sword back into its scabbard.

"We bought this house from the dentist's family ten years ago. The dentist had died. I read about his daughter in the **San Francisco Chronicle** all the time. She has turned out to be a very peculiar woman."

"What's her name?" I asked.

"Sylvia Lombardi. She married one of those east coast carpetbaggers who took over my city. She lives on Steiner Street. Why do you want to see her?"

"To get back the skull."

The witch sniffed, "Well, if there's a skull to be had, Sylvia Lombardi will have it."

"Why didn't you tell me about Sylvia Lombardi in the beginning?"

"I don't cotton to strangers intruding on my privacy, especially not a little fat Nazi and a red-headed floozy. Now, fat boy, this happens to be my home. Get out! I could have you arrested for trespassing and destroying private property," she said haughtily.

"Where I come from, everybody is welcomed into everyone's houses. In Hawaii, we don't keep people out, we welcome people in. We are polite to strangers and help them. You were brought up weird, if you ask me. It seems to me that you think that you're really something special but, beg your pardon, you sure don't look or act special to me."

"You know what I think, little boy? You were brought up in a pig sty. What's that smell?"

The smell was me. *The nits were dying on my head.* The overheated house was cooking them on my scalp. With my business finished, I walked to the front door, opened it and left a calling card. Standing outside, I picked an imaginary nit off my head and threw it inside the house. "Here," I said. "This nit is from the fat Nazi and a redheaded floozy."

The door slammed.

Aunt Momi walked me down the stairs, holding me close to her. "The dentist is dead, Aunt Momi, and it is Sylvia Lombardi we want. She lives on Steiner Street in San Francisco."

"Why did you leave me outside?"

"I was doing men's business, Aunt Momi. I was protecting my princess. Anyway, you were going to swear at the witch and sock her in the face and that would never do for a princess." I smiled because I had fought my first witch and won. I had joined the ranks of Dorothy of Oz.

Despite the army of nits dying in my hair, my aunt offered to let me sit with her in the backseat. I declined, "I'm going to ride shotgun. I have to keep an eye out for the outlaw that's been following us. Aunt Momi, I'm really glad I have nits. I predict that nits are going to be America's new secret weapon."

CHAPTER 36

GOOD AND EVIL ON STEINER STREET

Mr. Hamada drove faster than Batman and Robin for San Francisco. The red roadster tailed us again. Another hour had flown by and the skull was still not in my hands. The blood in my head boiled.

Charlie Chan stopped at a phone booth to look up the Lombardi address on Steiner Street. Finding his bearings, we flew over the Bay Bridge, leaving the red roadster in the dust.

Steiner Street is located on one of the many steep hills in San Francisco. It is a posh street where only very posh people live. Only San Franciscans who survived the crash of 1929 could afford to live on this street. The familiar prickly feelings of fear were whizzing through my brain, "If I don't find the skull on Steiner Street, if Johnny doesn't kill me: I will be cursed till the day I die."

The Lombardi house at 2234 Steiner Street was built of stucco and whitewashed like houses built on the Greek islands. We screeched to a halt at the curb and I quickly scurried out of the car to accompany Aunt Momi to the front door of the house. The concrete steps were much larger and steeper than those we had walked up on the Uplands. Catching my breath at the summit, I rapped on the door as Aunt Momi rested against a pillar. I overheard my aunt promising God that she was going to give up cigarettes. While I was wondering if another rubber band witch was about to answer the knock, the door opened wide. A lady, dressed in a green chiffon party dress and carrying a large straw hat in her white-gloved hand, greeted us with a cheery, "Aren't you two a sight for sore eyes. Come on in and tell me all your troubles." I thought Aunt Momi was going to faint.

Without letting us speak a word, the lady jabbered without interruption as she ushered us into her living room. Announcing that she was just about to sit down for her afternoon tea, she insisted that we join her. Aunt Momi looked at me curiously, a look as if to say we had fallen down the rabbit hole into Alice's wonderland. My aunt turned to the Queen of Hearts and asked, "Were you expecting us?"

"Of course not, my dear, what a silly question to ask, but one longs for company in the afternoons and since you both look so nice, I do insist that you have tea with me."

She was nutty as a fruitcake, but she treated us with such delicacy, you couldn't help but like her. Rushing around the room, she made sure we felt comfortable in her living room as she seated us in plush red velvet chairs and then tugged on a sash to call her maid.

Appearing out of nowhere, our hostess introduced Betty. She was one of the most amazing creatures I had ever encountered in my life. She stood well over six feet tall in her high heels, and wore a purple turban with an ostrich feather stuck in the middle of it. I whispered to Aunt Momi that she had to be taller than the Empire State Building. Her skin was as beautiful and black as any one of the three wise men who followed the Christmas star on a camel. The Queen of Hearts quickly instructed Betty that there would be two more for tea. Clapping her hands, the Queen of Hearts made Betty disappear as suddenly as she had appeared. Seated in the largest chair in the room, directly across from us, she closed her eyes and hummed. She was putting us under a magic spell.

While she was conjuring up her spell, I studied the room and my hostess. The living room was furnished as if Ali Baba had moved his tent from the Sahara Desert to Steiner Street. I was sitting under an Arabian tent with Persian carpets scattered higgledy-piggledy over an oak floor. Dark purple draperies with gold tassels dressed each window. All the couches and chairs were covered with animal skins from Africa. Not a whisper of fresh air could be felt anywhere, and the only sound I heard was from a fountain gurgling behind me. I felt I was floating down the Nile on Cleopatra's barge on a hot summer day. The smell in the room was the ripeness of a zoo at four o'clock in the afternoon. In the center of the room, a brass chandelier hung from the ceiling looking like an upside-down birthday cake.

The Queen of Hearts had a very pretty doll face for an old person. Her porcelain skin had never been exposed to the sun making her appear as fragile as a camellia. I feared that to touch her, would severely bruise her skin. Beneath her dress, a body burst out from every angle like the petals of a sunflower. Looking at her full figure, I felt a deep kinship.

Satisfied that all the spirits in the room had quieted down, the Queen of Hearts opened her eyes, wiped her chin with a lace handkerchief and fanned her face like a Japanese geisha girl. Aunt Momi and I waited politely for her to speak. Letting out two snorts, clearing the air in her nostrils, she announced that she was Sylvia Lombardi but we should call her Tasha, a name she had given herself recently after reading a very sad Russian novel. Letting out two more snorts, she asked, "And to whom do I have the honor of having tea with this afternoon?"

Aunt Momi introduced us and immediately explained our mission. As my aunt finished telling her story about the long-ago days on the Uplands, Tasha's eyes lit up like an electric light on a theatre marquee. When Aunt Momi asked, "Do you remember me?" Tasha clapped her hands and shrieked, "Of course, now I do. Your sweet mother was so dear to me. My father adored her. Mother was quite jealous of your mother, and now that I look at you carefully, of course, I remember you clearly. You and your sisters were always so sweet, so charming and so amusing. I was so jealous of you all next door because it always sounded like you all were having so much fun.

"Our house was so drib drab and dark. Dentists, my dear, as a lot, are dull as dishwater. I think it comes from looking at rotten teeth all day long. Frankly, my dear, it would drive me up the wall if I had to look into gaping mouths day in and day out, so I vowed to never marry a dentist or to even become one."

"I said to Mr. Lombardi before I married him, 'Sergio, if I marry you, you must promise me that you will let me create a wonderland of my own making. If you will let me do that, I will promise that you will never have an unhappy or boring day in your life. As you see, he kept his promise and I have kept mine. My darling, after a hard day making oodles of money, Sergio never knows whom he will find waiting for him at our front door. Doesn't that sound intriguing to know that one can count on not ever knowing whom or what you will find behind your front door?"

The exotic turbaned lady appeared again, this time looking as if she had just arrived by boat from the Bahamas. She wore a cloak of many colors. As she laid a silver tea service on a table in front of us, I asked Tasha, "Do you remember anything about the skull?"

"Oh yes, my dear, the skull? Let me think. I am sure that I didn't throw anything that interesting away, especially something so out of the ordinary that had belonged to my ever so ordinary and dreary father. Trying to remember where I stored it can be a conundrum. You know what a conundrum is, young man?" she asked.

I shook my head. She responded, "A conundrum is a puzzle — a riddle, like life itself. Life, my new little friend, is all about solving riddles. Do you know what the biggest riddle in life is?"

"I don't." I answered not having the faintest idea what she was talking about.

"Well, I'm not going to tell you. That riddle, like the one-eyed man said, is for you to find out for yourself. Do you know who you look the spitting image of?" said Tasha.

"Who? Not that ugly old Nazi Hermann Goering?"

"No, no, my dear, you are the spitting image of Mr. Tyrone Power, the most handsome movie star. You have his dark looks. Someday, you are going to look exactly like him. Now, as to the matter at hand, the skull, hmm, the skull." She stopped and directed a question to her maid, "Betty, do you remember seeing anything around here that resembles a human skull?"

Shaking her arms wildly at Tasha as if to ward off evil spirits, Betty moaned, "No, ma'am, and honey, if I'd seen something like that, I'd have thrown it out the window. Those things can curse you right down to hell. I mean right down to the black devil." Tasha's genie quickly disappeared into the kitchen waving her hands and mumbling about evil spirits.

"Don't mind Betty. She sees only the ordinary in life. I'm educating her to see life's possibilities, the possibilities that are all around us all of the time."

Tasha confided, "Betty appeared on my doorstep one wintry afternoon, wearing only shorts, a turban and not much else. She had no name but knew that God had sent her to me. I immediately named her Betty after my favorite movie star, Betty Grable. You must have noticed that both Betty's have great gams."

I pleaded, "Can't you think of any place, Tasha, I could look for the skull? I haven't much time left. Tomorrow, I will leave on a train for Baltimore to empty chamber pots for two old maids. Please, if you will give me permission, I will look around the house myself while you and Aunt Momi drink tea."

Tasha pointed to a staircase in the hall. "Go up those stairs to the third floor. I have boxes stored in a room to the left of the stairs. Start there. If the skull isn't there, go down to the basement-garage. Father's old dental things are in the closet next to the washing machine, right in front of my Mercedes-Benz. I put that car on blocks. I love that car but I won't drive it until this awful war is over. You see, Mr. Hitler rides in a Mercedes, you know."

I asked my exotic hostess if I could have Charlie Chan, who was sitting in the car, help me search for the skull. She agreed, thinking it was hilarious that I had brought along the famous detective to assist me. I didn't correct her because I wanted Tasha to think of me as a person of great possibilities. Leaving the living room, I heard Aunt Momi ask, "Tasha, you ain't got some of that Russian vodka in this house, do you?"

"I do, Momi. I could tell right away that you're my kind of girl, a person of real substance. Now, let me get some serious stuff into these tea cups." My aunt looked utterly pleased that she had found a playmate.

I brought Mr. Hamada up to the house as he kept reminding me to call him Charlie Chan. He informed me that he had on good authority that the owners of this house were on personal speaking terms with J. Edgar Hoover. After a quick introduction to Tasha, we climbed three flights of stairs to the third floor.

At the top of the stairs, I stood in a room built like a crow's nest on a sailing ship. From every window on this floor, the city of San Francisco spread before us. Charlie called it a widow's walk. The Bay Bridge was on one side and the Golden Gate Bridge was on the other. I even found the Aquitania's four stacks peeping over the roof at Pier 35.

Pushing Charlie Chan into the room on the left, we were stunned at what faced us. The room was chockfull of exotic costumes hanging on at least fifty clothes racks. The room resembled the women's section in a department store with one exception. Hanging on hangers were garments not found in any San Francisco department stores but costumes from India, Japan, France, Africa; in fact, all the countries of the world were represented by their authentic dresses. Uniforms from the Revolutionary War, the Civil War and the French Revolution were tucked into corners and hanging on racks all their own. A harem girl's dancing dress stuck out because it sparkled with precious jewels. I pointed out to Charlie a red cellophane hula skirt hanging next to Scarlett O'Hara's hoop skirt. Ladies' and men's hats of all sorts were stored on shelves above the costumes. A chipped blue and white rocking horse stood alone in the corner of the room, waiting for a little girl to ride on it. Tucked under the clothes was an assortment of boxes. We tackled the boxes right off but found only jewelry, belts, and feather fans in them.

While rummaging through this room, the familiar prickly feelings overcame me again in my thinking that Marigold and Uncle Lono maybe were right, perhaps I was on a wild goose chase! I sat on the floor and began to feel sorry for myself. Charlie Chan pulled me back on my feet, and suggested we head down to the basement-garage and keep searching.

As we passed the kitchen, off the dining room, Betty sat at the kitchen table smoking a cigarette. With the cigarette dangling from her mouth, she was cleaning her fingernails with a paring knife. We asked where the door to the basement-garage was located. She pointed to a brown door next to the stove. As we headed for the door, Betty pulled me aside and ordered my spy friend, "Go on down, Chinaman, I want to talk to this little person alone. Look in the room in front of that Gestapo car. That's where they keep the old doctor's things. The light switch is on the left when you get down there."

As soon as Charlie was out of hearing, she laid into me, and clutched my hands as if she was about to make a confession. "If you shore enough find that skull down there, you take it out of here. I want no skull around here scaring poor folks like me. I got plenty enough troubles without no skull bothering me none. You understand me, chile?"

"Yes, ma'am," I answered, trying to pull my hands away from her. I was anxious to join Charlie in the search.

"You wait just one minute," she said, releasing my hands. Taking off her turban and laying it on the table, she whispered, "Don't you believe what that crazy lady tells you about me. I never was in no way showed up here looking like Betty Grable. I just hired on like anybody else. No God sent me here — it was the devil that done that to me, especially for what I have to go through every day. She makes things up till I think I'm going crazy like her. Dress me up different every day. One day, I'm the Queen of Sheba, next day I'm a princess from India. It gets me all mixed up. One day, I'm Ginger Rogers, the next day she calls me Mary Pickford. That's one crazy lady in there. Imagine saying I'm Betty Grable, the movie star. I got my dignity. That I do. Now, I just don't want you to think I'm crazy like her. You tell that lady with you that I am not crazy. Now, skedaddle out of here and find that skull and get it out of this house. There are already more troubles around here than I can take. Now git."

I ran down to find Charlie. In front of Tasha's black Mercedes-Benz and next to the washing machine, Charlie was in a room moving cardboard boxes around. With a dirty rag, he swept rat doodoo off the tops of the boxes trying to look at the writing on them. Years of dust and rat doodoo faded the print on the boxes making it difficult for him to read. A rusted dentist chair stood alone in a corner, waiting for a patient to have a tooth pulled out of his mouth.

Mr. Hamada waved me over and called, "Come here, Percy. Look at this." Charlie held a cardboard box in his hand. On the box, in faded print, it read: Hawaiian Skull. 1923.

"That's it," I screamed.

"Let's open it and make sure." Mr. Hamada said rattling the box gently.

"Let me hold it," I said, almost losing my breath.

Charlie passed the box into my open arms, and I cradled it like a baby. "I'm gonna open it." I started to rip the cardboard box apart but I couldn't do it. The box was wrapped in wire. Wire held the skull a prisoner.

Charlie stopped me. "Go ask the lady in the kitchen for a knife. I don't want to scare her so you better ask. She doesn't like me and she looks the wild type. I saw a knife on the kitchen table."

Holding the box tightly to my chest, I said, "Please, Mr. Hamada you ask her. I don't want to leave the skull now that I have it in my hands. Please. She won't kill you." Mr. Hamada climbed the stairs from the garage to the kitchen as I concentrated at picking at the wire, trying to release its hold on the box. I sat down in the dentist's chair so I could get a better grasp on the box.

I heard a noise over by the Mercedes.

"Percy!"

The curse was never closer.

Johnny had found me.

CHAPTER 37

THE BETRAYERS

Standing in the doorway was the Angel of Death. He had dyed his hair black and wore a dirty brown sweater and frayed corduroy pants. He looked so scruffy that I would have passed him on Market Street without even giving him a second glance.

I cowered in the dentist's chair. "What do you want?"

"I'm here to pull out your teeth."

"What?"

"That was a joke, Percy. Have you already lost your sense of humor?" he said, standing in the door.

"You look like a praying mantis," I said, grasping the box to my chest.

"You look scared, Percy. What's that in your hands?" he asked.

"It's mine. One step in this room and I'm going to scream for Mr. Hamada."

"Is that what he calls himself now? Well, I don't think he'll return soon. Let's close this door so we can have a little conversation. No one will hear you scream down here."

While he was closing the door, I jumped out of the dentist's chair and stood behind it for protection.

Johnny stepped towards me saying. "This time, I'll be a little more careful with you. Percy, I know you won't believe me, but you and I are on the same team. I work for the OSS. It's a secret organization in Washington D.C. The OSS hunts for spies and counter spies."

"Now, you're a big spy. I thought you were King Tut. You know what you are, you're a big killer liar and I won't believe anything you say to me."

"I played King Tut to scare you," he whispered, giving me his charming Johnny smile.

"And what about burying me alive in that coffin?"

"I was coming back to get you, I told you that, and you had plenty of air. All I wanted was for you to tell me where the treasures were." He looked his charming self.

"You killed Mina and Mrs. Brown."

"Yes, I did that. Well, I had to. Mrs. Brown was on to my identity. She was going to expose me. She remembered seeing me at her husband's trial. I was investigating the money her husband stole from the government. It was money he had stolen from the U.S. Treasury. We are certain that money is now in Nazi bank accounts in Switzerland. Sometimes we have to do the expedient thing… and sometimes the expedient thing is killing. Suicides, we like to call it. I needed Mina to get to Toshi. Toshi was entering into the United States as a spy." His eyes had turned steely gray.

"Now what? Am I going to commit suicide? Is that what you're going to do with me?" I was holding onto the dentist's chair with one hand and the box with the other.

"Not if you tell me where the jade necklace is. I don't care about the rest of the stuff. You can keep the diamonds."

"Why the necklace?" I asked, looking for a weapon to use.

"We want it because whoever has the jade necklace can legitimately rule China. The necklace is the most powerful symbol in China for anyone who wants to rule that country. Up to just a couple of weeks ago, no one knew where the necklace was hidden. All the emperors in China have worn it since before the time of the Ming dynasty. Each jade is engraved with a symbol of the ancient sects that first ruled China. America wants to put Generalissimo Chiang Kai-shek on the throne of China after we have defeated the Japanese and Communists."

The necklace was in plain sight for everyone to see in a shop window at the St. Francis Hotel. Aunt Momi told me Uncle Lono sold it so he and Aunt Momi could live like a prince and princess in their San Francisco hotel suite.

Johnny sensed that I was waiting for Mr. Hamada to return, heard my thoughts. "I suppose you are waiting for your Mr. Hamada to come and rescue you. Did he tell you that he was on a mission for the Japanese government to sue for peace? That's a crock. He wants the jade necklace, too. The Japanese want it to set up a puppet government in China. You are a pawn in a very dangerous game. The game will be over and you will be safe and alive when you tell me where the jade necklace is."

I yelled, "Don't come near me. I have nits in my hair. They are catching and they will eat your brains out."

He laughed, "I have nits all the time and sometimes not on my head. Come on, Percy, tell me where the necklace is."

I made a face at him and said, "Being a true red, white and blue American, I am not going to tell you. As far as I am concerned, you're worse than stinking old Hitler."

"And you are a parasite like all your relatives, the rich living off the poor. I thought you were different; that's why I gave you the ankh. But you are like all the rest of them, thinking you're better than the rest of us. I want my ankh back."

"I don't have it. Mr. Hamada has it. Go get it from him. I bet when your so-called group hears that you lost your ankh, they'll kill you."

He smiled at me like a cat about to pounce on a mouse, and whispered, "I don't believe you. You have it on you. You leave me no other choice. And, this time, you're not going to get away from me." He held an ice pick in his hand.

The door opened suddenly, and standing in the doorway was Betty, all seven feet of her, totally covered in feathers looking like a voodoo doll. She held a knife in her hand.

Sounding like a siren, she wailed, "I wasn't going to give no Chinee a knife when youse were down here all by your lonesome." Seeing Johnny holding an ice pick and stalking me, she sounded the alarm, "Yeeeeeee! What you doing down here holding that thing in your hand? You trying to kill that boy?"

I screamed, "Yes, he's trying to kill me."

Johnny turned and pointed the ice pick at Betty.

I took advantage of the moment and shoved the dentist's chair into his behind. Catching him off balance, Betty lunged at Johnny and stabbed his arm. Johnny dropped the ice pick, slammed Betty to the ground and he ran out of the garage. Screaming, I followed him out of the room, jumped into the Mercedes Benz and blew the car's horn.

Picking herself off the floor, Betty, making the sign of the cross, put her head down like a bull and flew down Steiner Street chasing Johnny in her high heels. Betty was a wondrous sight to behold with her feathers flying in the air. A chicken was chasing a rooster. I charged up the stairs, bumping into Mr. Hamada, Tasha and Aunt Momi coming down the stairs to see what all the commotion was about. Showing them the box, I screamed, "Johnny tried to kill me for the skull."

I breathlessly told Aunt Momi, Tasha and Mr. Hamada what had happened and everyone took up the chase down Steiner Street following Betty who was now running in her bare feet. We didn't catch Johnny because he disappeared out of sight like a slippery eel into one of the back alleys off the street.

Back in the house, out of breath, and because Tasha's hundred-proof vodka had taken its effect, Aunt Momi slurred as she spoke, "I don't thinkish we should call the police, Tasha. No one hash been hurt and nothing wash stolen. And they justsh might not believe ush." As she was talking, she swayed as if the Arabian tent was spinning around her like a merry-go-round.

Mr. Hamada agreed with Aunt Momi's proposal. I took a good look at him standing at the front door, agreeing with my aunt, and saw another betrayer in my life. No one asked him what he was doing while I was fighting for my life. I had the horrible thought that he wanted me dead, too.

Standing on my tiptoes on a chair, I gave Betty the longest kiss I could muster for saving my life. Betty gave me the knife as a parting gift to open the box with the skull in it. After Tasha insisted that Aunt Momi tell her my train departure time, she escorted us to the front door. She gave us an effusive farewell that lasted a good five minutes which included lots of kisses on both cheeks. Charlie Chan had now become her "darling Charlie." She released us, fluttering her handkerchief in the air, crying, "Adieu, adieu."

We walked down the front steps. I carried the box with the skull in it. I promised to write Betty and Tasha after the skull was safely buried in the sands of Kapake. Aunt Momi's parting words were, "Tanks for the vodka, Tashi honey. You is a real sport. Sorry we caused you some unnecessary commotion. Oh well, my life seems to go that way." With that, she began singing to herself, "I'm an old cow hand from the Rio Grande."

Seated back in the panther, Aunt Momi sighed, "Jesus, that vodka hit me." Charlie started the limousine and put the car into first gear and headed us back to the hotel. Out of the corner of my eye, I discovered that Johnny's red roadster convertible was parked on the other side of the street. I closed my eyes and prayed to God that Tasha had enough magical powers to make Johnny and his car disappear forever.

While holding onto the cardboard box, my blood bubbled in my head. Aunt Momi called from the backseat, "Aren't you going to open the box, Percy? It could be empty."

Without another word, using the knife Betty gave me, I cut the wire and pried the box apart. Pulling out old newspaper stuffing, I saw something round like a beach ball wrapped in an old dishcloth. I had seen lots of skulls in scary movies and a part of one on a Hawaiian beach, but I had never actually touched one. I unwound the cloth carefully and lifted the skull out of the box. I was sure it was the skull that Grandma had taken because it had a perfect set of white teeth. I kissed the skull and told the skull it was going back home.

Gripping the skull with my fingers, my face became red as a beet. I groaned, "I can't breathe, Aunt Momi. The curse has got me!"

The lobby of the Westin Saint Francis Hotel circa 1942.

CHAPTER 38

TRUE IS TRUE... OR IS IT?

Opening my eyes, I lay in a bed, holding the skull close to my chest. Aunt Momi was standing over me.

I looked up at her and asked, "Am I dead?"

"You're very much alive, Percy," my aunt replied, no longer slurring her words. She removed a wet compress from my forehead.

"I'm in a morgue. Just like the one they put Mother and Hatsuko in." I looked around the room at my surroundings.

"You're in my bed at the St. Francis Hotel," she murmured, passing the compress to a stranger behind her.

Trying to remember what had happened, I asked, "Where am I?"

"You fainted, Percy dear. Why don't you let go of the skull? I'll put it on that bureau for you. The skull will be safe there and you can watch it from here," she said gently.

"I want to keep it with me," I answered, not sure my fingers would ever let the skull go. "Who's that behind you?" I asked.

"Dr. Palmer. He's the hotel doctor."

"Did you tell him I am cursed?' I said, looking at the gray-haired man closely.

"Yes, dear, I told him you are cursed. I also told him that we have found the skull and that you are no longer cursed. Now, let the doctor examine you."

Resembling a St. Bernard, the doctor thumped on my chest as he advised, "Now, son, I think it would be wise to listen to your aunt and let go of that skull. The skull is what is making you feel so funny. You're making yourself sick believing the skull has magical powers. It's the reason you fainted. Now, let me have it."

I clutched the skull closer to my chest and said, "I want to keep it with me. Don't touch it or you'll get cursed just like me."

He nodded, "I see. I'll leave you a bottle of white pills. You are to take them when you start feeling funny again." He reached for the skull.

Turning away from him, holding onto the skull, I said vehemently, "I will!"

The doctor looked at Aunt Momi, shook his head, and advised, "Let him rest awhile more. Get him up and get something into his stomach. Did you have lunch, young man?"

I looked at Aunt Momi, trying to remember. "We forgot to eat, didn't we, Aunt Momi?"

Patting my hand, she concurred, "Yes, we forgot to eat."

The doctor brought out a small bottle of pills from his black bag. Giving Aunt Momi the pills, he said, "Phenobarbital. Have him take one of them if he gets nervous again. A quarter of one will be more than adequate. Too many of these pills are dangerous, so be careful."

Aunt Momi replaced the washrag on my forehead and told the doctor I was infested with nits.

I called to the doctor as I tightly held the skull.

"Yes?" he answered, questioning the look on my face.

"I'm a nit case!" I smiled like Johnny.

The doctor closed his bag, smiled back and left the bedroom.

The bedroom was quiet, too quiet. Something strange was happening in the next room. Aunt Momi and Charlie Chan were speaking in whispers. I heard my name spoken more than once. Taking the washrag off my forehead, clutching the skull, I tiptoed to the door to eavesdrop. Feeling lightheaded, I wobbled as I stood at the door.

Squishing my ear against the crack in the door, I heard Aunt Momi whisper in her low baritone voice, "Dr. Palmer had some nice things to say about you, Charlie. May I fix you a drink?"

"I'm on duty, ma'am," said Mr. Hamada.

"I won't tell."

"No, thank you, really ma'am," speaking ever so politely.

Pressing my ear closer into the door, I heard Aunt Momi fill a glass at the bar with ice cubes. After a short pause, my aunt said,

"May I be frank with you, Charlie?"

"Of course, ma'am," he whispered.

Aunt Momi said, "I've been worried for a long time about Percy. He hasn't been right since the day his mother died. After the attack on Pearl Harbor, after my sister died and his best friend Hatsuko died, he hasn't been right. They were his only friends. After Hatsuko killed herself and my sister died, he blamed everything on the skull he's holding on his chest. My mother took that skull away from a Hawaiian burial ground. Percy feels that the skull curses our family. He believes that strongly. We didn't know it, but weeks before we left on the Aquitania, Percy skipped school and went to the movies all by himself. Day after day, he wandered the streets of Honolulu alone, and we didn't know about it. He later told us that sometimes he'd seen the same movie over and over again. But that is all he has said about that experience. That period of his life remains a mystery to his father and to me. I do know that after his mother died, he began acting as if he was in a movie, a movie of his own making, and he made everyone around him into movie stars. On the ship, he ran around saying that he was the Scarlet Pimpernel, a film shown on the ship. I thanked my lucky stars that he didn't see a movie about Jack the Ripper. One of the passengers, he nicknamed Tarzan."

Charlie interrupted, "May I be frank with you?"

"Of course, Charlie," she answered.

"Driving over here this morning, Percy thought I was a Japanese spy. I went along with him, thinking he was playing a game, but as he talked on I could see that he was very serious, especially when he talked about this Johnny person. He became very excited when he showed me a charm that belonged to this person. I took it away from him and that seemed to relieve his unsettled mind. He believes that this Johnny fellow wants to kill him and, from what we have just witnessed, he may be telling the truth."

"Johnny?" asked Aunt Momi.

"It seems this Johnny person is running around San Francisco wanting to kill him, or is this one of his movies, too?" Charlie asked, sounding concerned.

Aunt Momi responded, "Johnny was an officer on the ship. He was very sweet to me. If ever I wanted to know where Percy was roaming on the ship, Johnny found him for me. I have no complaints about Johnny, but Percy towards the end of the voyage called him the angel of death. I believed it to be more theatrics on Percy's part but, after what I have learned from the captain of the ship and what happened just now, I'm not so sure. I was shot at and I know I received several notes from a crazy person, but they could have been written by Percy to keep the trip exciting. We found him in a coffin, but that, too, could have been Percy's own doing. A friend died suddenly on the second day out, which remains a mystery, and yesterday, I learned from the captain of the ship that an acquaintance of Percy's was found dead in her cabin after I had left the ship. Both deaths, I am quite sure, are quite explainable as accidents or due to natural causes. This youngster lost his mother and his best friend whom he adored at an impressionable age and, I fear, he has now acquired an unnatural obsession with death. His sister, Marigold, and I had permission to leave the ship early before it docked, so the second death was a shock to me. The woman was well connected in Honolulu but was involved, not of her own doing, in an unfortunate scandal." Aunt Momi paused to sip her drink.

She began again, "I don't take too much stock in what Percy tells me anymore because he likes to cry wolf."

"What's going to happen to him?" asked Charlie.

"His father wants me to send him to a military boarding school, but I convinced his father to let these relatives of mine, who live in Baltimore, have him till the end of this school year. If that doesn't work out in Baltimore, I'll put him in a Catholic military boarding school here in California," replied Aunt Momi.

"What about his sister?"

"She's also a very sad case. Since my sister died, Marigold feels abandoned not only by her mother, but by her father, who has remarried and has another child. She adores her father. Marigold has latched onto my husband and won't let him out of her sight. Right now, he's taking her on a horseback ride through Golden Gate Park. Lono is being very sweet to her. Frankly, he treats Marigold a hellava lot better than he treats me, Percy, or my children. But that's just between us."

Taking a long pause, she began again, "I'm going to fix another drink. You're sure you won't change your mind?" my aunt said.

"No, ma'am. May I be frank again?" Charlie said, lowering his voice, making it hard for me to hear what he was going to say next.

"Be my guest." she said, putting ice cubes in her glass.

"I'm not Charlie Chan."

"Well, it is a very improbable name. What's your real name?"

What he answered shook the very last foundations of our friendship. "Patrick Leong. I'm a graduate student at the University of San Francisco."

"Why the silly ruse, Patrick Leong?" my aunt asked.

Clearing his throat, he said, "I needed a part-time job that paid well. I ran out of money to pay my tuition and needed a job to fit into my schedule at school. A chauffeur's job has lots of flexibility. I also knew that no one wants a chauffeur speaking like an English professor. They prefer a dumb Chinaman driving their cars, or I should say uneducated. That's why the Charlie Chan ruse."

Aunt Momi responded, "Do me a favor. Stay Charlie Chan until we get Percy on the train for Baltimore. It would be a terrible blow to him to learn your true identity. He's had too many disappointments lately."

"He calls me Mr. Hamada, a Japanese spy."

"Well, cheers, Mr. Hamada." Aunt Momi said, sipping her drink.

Wanting to cry out in anger, I accidentally hit my head against the door.

Aunt Momi whispered, "Shhh. Did you hear that? I hope that wasn't Percy listening to us. He's a great eavesdropper."

I jumped back into bed just as Aunt Momi walked into the room. My eyes were closed when she asked, "Are you ready to get up now?"

"I am," I said, looking at her as I adjusted the skull on my belly.

Pulling the covers off me, she announced, "Well then, it's time to get up. We're going across the street to the Golden Pheasant and have something to eat. Are you up to a chocolate milkshake?"

Sitting at a corner table next to a window in the Golden Pheasant restaurant, I watched people strolling up and down Geary Street. It was early evening. Watching them look so happy made me feel empty inside. Since I had heard the conversation between Aunt Momi and Mr. Hamada, a cloud of sadness had covered me like the rain drizzling on the street. I should have been happy because I ordered everything I loved: a tuna salad sandwich, a chocolate milkshake, and a chocolate sundae that arrived with a tall glass pitcher of hot fudge to pour over the vanilla ice cream. The meal in front of me looked as uninteresting as a bowl of wilted lettuce. I felt too sad and too empty inside to eat.

With my feet, I held the skull in its box under the table. Aunt Momi and Mr. Hamada talked gaily across from me as if they were attending one of Tasha's tea parties. Every so often they'd give me a furtive look. By their looks, they were checking my reactions to see if I had overheard their conversation. They reminded me of Peter Rabbit and Mopsy coming out of a rabbit hole to check to see if Mr. MacGregor had left the garden patch. They feared, and correctly so, that the child had become the wiser.

Aunt Momi chattered endlessly about things of no consequence to her, to me or to Mr. Hamada. They were the babblings of someone who was trying to keep a stiff upper lip though the Titanic was sinking. The silver tongue kept me from screaming, "I am drowning in a pool of confusion, Aunt Momi." The meal progressed slowly, making time almost standstill. Throughout it all, Aunt Momi kept fishing in roundabout ways if I had overheard their conversation in the hotel suite. I playacted that everything was normal.

Within myself, inside my head, I kept thinking that my pretense at being normal was failing miserably because my imaginary world had shattered and it showed. My brain had burst into little pieces of glass and the pieces of glass were scattered out into the restaurant and everybody could see that I was falling apart. After hearing that nobody believed me, my motion picture projector had stopped running. I was sitting alone on the dark side of the moon. The stars in the universe that had guided me since the day I was born had disappeared into a black hole.

"Aren't you hungry, Percy?" Aunt Momi asked, staring at me wondering where my mind had wandered. I didn't respond and watched a passersby look into a shop window.

"Percy, where are you?" Aunt Momi's voice brought my senses back to the table. Not making any sense, I replied, "I was thinking about what the captain said, 'Horatius saved Rome. He really did!'"

"What do you mean, Percy? Oh, never mind about the captain. How are the nits? Are they still troublesome?" Hearing the captain's name mentioned, she reached for a cigarette.

"Dying," I said flatly, knowing where her mind had drifted to.

Taking my hand in hers, she asked, concerned, "Do you need to take a pill?"

"I'm fine," I said, dipping a long spoon up and down in the chocolate milkshake.

With a face of a Buddha, Charlie kept watching me, not revealing what he was thinking. I kept away from his glance by turning my head looking out the window. I was thinking how he had betrayed me and also thinking that it served me right for making a traitor to my country my best friend.

"Percy," Aunt Momi said, eating my chocolate sundae, "were you sleeping soundly before I woke you?"

"Yes," I smiled. I can't even trust Aunt Momi. She, too, betrayed me.

Swallowing a large spoonful of my sundae, she revealed, "The day after tomorrow, I'm leaving on the Aquitania. I'm going back to Honolulu to pick up my girls and bring them back to San Francisco. I'm putting them in Dominican in San Rafael. It's a very fine Catholic boarding school. Would you like to go to a Catholic boarding school?"

"No, Aunt Momi! Is Captain Spaulding going to be the captain on the Aquitania when you go back to Hawaii?"

She fluttered her eyes nervously and switched to other matters. "Uncle Lono wants me to take the treasures back to Hawaii. I'm putting them in the ship's safe because this time you'll not be there to protect me. And, young man, I want to take the skull back to Kauai and bury it before I return with the girls. We want to get rid of the curse, don't we? Will you let me have the skull?"

"Maybe," I said, feeling even lonelier. It was a new kind of loneliness that I couldn't explain because it just felt dark. I had never felt so dark in my life, not even after Mother died. Not even the voice in the closet had an explanation for the confusion I was feeling. I was no longer living on the dark side of the moon but in the dark hole with the dead stars.

After eating my sundae, my aunt continued, "I don't think we should take the skull back to Cousin Oliver's flat. Let me have it. I'll keep it in the hotel room and I promise I'll protect it with my life. Cousin Oliver can be sticky about those things."

"Like my nits," I said, looking at the empty sundae glass.

"Like your nits," she agreed, wiping a dribble of chocolate off her chin.

I asked Mr. Hamada, testing him, "What would you do, Charlie Chan?"

Without an accent, he answered, "Let your aunt have the skull, Percy. It's a wise decision."

Feeling my child world had just shattered, I listened to my inner voice. Making up my own mind, I reached under the table and handed the skull to my aunt predicting: "Aunt Momi, whether you believe me or not, Johnny is not through with me."

Before driving back to Cousin Oliver's with Mr. Hamada, I excused myself from the table saying that I had to go to the bathroom. I snuck back to the hotel and ran through the lobby and down the hallway to the hotel shops. I found the shop where I had remembered the jade necklace was displayed in the window. The necklace was gone. I asked the clerk what had happened to it. He said that a very rich looking Chinese woman bought it that afternoon. I was relieved thinking that the necklace might have gone home to China but, most importantly, Johnny didn't have it.

Riding in Cousin Oliver's car, Mr. Hamada driving, I looked for the red roadster. It wasn't following us any more.

I made two requests to Charlie Chan. I asked, "Charlie, I want the ankh back." He reached into his pocket and put the ankh into my hand without comment.

As I shoved the ankh into my pocket next to the amethyst brooch,

I made a second request. "Mina's scarf? Is Toshi going to get it? If he isn't going to get it, I want that back, too."

"I promised you that Toshi will receive the scarf tonight and I will see to it that he gets to his sister in Washington, D.C. Don't you trust me anymore, Percy?" Mr. Hamada asked. His eyes were on the car in front of us.

I said, truthfully and deliberately, "No, Mr. Hamada. I don't trust anybody anymore."

Arriving at Cousin Oliver's flat, the street lights were turned on and the air was swirling with mist. The mist made the street look ghostly. Charlie parked the car against the curb and announced, "Your aunt is taking you shopping tomorrow morning. I'm to deliver you at nine."

Getting out of the car, I reminded him, "Don't forget about the scarf." I slammed the car door and, as I was about to enter the apartment building, I turned around and said to Charlie Chan, student, Patrick Leong, "I grew up today, Mr. Hamada. Goodbye."

Cousin Oliver had been invited to dinner at the Bohemian Club. Before he left, I caught him in the hallway, scratching his head.

Ellen and I dined at her kitchen table on Swedish meatballs and leftover mayonnaise dips. The conversation was on the weather because I was afraid I'd blab to her about the nits in my hair, and I didn't feel like talking because I felt sad. Sniffing the air throughout our dinner, she said she loved the smell of my hair tonic. It reminded her of her mother's kerosene stove in Sweden. While eating my dessert, banana cream pie, I looked out the window and caught a glimpse of a red roadster parked under a street lamp near a fire hydrant.

St. Francis Hotel on left. Circa 1942.

CHAPTER 39

GONE AGAIN

I reported to Aunt Momi promptly at nine. Cousin Oliver sent me over to the hotel in a Yellow Cab. Charlie had called in sick.

The Kamehameha suite was the usual colossal mess but this time hats and hatboxes were in amongst the empty plates and gin bottles. Uncle Lono's clothes were strewn everywhere telling me that Aunt Momi and Uncle Lono had been fighting all night. Aunt Momi and Princess Alice were on the floor, sitting cross-legged, giggling like twelve-year-olds, trying on hats.

Standing at the open door looking bemused, Aunt Momi waved me over as she stood up. In front of a mirror, she adjusted a goofy hat on her head. Tilting the hat forward, she sighed, "Percy, what do you think of this very, very expensive Lily Dache creation?"

The creation was shaped like Marigold's birthmark and made of black velvet. It had bunches of red cherries that cascaded down the right side of her face. A lace veil was attached to either side of the velvet tower, crossing over her eyes, making her into a cherry-picking Zorro.

"It's very katish, Aunt Momi. It's really very katish!" I lied enthusiastically, pressing my fingers on the silver tongue.

Taking off the hat, Aunt Momi shrieked, "I knew you'd like it. Alice, I'm off to the White House Department store to shop with Percy. We'll be back at the hotel before lunch."

Picking her purse off the couch, Aunt Momi said too cheerfully for someone who was not a morning person, "Today, you are going to have the best day of your life, Percy. I'm going to buy you the most wonderful things at the White House. We're going to charge, charge, *charge* everything to your Uncle Lono, the bastard. Doesn't that sound just too, too wonderful?"

"No," I said, looking her straight in eyes. An alarm had gone off inside my head. Something smelled in this hotel suite and it wasn't the dirty dishes or the nits dying on my head; the atmosphere in the suite stunk as rotten as Denmark.

"No?" she answered, flummoxed at being caught off guard.

"No," I said again, "You're acting 'too, too,' grand with me this morning. What's up, Aunt Momi? 'Fess up."

"Tell him, Momi. He's going to find out soon enough," shot Princess Alice, pulling a large gray veil over her made-up clown face. Her hat looked exactly like the one Edwina wore at Aunt Rose's funeral, the same hat Johnny escaped in.

I asked again, "What's wrong, Aunt Momi?"

"Maybe you should take a white pill before I tell you," my aunt said, fixing a Mimosa at the bar.

"I don't need to take a white pill. Tell me," I said, facing her squarely making sure I could see the whites of her eyes. Mixing the gin and the orange juice with her finger, ignoring my stare, she faced the window that looked out on Union Square and drank her breakfast in one continuous swallow.

Watching her down the drink, waiting for her to speak, my mind traveled into my dark hole. The room was quiet except for an ambulance siren screaming on the street. The siren beckoned me to jump out the window.

"Are you all right, Percy?" Aunt Momi said, studying my face. "You sure you don't want to take a pill?" Her voice had lost all its forced gaiety.

"Tell me what happened," I demanded. I searched her eyes waiting for the answer that was slow in coming.

She blurted out, "We were robbed last night. Someone stole the skull. It's all your Uncle Lono's fault. He forgot to lock the door. I'm not speaking to him. He's so scared of me right now that he took two bell men over to Ransohoff's before they opened and got me all these hats to make up." As she talked, she searched my face to see if I was going to faint again. "And, that's why I'm going to buy you anything you want at the White House, on Uncle Lono, of course. I'm so mad at that dingbat I could spit. We had the worst fight of our marriage, as you might notice. Poor Marigold, she was a witness to all of it. I couldn't believe that he could have been so stupid. I threw all his clothes out into the hall and told him never to come back. He threw them back in. Not only is the skull gone, but the bastard stole my mother's engagement ring. All of San Francisco must have heard us fight, at least this floor did. Alice heard it."

Seeing the look of horror on my face, Aunt Momi's eyes moistened as she asked, "Please, please, please, forgive me, Percy."

Not knowing how to respond, I asked, "Where are Uncle Lono and Marigold?"

"Your uncle didn't want to call the police. He doesn't want reporters dredging up the time he spent in prison here. He's scared spitless that someone in the press will make a big fuss over him if we report the robbery. The royal pain-in-the-ass is meeting with a private detective and, after that, he's taking Marigold sailing. I told him I never wanted to see him again if he didn't bring the skull back to the hotel with him. Don't worry, he'll find it." My aunt's voice didn't sound at all convincing.

I grabbed one of the hats, squashed it on my head, and paraded around the room, singing, "Johnny stole the skull. Johnny stole the skull. He was looking for the treasures. He was looking for the treasures. He didn't get the jade necklace. Johnny got fooled."

I began to laugh hysterically as I sang, "The joke is on Johnny now. Now, he has the curse. We're free, Aunt Momi! We're free! Whee!" I plopped down on the floor after sailing the hat on my head out the open window.

Aunt Momi screamed, "That hat's not paid for."

Golden Gate Bridge in fog.

CHAPTER 40

PUTTING IT ALL TOGETHER

I told Ellen that leaving for far-off lands has many benefits. One of them is that you meet new people who haven't a clue you are cursed. Another benefit is that leaving by train you travel across new lands like an explorer. Most importantly, people give you lots of money before you leave in hopes that you never come back. I figured that if I came back to San Francisco and then went away, at least once a year, I could be as rich as Cousin Oliver. I told Ellen that I planned to make leaving on a train a profession like being a fireman. Cousin Oliver gave me ten silver dollars to tip the porters and eat meals in the dining car.

It was evening. The fog had lifted. I was packed and ready to leave Cousin Oliver's flat for the train station. Marigold and I had reservations on the "City of San Francisco" for Baltimore. It left at nine. At the end of our train journey, two old maids in Baltimore were waiting for us to empty their bedpans and to live in their stuffy old attic like Shirley Temple paupers.

Ellen packed my suitcase twice and gave me a basket of "goodies" to take with me on the train. Cousin Oliver gave a final inspection of my person. He was farsighted and had a stuffy nose so he missed the nits and the smell of turpentine. All of us, including Ellen, rode a Yellow Cab down Market Street to the Ferry Building. At the Ferry Building, we met Princess Alice, Aunt Momi and Marigold. They were waiting to take the ferry with us to the train station. I told them that the best part about leaving San Francisco by train is that we traveled by a ferry across San Francisco Bay.

Uncle Lono and Charlie weren't with us. Uncle Lono was still in the doghouse. Neither skull nor ring had been recovered. Charlie was still sick. He had an upset stomach.

The Oakland train station was a letdown. The station wasn't the grand palace that I had imagined. It was a long wooden shed that resembled a barn that stored hay for Iowa farmers. I told Marigold it reminded me of the rickety train station in Dodge City where the Cole brothers "shot it out" with Errol Flynn.

Aunt Momi and Princess Alice wore their new hats. Aunt Momi's had cherries down the side of her face and Princess Alice had green grapes down the side of hers. Other than the color of the grapes, the only difference between hats was the light green veil that covered the brown skin on Princess Alice's face. I told them their hats made Carmen Miranda's fruit basket hats in 20th Century Fox musicals look pale by comparison. That pleased them greatly.

The "City of San Francisco," our train, resembled a long silver bullet. Marigold and I were booked in one of its sleeper cars paid for by Cousin Oliver. Arriving at the train station, Cousin Oliver showed our tickets to a red cap and tipped him five dollars to take our suitcases to our seats.

There was a great deal of hullabaloo going on in the station as we arrived. People were rushing up and down the platform, getting on and off the train, looking for friends and buying food, magazines, and Cokes from hawkers with trays strapped around their necks. We screamed to be heard. Everyone stared at us because Aunt Momi and Princess Alice looked like movie stars from Hollywood. To add to their glamour, they carried bouquets of gardenias in their hands. The gardenias were from Podesta Baldocci, San Francisco's famous flower shop. They were sent to Aunt Momi from an unknown admirer. Even Marigold held a bouquet. I whispered to Aunt Momi that all that Johnny had to do to find us was to follow the gardenia scent.

Marigold hadn't spoken since we had met at the Ferry Building. Aunt Momi and Princess Alice flanked her like prison guards. A dark cloud clung over her head as she kept looking around. Speaking for the first time in a little girl voice, she asked, "Isn't Uncle Lono coming to see me off?" It was the same hurt look in her eyes when Daddy abandoned us on the pier in Honolulu.

Aunt Momi shook her head.

She wailed, "He promised me that he would come. I was counting on it. I'm not going to Baltimore. I'm not going to some damn place where old ladies don't know how to play baseball. I'm going to hate it. I know it. They won't be any fun at all."

"You are going to Baltimore, Marigold, and there are no ifs, ands, or buts." Aunt Momi tugged her arm like a prison matron towards our car.

Marigold whined, "You wait. I'm going to run away as soon as I get there and meet Uncle Lono in Chicago. I promise that's what I'm going to do."

A hush fell over the train station as a nurse pushed a wheelchair past us. In the wheelchair sat a sailor whose face was bandaged like a mummy. Someone behind us said that the sailor was one of the survivors from Pearl Harbor. He was going to Johns Hopkins Hospital on the East Coast to treat his burns. As he was being lifted into our sleeping car, something fell from under his blanket. The nurse quickly picked it up and placed it in his hands. Someone in the crowd feeling very patriotic sang **God Bless America**. We saluted the sailor as he disappeared into the train.

"It's time to get into your car, too, children. The train's scheduled to leave in fifteen minutes," Cousin Oliver instructed. "I don't want you on this platform when the stragglers arrive."

"I'm not going until Uncle Lono comes," Marigold said defiantly, looking at Aunt Momi as if she wanted to shoot her.

"Listen to Cousin Oliver, Marigold. It's time for you and Percy to get aboard. Uncle Lono isn't coming," declared Aunt Momi.

I kissed Ellen and Princess Alice and shook hands with Cousin Oliver, hoping he'd slip me more silver dollars. (He didn't.) Aunt Momi led Marigold over to our sleeper car. I followed them with my hands behind my back.

As steam whooshed from under the train, Marigold took her first step up into our sleeping car. She clomped down hard on it. She clomped down hard on the second step and each step that followed sounded her pain leaving Uncle Lono in San Francisco. When she stood on the landing of the car, she turned and yelled at Aunt Momi, "The reason Uncle Lono isn't here is because you're mean to him all the time. I wish you died in your sleep."

My sister stomped into the car, leaving me standing with Aunt Momi. Seeing my aunt's lips quiver, I whispered into her ear, "Marigold tells me that all the time, Aunt Momi. She doesn't mean it. She only says those things to people she loves."

Reaching the first step as I adjusted the basket of Ellen's treats on my arm, I said, "Aunt Momi?"

"Yes, dear?" she said, looking at me tearfully.

"Say hello to Captain Spaulding for me." I winked. My aunt blushed redder than Dracula's blood.

Seated in our reserved seats, looking out the window, we watched the latecomers pour onto the platform. The last ferry had arrived from San Francisco. The hordes drove the porters crazy asking them to handle their suitcases all at the same time. The latecomers became hysterical when the train whistle warned them that our departure was imminent. Cousin Oliver, Ellen, Princess Alice, and Aunt Momi huddled to protect themselves from the stampede. I kept waving at them giving them a sappy puppy-dog look, hoping they'd change their minds and take Marigold and me off the train. Watching them, I noticed the gardenia bouquets had turned brown. Marigold sat on her gardenias. She was too miserable to notice and kept on looking for Uncle Lono.

A porter with sweat pouring down his face ran down the aisle, calling, "Mr. Percy. Mr. Percy. Where iz you?"

I raised my hand and said, "I'm Mr. Percy."

Out of breath, he handed me a box and said, "This iz for youse! It'z a present from a gentleman standing out on the platform."

I recognized the cardboard box at once. The feeling of dread that I had hoped to leave behind me in San Francisco was with me again. "Does he have red hair?"

"No sah! Except on his arms. He says youze got something zat belongs to him and he sez I'ze to git it from youz and givzs it back to him."

I reached into my pocket and pulled the ankh out as the porter said, "I'ze wouldn't let him aboard bedcaz he haz no ticket and hez an all over crazy look." The porter watched me swing the ankh back and forth in my hand.

I said, speaking slowly, "Tell him that if he wants his stinking ankh back, he has to come get it from the Scarlet Pimpernel. And if he's too chicken to do that, tell him to go back to Egypt and to get himself another one and to leave me and my family alone."

"I'ze tells him that for you, sho enough, if I can remember all that.

He scare me good wiz all that fuzzy black hair and mean eyes. I can tell he aint goin to like that answer. No siree." The porter shoved his hand at my face, waiting for a tip. I reluctantly pulled out one of Cousin Oliver's silver dollars from my pocket and gave it to him. I had planned to keep most of the silver dollars for chocolate milkshakes in the dining car. With the silver dollar in his hand, the porter ran back down the aisle. Putting the ankh back into my pocket, I prayed the porter remembered to give scummy Johnny my message word for word.

Holding the skull on my lap, I shivered because I was it again.

Marigold hadn't paid the slightest attention to what had gone on because Uncle Lono had arrived with the latecomers. My sister was jumping up and down like a Zulu on the warpath, waving at him. The dark cloud over her head had miraculously disappeared.

On the platform, next to Ellen, stood Mr. Hamada, giving me the "thumbs up" sign. I figured he must have come with Uncle Lono.

Poking Marigold on the back, I said, "Look what I got back — the skull." I pushed the box next to her face to show it to her. I mouthed and pointed to Aunt Momi, "The skull. The skull." I ripped open the box and pulled the skull out of the box showing the skull to my friends on the platform.

When Marigold saw the skull in my hands, she screamed louder than ten air raid sirens, "Uncle Lono found it. Look, Aunt Momi sees it. She's kissing Uncle Lono."

"It wasn't Uncle Lono, Marigold. It was Johnny who gave it back to me."

A man with black, bushy hair and a beard stood directly behind Aunt Momi holding a wire stretched between his hands. He grinned wickedly at me. I stuck out my tongue. Nudging Marigold, I said breathlessly, "Look behind Aunt Momi. That's Johnny, the man with a wire in his hands. He's going to kill Aunt Momi."

"Stop kidding, Percy," Marigold ordered, elbowing me in the ribs.

"I'm not kidding." I yelled, pounding on the window making faces. I mouthed "Johnny is behind you" pointing to the man standing behind Aunt Momi. Everyone, thinking I was crying wolf, made faces at me.

Mr. Hamada disappeared.

"Marigold, you stay here," I said. "I'm getting off the train." I placed the skull on the seat next to Marigold.

She grabbed my sleeve and yelled, "You're not leaving this thing with me."

In a blaze of color, Tasha from Steiner Street arrived on the platform. Betty held an umbrella of reds and blues over her head. Betty, while making her entrance, accidentally pushed Johnny out of the way. Tasha kissed Aunt Momi on both cheeks. Swathed in black sable, looking like a countess from the steppes of Russia, Tasha kissed everybody on both cheeks, even people she didn't know. Betty, holding the umbrella over Tasha's head, stomped on her high heels because her yellow coat kept riding above her knees, showing her purple panties.

Johnny vanished.

With Tasha's arrival, everyone forgot about us on the train. It was obvious that Princess Alice took an immediate liking to exotic Tasha because they held hands like cousins from Russia. Cousin Oliver's cheeks turned a primrose pink staring at Betty's purple panties.

A perspiring, Mr. Hamada rejoined the group. He held up a black wig in his hand. I mouthed, "Where's Johnny?" Before he could answer, he disappeared back into the crowd.

The train lurched twice, then once more. The train whistle blew, and we began to rumble slowly down the tracks. Hearing the whistle, everyone turned to us and waved madly as the train moved away from the platform. Marigold blew kisses to Uncle Lono. My uncle's eyes were only on my sister. Marigold pointed to Aunt Momi and yelled, "I love you, too, Aunt Momi." Our train picked up speed and, in an instant, we were out of sight.

Good-byes are confusing, especially to an eight-year-old boy. You hate losing the familiar even if the familiar was uncomfortable. I wanted to say so much to everybody and I wanted to hear their answers. Good-byes were like my mother's death: sudden, abrupt, and as if someone punched me in the stomach.

I had become familiar with those dark feelings during and after the attack on Pearl Harbor. They were the same feelings I felt when the bullet shot into our cabin, and the same feeling I had lying on top of and in the coffin, each time facing death. It was the same feeling I had eavesdropping on Aunt Momi and Mr. Hamada. Goodbyes are like that, too, especially when you realize that you might never see the people you love ever again. I was living in the dark hole of my soul.

I sat back in the seat, feeling the train shifting tracks as it passed Southern Pacific freight cars waiting for their morning run to Los Angeles. We passed telephone poles and empty grassy fields, and soon we were riding out into open country. With both my hands, I rubbed the rough texture of the faded crimson seat and pressed my finger on a repaired tear, wondering who tore it. Putting my nose into the cushion behind me, I smelled other journeys.

Before I replaced the skull back in the box, I wrapped it carefully in a clean dishcloth that I borrowed from Ellen's food basket. I stuffed the box with newspapers to hold the skull firmly in place and hid it under my feet so it would not frighten a lady with prying eyes sitting across the aisle.

Marigold's nose was still pressed against the window.

"It can't end like this," I said, sitting back and feeling as if I had been shot with an arrow. "Is this it, Marigold? One minute here, the next minute going somewhere else. Since Mother died, I have not stopped running. When will I stop running from place to place?"

Curling herself up into a ball, Marigold mumbled, "What do you mean?"

"I don't know. Is this how our life is going to be? Running for the rest of our lives? And where do we end up? When do we stop? Who wants to love us?"

"End?" she asked.

"I don't know. Everything: Johnny…Charlie…Mr. Hamada…Uncle Buster… Marigold, was it real or did I make it all up like I heard Aunt Momi tell Mr. Hamada? Please speak to me." I looked straight into her eyes, fearing her answer.

Marigold sat up as we passed the lighted street lamps of a small California town and answered, "What do you want to know?"

"Did I fall overboard on the Aquitania?"

"Yes."

"Did Buster Crabbe rescue me?"

"Yes," my sister answered.

"Was Johnny the killer?"

"You can answer that, stupid."

I pulled Aunt Rose's amethyst brooch out of my pocket. "This is proof of that. It proves that he was the killer. He killed Edwina, too. He nailed me in a coffin. But the question is: where is he? He disappeared at the train station. Now, he says he's an American agent. All I know is that he's crazy and he makes me crazy with his crazy words. What is he doing now? Maybe, he is on the train. I have his ankh. Is it part of a secret club? How come Charlie had his wig in his hand? It's not fair, not knowing everything and Aunt Momi thinking that I have been crying wolf all the time. Here, take the brooch. Brooches are for ladies. If anything happens to me, if someone kills me, you'll have proof that I was telling the truth. I'll keep the ankh because someday Johnny is going to try to get it back from me and I want him to."

Marigold sighed, "Percy, will you stop thinking. Leave me alone." She curled up into a little ball and went back to pressing her face into the window daydreaming she was on a roller coaster ride with Uncle Lono.

I poked Marigold trying to comfort her, "I bet you had a good time with Uncle Lono."

"Get your finger out of my back," she growled.

I opened up Ellen's basket and ate an egg salad sandwich. I pinched Marigold's arm pointing to the basket, and asked, "Do you want something to eat? A cookie?"

"I'm not hungry," she grumbled.

"Marigold?"

"What?"

"I have something important to tell you."

"What is it?" she said impatiently.

"Now, don't get goofy on me."

"What do you want, Percy? Can't you leave me alone for one minute, and don't get too close to me. I don't want your nits." Marigold was back in her old grumpy voice.

I was stunned. "How did you know I had nits? I was just about to tell you that."

"Aunt Momi told me," she answered, taking the cookie out of my hand.

"Boy, does Aunt Momi have a big mouth. She told me not to tell you till we passed Chicago. That really upsets me because I wanted to tell you about my nits myself. I wanted to see the shock on your face."

"Was that all you wanted to tell me?" she asked, eating the cookie.

"It proves my point, Marigold. You're the only true friend I have because you stick to your word and take the good and bad in me. You take me just as I am and I take you grump or nice. I love you."

Making a sour face as she brushed the cookie crumbs on the floor, she sighed, "Please be quiet."

"In fact, you're the only friend left that I can trust, so don't die."

"I can't die if you keep interrupting me all the time. If I tell you something will you leave me alone?"

"I promise."

"I like you better than Uncle Lono. Now, leave me alone, will you?" Marigold turned to the window and watched a train passing us going to where we had come from.

Marigold was smiling to herself.

Before we turned in for the night, we went into the dining car to drink a cup of hot cocoa. I placed the skull and Ellen's basket next to me. I confided to my sister, "Marigold, we are about to start a new adventure."

"Please. I'm tired of your adventures. I want to have a little peace and quiet." She looked as if she wanted to drown me in her chocolate.

Watching her return to her daydream, sipping my chocolate, I gave her my most mischievous look and said in a confidential voice, "You'll really love this new adventure."

She slapped my hand because I had interrupted a daydream about Uncle Lono.

Trying to get her mind off the Black Prince, I put myself in peril and said, "Did you see the sailor in the wheelchair getting aboard the train, the man who was bandaged up like a mummy?"

Her eyes smoldered as if she was just about to catch on fire and, instead of hitting me, she answered, "Yea, and give me one of Ellen's egg salad sandwiches, you pig." I reluctantly passed the basket over to her.

I whispered across the table, "It's Toshi!"

Picking a sandwich out of the basket, she scoffed, "Come on, Percy. Next you'll be telling me that Tarzan is the conductor."

"REALLY AND TRULY! Toshi is on the train. Didn't you see what fell from his blanket when they put him on the train?" I said insistently.

"No," she answered, throwing the egg salad sandwich back into the basket after she took a bite into it. Instead, she grabbed a cookie and dunked it into her hot chocolate.

I hissed, "It was Mina's red scarf."

Marigold looked into my eyes to see if they were blinking and if my mouth was twitching. "Honest to God, it was, Marigold."

"I don't believe you," she said, munching on the cookie, sounding as if she was about to shut me out of her life.

I argued, "If you ask me, you're acting like an adult, Marigold, and that's real bad. Toshi is sleeping in our car and that's the truth. I don't care if you believe me or not because true is true. With or without you, I'm going to help Toshi get to his sister in Washington, D.C. and, while you're feeling sorry for yourself and acting like a poopy old grown-up, I'll be having another wonderful adventure. Mr. Hamada is the cleverest spy in the whole wide world. That's what he really is. I knew he wouldn't let me down. I knew he was just playing with Aunt Momi."

I looked down at my stomach and saw that I had changed. I was beginning to look like Tyrone Power. I sighed, "Marigold, you will never understand me. We're different as night and day. You were born strong as an Amazon. Even your measles disappeared in a day. The only time you're sick is when you're on a ship sailing over the sea. Marigold, you're strong like Mother because Mother never had a headache in her life. You don't understand people who have headaches and are hanging onto life by a thin thread."

Marigold didn't hear a word I said.

We changed trains in Chicago for Baltimore. Waiting to board our new train, I watched Marigold feed Toshi the last of Ellen's cookies as Eddie, the porter, adjusted Mina's red scarf around his neck. At the newsstand, I read the headline in the Chicago Sun, "Ship Murderer Caught in Oakland Train Station."

EPILOGUE

Johnny was too smart for his britches. He couldn't go around killing people without getting caught. Thinking back on it, I was lucky that he didn't kill me. With or without the curse, I will always have an evil Johnny showing up somewhere in my life. God likes to test me. I knew even in Chicago that if Johnny escaped from prison, he'd come after me in Baltimore. This time, the Scarlet Shadow would be ready and waiting for him.

In the meantime, I had other adventures to think about. I was going to see Toshi reunited with his sister in Washington, D.C. Eddie, the porter, my new best friend, was going to help me contact Eleanor Roosevelt. He told me that the First Lady was a friend of every cursed person in the world. My plan was, after I had Toshi settled with his sister, I would escape from the two old ladies and take Kaina, the skull, (I named him after a Hawaiian friend of mine) to Kauai, myself. I knew, by then, that curses were made up stories but, if you believed in them, you made curses come true. My mother warned me about that. I hoped, that before the war was over, Marigold would be home again with our father because that's where she belonged. After I got Marigold back to Honolulu, I would travel to Hollywood and eat a huge bowl of spinach at the Brown Derby with Uncle Buster and Alice Faye. You see, I still wanted to sing and dance like Alice Faye in Hollywood musicals.

When Ellen showed me the secret ingredient to her egg salad sandwiches, I almost had a heart attack. The special ingredient that I had been searching for since the day Hatsuko died was Miracle Whip. Knowing that made it okay for me to believe in miracles and have the power to change my mind when I had to. My father would have said, not believing in miracles himself, only in coincidences, that changing one's mind was a big part of growing up. My father changed his wives three times.

I also believed that it was God's voice that I heard inside my head. I listened to that voice more often because that voice never betrayed me. I learned to count on myself more and not on others.

Neither Marigold nor Mr. Hamada ever betrayed me.

I learned from Mr. Hamada and Marigold about truth: truth was in the mind of the beholder, and everyone lied to himself and to each other. The people who lie best are those who believe the lie they are telling is the truth.

I wasn't as scared anymore. I was no longer the little boy who spit on towels for luck. Though, once in awhile when dark feelings about Johnny simmered in my brain while walking alone on the streets in Baltimore, I looked into dark corners and crossed the street to keep out of the path of black cats. Feeling the ankh in my pocket, I waited for Johnny to show up in my life again.

As I traveled on the train across the United States, I knew certain things. I loved being the Scarlet Pimpernel (Shadow) and now adored Miracle Whip. I hated people like Hitler and Johnny. Hitler and Johnny taught me that when people with orange eyes tell you that they speak from their hearts, I'd better watch my back.

Once in awhile, I would indulge myself and eat Best Foods mayonnaise on peanut butter. I only did that when I was depressed.

I understood, a little, what fiction was and what fact was in my life. Still, a question remained: was all life an illusion? To find the answer to that question, I asked God for the answer. God never answered me. More than likely, I wasn't listening.

Finally, I learned that I wasn't the center of the earth, just part of it. I was some of the bad part and some of the good. The voice in my head kept telling me to keep on the alert and be careful. If I wasn't careful and didn't remember the silver tongue around my neck, I, too, would become one of the betrayers.

Hopefully, I didn't.

By the way, Aunt Rose's coffin did land on a Hawaiian beach in April of 1943. She was perfectly preserved. Those who found the coffin reported that she had a smile on her face. She was holding a fur coat.

True is true.

Photo Credits

All photos of the Aquitania from Ocean Liners of the Past – The Aquitania. 1971 Patrick Stevens Limited, Bar Hill Cambridge, CB3 8EL, England.

Buster Crabbe – Columbia Studios Photo.

Charlie Chan and Tyrone Power – 20th Century Fox studio photos.

Westin St. Francis photos – courtesy of Marsha Monro and Steve Wong.

ABOUT THE AUTHOR

David P. Penhallow grew up in Hawaii and is a graduate of Stanford University. He presently lives on the island of Kauai.